I0662569

DRUID'S DAUGHTER

***

By Kelly Peasgood

A Kelly Peasgood Publication

"You won't get away with this," the Guardian cried.

He raised his hand, a jet of flame extending from his outstretched fingers. Karen took a step back and raised both her hands, palms out like a shield. The flames stopped a hand's width from her face. Manfred raised his arm to shield his head and turned to avoid the heat. Karen flicked her wrists forward, palm down. The flames turned, then shot back at the Guardian. He screamed, trying to dodge out of the way, but with only partial success as tongues of flame licked at his cape. The remaining fire sailed toward an occupied table, much to Karen's alarm. The patrons sitting there screamed and scattered. For a moment, chaos reigned.

The Guardian tore off his cape and screamed in fury. Karen lowered her arms. She retrieved her cloak and clasped it about her shoulders, then stood watching the Guardian. His eyes narrowed. He made a gesture with his hands and three wild dogs materialised before the girl. Manfred gripped his sword tighter and swung at one as it attacked. The beast yelped as the blow hit home. It fell limp and a foul stench arose from its broken body.

The other two leapt at Karen.

To all who helped make this book a reality, including my cohorts from Muses Ink, my Mom & Dad, and especially Mike. Thank you all for your support and belief.

Also by Kelly Peasgood

Spirit of the Stone
In Dreams We Live
The Forgotten King (Book 1 of The Forgotten)

Prologue

I've seen too much. Manfred took in his surroundings with a dissatisfied scowl. A haze of smoke hovered in the air and The Golden Rest held such a pungent odour, he wondered how anyone could keep coming in, night after night. Like too many inns he had frequented in pursuit of one person or another. They all began to blur together in his mind. A sure sign he needed a break, at the very least. Though in truth, he wondered why he bothered at all anymore.

In the past, people respected trackers, and one with Manfred's skills never lacked for employment. But now Guardians corrupted everything, and the need for honest guides had become scarce. The criminal element held power, and the only souls they wanted tracked were the good and honourable ones. Yet these criminals went one step beyond even the worst cutthroat in Sandroga, far to the east; these depraved Guardians eschewed pure evil. Manfred refused to hunt down the good so that the evil could profit. Unfortunately, not all trackers had such standards.

Things weren't so bad even a year ago, Manfred mused. Guardians hadn't moved this far west yet. In fact, that had probably proved Manfred's most profitable year, if he discounted the reward payment from Queen Chipia for finding her son a few years back.

It had taken most of eight moons to track the prince's abductors, and all Manfred's resources had gone into the hunt. That had limited any other assignments that had come along. To Manfred, it all lay in the search, the constant change of scenery, the ability to work on his own terms and answer to no one but himself. The money came secondary. And so, while the Queen had offered generous payment, the time lost had grated on the tracker.

But last year, he'd had good and numerous contracts. Many decent citizens had fled west, hoping to avoid the tyranny of the Guardians. However, corrupt people, twisted by the influence of those same Guardians, had also thought to find a safe haven closer to the mountains. His last hunt of such a person though remained too recent for his own peace of mind.

Trayon, he'd named himself, a thief and a murderer. He had looked harmless enough; of medium height and build, well-kept by all appearances, and seemingly very good natured. Manfred had even shared a cup of ale with the man before learning his vile nature. Right here in Ildare, as a matter of fact, though at a different tavern.

Manfred had woken to a blood-curdling scream. A serving wench had found a body, twisted into such a grotesque display that it had taken three tries to revive the poor girl. The victim's kin, merchants from the north, were outraged. So too was the innkeeper, even before he discovered his coffers stripped bare and his other serving girl missing. That anyone could perpetrate such a horrendous act without raising any sort of alarm frightened them all. Especially when they found the only other person missing was the amenable Trayon, whom everyone had liked, and who had so thoroughly fooled them all.

They had turned to Manfred then. These people knew the laconic, impassive Stalker with his lethal reputation, and while they feared him, their new-found hatred of Trayon overcame any qualms they might have had about approaching Manfred. He agreed to track down Trayon and return the girl for a fair price, though in all honesty, he would have searched out the man on his own. After all, Trayon's geniality had fooled Manfred also, and no one made a fool of the Stalker. He did not approve of such senseless murder, and the girl remained in great danger so long as Trayon had her.

By noon, Manfred had picked up Trayon's trail and headed deeper into the mountains, into the wilderness where few ventured and fewer lived. By evening, Manfred knew that Trayon had expected pursuit and had attempted to compensate. The man had re-crossed his own tracks more

2

than once, sometimes even backtracking to confuse the path—all the more difficult with an unwilling hostage. But Manfred persevered. All signs pointed to the girl's constant struggle, a positive indication to the Stalker. It meant she still lived. It also made his job easier, despite Trayon's efforts to mask the trail.

When full night arrived, clouds had swept in to swallow any guidance the stars or slice of moon might have provided. He debated lighting a torch, but feared for the girl should Trayon note any sign of pursuit. He stopped to wait for first light, lest he miss any signs. This would give Trayon a greater lead, but surely the man had to rest some time too. Manfred hoped the criminal paused long enough to negate any advantage night-travel would gain him.

It took three days to catch him up. On that third morning, Manfred woke before dawn, as usual, but within an hour, he knew something was wrong. No sound reached his ear—not a bird cry, the scuffle or scurry of small creatures around the rocks or through the vegetation, nothing. He soon discovered why.

The smell hit him first. A strong metallic tang with an overtone of a privy. And the air felt heavy with the remembrance of fear and pain. Manfred knew what he would find before he saw her, though it didn't quite prepare him for the horror. Perhaps Trayon had found his hostage too much, or he believed any pursuit long lost and thought he could now enjoy his demented pleasures. Manfred knew the man had lost him mind.

She hung naked by her wrists in a scraggly mountain ash. Blood dripped slowly down her body, gathering in a sticky pool beneath her. She had died perhaps two hours before dawn, and her blood only now began to thicken. Trayon had sliced her up, left parts of her dangling and others parts missing completely. He had peeled the skin on her right side and left it to flutter gruesomely in the breeze. The other half of her remained mostly untouched, showing a comely body and a once pretty face now frozen into a rictus of disbelief and terror.

Manfred had fought in war before, had seen death in more ways than he could count, but this appalling display of torture for torture's sake turned him nauseous, forcing him to swallow back the bile that crept into his throat. He burned with a cold

3

fury.

And with wariness. Two hours was a long time for death to go unnoticed by scavengers, especially considering the amount of blood soaking the area. He looked around, sliding his sword from its scabbard. If Trayon lingered in the area, it would take a while before scavengers worked up the nerve to approach such a feast.

That was when Manfred heard the growls. He spun to find himself the centre of a half-circle of jakotes. Although they sometimes hunted in small packs, jakotes rarely had the coordination these five showed. Thin, sleek creatures, their rounded ears now laid back against canid heads, and their long muzzles pulled back to display rows of sharp, yellowed teeth.

A maniacal laugh reverberated through the mountains. Manfred glanced past the jakotes to see Trayon materialise out of nowhere. He wore brown and grey clothes that faded into his surroundings with amazing ease, adding to the illusion of invisibility.

"I knew they'd send someone after me," he said, sounding like the genial man with whom Manfred had shared a drink not long ago. But the light of insanity in his dark eyes and the stain of blood on his hands put the lie to that image. "I had even hoped they'd send you, though I didn't really believe they'd have the nerve to approach the Stalker."

"Well, they did." Manfred replied, his voice cold and clipped. The jakotes hadn't moved. Did Trayon control them somehow?

"Yes, so I see." Trayon grinned. His teeth had traces of red, as though he had taken a bite of the girl. Manfred's stomach recoiled at the thought.

"So," Manfred forced himself to sound calm. "Why are we here?"

"I told you. I was hoping they'd send you."

"Why me?" Manfred demanded.

"Why?" Trayon sounded baffled. "To test you, of course. See how good you really are. To pit myself against the best!"

Manfred shook his head in disbelief.

"You killed these women to see if I could track you?"

Trayon glanced at the grisly mess flopping loosely from the tree, his face impassive. Then he frowned.

"What are a couple of silly whores to a man's strength?"

4

Manfred bit his tongue to keep an outraged retort from flying out. Even so, he could feel his muscles vibrating with the effort of holding still, and his knuckles whitened with the strain of his grip on the sword hilt. The girls were innocent, caught in a madman's distorted view of the world. It made their deaths all the more tragic, but no less real.

"They are not important," Trayon continued, his voice still eerie in its false rationality. "We are important Stalker, you and I. Times are changing and we must take advantage of it."

Now Manfred frowned. He had no idea what the man meant.

"You are very good at what you do," Trayon stated. "I am most impressed. Just think what we could accomplish together!" He gestured to the girl, though his eyes stayed riveted on Manfred. His tone took on an excited lilt. "You could track them; I could take them. Together, we could rid the world of their foul presence. Think of the possibilities!"

Manfred stared at him in horror. Had he seriously suggested they become partners in murder?

"So what's in it for me?" he asked, stalling for time, wondering if he should just rush the man now, or if the jakotes would try to stop him.

Trayon shrugged. "I suppose you could take a few of them, if you wanted. I hear you're good with a weapon."

"You really are mad!" Manfred blurted, indignation overcoming caution. Big mistake. Trayon's eyes narrowed.

"You refuse me?" The man had the nerve to sound incredulous. The jakotes growled again.

"Call me crazy," Manfred replied, shifting his stance and affirming his grip on his sword hilt.

Trayon snarled, his face finally matching the insanity of his eyes. But in the next instant, he returned to the reasonable-looking fellow.

"So be it," he said, and swept his arms forward with a mumbled command. The jakotes started moving again. Manfred silently cursed himself. The man had magic. It explained so much, yet he had failed to see it before. This was how Trayon had managed to kill the girl back in Ildare without raising an alarm. He had covered the sound of his acts with magic. Perhaps he had even accomplished the foul deed in the same way. The girl could have screamed for her life and no one would have heard. How much more terrifying for her, crying for help, praying for someone to save her, never knowing those in the next room hadn't heard a peep. The despair of realising her pleas would go unanswered as she died.

And now, the jakotes Trayon had silently held off from their feast leapt forward, all the more eager for the taste of meat.

They attacked all at once, a pack intent on taking down prey larger than themselves. It almost seemed they shared the same thoughts, acting as one being with five parts. Manfred could hear Trayon cackling not far off, but he spared little thought for the man. He needed all his concentration to counter the jakotes as they lunged.

Manfred slashed and thrust with his sword, all pretence of civilised combat put aside as he fought for his life. He sliced one jakote in half and maimed a second, but the others continued their assault, heedless of their fallen companions. Vicious and blood-thirsty, fast and relentless, they flew at him in a kind of dance. More often than not, Manfred could only force them back, not having the time or the angle to use his blade as he needed. He kicked, he slashed, and even roared at them, but still they came on, seeming more like thirty than three.

Their attack didn't suit Trayon. Manfred suddenly found himself facing four opponents. While the jakotes fought with tooth and claw, Trayon leapt in with bare hands. His teeth bared in a rictus of fury, ready to bite into Manfred at the earliest possible opportunity.

All of which probably saved Manfred's life. A human adversary he understood, even one so completely deranged as Trayon. With a stab to one of the jakotes, Manfred's sword tore from the beast's hide, crunching through bone, and swung around into Trayon's mid-section. For a surprised moment, the two men stared at each other. The remaining jakotes yelped in panic and rushed for whatever cover they could find, Trayon's magical hold on them shattered.

There are moments in life when time seems to slow, and events that take seconds seem to last for hours as every minute detail is stored in the brain. Trayon's death left such a stain on Manfred's mind.

Trayon studied the blade in his gut with great fascination, his hands moving with painful slowness to touch the blood-stained length of steel. A great drop of blood fell with a wet splat. Trayon sank to his knees, his head coming up as his body went down, his weight angling the sword toward the ground. His eyes met Manfred's, a moment of clarity lighting them in the depths of his pain. He smiled then, as though released from some great torment. A trickle of red escaped his nose and he coughed a spittle of blood. Then the light faded from his face as death clouded his dark orbs and Trayon's corpse slid from the sword to land in a gentle heap in the dirt.

Manfred stared down at the body for a time before cleaning his sword on the dead man's shirt. He headed to the remains of the girl. Trayon he would leave for the jakotes, or whatever creature cared to claim him, but not the girl.

He cut her down with great care and buried her as best he could in the rocky ground. He layered some of the larger rocks over her grave until he had built a reasonable cairn. Scavengers might try to dig her up again, but Manfred hoped the weight of so many stones would deter them. In other circumstances, he might have brought her body back to her kin, but no one should see what Trayon had done to her. It was just too vulgar.

After a moment's hesitation, he cut off Trayon's hands and wrapped them in the man's torn tunic, along with the money he had stolen which Manfred found tied to the dead man's belt. Punishment for a thief and proof of his end. Then Manfred turned and left, taking his scarred memory with him.

When he returned to Ildare, he produced the hands with the gold, and told his story, his voice oddly flat. The kin of the first girl found comfort in Manfred's actions, but the innkeeper was horrified. He was not sorry to see Manfred go.

But when the Stalker left, he found himself in need of a drink. Which brought him to this nasty little inn on the edge of town—The Golden Rest seemed a laughable name in the dim interior—sitting next to a fire that did little to warm him, and trying to forget the past.

Seen too much pain, he thought to himself. *What's the use when people like Trayon roam the world, and people fear you because you know how to deal with the likes of him?* Manfred shook his head, trying to lose himself in the shadows and his ale. *No more,* he decided. *I've had enough.*

And then *she* walked in, and everything changed.

Chapter 1

The patter of rain drumming on tiled roofs nearly washed out the dull murmur of conversation. Following the sounds of the voices, Karen came to an inn. A sign creaked mournfully over the wooden door. Though the elements had weathered the paint, Karen could still make out the images of a pickaxe and a gold nugget next to a bed, and roughly scratched below these, the name The Golden Rest. A structure of mud bricks rather than stone or the more common wood set this building apart from the rest of the town.

She paused by the door. If she took this last step, she knew she could never go back. Her ignorance of the world of man would be forever shattered. But she knew she would have to deal with humans in the future, and to continue her journey in this storm at night was foolish. Besides, she was running low on supplies. So she took a breath and pushed open the door, allowing her solitary fantasy to fade forever.

A few dirty old oil lamps did their best to illuminate the interior of the smoky inn, yet the corners remained swathed in darkness. The smell of stewing meat wafted toward the open door, almost enough to overcome the odour of mouldy straw covering the ground and the stench of sour ale and stale sweat. Karen stepped out of the rain and gently closed the wooden door that wanted to slam behind her.

Pulling back the hood of her taupe cloak, the coarse material heavy with rain, she examined her surroundings with interest. A few weary eyes glanced in her direction; none looked away. The floor space of the inn covered about the same area as her stone house that lay so far away now. She wished for a moment that she had never left her familiar surroundings.

Wooden tables and rickety benches lay in rows taking up most of the space. Men and women partaking of an evening meal crowded around most of them. Three men sat leaning against a ratty bar, one too short to properly see above the wooden counter top and the other two in want of better clothing if the rips Karen could see gave any clue as to the rest of their wardrobe. A wash of earthen colours met Karen's gaze, much like her own beige tunic and brown trousers, along with one or two more brightly coloured outfits. But not even bright clothing could hide the edge of despair mirrored in their eyes, reflections of the misery most of these people seemed to share. Rather than joining together in camaraderie, these people crowded together for a sense of safety, the reassurance that they were not alone. Karen's map had shown Ildare as a trading town, but if the faces of these townsfolk provided any indication, then it seemed trade was not as profitable here as it once had been. Or perhaps it was something deeper?

Voices rose and fell all around the inn, sounding more like a babble of irate birds than conversation. A stone fireplace built into the far wall had a fire roaring within its confines. Karen moved toward it, seeking warmth. A man in a stained apron straining around his wide girth blocked her path.

"Good evening, pretty one. Perhaps I may be of some service to you?" he said peering up at her with a grin that lacked a tooth.

"I do not think so, sir," Karen replied, trying to hide her displeasure at the smell of the man. "I wish merely to go to the fire and dry off, and then acquire a room so I may rest from my journey."

The man's smile widened.

"Then, indeed I can help, pretty one, for I have such a room."

Karen regarded the man warily. She didn't like the way he kept calling her pretty one. About half the people in the inn had paused in their meal to watch her and the paunchy man.

"I think not, sir. Please allow me access to the fire."

"No, no! You misunderstand me," His eye held a

9

mischievous spark, as though he enjoyed misleading people. "I am the innkeeper and can arrange a place for you to stay. However, should you require anything else," He paused meaningfully, his eyes straying to her chest, "Just come to me."

Karen edged around the pudgy man. Her drenched cloak clung to her body. The damp had seeped through to her clothes and chilled her flesh. Nearly all eyes in the establishment followed her movements, as did curious whispers. Karen heard fragments of various conversations as she walked past these tables to the fire.

"... Elfin, yet not quite ..."

"... so lovely, and young ..."

"... never seen her before. Where ..."

"... not like us."

A table stood directly in front of the fire, this one boasting chairs instead of benches, though they appeared equally worn. A large man sat at this table, studying Karen as she approached. She stopped and looked at the empty chair across from him. There were no other places near to the fire and she shivered with the cold and damp. Touching the back of the chair, Karen glanced to the big man. He stared back, hooded eyes considering, not quite hostile, but wary. Finally, he gave the barest of nods and said in a deep and powerful voice,

"You might as well sit. No one will stop you."

The whispering stopped. The room grew silent. Only the crackling of the fire disrupted the stillness. Karen glanced about uncomfortably. No one met her gaze. Was this what the outside world was like? Mysterious and untrusting? Again, she longed for a return to her isolation, back where she understood the behaviour of nature.

She looked again to the tall man. He sat in the shadows created by the fire, but Karen's half-elf blood had given her excellent night vision. The shadows hiding the man's face from the other humans did little to hinder Karen's appraisal. His expression was grim and just a little haunted, yet the beginnings of a smile tugged at the edge of his lips. Vast knowledge lay in his light grey eyes and a gentleness that belied his great bulk and gruff manners resided in him. Something in those pale eyes called out to Karen, told her that this man would not harm her. Still, she felt uncomfortable under his close scrutiny, and she sensed the fear others had toward this stranger. Karen forced her misgivings aside, trusting the honesty his eyes promised even if his words were less than encouraging. She moved to the empty seat and sat without looking away from the man, leaning her walking stick against the table and dropping her travelling bag to the floor. Slung across the back of the man's chair, Karen noticed a broadsword encased in a worn yet intricate brown scabbard just peeking past the elbow of his creamy tunic.

The innkeeper strode forward warily as the large man called for ale, though judging from the two empty mugs, it was not his first drink of the night. The big man raised an eyebrow at Karen, pushing at one of the mugs. "You want anything?"

"No ale, thank you."

The innkeeper went to fetch the man's drink, hurriedly leaving them. The other patrons started to talk quietly among themselves. From time to time, some stole a glance at the two beside the fireplace then looked quickly away.

Karen turned toward the fire and removed her cloak, brushing stray water droplets from her shirtsleeves. She tried to ignore her discomfort at being the centre of attention. The man spoke, his voice surprisingly soft now.

"You're not from around here. What's your homeland?"

Karen paused to study him. A couple of battle scars marked his tanned, clean-shaven face. Frown lines etched themselves around his eyes and mouth, but Karen could detect some almost hidden markings of a smile, of laughter. He was older than she, though it didn't seem like many years separated them. Yet Karen sensed that the man's experience had aged him.

"I am from the countryside beyond the Farrange Mountains," she said.

"I have, on occasion, wandered in that direction, although I've seen few establishments in the area," he mused. "Perhaps you have heard of me. I am Manfred, but most folks know me as Stalker."

Karen shook her head, reminding herself of the customs and manners of men that her father had taught her so long ago.

"I have not heard of you before, but I am pleased to make your acquaintance." She hoped she had said that correctly.

"You've not heard ..." Manfred paused as the innkeeper

brought his ale, removed the empty mugs and left again. "Just where over those mountains do you live?" he asked suspiciously.

"Near Cleaver Point."

"That far? No wonder you've not heard of me. You must have known of the Druid though. Rumour said he lived near there."

Karen nodded, surprised. This man knew of her father!

"Never met him myself," Manfred continued. "Heard of him, though. Spirits! Who hasn't heard of the old fool? Exhausted his powers to fight all of Hell's offerings. Died in the end. Humph. That must have been some magic. Can't trust such power, and Druids are the worst. Always using people, never telling them the whole truth. But that one ... no, he was different." He looked at Karen as though realising that he rambled. A tear slid down her cheek.

"Hey, sorry girl," he said uncomfortably. "Didn't mean to upset you. Close to him?"

Karen nodded again. "I knew him." She said no more, instead turning back to the fire.

Manfred sensed she didn't want to speak further of the Druid, so he asked in a more gruff voice,

"What's your name?"

Karen did not turn, but replied, "Karenrana. My father called me Karen."

"What're you doing so far from home, Karenrana?"

Turning to face him, the glow of the fire reflected in her eyes. She did not want to reveal too much about herself or her mission. Yet she found herself more and more willing to trust this man. She had learned to trust such feelings long ago.

"I travel to Nearbrook."

"Nearbrook," he grunted. "That's a long way off! What's to do in Nearbrook? Nothing but a bunch of down-trodden wretches."

Karen remained silent a moment before replying, choosing her words carefully.

"I must find someone who lives there."

She gazed back into the flames. Several images played themselves out through the tongues of the fire, reminding her of the times her father had taught her control over her own red flames of power. She remembered the day when she was but

12

ten years old and her father, Draimar, had taught her about protective magic. They had gone to the secluded clearing just out of sight of their little stone house. Karen had a shield of magic surrounding a simple wooden rod and Draimar once again explained how to keep her power focused.

"That's it Karen, you are doing well," came her father's voice, a deep richness in the quiet morning air. "Control your strength, focus your power on the line. Gather energy from what you see around you, the trees, the grass, the earth itself. Be aware of the strength they give you and bind with it. Let the power flow through you and return your own strength to that from which you borrow."

Karen glanced at her father, mauve eyes a study in concentration, then refocused her attention on the beam of red extending from her right hand—her line of magic. The red glow encompassed the wooden pole in a protection shield.

"That's right. Now, prepare for a counterattack." Karen nodded, her golden hair bouncing lightly with the movement of her head. She watched from the corner of her eye as another beam of magic came from her father, this one blue, the power of the Druids. It reached the pole and began to move past Karen's shield. Red flames licked at the blue, but the blue kept pushing, moving closer to the pole, threatening to reach the object Karen protected. She could not allow that to happen again. They had practised this exercise for most of the morning and each failure frustrated her. Although she had improved significantly, Karen had yet to keep her father's flames from touching the pole. This time, she told herself, he would not succeed. She would prove that she could protect something, that she could learn, make her father proud. Closing her eyes and focusing all her energy upon the magic alone, she willed her power to protect her charge, to fight her father's line of magic. A moment passed as the two powers vied for dominance.

Suddenly, a burst of red flame enveloped the blue fire of the Druid and exploded in a brilliant flash. Both lights ceased in a clap of thunderous sound. Draimar stared at his daughter and she stared down at her shaking hands, astonished.

"What—" she started, looking up. "What happened, father? What did I do?" Nothing like that had ever happened before.

Draimar shook his head and replied,

"You defended yourself against attack. Excellent, Karen! That's all for today. Go and rest now."

Karen nodded, still gazing at her hands, her fear abated somewhat by her father's reassurances. She began to walk toward the small two-bedroom dwelling, hidden by the nearby trees that watched over the clearing. When she reached the wooden porch leading to the door, she paused and turned back to her father.

"It is because of Mother, is it not?" she asked in a voice like soft chimes. Her father met her gaze, but said nothing. Karen continued in a whisper, "It is the magic of the Elves that caused so great an explosion." She turned and entered the house.

That was before she really understood the sacrifice of her mother; how Sadricha, High Priestess of the Elves, had given up her life and her power to her daughter so that Karen might live. Before she truly knew that her magic differed in more than colour from that of her father, for her power combined the strength of Elf and Druid, and her mauve eyes constantly reminded her of the blending of those two powers.

"You'll need a guide to reach Nearbrook unharmed," Manfred stated, bringing Karen out of her reverie and back to the smelly inn of Ildare, away from memories of her father. "Any woman alone would," he continued. "You might even find someone here willing to take you there for the right price." He glanced around the inn, his manner clearly stating that he doubted she'd find any such help.

Karen regarded him. Instead of responding to that, she asked,

"Why do they call you Stalker?"

His blink brought his scrutiny back to her, perhaps surprised at the question, or maybe just unaccustomed to being questioned in turn. After a moment, he answered.

"I suppose it's the way I do things. With stealth. I've hunted men down without anyone knowing I was there. Until the last minute, when I've got them."

"You hunt people?"

"I'm a tracker."

"And you know your way around the land?" she said, barely making it a question.

14

His open stare said, *Of course,* but his lips said nothing. Karen thought quickly. Travelling with a companion might draw less attention to herself on her journey. She recalled her father telling her that women seldom travelled alone in this world and Manfred's own words confirmed it. Though she knew nothing of him, Karen did not sense any danger to herself from Manfred, and she found herself trusting him. His fear of magic—of Druid magic—she would address later, somehow. Assuming he agreed to help her.

"Then you know the way to Nearbrook," she said. "And you can take me there."

"Now just wait a minute," Manfred objected, his eyes widening slightly. "I don't have time to baby-sit a girl to some pitiful little hovel they call a town—"

"And you could navigate me around dangers," Karen continued over his objection, her tone reasonable. "I do not know enough about this land and I could find no better guide than a tracker feared even in this small trading town. Of course, you would have to be able to move fast." She met his challenging gaze as though considering his worth. "Do you think you could move fast enough?"

"You'd have trouble keeping up with me, girl." It came out almost as a snarl, but one delivered with a sense of pride. "Such a long trip, you wouldn't last more than a day without slowing me down."

"Then it is agreed," Karen stated, much to Manfred's surprise. "You will take me to Nearbrook, and I will not slow you down."

"You ..." he started, but the words caught in his mouth. He clenched his teeth, the muscle in his jaw throbbing furiously. Then he tried again. "But I never ..." Again, his lips moved in soundless outrage. Finally, he shook his head and a slow smile spread across his face. He gave one quick bark of laughter. "You're really something, you know. I've never had a man who could ring me in so easily, let alone some little slip of a girl. Oh, what the Hells," he concluded, taking a swig of ale and slamming down his mug without spilling a drop. "I'll get you to Nearbrook. But understand this, you pay all our expenses, and I say what those expenses are. Agreed?"

Karen merely nodded as though she had expected such a decision. Inside, she heaved a great sigh of relief. Having

15

someone as world wise as Manfred seemed could only help her, although she wondered briefly at her own ready acceptance of this stranger. Having never encountered anyone from the outside world—that was how she looked upon this land beyond her familiar mountain home—until this very inn, she had to trust her instincts considering her lack of experience. In the past, her instincts had kept her away from the dangers nature could impose. Now they had led her to this man who feared magic and whom she had to browbeat into helping her. She hoped these instincts proved her right now.

"Innkeeper!" Manfred bellowed, still shaking his head slightly, a bemused smile on his lips. "Bring some food."

The noise level in the room had risen steadily in the time they had spoken, but the innkeeper had no trouble hearing the Stalker's voice.

"So, who is this person you're looking for?"

Karen thought for a moment, considering just how much she should tell this man. Despite her growing trust, she did not want to say too much, especially about matters concerning magic. She didn't want to frighten him away.

"Just a lad," she replied finally.

"Just a lad? No more?"

"I can tell you only what I know. His name is Jans. He is a half-elf and he lives in Nearbrook."

"Why do you look for him?"

She stared down at the tabletop. Why did she seek him? Because of a vision? A waking dream that warned of danger? But her father had told her the day he left that she too would have a vision that would bring an end to her days of solitude. And that vision had come, leaving her more than a little afraid.

"I look as part of a promise," she said finally. "I was instructed to find him."

"By whom?"

"Is that important?" She looked into his steely eyes, struck once again by their unusual paleness considering his dark hair and tanned skin. He held her gaze for a time, lowered his eyes and replied,

"Not really," He raised the mug to his lips and drained the rest of the liquid. "I was just asking."

At that moment, the innkeeper arrived with some food. He placed scarred wooden bowls little more than half full of

16

something vaguely stew-like, and a chunk of bread before the two of them. He looked from Karen to Manfred as though waiting for something. Manfred studiously ignored the little man, tearing off a bit of bread instead and scooping up some greenish-brown slop with it. Obviously this was one of those expenses he had mentioned. Karen was reminded of her father's stories of how the outside world used coin in exchange for goods. Maybe they called them expenses now rather than goods. For that purpose, Draimar had left Karen a pouch filled with such coin, for when she had to leave the Point for this other world. She pulled out a small gold piece from this pouch around her waist and pushed it toward the innkeeper as payment, hoping it was enough. The man's eyes grew so wide that she thought perhaps they might pop out of his head. He snatched up the coin in fat fingers and put it to his teeth, biting down hard. Then he gripped the gold and examined it before turning a grossly pronounced smile to her.

"Perhaps you'd like a drink now?" the innkeeper offered in a tone Karen thought of as unctuous, the sort of whining a wolf pup used when it wanted something. The whole procedure completely baffled her. "I have some fine sweet wines."

"Thank you, sir," Karen said. "But no."

"Another ale," Manfred said, keeping his eyes on Karen. "And bring the lady's change. And remember," his stare swung briefly to the tubby little man, "I know how to count, so there better be enough coins returned."

The innkeeper gave Manfred a subtle, fearful look. He glanced at the gold piece in his hand, smiled again, then left to get the drink. Manfred shook his head ever so slightly and drew a dagger from his belt with which to eat, glancing at Karen.

"You got a dagger? The goat's tough as a Guardian's hide."

Karen nodded and drew a bejewelled dagger from her tunic, wondering what manner of animal a Guardian was. She smiled sadly. This dagger had once belonged to her mother. Karen's father had gifted it to her on her eleventh Birthingday. The hilt shimmered bronze, but the metal of the sharp-edged blade was harder to place, a mix of ores that formed a unique and strong surface in a style long forgotten. Golden runic letters, an alphabet her father had taught her, lined the folds of the blade, clearly indicating its Elfin origin.

The gems that bedecked the handle of the dagger reflected the flickering fire in the hearth. Manfred had raised his brows at the sight, for she had hidden the weapon well in her tunic. He returned his attention to his meal with a shake of his head.

Karen stabbed a slice of steaming meat out of the stew—Manfred had named it goat, and she was willing to believe him—and placed it in her mouth. Though fairly tough, the broth swamping it was wonderfully hot if strangely spiced. It had taken most of a week to reach this small village from Cleaver Point; a week of cold meals, so the warmth did much to revive her spirit. She looked toward Manfred. He held some bread in his hand and chewed it thoughtfully. Karen swallowed her piece of meat with a gulp. Warm, perhaps, but not altogether palatable.

"Where do you come from?"

Manfred gazed at her and slowly lowered the bread. He looked down at his bowl and said, "A lot of different places, I suppose." He hesitated. "Yeah, a lot of different places."

Chapter 2

The innkeeper sauntered up and placed Manfred's ale on the table. His eyes glittered when he saw the sparkling gems on Karen's dagger. At Manfred's glare, he reluctantly relinquished Karen's change, a handful of silver and copper pieces.

A cool breeze spread through the room as the door opened. Karen and Manfred glanced toward the entrance, as did the innkeeper after ripping his gaze from the knife. A flash of lightning lit the dark sky, making the rain look like hundreds of driving daggers falling from above. Silhouetted against the frame of the door stood a large man, heavily muscled, nearly the size of Manfred. He stepped through the entrance and headed to the bar, the door slamming shut in time to the thunder behind him. All voices hushed to tense whispers, the air thick with apprehension.

"Sweet Spirits," the innkeeper breathed uneasily, Karen's knife quite forgotten. "A Guardian." He moved off quickly to serve the stranger.

A Guardian? Karen wondered. Not an animal then, as she had thought from Manfred's earlier comparison. How could one equate a goat with a human?

A curved sword hung from the Guardian's belt and Karen could see several throwing knives adorning his clothing beneath the silver cape that matched his gloves. His scarred face seemed rough and worn, and his dark eyes glowed unnaturally in the dim light of the room.

"Guardians are hated hereabouts," Manfred said softly,

leaning to get a better view of the man while effectively hiding himself in deeper shadow. "But they are feared more."

"Why? Who are they?"

"They're from the East, where the Ebbrings rule." Ebbrings, she thought, the name sending a thrill of fear through her. The dark forms of her vision perhaps? "They're the minions of evil," he continued. "The Guardians seek and destroy anyone who could be a threat to their masters. They're coming further west every day. Since the war, they've just taken more of a hold in our lands."

"The war?" she whispered.

Manfred spared her a brief glance before returning his hate-filled gaze to the Guardian.

"You know, the war led by the Druid. Ten years ago. When he gathered the nations together and pitted himself against those who serve the Ebbrings. Many died, a lot by magic. Even the Druid didn't escape the fury of the Guardians. This one thinks much of himself to come into an establishment such as this on his own."

"How do you mean?"

"There are always those who would like nothing better than to see an end of them and their tyranny." Manfred punched his fist into the palm of his open hand, clearly showing he stood as such a one. He looked around at the cowering people of the inn in disgust. "Only problem is, there are others too damned scared to do anything."

Karen looked again at the Guardian. The man leaned against the bar, surveying the room, a mug held lightly in his right hand. A dirty grey light with angry red flashes outlined his form, a magical aura tainted with evil, visible to Karen if to no one else. Had this person used that magic against her father? She had never really known how Draimar had died, nor whom he fought. She only knew he was dead, and had been for ten years. Yet now, according to Manfred, she looked at someone who might have had a hand in extinguishing the life of her beloved father. The thought sent a wash of fear through her, but more than that, it brought sadness and anger.

"He's waiting for someone to challenge him!" Manfred exclaimed. "That arrogant ..." His voice trailed off and he mumbled something uncouth under his breath.

"Is that how they find those who could be threats? By

waiting for a challenger?" Karen asked incredulously, wondering anew about the customs of this world.

"That's just one way. It's rumoured they can detect magic too. That's how they find their greatest threats."

Karen tensed. If Guardians could sense magic, she would not be safe. She had thought the ability to see magic auras rare unless the user had already gathered his power. Gorlon, her father's teacher, had been able to find magic in others regardless of their strength. To him, seeing an aura was a simple matter. That was how he had found her father and trained him in the ways of the Druids. Draimar had once told her that he could only sense the auras of stronger users, although he had at least as much strength in magic as Gorlon. She wondered now if she were more like Gorlon or Draimar. Was this Guardian a powerful user, or merely someone with a slight ability? She did not want to encounter any trouble, not now, not when she had only begun her journey.

"How?" she asked softly, glancing quickly at Manfred then away. "How do they detect magic?"

"No one knows. They have magic of their own, so it has something to do with that. Why?" He glanced sidelong at her. Whatever he saw in her face made him frown. "You have magic, don't you?" More an accusation than a question.

"Yes," she whispered. She peered back to the bar. The Guardian stared at her. Could he see her aura as clearly as she saw his? The man took a gulp of his ale and swaggered toward her. Karen gazed at the tabletop in front of her, her hands pressing hard into the table, her meal forgotten.

"Well, what have we here?" a sharp masculine voice drawled in a hard, clipped accent. The Guardian stood at the table, looking down at Karen.

"Just two weary travellers trying to enjoy a meal in peace," Manfred said between clenched teeth, a scowl upon his face as he leaned back in his chair. The Guardian turned to face him.

"Ah, you, then, must be the Stalker. Yes, the innkeeper mentioned you were here, warming your toes by the fire." The Guardian glanced down at Karen, but spoke again to Manfred. "Although I see that's not all you're warming."

Although Manfred did not reply, his thoughts seethed. Did the bastard expect him to rise to that flimsily veiled challenge? And in defence of a near stranger who had just admitted that

21

she had magic? Sure, he had been willing to help a woman in need—and judging by the gold she flung about so carelessly, she could afford the expenses he would extract for her so easily duping him—but a woman with magic? And no matter what she looked like—*Spirits she was beautiful*—how could he trust anyone with the powers that had turned the world into the disaster it had become? Someone perhaps like Trayon. Not a chance. The Guardian laughed, his voice rough.

"Something wrong, Stalker? Please, don't let me interrupt your meal."

Manfred pushed his bowl away. He had one magic-user sitting quietly across from him and one standing over him, taunting him. What a sorry way to spend an evening.

"Oh, is something amiss with the food?" the Guardian asked sardonically. "I'll be sure not to order it."

"There's nothing wrong with the food; it's the company." He glared up at the man.

The Guardian laughed again. He turned back to Karen.

"Tell me, who's your silent friend, Stalker?"

Manfred, about to dismiss any connection to Karen, made the mistake of looking at her. She sat seeming so composed and sure of herself. But her hands had mottled white and red from her death-grip on the edge of the table. And although her body said she could handle herself, her eyes, a most unusual shade of purple, spoke volumes of fear and uncertainty to the trained eye. And, he was disturbed to see, an absolute trust in him. *Damn-it all to the nine Hells,* Manfred cursed to himself. He couldn't just leave her to the mercy of a Guardian, magic or no.

"A travelling companion," he answered with more steel in his voice than he'd intended.

"Really? Then how is it that she is wet and you remain dry?"

"We had to part a few days past and agreed to meet here," Manfred spat. "I arrived before the storm. She did not."

"And are you aware of your companion's magic?"

Manfred grunted but said nothing. Of course he knew—now. How did he manage to get himself into this mess? Confrontations like this were just one reason he worked alone. He should just cut his losses and run now. Leave the girl to her own fate. But looking into Karen's eyes again, he just couldn't.

And he didn't have the slightest idea why. She must have used a spell on him.

"Ha! Companion indeed. What's your name girl?" he demanded. Karen ignored the imposing man beside her, staring hard at Manfred instead, as though drawing strength from him.

"I asked you a question!" the Guardian snarled.

She looked up, meeting his black-eyed gaze with her own mauve stare, her fear hidden now beneath a defiant determination. "So you did."

Rage showed in the man's eyes.

"How dare you!" He placed a large, gloved hand on her shoulder, his fingers flexing like talons. Before he could think about it, Manfred jumped to his feet, his chair falling with a clatter. He grasped his sword with a steely ring in the blink of an eye even before the chair hit the floor. The room went still. Manfred and the Guardian glared at each other.

"Your move Stalker. Attack me, and the girl dies, you with her. Let me take her, and I will spare your life—for now." The Guardian snarled, lips pulling back from his teeth like an angry beast, so like Trayon's maddened grimace that for a moment, Manfred could almost see the dead man's features on the Guardian's face. "So, what's it going to be? Her life or yours?"

The Guardian grabbed Karen's arm and jerked her to her feet. A knife flashed in his hand and he held it to her throat. Manfred barely flinched, though his stomach lurched. *She's got magic,* he thought to himself. *She can take care of herself. So what are you doing?*

"You won't get out of here alive," Manfred hissed, ignoring his own thoughts.

"Oh no? Who's going to stop me? I see no one else moving. You might kill me, but not before she dies."

Manfred glanced briefly at Karen, standing calmly in the Guardian's iron grip even though her eyes flashed wide with fright. As he watched, she began to glow, a soft red at first, but quickly brightening.

"What the—" The Guardian dropped his blade and pushed Karen away toward the table, grabbing at his hands. He screamed in pain. "My hands! What have you done?" He glared at Karen. "Water," he bellowed. "Bring me water!" He peeled off his gloves, revealing burned and blistered hands.

23

The innkeeper rushed up with a pitcher of water and a glass. The Guardian knocked the glass to the floor in his haste to get to the pitcher. He plunged his smoking hands into the water, which promptly steamed and hissed at the contact. He stared at Karen. She appeared normal now, the red glow gone. Manfred stood at her side, towering over her.

Yup, Manfred thought, *she can take care of herself just fine.*

"You won't get away with this," the Guardian cried. He raised his hand, a jet of flame extending from his outstretched fingers. Karen took a step back and raised both her hands, palms out like a shield. The flames stopped a hand's width from her face. Manfred raised his arm to shield his head and turned to avoid the heat. Karen flicked her wrists forward, palm down. The flames turned, then shot back at the Guardian. He screamed, trying to dodge out of the way, but with only partial success as tongues of flame licked at his cape. The remaining fire sailed toward an occupied table, much to Karen's alarm. The patrons sitting there screamed and scattered. For a moment, chaos reigned. People ran for the walls, hoping to find safety. Some went out into the rain and others cowered under their tables. No one wanted to be a part of a magic duel. Finding themselves in the middle of one, they wanted only to escape. The Guardian tore off his cape and screamed in fury. Karen lowered her arms. She retrieved her cloak and clasped it about her shoulders, then stood watching the Guardian. His eyes narrowed. He made a gesture with his hands and three wild dogs materialised before the girl. Manfred gripped his sword tighter and swung at one as it attacked. The beast yelped as the blow hit home. It fell limp and a foul stench arose from its broken body.

The other two leapt at Karen. She spun away from the first, but the second hit her full on and she toppled back. It bared its fangs, growling, and dug sharp teeth into her arm.

The Guardian sent his flames toward Karen and Manfred, but hit some frantic patrons in his path instead. He yelled in outrage as Manfred rushed the dog that had missed Karen, swinging his broadsword. The beast avoided the first sweep of the blade and pounced at the Stalker. But Manfred was faster. He brought his sword up in front of himself, impaling the creature. *So much easier to kill than Trayon's jakotes.*

24

Meanwhile, Karen kicked off the dog assailing her and grasped her walking stick which had fallen to the floor. The dog lunged again, and met with a powerful blow. Dazed, but still alive, it tried to reorient itself on Karen, but she swung the stick once more, splitting its skull. Her staff cracked with the impact and broke. The beast whimpered and crumpled to the floor, unable to rise.

"No!" the Guardian cried. He started to gesture again. Karen sent out a burst of red from her hand. It met the Guardian full in the chest, sending him flying to the wall near the door. He landed heavily, eyes wide with the knowledge of death, a smouldering hole through his body.

"What's going on here?" a commanding voice called. Two more Guardians stood framed in the doorway. Manfred grabbed Karen's arm.

"Come on," he whispered urgently. "There'll be more here in no time. You can't fight them all."

Karen glanced at the door, then turned to follow Manfred. She grabbed her dagger as they passed their table and tucked it in her belt. Scooping up her travelling bag, she trailed Manfred as he led them to a back door beyond the kitchen and out into the rain. The confusion at the inn held off any pursuit for now.

Darkness closed about them. The rain fell hard and fast, blurring their vision and washing the stench of the inn away. Manfred took them through the streets, down foul-smelling alleyways and around various wood and brick houses and stone buildings.

He finally stopped at a small wooden structure, an old shed with a slight lean to it. He opened the rickety door and the two entered, gasping for breath. Rain pounded on the roof, but surprisingly none came in. Manfred closed and bolted the door while Karen searched her surroundings in the darkness. Several crates lay strewn about, most of them empty. Her hands encountered cobwebs, but she brushed these aside and collapsed on one of the crates. Darkness enshrouded this building as it did the streets outside, even to Karen's exceptional sight, yet she could sense Manfred's tension from across the small room.

"Did he teach you that?" he asked, a tremor in his voice.

"Who?"

"The Druid. You said you knew him. Is that where you learned your magic?"

Karen remained quiet for a short time, remembering the protection lesson with the pole, then replied, "He taught me control. The magic is mine."

"You must have powerful ancestors."

Karen nodded to herself in the gloom. "Yes, you could say that," she murmured.

"Karen, what are you doing here?"

"What do you mean?"

"I mean why are you here, so far from home?"

"I travel to Nearbrook."

"To look for some guy named Jans, I know," Manfred said. "But why? Why is he so important? What will you do when you find him?"

Karen did not reply. Instead, she thought back to her vision, the reason she had left her peaceful isolation where she had never met another soul besides her father.

The vision had come like a thought unbidden, its intensity making it impossible to mistake, or to ignore.

Evil wrapped cold fingers in a stranglehold around the East, threatening to destroy all creatures of good as thickening tendrils of hate reached greedily in all directions. A powerful force with many servants, the numbers of followers of this dark chaos grew daily. Seven shadowy shapes, impossible in their beauty, unimaginable in their hatred, rose from silvery waters and commanded cowering humans, thousands of servants, to carry out their malicious purpose. Karen watched as city after city, village after village, fell into ruin. Burnt-out husks of a once joyous civilisation crowded the land. She saw the future this darkness could bring, the death of all good unless evil was stopped. All turned black and barren, withered into decay and black tyranny. The only creatures left alive lived in despair, bearing tremendous burdens and torment that bent them to the ground under its weight. She gasped at the stifling oppression she felt from this future.

The vision altered, showing the present day. In a far off village in the world of man—Nearbrook, sighed a breeze that only existed in her mind—she saw a boy. He stood out in stark detail against the shadows around him, surrounded by an aura of white light. His blond hair just covered the tips of his pointed

26

*ears and his eyes shone blue. For the most part, his features seemed human. Only the sharpness of his ears, his high cheekbones, and the slight slant of his eyebrows betrayed his Elfish descent. A beige cape draping over a white tunic fell to the backs of his knees. He boasted nutmeg pants and dark brown doeskin boots, folded to the middle of his calf. Around his waist he wore a belt from which hung a hunting knife and a short sword. A voice whispered his name—*Jans. *To stop a future of darkness, she must find this boy._*

"Karen?" Manfred's voice sliced the vision away from her. "Karen, I have to know if I'm going to help you," She turned to face the direction of his voice.

"I have to do what I can."

"I don't understand. Do what you can for who? Against what?"

"The Ebbrings." That was the name of the creatures Manfred had said fought her father, and she thought they might be the same creatures her vision had revealed.

"You're crazy. What can you do? Kill them? All by yourself? And why should you need this Jans person?"

"This is what my father trained me for. I must destroy the Ebbrings. Jans can help. I need his power."

"He's got magic too? Like yours?" A mixture of disgust and fear tinged his words, with a hint of awe.

"I do not know. But I will need his help."

"And what do you plan to do?"

"Everything I can to dispose of their evil."

"Just you and this boy? Destroy all the Ebbrings? You have a lot of confidence in your powers!"

"My father taught me everything he knew and I have my mother's magic within my blood," she said defensively. "I was born to do this. I have powerful ancestors."

"How powerful? Who are your parents?"

"My mother was the Elfin High Priestess Sadricha. Through her, I have the magic of the strongest of Elves. She sacrificed her life to give me those powers." She paused, almost afraid to go on.

"And your father?" Manfred urged quietly, although his tone suggested he already knew the answer.

Karen struggled to maintain her composure, not wanting to break down now. In her mind she relived that last day with her father, seeing it as though they stood in that clearing once more. Her last lesson in caution and defence; her final instruction to combine knowledge and wisdom with the use of her magic. She watched again as Draimar walked toward the trees without looking back, following his own vision. She saw again how her father had disappeared into the depths of those woods as though swallowed. Through the eyes of a twelve-year-old who would never see her father alive again, Karen saw her father's image fade into mere memories, though his life had lasted another year. For that year, she had known he still lived, but the moment he died, Karen had felt his spirit seek her out to say goodbye.

With a deep breath, she looked toward the man who had helped her back at that inn, this large man who had no liking for Druids and feared the use of magic. She looked to Manfred and said sadly,

"My father was one of the most powerful men ever. He prepared me for this since I was a young child, and yet, I do not know how I am to complete this quest. My father was the Druid Draimar."

***

An awkward silence followed Karen's statement. Manfred had known, or at least had guessed. Her sadness when he had mentioned the Druid, his teaching her how to control her magic. Still, the revelation hit him like a blacksmith's hammer. Not just a girl with magic, but a Druid. Again he saw the Guardian struck by Karen's magic, how she had eluded the man's grasp with so little effort. She didn't need help to get to Nearbrook. Anyone mistaking her for a helpless woman travelling alone would soon learn his error. But then he thought of those dogs the Guardian had called. Without Manfred's help, would she have come out the other side of that battle?

But a Druid? He couldn't seem to get past that thought. He could hear her shifting in the darkness. He wondered if she were as uncomfortable as he was.

"Why—" Manfred took a deep breath. "Why didn't you tell me before?"

"Would you have accepted me had I told you? You already told me you do not trust magic, especially Druid magic. If you

28

had known who and what I was, would you have even wanted to talk to me, let alone help me?"

"I ..." He stopped. *No,* he thought to himself, until he remembered the look in her eyes, the uncertainty. A Druid perhaps, but a hesitant one, one that needed help and could admit that. "I don't know."

"When I first learned the strength of my power, what it could do, it frightened me. Even now, I remain wary of using it because of what I know it can do. You saw what happened to that Guardian and it was terrible. I could have done much worse. If I am afraid of my power, and I have to live with it, I can only imagine the fear others will have. You were right; Druids did use people. My father did not agree with that, so he tried to help others on his own, to accomplish what he could alone, and that killed him. I cannot use people, but I also cannot accomplish what I must on my own. So I must trust that people will help me of their own accord." Even as she spoke, Manfred could hear the truth of her words.

They did not speak for a while. The rain subsided outside and they could soon see the outline of the door as moonlight seeped through the breaking clouds. Karen shifted again, readjusting a small cloth she had tied around her arm. Manfred just had time to wonder about that when she spoke again.

"I have never before had to deal with the outside world. The inn was the first place where I ever had contact with men and their ways. Father tried to prepare me, but I was afraid. I did not know what to tell you, so I told you almost nothing. I am sorry, Manfred."

In the distance, a dog barked. Manfred started, looking to the door. He drew his sword.

"We have to go. They're getting closer."

"Who?" she asked, although she could sense something strange in the air. It startled her to realise that she had sensed this same wrongness when the Guardian at the inn had spotted her. Perhaps an aspect of how Guardians found magic users.

"The Guardians," Manfred confirmed. "They're searching for us. Come on, Karen, we have to hurry."

"You will still help me? Even after I tricked you into coming with me? Now that you know I am the Druid's daughter? That I have magic?"

The baying of another hound soared through the air.

"They're getting closer," he repeated, not directly answering her. "Come on."

He moved to the door and opened it. Moonlight spilled in. Karen stood and went to his side. She could not imagine his thoughts right now, but at least he hadn't abandoned her. For that, she was grateful.

Together, they peered into the shadowy streets. Nothing moved nearby. Manfred took Karen's wrist in his rough, callused hand and started off away from the town.

***

Distant voices murmured amidst the growling and whimpering of the dogs. Pinpoints of light from flaming torches bobbed up and down with the movement of several men.

Moments later, led by three leashed hounds, Guardians arrived at the empty storage shed. The dogs sent up a frenzied howl, the scent of their quarry filling the air.

"They were here. And they're vulnerable," one exclaimed after briefly searching the building.

"Are you sure?" a shorter man replied.

"Look here," The first Guardian pointed to the crate where Karen had sat. He lowered his torch. "They paused long enough to leave a trail."

On top of the crate, near the edge, a few drops of fresh blood had fallen.

Chapter 3

Amrah slid to the next shadow created by the overhang of The Sleeping Dog. An apt name for such a sleazy establishment, she thought. While outwardly The Dog provided food and rooms at the cheapest rates in Sandroga—fare not worth the price, in Amrah's opinion—in truth, it catered to the most twisted whims of the sexually depraved. *What in all the Hells is Yagoth doing here?* she wondered.

At first glance, people found Amrah an attractive woman, perhaps thirty summers old or so. But when they looked closer, they found hers a double-edged beauty. Though the angles of her face were more than pleasant to look upon, they were hard and brooked no nonsense. Her eyes, the colour of summer grass, were jaded in a way that said she had seen far too much and none of it impressed her. And while she had a lithe and graceful form, she moved with such deadly intent that none could mistake her for anything but a dangerous woman.

The people of Sandroga knew Amrah well. To all intents, she and her brother Toron ran the town. Sure, there was a mayor and an enforcement squad, but they were as corrupt as anyone. They got rich in pretty much the same way as any cutthroat in town, only they had the 'law' behind them. They also had enough brains not to use that 'law' to interfere with Amrah and Toron's activities.

The Sleeping Dog hunched as deep in the worst section of Sandroga as one could get, but Amrah had no fear of the place. If anyone saw her in the shadows—as unlikely as that seemed, especially at two hours past deep night (although the town never really slept, save perhaps around noon when the full light of the sun laid bare even the darkest soul)—they knew enough to stay well away. Amrah on a hunt proved even more dangerous than usual.

And she hunted now. Yagoth was more than a good friend. They had shared blankets often enough. But he had started acting strangely a few days ago. At first, she had thought he was seeing someone else, and she would have let him go despite the stab of pain it caused her. Yet the signs pointed to something more ominous. His whole manner had changed. Granted, at the best of times he was a liar and a thief, but who wasn't in Sandroga? But he had never been cruel.

Until about four days ago when he began to withdraw into himself and grow abusive—toward everyone, though he remained cautious with Amrah. She knew how to take care of herself better than most, and Yagoth had suffered a black eye and a broken nose when he thought to challenge her. She hadn't meant to hurt him so, but he had an odd cast to his eyes that evening, as though not entirely himself, and Amrah didn't take chances. When it came to a choice, *him or me,* she always put herself first.

What disturbed her most about Yagoth's abrupt change was the timing. A group of Guardians had passed through town, ostensibly to gather recruits into their ranks. Amrah didn't know what they expected to find in a place where people would rather cut your throat than look at you, especially if you had magic, but they had come nonetheless. They had wisely kept together—a group of eight magic users with the vile reputation every Guardian shared was less likely to be set upon by even the boldest criminal than Guardians roaming the streets separately. No one Amrah knew wanted anything to do with such loathsome wielders of magic—men even a cutthroat went out of their way to avoid—and the sooner the Guardians left town, the better.

Yagoth, and a few others sharing his speciality for ferreting out secrets, had gone to learn what they could of the Guardians' real purpose. He had taken longer than Amrah thought necessary yet had returned unscathed, which had sparked her belief in his infidelity. But now she knew something else had gone wrong. She could point out the symptoms, the

32

differences only someone who knew Yagoth as well as she did would see, but she couldn't find the cause. It infuriated her, and she had determined to find the problem and put an end to it. No one else who had scouted out the Guardians had changed like Yagoth, although Amrah couldn't claim they weren't different in some way. The spies had always remained a secretive bunch, though they seemed more so now, keeping to the darker parts of themselves as much as the dingier sections of Sandroga. But maybe she read more into the situation than existed. It just showed her worry for Yagoth.

So here she stood, clinging to the shadows of The Sleeping Dog, following the man who might give her the answers she sought.

Yagoth slipped inside the wooden structure with its peeling whitewash walls with barely a glance at his surroundings. Amrah waited before following, and as well she did. A second figure moved into view, sharp eyes searching the area. Although cloaked and hooded, Amrah recognised the slender new-comer. Vilna, one of Yagoth's network of spies, her speciality lying in the fact that few men could withstand her looks and charm. What was she doing here? Suddenly, Amrah rethought things. Perhaps Yagoth *had* found someone else to share blankets with, though why he would choose someone as two-faced as Vilna, Amrah couldn't fathom.

But a nagging suspicion itched at the back of Amrah's mind. Although secretive by nature, the pair exercised more stealth than a simple romantic rendezvous warranted. At least to Amrah's way of thinking.

So she moved ahead into the cheap little inn. *The trick with not being noticed in such an establishment is to look like you belong.* Amrah strutted in, through the noisome bar area and toward the back, where rickety stairs led up to the sleeping chambers. No one gave her a second glance, and any who gave her a first look-over merely registered a woman with a purpose, no more.

Now to discover where Yagoth and Vilna had gone.

Unlike the stone walls and flooring of Amrah's own dwelling across town, The Dog was made completely of wood. This whole section of Sandroga was, giving rise to the many fires suffered throughout the year in this Quarter. The only stones around here were the ones you might trip over in the muddy street. The Dog creaked incessantly, both from human movement and from improperly treated wood ever swelling and warping. It made silence more difficult for the unwary than tromping on stone floors did, but Amrah had exceptional skills, even among her own people.

On silent feet, she slid to the first door along the landing. She listened but a second to the torrent of groans and high-pitched squeals before moving on. The second door boasted the rattle of chains and some very colourful talk, none of which came from her quarry. Opposite, the door held back what sounded like a whole barnyard of animals. Amrah grinned. That was the head enforcer with his mistress—everyone knew those two staged elaborate scenes with every sound imaginable. She spared a moment to wonder if the sounds now were real or faked, then decided she really didn't want to know.

Further along the hall, she found an astonishing array of sexual depravity encompassing a few noises even Amrah couldn't find a name for. Then a couple of empty rooms, and finally a voice she recognised coming from the second to last chamber on the right.

"About time you two showed up," said Gorath, another of Yagoth's network. Amrah could easily picture the little man as he spoke. Broad-shouldered and bow-legged, black scraggly beard and unkempt hair, his piercing eyes usually hidden behind a thin cloth to add to his disguise. Gorath worked the beggar's area, gaining useful information by the simple fact that most people ignored his presence. He was neither blind nor needed to beg, but few knew that. And his voice, pitched high and nasal on the streets, was in truth a deep rumble—a detail the spies thought they hid well, but little in Sandroga escaped Amrah and Toron. It always amused the siblings when the spies thought to fool them by using Gorath as his true self to learn some secret better kept unknown.

"I've been waiting for a quarter hour," Gorath complained.

"And you're lucky I didn't make you wait another quarter hour," Vilna replied sourly.

Amrah slipped on to the last chamber, which she thankfully also found empty. The lock was laughable and she quickly let herself in. Pressing herself up to the wall joining the room the spies had claimed, Amrah settled herself to listen and learn what she could.

34

"What have you found out?" Vilna demanded.

Yagoth merely grunted.

"You mean you've learned nothing?" This from Gorath.

"How hard can it be?" Vilna said over the older man. "That bitch Amrah and her oaf of a brother trust you, don't they? Just get the whore to talk under the sheets."

Amrah gritted her teeth. She and Vilna had never seen eye to eye, but the level of hatred in the other's tone seemed beyond reason, and Amrah knew how to hold a grudge.

"They're not stupid, Vilna," Yagoth growled. He sounded so strange to Amrah; not at all the cheerful man she had come to know. "I can't just ask where the rebels are without good reason."

They want the rebels? Amrah willed them to say more, to let her know what was going on.

"I got the mayor and his cronies out of the way—" Vilna began.

"Yeah, like it's hard to pay off that scum," Yagoth said.

"The point is," Vilna continued, ignoring him, "that I did my job. The mayor won't interfere when they come back."

They who? The mayor hadn't left town. The Guardians, then? Or something worse?

"And I'm making inroads with Toron's people," Gorath said. "It's slow, but that's to be expected."

Amrah smiled at that. Gorath only thought he accomplished something. Several of her brother's network had already reported Gorath's attempts to put an advantageous face on an alliance with the Guardians.

"So it seems," Gorath continued, "that you're the only one who hasn't done what you promised."

"You're not planning on double-crossing us, are you?" Vilna's voice had dropped into a deadly whisper, barely audible to Amrah in the next room.

Yagoth began to laugh, an unpleasant sound, touched with a bit of madness, or so Amrah thought.

"I've no desire to feel the sting of Guardian magic again," he said bitterly. "I'll have the information soon."

"You'd better—" Gorath began, but Yagoth's astringent snigger cut him off.

"Or what, Gorath? You don't have a threat vile enough to top what a Guardian would do to me. Nor you, Vilna, so you might as well stop scowling and leave off playing with that little knife of yours. I said I'd get it and I will."

Footsteps stormed across the room and the door creaked open, then slammed shut. Silence followed him. After a moment, so did Vilna and Gorath.

Amrah sat back, her thoughts awhirl. They wanted to know where the rebels were, information only Amrah and her brother were privy to. Why? The Guardians *were* involved, as suspected, but exactly how remained a mystery. Yagoth had suggested the Guardians had already worked some kind of magic on him. It explained his change in behaviour, but what had they done? Something painful, and frightening enough to keep him in line.

Amrah shook her head. She had followed Yagoth to get some answers, but it seemed what she had learned only led to more questions. Well, if Yagoth was supposed to find the location of the rebels, perhaps she could use him as he sought to use her. The thought of slotting Yagoth into the position of merely a useful tool saddened her, but only for a moment. He had betrayed her. An affair, she could have forgiven. Outright betrayal angered her. But what brought the sense of pure outrage burning in her throat was the knowledge that the Guardians could subvert her own people so easily.

Amrah left The Sleeping Dog with one thought blazing above all others in her mind.

The Guardians would pay.

Chapter 4

A forest of pine and fir interspersed with silverleaf and oak lay to the south of Ildare, far to the west of Sandroga. Karen leaned against the broad trunk of an ailing oak tree and checked the cloth she had tied around her right arm; then she studied the plants growing around her. Manfred sheathed his broadsword and glanced over at Karen. Dawn had begun to lighten the sky, though the sun had yet to awaken the day with its brilliance.

"We've lost them for now, but ..." He stopped, noticing her arm. "What's wrong?" He moved closer, his eyes widening as he noted the bloodstained cloth through a rip in her tunic. He hurried to her side. "What happened?"

He reached for her arm, but Karen pulled away.

"I am all right. It is not deep." She knelt and plucked some leaves from a nearby calenda plant and crumbled them in her hands, knowing they would help guard against infection.

"What happened?" Manfred repeated.

Karen sighed. "The Guardian's dog." She removed her makeshift bandage and looked around for something better to use as gauze.

"Why didn't you say anything?" Manfred ripped a piece of cloth from his own light tunic and took the crushed calenda leaves from her to make a compress. Despite her protests, he tied it around Karen's wound.

"It will heal." She regarded Manfred for a long moment. "Thank you," she said softly.

Manfred glanced up from her wound. "For what?" he

grunted, looking down again.

"For helping me get away from that inn. For still helping me get to Nearbrook." She sighed again. "For accepting me."

Manfred kept his eyes downcast, busying himself with dressing her wound. After a short time he stopped and looked up. Karen's mauve eyes found his. He shrugged, shifting uncomfortably.

"Don't mention it. I was ... just trying to help. Besides," he went on gruffly, avoiding her gaze now, "we've got a deal. Doesn't work if I don't keep up my end." He peered up through the boughs of the trees. "We should get moving. The further we go today, the better. They will still search for us, but we can stay ahead of them if we get moving." Then, under his breath, he added, "I hope."

***

They emerged from the concealment of the forest around noon. Manfred set a good pace and Karen easily kept up. Neither having slept the previous night, they nevertheless continued on their way, pushing weariness aside. They began to cross a wide desolate plain, but Manfred paused and looked around them. The grass cover, like an entrance rug to the forest floor, had petered out, leaving dry-baked ground. Ahead, deeper into the barren plain, forests of rough boulders replaced the trees. Yet he could sense life, something out of place in such a wasteland.

"What is it?" Karen asked, her hushed tone indicating that she, too, sensed something wrong. Manfred raised his hand to silence her. He glanced at her quickly and, with his eyes, indicated the vast rock-plain beyond.

"There's something out there."

Manfred scrutinised the land and drew his sword, though he still saw nothing.

"Where? What is it?" Karen whispered.

"I don't know, but it's coming, and fast."

The two searched the emptiness, waiting for something to happen. Manfred felt tension in the air and sensed someone approaching, but suddenly realised that danger lurked both ahead and behind. It felt like someone watched him; that eerie sensation that crawls up the spine when hidden eyes study

38

every move. They had nowhere to hide. They'd have to stand their ground against whatever approached. They did not have long to wait.

"Drop your sword."

Manfred disregarded the point of a blade at his back and spun, grip loose but ready on his sword. The long knife suddenly at his throat did not slow him, but the sword at Karen's back did and he paused. Then he cursed himself for hesitating, but the damage was done. He had lost any advantage he might have had.

"I will advise you again, drop your sword," the man with the knife repeated with chilling calm. A slender man, he stood shorter than Manfred by a head. A faded green cape that would blend well with the forest sheltered his arms from the sun, and his lean unprotected face had only the hint of a tan. His dark blond hair held no signs of bleaching by the elements. Strange for someone who seemed quite at home in this barrenness where the intense sun had long ago dried and cracked the landscape. An older man in a brown cape stood with him and a third, gaunt yet not without brawn, rose from the dusty earth in front of Karen, flinging back the sandy cloak that had hidden him so effectively. He moved to join his companions. The older man with greying hair framing a round, creased face, told Karen to turn around. As she did so, Manfred noted the similarities in facial features between the older man and the one who had spoken before. The third man had shoulder-length brown hair loosely held back by a leather cord. It only served to emphasise the severity of his face. He now stood a step behind his companions, his body fading eerily into the background where his sandy cape hugged him. The sword in his hand hung loosely by his side, but Manfred had no doubt he would use it swiftly if needed.

Manfred looked to Karen. She appeared calm, though somewhat surprised that they had been taken so easily. Manfred fumed at himself for failing her, then paused in his thoughts. Had he hesitated because of her magic? Knowing she could take care of herself against Guardians, had he dropped his guard, depending on her powers? No, he thought. He had been ready to cut into the stranger at his back until he saw Karen's danger. How could he protect his client if he hesitated when danger threatened her? He would have to practice more caution in the future once they had escaped this mess. And yet a small voice whispered at the edge of his thoughts; why should this client be any different from others he'd taken on? The knife at his throat dug in just a little, a reminder of his present danger. He'd have to examine the reasons behind his failure another time.

***

Manfred lowered his hand and dropped his sword. The lean man behind his companions stepped forward and bent down, retrieving the discarded weapon. He straightened slowly and met the angered eyes of the Stalker with his own dark gaze. Challenge flared between the two, an invisible threat vibrating in the air.

"Joanha!" the older man called sharply. The gaunt man before Manfred glanced in annoyance over his shoulder, causing a strand of hair to escape the leather cord, but he obeyed the unspoken order. He stepped back, his sight again trained on the Stalker.

"What, if I may inquire, is the meaning of this?" Karen demanded.

"You're in no position to be asking questions, wench!" Joanha exclaimed, his glare turning to her.

"Joanha," the younger man snapped. "Hold your tongue." He regarded Karen a moment, then said, "I apologise for Joanha. He is not well mannered among strangers."

"And rightly so," Joanha spat. To the older man, he said quietly, "They could be with the enemy."

"And which enemy is that?" Manfred interjected, menace in his eyes.

Joanha shot him an embittered glare. "Ours is the only enemy. The Ebbrings and their bastard minions, the Guardians," he replied with venom.

"Then it seems we have something in common, for they are the enemy we fight," Manfred shot back, the menace fading only slightly.

"We are not with the Guardians. We have run from them since early this morning," Karen added.

"From where?" Joanha demanded with suspicion.

"Ildare. We had a difference of opinion with a Guardian

there," Manfred said, a slight twinkle in his eye now. "The others did not approve of the way we dealt with him, so we've been avoiding them since."

"How did you deal with him?" the older man spoke up, his eyes intense.

Manfred glanced silently at Karen.

"With magic," she said quietly.

"What sort of magic?" Joanha's scepticism was so heavy that Karen found herself straightening her shoulders as though to throw off a burden.

"Strong magic," she said.

"What did you do to him?"

Karen merely stared at him, not replying. She stifled an urge to run back to the forest, back to somewhere in solitude, away from such suspicions and mistrust.

"Magic indeed," Joanha snorted, dismissing her with a curt wave. "There was no Guardian. They're no good to us, Will."

"Don't be so quick to judge, Joanha. There could be some truth to it all," the older man said thoughtfully.

"Oh, come on Will. They'll be more trouble than they're worth," Joanha replied, gesturing obscenely with his sword.

"If they have magic, then they're worth a great deal!" Will shot back. He turned to face Manfred. "What manner of magic do you possess, friend?"

"Friend?" Manfred chewed on the word as though tasting something bitter in his mouth. "You insult us, take our weapons, hold us captive, and yet feel free to call me friend?"

"I do apologise, but we have yet to establish your reason for being here and to decide if you are a threat. Now, I ask again; what manner of magic do you possess?"

"I, myself, have none," he said, and indicated Karen. "She's the one who blew a hole the size of my fist through the Guardian." Will's eyes widened as he turned to regard her.

"*Y-you* seared a Guardian?"

"You are quick to accept him as the one with power, but ready to disbelieve I could have the strength to destroy the enemy," Karen replied evenly, calling to mind the memory that few would trust power in a woman. She wondered at his words though. Seared the Guardian? There was a word for what she had done? She spoke on: "Is it so hard to accept that I have such power?"

Will searched her features.

"You are of Elfish descent. That much is obvious." He eyes remained sceptical.

"What's your business here, so far from Ildare?" Joanha interjected. "Why this direction?"

Manfred and Karen exchanged uncertain glances before Karen answered, "We travel to Nearbrook."

"Nearbrook! You have far to go then," the unnamed man said.

"Then perhaps we may continue on our way," Manfred voiced for both him and Karen.

"Oh no. Not yet, I'm afraid. We don't know what dangers you bring," Will said.

"We are not a threat to you," Karen insisted. "But they may still followed us. Is there a safer place to talk than the open plains?"

The three men exchanged glances, Joanha's openly mistrusting.

"This way," Will said eventually, and led them deeper into the forest of rock.

They soon approached a cluster of boulders. Karen and Manfred found this pile of stone indistinguishable from all the other rocks. Joanha and the other young man moved one of the smaller boulders, revealing an entranceway leading to darkness. Will, in the meantime, spoke with Karen and Manfred.

"I am Will and that, of course, is Joanha," he said, pointing. "This is Shawlen," The third man of their company nodded briefly. "We are part of the rebellion against the Ebbrings and their minions." Karen saw Manfred's brief nod, as though confirming something to himself. "Know that, although we bring you to this place freely, should you betray us, you will not escape here alive."

Joanha and Shawlen moved into the darkness of a tunnel beyond the entrance carrying torches left for such a purpose.

"This way," Will said, waiting for them to enter. Karen looked at Manfred, who shrugged and extended his arm toward the darkness.

"After you," the large warrior said wryly. Karen walked in, shadowed by Manfred. Will turned to seal the entrance, then they were off. The tunnel felt cool and slightly musty, a thing of nature carved long ago. A thin mat of lichen covered the stony walls. Karen wondered how it grew without a hint of sunlight. However it survived, the lichen did little to reflect the torchlight, making the tunnel walls feel closer than they were.

Their little group descended into the depths of the passageway. Now and again, the flames of the torch licked the blackened ceiling, and more often than not, Manfred had to walk hunched over so as not to hit his head. Twice, they turned and followed an adjacent passage, and finally stopped in a large chamber illuminated by several torches.

The ceiling here rose eight or nine feet and various signs of occupation—blankets, pots, weaponry—cluttered the edges of the stone room's ample floor. Several people stopped whatever they had been doing and watched warily as Karen and Manfred passed, surrounded by the trio guarding them. Karen peered uneasily at the rebels. She felt no danger, but was still unused to encountering people. Ildare had not provided a pleasant introduction into the outside world.

Their procession halted, brought up short by a dark-haired, middle-aged man in a dark tunic and faded pants. He had a strong build and held himself with assurance. He had a lived-in face, rough and scarred from an old burn, but his eyes spoke of laughter not so long forgotten.

"Who are these strangers, Will?"

Movement resumed as the people in the cavern went about their business, apparently confident in the skills of this man. Will moved off a few paces with this new person, but Karen could still hear their exchange.

"We found them in the flatlands to the north. They claim to be running from Guardians," Will whispered.

"Why?"

"Apparently, they killed one back in Ildare. Now they're travelling to Nearbrook."

"Killed one eh? In the town?" His gaze barely flickered to Karen and Manfred, but Karen felt the man had taken their measure in that brief glance. "If they're running, then there was more than one Guardian. How did they escape?"

"The girl says she's got magic. Apparently she seared him. But how she avoided retaliation ... Unless they caught the Guardians completely by surprise—and we all know how hard that is—I don't know how they escaped unharmed."

"They didn't," the man said. Will took their measure himself, his eyes finding the rip in Karen's tunic.

"Perhaps they lured him away from his companions with magic and then slew him," Will mused. "It's possible, but they haven't told us just what happened."

"Hmm. And their threat value?"

"If they killed a Guardian, we're on the same side. If it's just a story to get to us, then we're better protected here," Will replied. "However, if any Guardians do follow, we could find ourselves in more immediate danger."

"And knowing that, you brought them here," the man stated.

"Listen Chanet, it's safer here. There's enough of us to defend ourselves. Besides, we kept a careful lookout."

The other man, Chanet, sighed heavily and turned to face Karen and Manfred.

"Very well." Moving back to them, Chanet pointed at Manfred and commanded, "You. What's your name?"

"I am known as the Stalker. This is Karen." He squared his shoulders. "Why do you keep us captive?"

"You could be a threat to us. You, girl. You have magic?"

Karen nodded, but said nothing. Chanet stepped closer to her, studying her.

"Strong magic? Enough to overthrow a Guardian?" Again, Karen nodded. "Were you born with magic, or taught it?"

Karen hesitated before answering. This Chanet did not possess magic of his own, but he obviously knew at least some of its workings. So did the enemy. Surely these rebels did not intend her or Manfred any harm, especially if they looked for help in their fight, yet she could not fully bring herself to trust them.

"Both," she replied finally. "My parents held vast powers and my father taught me how to use them."

"Held? I assume they are dead, then?"

Karen nodded slowly.

"Then there is no harm in telling us who they were, for it could not possibly harm them."

"No, but it could harm me," Karen replied.

"In what manner? If you've power enough to destroy a Guardian, what possible threat could we pose?" He kept his tone gentle, but it demanded an answer.

44

Karen's eyes flickered to Manfred before she replied. Something in Chanet's voice convinced her that she could reveal her past without threat, at least here. She found her doubts easing.

"My mother was High Priestess of the Elves. Her name was Sadricha. My father held the power of many, for he was a Druid."

"A Druid?" Joanha demanded suspiciously. "What Druid?"

"The last of the Druids to have walked in this world of men. The Druid Draimar."

Karen stared in surprise at the reaction her words brought. Both Will and Shawlen had fallen to their knees, heads bowed. Joanha glanced at them too, then looked to Chanet. The rebel leader, also down on one knee, raised his eyes to meet Joanha's.

"Have a little respect," he hissed.

"Respect? Respect for what?" Joanha whispered harshly.

"You stand before the daughter of a powerful man."

"Wha ... you believe her?" Joanha shot back incredulously.

"None would dare claim to be the offspring of such unless true," Chanet explained through clenched teeth. "And she does bear his resemblance. At least bow your head in acknowledgement of the truth." He lowered his own eyes again. Will and Shawlen watched this spectacle furtively, awaiting its outcome, yet their heads remained bowed.

With a scowl upon his face, Joanha slowly lowered his eyes and gave a quick bow of his head. Karen gazed in wonder and confusion at the four men, and then at Manfred. The warrior shrugged, unsure of what to do or say next. He opened his mouth, about to speak, thought better of it, and brought his lips together. He shrugged again.

"Please," Karen began. "You need not fear me. I will not harm you. That is not why I am here." She paused, gesturing to them to stand, not knowing what else to do. On their feet, Will, Shawlen and Joanha had raised their heads slightly, yet their eyes remained downcast. Joanha's scowl said louder than words that he did not like that fact.

"Why, then, are you here?" Chanet inquired, unable to meet her gaze.

"We were on our way to Nearbrook when your men brought us here. Now, if you are through with us, we have little

45

time," Manfred said.

"Will you at least honour us by staying to eat? Our tunnels approach Nearbrook and can ensure cover from pursuers for a great distance."

"Thank you, Chanet," Karen said, remembering that neither she nor Manfred had eaten since the inn. "We will stay to eat, but must leave as soon as possible."

Chanet nodded and ordered preparations for what little food the rebels could provide.

Chapter 5

An hour later, after some much needed rest, Karen and Manfred sat in a small room around a makeshift table with various members of the rebellion, Will and Chanet among them. Both Joanha and Shawlen had disappeared to go about their duties, Joanha gruffly and Shawlen very politely.

Some dried fruit accompanied the rabbit meat that Chanet distributed. He apologised for the meagreness of the fare, explaining how many of the farmers who had provided them with food had met early fates.

"The Guardians somehow discover who supplies us. The bastards show no mercy. Kill families, take livestock, burn down entire homes. We've lost many good men. Now we acquire what we need any way we can." He spoke with great sorrow while the room remained sheathed in silence.

At last, Karen spoke.

"You said I bear a resemblance to my father. You knew him, Chanet?"

Chanet nodded as he chewed his food.

"I was a lieutenant in his army. Only met him the once, but he's not one you quickly forget. You have the shape of his eyes and something about how you carry yourself reminds me of him. I didn't really notice until you named him your father, though."

"Did you ... how did he die?"

Chanet regarded her with dark, sad eyes.

"He had us gather in the field for battle, then went off in search of the enemy leaders, the ones with magic. He planned to stall them long enough for us to have a chance at victory. I heard a lot of noise and saw flames and flashes, but we never saw him again. We were too busy trying to survive. But they were too many and had more magic users than we did. The story goes that he held off the Evil long enough for the few of us who survived to escape. Then, weakened by the drain of magic, he gave his life in a brilliant explosion that destroyed the enemy for miles around.

"Most of the survivors fled, hoping to find refuge back home. The enemy had faltered at the end, but the Guardians exerted control soon after that battle. We had lost our leaders. Fear of magic strong enough to destroy the Druid made it that much easier for the terrors and dominance of the Ebbrings and Guardians to gain a foothold. Those of us who still had the will to fight were shunned and no longer welcomed in the cities and villages. So we ended up here, holed up in tunnels and caverns across the land, branded as outcasts and rebels. But we fight on. Draimar's cause lives on in us. He gave his life for our freedom, and what you see around you are the men and women willing to die for that freedom."

The others at the table, determination burning in their eyes, added their agreement. Freedom from tyranny was all these people had left, and a tenuous freedom at that. But as they struggled to hold on to that ideal, they never forgot their past, how they came to this point in life. Draimar had opened the door to a life free from the horrors of the Ebbrings and their followers. These people had but to keep that door open long enough for the world to recognise the beauty of that freedom which lay beyond.

Partway through the meal, Joanha returned, a longbow at his side and a quiver of arrows slung across his back. He went directly to Chanet and whispered something to him. Chanet rose and all eyes turned to him.

"There are Guardians at our borders and approaching fast. They've Death Hounds with them. It's likely they'll discover this entrance." He paused, surveying the occupants of the room. "Put the plan into action."

All stood except Karen and Manfred and prepared for the coming danger. Joanha slipped out after a quick glare in Karen's direction. Chanet moved to speak briefly with Will, his jaw clenched. He came and stood before Manfred and Karen

48

as Will left the room.

"We'll barricade the entrance hall to Tunnel Three here a few feet in. It'll look like a solid wall. Tracks will be made to Tunnel Five, and that'll be blocked also. This should confuse them at least long enough for us to evacuate. We'll make the caves look uninhabitable and erase all traces of our passing. We have to move fast and would appreciate any help you can provide."

"We'll do whatever we can," Manfred said. "Where do we start?"

"Follow me," Chanet replied. Torch in hand, he led them back through the large chamber, now alive with motion, then up through the familiar tunnels to where they had first entered the rebel base.

"It's your scent they'll search for. Go with Will. He'll bring you to the other entrance where you can help block it off. From there, someone will guide you to the tunnels leading to Nearbrook."

"You are going?" Karen asked, suddenly not wanting to leave this man who had known her father, though only briefly.

"I must oversee operations in the main hall. Everything has to be exact." He turned to go, but Karen held him back a moment.

"Thank you for all your help Chanet. Perhaps we will meet again."

He looked into her eyes. Slowly, he smiled and, without another word, retreated confidently back through the dark tunnel, leaving them the torch.

"We'll have to hurry," said Will as he approached from behind. "This way." They moved through a tunnel neither Karen nor Manfred had seen earlier.

Ten minutes passed before Will stopped them and spoke again.

"This is the other entrance." Both Karen and Manfred looked, but could see no distinguishing features to mark the way.

"Here," Will held up the torch he had taken, indicating a very faint outline. "Would you help?" he asked Manfred. Karen took the torch as Will and Manfred pushed at the wall. It gave way, causing a few particles of sand to loosen and drift into the tunnel.

"You'll have to go out a little distance, then retrace your steps and hurry back. This will confuse their hounds, but not for long."

Karen nodded. Followed by Manfred, they went out. They stood in the lifeless rock field. Boulders and dry earth stretched into the distance. They could not even see the forest near Ildare. They did as Will suggested, circling a rock or two to leave their scent, then quickly returned to where he waited. Will sealed the entrance once more and turned to them.

"Now, the difficult part is getting to Tunnel Five without leaving a trace. We'll use these."

He reached up and pointed out something on the ceiling of the tunnel barely within arm's reach. He had to stand tiptoe to get a firm hold onto what appeared to be some sort of bar attached to the roof.

"There are various support bars hidden up here, like a horizontal ladder. So long as you don't touch the ground, no proper scent should be left for their dogs. Hopefully, it will stall them, confuse them enough to give us more time," Will explained. "You'll have to leave the torch. But don't worry," his lips quirked in a momentary smile. "The bars are evenly spaced."

With that, he started off on the bars, knees bent to keep them as far from the floor as possible. Manfred looked askance at Karen, but she had already reached for the bars above her head and swung off after Will. Manfred shook his head, looking back at the entrance. With a sigh, he doused the light, and awkwardly followed his companions.

It took nearly five minutes before they saw light from where rebels worked at the other entrance. By then, agony screaming in abused arms, all three breathed heavily.

Shawlen appeared from the mass of people piling rocks and debris to cover the tunnel.

"Glad you're here. We can use the help. Now," he regarded Karen. "I know you can't use your magic to help for fear of Guardian detection, but we'd appreciate any physical labour. From both," he added, looking at Manfred.

They nodded and moved to help the other rebels camouflage the entrance. Shawlen, meanwhile, took Will aside to discuss the progress of the Guardians.

"They'll be at the other entrance in about twenty minutes,"

Shawlen said.

"That soon? How's the other blockade coming along?"

"Near completion. Five minutes, tops."

"How long for this one? Ten?"

"I figure that's long enough. It has to be." Shawlen looked anxiously to where Karen and Manfred worked. "Who's leading them out?"

"Chanet wants Joanha to, but I don't know. Joanha doesn't trust them. Besides, he's not here and we can't wait for him to show." Will shifted his weight restlessly. "No, it has to be someone else, someone on hand and nearby."

"I know the way," Shawlen said. "I can move fast and you don't really need me here."

"Are you sure?" Will's eyes tracked the working rebels. "You want to take the risk?"

"That's why I joined," Shawlen replied with a grin, drawing Will's attention.

After a moment of hesitation, Will nodded.

"You'll need the supply kit we arranged. It has food rations that should last for part of your journey, but you'll have to stop for more in a few days. Use the water smartly; it's all we can spare." He paused. "After Nearbrook, go on to the Sandrogan tunnels and let them know what's happened and to avoid this area for a while. Some of the others will follow you later. The rest of us will go to Rischa or Incarn. Someone will have to let those north of Sheol know too." He looked fondly at the younger man. "Well, see you soon then." He offered his hand. Shawlen clasped it, mid-arm before pulling the older man into a hug.

"Good luck, brother," Will said, pushing away after a moment. Shawlen nodded solemnly, then turned and called to Karen and Manfred.

"It's time to go. We'll come upon Nearbrook before you know it."

Will called after them: "Thanks for the help." Karen smiled as she and Manfred followed Shawlen into the dark recesses of the network of tunnels.

Chapter 6

The torch Shawlen carried did little to chase away the darkness. Karen and Manfred had to stay close to him, lest they lose him in the shadows. They followed the many twists and turns of the tunnel for hours without break. But they pushed on in spite of exhaustion, hoping to cover as much distance as possible in this first day. After several hours, it became a chore just to put one foot in front of the other. Karen recalled her many excursions into the forest and mountains around her home. She thought back to the times that she had spent climbing Cleaver Point and hiking around the distant, quiet countryside. She had often spent many days in such exercise, yet this journey found her stumbling. She reminded herself that she had only rested that brief hour earlier, and not much more than that for two days. The near darkness closing in all around, the oppressive dampness turning her flesh clammy, and the underground chill seeping into her bones did not help either. Finally, Shawlen called for a halt.

The rebel took out the supply kit Will had given him. Unwrapping it to reveal some food and a canteen of water, he dispensed equal rations.

"I'm afraid these kits only contain the bare essentials for such trips," he sighed. "At some point, we will have to go above ground to replenish supplies. I know a place along the way that will do."

Shawlen took out some dried meat, a little cheese and some bread. He put aside a small portion of dried fruit for a morning meal. In the gloom of the tunnel, morning and night would soon become indistinguishable.

Karen checked her injury. Her Elfin blood carried self-healing qualities, a trait she had discovered as a young child eagerly exploring the world. That, combined with the calenda leaves, had nearly healed her wound and she decided to forego any additional bandages. Manfred spoke, breaking the silence.

"Your tunnels are extensive. I had no idea they went so far as Nearbrook."

"Are you saying you've been in them before?" Shawlen asked.

"Not in them. I have heard of them though."

"Ah, yes. The Stalker, best tracker to be found. I had heard you worked alone. Why do you go to Nearbrook?"

"These are hard times my friend," he replied simply. "The odd job now and then keeps a man in shape, especially one against Guardians." He looked away. "Actually, I go to help Karen."

"But why Nearbrook? What's there?"

Karen explained briefly. Shawlen raised a brow.

"Yet, what kind of help does the daughter of the Druid need?"

"I do not know yet. But one can never have too much help, no matter the nature of one's father."

Shawlen smiled, laughing faintly. He looked down the passageway. "We should get moving. We have a long way to go."

"How long will it take?" Karen asked. She remembered how far Nearbrook looked on the runic maps she had studied from one of her father's scrolls.

"Just under two weeks if we keep the pace steady."

They continued on then, saying little. At times, the scurrying feet of a tunnel rat rushed past. The occasional drop of moisture from overhead interrupted the silence. The three stopped only when necessary, meals being scarce and eaten quickly, with rest breaks just long enough to grab a small nap. These caverns held little comfort for extended periods of sleep, but Karen welcomed the breaks even if they doused the torch and were lost to the oppressive darkness at these times. After a while, she grew used to her weariness and the quiet provided her time to think, and to accustom herself to being around other people.

As she walked, she thought about the last time she had seen her father. She remembered standing among the tall leafy trees of the woods that sheltered their little cottage, a gentle breeze stirring her hair in the early morning.

Karen crouched low in the sparse forest grass, sharp Elfin eyes searching her surroundings. She spotted movement again, a fleeting shadow passing quickly from one silverleaf to the next, and disappearing just as fast. With the quiet stealth of a wildcat hunting its prey, she crept forward, nearing the wooded area that last concealed her quarry. In this exercise, stealth and caution mattered as much as magic. Even at twelve, she understood how these concepts melded together. Along with wisdom and knowledge, she reminded herself. The ability to use magic was nothing without knowledge and the wisdom to understand that knowledge.

The earth began to shake all around her, bringing a flurry of foliage cascading down around her head. She dropped to a crouch. Three blue fissures rent the ground ringing her like miniature volcanoes. Several rock stalactites spewed from them at sharp angles, shooting chunks of dirt and rock in all directions, forming a stone cage dense enough to trap her. The trembling ground grew still as the cage completed its enclosure. She raised her arm slightly and unclenched her hand as a bubble of red energy shot out from her palm, creating a small explosion, but one more controlled than in years past. The stones crumbled, allowing her to escape.

Awaiting her beyond the cage stood a handful of wild creatures, each a jumble of fur and fangs encompassing red-brown eyes. Some had the pointed ears of felines while others possessed the elongated jaws of canines, yet no one name could approximate the nature of these magical creatures. She stopped and tensed, preparing for the attack. The beasts neared. She gathered her magic, creating a soft red glow around her. The aura grew more intense as the animals advanced. They paused, unsure. One, braver than the rest, kept moving forward. It leapt with a growl rising from its dog-like throat, but burst into flames before it could reach her. The others attacked en masse only to meet a similar fate. The glow around Karen faded with the demise of the last creature and she looked to the trees once more. She could easily destroy such simple conjurings , but they often hid the creation of something much more sinister. She waited but a moment for that something to appear.

A figure detached itself from a clump of leatherleaf and lumbered toward her, towering to a dizzying height. Broad shoulders dwarfed muscle-laden arms that curved into sharp claws. It growled, steaming saliva dripping from razor-sharp fangs, but it did not attack like the other beasts had. Instead, it began to circle her slowly. She leaned away, ready to run for cover. In a blur of movement, its speed belying its great bulk, the figure appeared before her, blocking her path of escape. A bright red flash forced the creature to step back, but its eyes found Karen once more, standing motionless before it. It growled again and approached in a tightening circle, cutting off any chance of retreat. Barely a breath away, it reached out a claw with unnatural speed, but it passed harmlessly through her. At that moment, a searing streak of red lightning emerged from the air behind it, tearing the beast apart before it could react. It crumpled to the ground with a horrifying wail, then faded into ash. Silence gripped the woods a moment before a man in dark robes stepped into the light, the shadow of his hood not quite hiding the proud grin upon his face. Karen released her mist of concealment and dispelled the illusion of herself that had fooled the giant beast, her own smile a reflection of the man's.

'Excellent, Karen,' She heard the words spoken in her mind, a method of mind-speech that her father had taught her. 'Your powers are very well advanced.'

'Thank you, father,' Karen replied, also using the mind communication. She had grown confident with this method of speech and felt she fully understood her ability to project mere thoughts into mental language and transmit them by a psychic link of magic.

'Now, I want you to ...' The Druid stopped, listening to something in the distance. Karen looked around but saw nothing. Images of events in a far away place clouded Draimar's dark eyes. A vision, a premonition or foreshadowing of events to come.

He had told Karen about this—when he had spoken of the outside world, the world of man. What he saw now reflected trouble in that world. Visions always did. Her father had explained how nature could see an imbalance before mortals *could. To rectify these problems, the forces that guided magic sought out those who could put things right. In the past, Druids often provided that solution. And Draimar was the last in that line. Karen knew what would follow this vision. This was a day she had always feared, the day that she would lose her father.*

"Karen," Draimar looked upon his daughter with a clear, determined resolve. "I must leave." Karen shook her head, but he continued. "I told you the day would come when I would have to go. I fear I may not return."

"Father, no! Why must you go to your death? Can we not forget the world of man?"

"No." His answer came sharp as a whip. He took a deep breath, his eyes sad. "If I do not help, the danger will eventually reach us and by then, it will be too late. Although I have no wish to die, I must go."

"Can I come with you?" Her voice trembled despite her best attempts to control it. Draimar looked at her for a long time in silence, as though trying to overcome some inner turmoil. He hugged her, then stepped back, his tanned hands still resting on her shoulders.

"This is not your time. Soon, you will see your own destiny. Don't be afraid of the visions. Follow your instincts and remember what I have taught you." He touched her cheek and smiled sadly, kissing her forehead. "You remind me very much of your mother. You have her beauty, and her heart. Good-bye, my lovely child."

He walked toward the trees without looking back, disappearing into their depths as though swallowed. Karen watched him go and, choking back tears, raised her hand in a wave.

"Farewell, father. I love you."

The guttering of the torch in the rebel tunnels brought her back to the present. She wiped at her tears before they had a chance to fall. She was glad of the dimness because it hid her weakness.

When the torch finally gave out, Shawlen had them tie a length of rope about themselves so that they did not become separated, rather than lighting another torch. That suited Karen. The smoke from the pitch hurt her eyes in the close confines.

***

"We'll be at the Goran entrance in minutes. We need more supplies and this is a good spot for foraging."

After three days of walking in virtual silence and darkness, Shawlen's voice pierced the air as he stopped them.

"We'll have to wait a bit. The entryway is concealed, but it's busy around midday. It wouldn't do us any good for someone to see us pop out of nowhere."

Karen stopped a second before Manfred did and he bumped into her. He apologised, his hand on her back to steady her as he addressed the rebel. "How can you tell what time of day it is in these tunnels?"

"Having lived here as long as I have, you get a feel for it," Shawlen replied with a chuckle as he lit a torch.

"Right now, I'd believe you if you said it was midnight," Manfred said lightly, his hand falling, though his presence remained a constant heat at Karen's side. He seemed distracted for some reason.

Shawlen divided up the last of their supplies for a quick lunch. As with most of their meals, this one began in silence. They untied their connection rope, laying it aside for later. Then Karen asked:

"How long have you been here?" Shawlen thought for a moment before replying.

"'Bout five years. I'd been helping my family take care of the farm until the mayor confiscated our land for the use of the Guardians. My parents disappeared for arguing the matter. A holiday, I think the mayor called it, the kind you don't return from. I didn't plan to follow them to their graves without a fight, so I joined my brother with the rebellion." His voice grew distant. "Will's more like a father than a brother sometimes. But I've proven my value." Shawlen paused, then said in a business-like tone:

"I'll go into town, see what food I can get. I'll check if there's been any sign of Guardians. You two stay under cover until I return. If Guardians do come this way, they may have a description of you. I've been here before, so I'm less likely to cause suspicion. There are some edible wild plants nearby you could gather. And if you don't know what they are—" he shrugged. "Don't bother—no time to show you which are safe."

57

Karen smiled to herself at that. She knew how to identify the edibles from the poisons. "I'll return soon. Try to keep out of sight." Shawlen moved toward the entrance. Karen stopped him with a hand to his shoulder before he had the doorway more than a crack open.

"Take this," she said, handing him her gold pouch. She had already removed some for her and Manfred to use later in their journey. "You may need some." Shawlen looked at the money, his eyes nearly popping, then glanced up at Karen.

"Where did you get this?"

"My father left it for me." She cocked her head. "Why? Is it not enough?"

"Not enough?" Shawlen nearly choked on the words. "Why, there's enough here to buy the whole town! I can't take all this." He tried to push the pouch back into Karen's hand. She had no idea that gold would cause such excitement. Now she better understood the reaction of the innkeeper back in Ildare.

Instead of taking the gold back, she wrapped Shawlen's fingers around the pouch. "Take it," she said. "Use it in your fight."

Shawlen tried to object, but the look in Karen's eyes changed his mind. He carefully tucked it into his belt.

"Thank you," he murmured, shock and gratitude vying for dominance.

He turned to the entrance again and cautiously pushed open the door the rest of the way. Peering about in the sudden glare of midday, he saw no one from the concealment of bushes protecting the entrance. On his knees, he looked back down at Karen and Manfred.

"The town is just over there," he pointed to his right. "If you come up, the cover is thicker over here," he gestured left, "but don't wander too far." He turned his gaze to the right. Without looking back at them, he said, "I won't be long, but if something does happen, get out of the tunnels and leave me. Nearbrook's nine days in the tunnels, but unless you know them, you'd be lost in two."

Shawlen glanced back. He quickly averted his gaze from Karen, watching Manfred instead. "Give me an hour." Then he was gone.

Manfred turned to Karen.

"Nine days. That's good. If we travelled over the land instead of under it, it would take us twice that time to reach Nearbrook. The paths through Alberion Woods are long and not very straight, and then we'd have to cross the Alberion River beyond that." Karen nodded, picturing in her head these familiar names from her map. "The river is difficult to cross at the best of times, and treacherous now, with the spring thaw. But the tunnels must go deep to go under the river." He paused in silent contemplation.

Karen took in their surroundings from the tunnel entrance. She could see little other than the bushes hiding them, but she could hear the chatter of birds and, more distantly, the creak of wagon wheels slowly moving along a dirt road. She pulled herself out of the tunnel, Manfred close behind, and stopped, listening for any other signs of life. When she heard nothing else, she went in search of some of the wild plants Shawlen had mentioned.

Chapter 7

Shawlen sauntered into town, passing some of the smaller carts offering wares that did not interest him—jewellery, clothing, blankets, medicines sworn to cure all ailments, and other items overpriced for their quality. He passed some of the shabbier wooden houses with their thatch roofs until he came closer to the centre of town. Further along the main road lay the finer brick and mortar dwellings topped usually with tile, though some still had thatch. But that part of Goran didn't interest him. Here, at the centre of town, stood the Market.

He paused at some of the carts, inspecting the food items, calculating in his head how much they'd need to get them closer to Nearbrook. He didn't want to buy too much for fear of raising suspicions, but he didn't relish the idea of having to stop later on for more supplies either. He already putt Karen and Manfred at some risk by stopping here, but they needed food. Using the gold Karen had given him would invite questions, but perhaps buying in quantity would ease any problems. Besides, he looked for someone specific who would ask few questions and give him little hassle.

He moved from one cart to another, surreptitiously searching for the woman. At last he saw her, long hair tied back and dark skin flushed in the heat of the spring day, a few carts further on. She had her usual foodstuffs on display: fish, nuts, figs and cheeses. That would go well with the meat and bread he had already purchased. He eased his way over to her, gave her a subtle wink, and carefully studied some cheese. With a smile that lit her tilted green eyes, she took some coppers from a customer and his wife in exchange for some nuts and shooed them away. She came and stood beside Shawlen, gently nudging him with her shoulder.

"Well handsome, been a long time," her voice, silky smooth as always, presented a pleasant contrast from the crass calls of her fellow hucksters. "What's up?"

Shawlen grinned. Miranda always did get to the point.

"Need some things, Mira. A supply of food for a week or so."

"Some kind of trouble, sweetie?" Her easy style never ceased to amaze him. Though happily engaged with another, Miranda constantly put forth her flirtatious side to keep people off guard. It could be a great advantage against those who didn't know her. That was one way she found much information useful to the rebels. Her open nature to friend and foe alike kept people oblivious to her association with the rebellion.

"Just travelling for a while out of the heat of the sun."

"Ah," she hummed. "Then you must be lonely."

"I have enough to keep me occupied. Sometimes I feel I could eat enough for three people."

She smiled, easily understanding him. A man came to look at her wares, but the scent of fresh bread and smoked meat from the cart next to Miranda's enticed him away. After the stranger moved on, Miranda turned to Shawlen again.

"For such a healthy appetite, you've come to the right woman. I think I can fix you up with enough that even your palate would approve. But I'm afraid it will cost."

Shawlen's grimace melted easily into a smile.

"Always does." He glanced around, making sure no one stood close enough to hear him. "Listen, Miranda, I need information too. And I've got enough to make it worth your while." He carefully slipped a gold piece out of the pouch and pressed it into her palm. "There been any Guardians about?" She looked down at the coin, then raised an eyebrow to Shawlen.

"Nothing more than usual, sweetie, but they're watching a little more than normal."

"Any idea why?"

"Well..." She took a breath as Shawlen handed her some cheese and nuts to wrap for him, keeping up the pretence of being no more than a customer. "You know how rumours go.

Some say they're looking for informers, others claim they want recruits. Seems to me they search for someone in particular. You ever heard of the Stalker?" Shawlen nodded, his muscles tensing ever so slightly. "I've heard tell he's the one they're after, though I don't know why. Seems he took off with something they want. Someone's more like it, though."

"What do you mean?"

"Guardians aren't too subtle about their questions. They've warned us to watch for this Stalker and then, in the next breath, ask us about some girl. They claim the events are unrelated, but I have my own views. We're supposed to report anyone out of the ordinary. Lucky for you, your face isn't entirely unknown hereabouts." Her slap on his bottom caused him to jump, his face flaming crimson. She laughed and motioned with her eyes. Shawlen grabbed her around the waist in a tight squeeze, adding his own laugh when he saw the two Guardians she had indicated. One equalled Shawlen's height with very short-cut dark hair; the other stood somewhat shorter and walked with a limp. They had approached Miranda's cart, their eyes on Shawlen, but her show of familiarity with him seemed to make them pause. But not for long.

"A friend of yours, Miranda?" the smaller man asked, his voice a raspy whisper. Shawlen noticed a scar along his neck.

"Sure is. Johnny's from the outskirts of Alberion. He comes by now and again, keeps a girl's spirits up he does." Miranda's smooth lies made Shawlen grin, an act entirely befitting his supposed role. The Guardian looked at Shawlen again, considering.

"Johnny, is it?" The tone was sharp. "Where you headed?"

"Well, sir," Shawlen kept his tone jovial, but not disrespectful. "I had planned to go on to Renchau, but Mira here has a way of lengthening stays in Goran." He hugged her again, giving a quick nuzzle to her ear. The Guardians studied him a moment longer, then turned to leave. The larger one stopped and turned back, his silver cape swirling.

"Should you happen to continue your journey, I'd advise that you watch out for strangers."

"Well, now, it's hard to avoid meeting people on the roads, sir." Shawlen adopted his most innocent face. "What would you have me do?" Dangerous to get information this way, but perhaps more dangerous to appear unconcerned about

62

Guardian warnings. When the Guardian smiled, Shawlen knew he had said the right thing.

"Any good citizen will inform one of us immediately of any suspicious activity."

Shawlen nodded. "I'll do that, sir. Thank you for the warning. Anyone in particular I should watch out for?"

The Guardian raised an eyebrow. "You want to especially stay away from large men. No telling what kind of danger they might pose. You would also do well to tell us if you should encounter any pretty young women who seem out of place. I hear blondes are the worst." Shawlen kept his jaw from dropping with an effort. He could see the lack of subtlety Miranda had mentioned. Obviously the Guardians were more concerned with catching their quarry than with being secretive. "Anyone coming from the west could be dangerous. Do you understand that, Johnny?"

"Oh, yes sir. I'll be sure to keep my eyes open."

The smaller Guardian snorted. "See that you do, Johnny." He turned back to Miranda before leaving. "Keep yourself out of trouble." After they had passed out of hearing, Miranda leaned over to Shawlen.

"Any idea what that was all about?"

"Some," he replied with a short nod. "Thanks, Mira. I have to get going."

"Here," she put some extra food into a pouch and gave it to him. "You take care of them." He gave her a quick kiss on the cheek, slipped another gold piece into her hand and left before she could protest.

***

"So news has certainly preceded you," Shawlen finished. He had returned to the tunnel just after Karen and Manfred. They had gathered a good supply of narong roots and carnda leaves to supplement their diet, and Shawlen judged that they had enough to get them to Nearbrook. They had started out again as soon as Shawlen returned, and he now spoke to them in the renewed darkness of the tunnels.

"It seems unlikely that the Guardians from Ildare could have moved so fast. They don't have access to anything like our tunnels, so they must have sent word ahead. We have a couple of magic users who can send out word without having to leave one place for another. My guess is that's what happened, so it's less likely that any hereabouts know what you look like, Karen. Their description certainly didn't help much. Miranda says they're looking for you, Manfred, but they're less clear about Karen. I'm hoping that by the time we reach Nearbrook, word won't have reached there yet. Maybe they won't think to look so far afield for you. Still, I'd like to get there as quickly as possible, keep them off guard any way we can."

"I agree," Manfred said. "If there's any way to shorten the trip, that's more time on our side."

"In a couple of days, we go under the Alberion River. I was going to keep left to the easier tunnel. It has a lot of switchbacks to make the descent easier, but it also takes longer. If we go through the right tunnel, we can knock off a day, but it's more dangerous. The way is much steeper, especially going back up, and it gets pretty tight. One wrong step and we won't be worrying about time anymore. We've lost more than one person down there. But if you want to risk it, we can give it a go."

Karen thought about her vision, about the sense of urgency she had felt when she saw Jans. She had dealt with the difficult paths of Cleaver Point almost her whole life. Steep and narrow did not even begin to define those paths.

"I think the time saved is worth the risk," she said. "We'll take the right tunnel."

Shawlen nodded in the dark and the three continued on in silence.

***

The ground began to fall swiftly. They had lengthened the distance between themselves on the rope, but only enough so that if one should fall, the other two would not tumble also, taking all three into an uncontrollable plunge. Shawlen led them with one hand gripping a torch to light the way and the other constantly using the wall as a guide. He warned them of the sudden drop-off at the bottom of the incline.

The increased moisture in the air and trickling down the walls spoke to the proximity of the Alberion River. The tunnel grew particularly slippery in spots and a small dribble of water wound down a groove in the middle of the path—if one could call the tunnel floor a path—to the drop-off Shawlen said lay ahead. They could hear the sound of that small bit of water cascading over the precipice. The height of the tunnel and the depth of the drop-off amplified the noise to a steady roar, but Shawlen led them confidently. The incline made it almost impossible not to run, which helped speed them along, but also made it more dangerous the closer they got to the edge. The sound of dripping water grew louder the deeper they went, a constant reminder of the river above pressing down on them.

When Shawlen signalled with the torch to the side, the three dropped to a crouch, trying to slow their progress. Karen slipped, but quickly regained her footing, only to have Shawlen slip in front of her. Karen and Manfred leaned back, pulling on the rope to stop the rebel's motion. The torch slipped out of his hand and disappeared over a drop just ahead, following the fall of the trickling water into a deep canyon. In the sudden darkness, Shawlen climbed to his knees, his momentum halted by the pull of the rope. He cursed under his breath at the loss of their light, but thanked his companions for not losing him.

"I could try to light the path ahead," Karen called loudly over the din of the waterfall after a few minutes of silence had dragged by.

"The Guardians can sense magic. They might find the tunnel," Shawlen called back.

"Then let them come down and fall into oblivion," she replied. "We are far enough underground and the river runs deep. Surely they will not sense much down here. Even if they do, we will not linger. We have you to tell us of the dangers, Shawlen. They have no one. If you think we can find the way in the dark, then proceed. Otherwise, we only have one torch left. If we lose that, then what? We will need that torch later. But now, we will use magic."

Shawlen sighed in the darkness. "You're right. I'm sorry. It will be easier with two hands anyway. I have nothing to light, though."

"I do not need anything." She lifted her hand, a small red ball of light forming in her palm. It grew to about the size of an apple, giving off at least as much light as the torch had. She sent the ball past Shawlen's amazed face to the drop-off and let it hover there. Shawlen looked Karen's way, then back to the red ball with a slight shake of his head. On hands and knees, he began to crawl forward, Karen and Manfred right behind. Just before reaching the light, Shawlen veered to the right to a small ledge ringing the canyon beyond. He eased himself back to his feet, keeping his back pressed firmly against the wall. Karen and Manfred followed suit. Karen's ball of light followed them as they inched along this narrow ledge. They could not see the far wall, and the canyon fell into a black, fathomless pit. The sound of their own breathing, mixed with the thunder of the water, filled the cavern with eerie echoes. Bits of stone slid under them, adding their own disproportionate noise to the canyon, but the ledge remained solid.

At last, they reached the other side, and true to Shawlen's word, the tunnel back up rose nearly vertical, really more of a hole discovered by accident than a tunnel.

"There. Do you see them?" Shawlen's words echoed. They had moved far enough from the water that it had become a distant rumble now, making their voices seem much louder. Karen and Manfred looked to where Shawlen pointed. In the dim glow of the globe of magic, little notches, no more than an inch across, threw shadows against the otherwise smooth surface of the tunnel. Hard going indeed. Karen moved the light up a few feet to outline where the tunnel hole became close enough for a person to touch either side.

"That's it," Shawlen said. "We get up that far and we can use the walls themselves as support. But getting there is tricky. Those handholds are small."

"I will make sure we make it," Karen said. The men turned to her, questioning. She continued to look up, judging the distance. "The holds will support us and will not let us fall." She glanced back at them. "Unless you would prefer me to levitate us, but that would leave a heavier trace of magic."

"No," Shawlen spoke quickly and Manfred rapidly shook his head. "I'd rather not have to fly. Besides, it takes a sharp turn up there." Karen smiled. His fast rejection and hasty reasons spoke more of anxiety than anything else.

"Then we'd better get started," Manfred said, not sounding fazed in the least, though his eyes looked a trifle wider than usual. "The sooner we begin, the sooner we'll be back in more reasonable terrain."

Karen cast a small field of stability on the notches, then,

66

after checking the retention of the rope, nodded to Shawlen to begin the ascent, following the luminous ball up. As they climbed, a slight pull on their hands like a magnet to their flesh kept their grip firm as Karen's magic kept them safe from a fall. When they had reached a position where the walls closed in on them, Karen paused and gestured down past Manfred as best as she could given the tight space.

"What was that?" Manfred asked as the air shimmered briefly below him before returning to normal.

"I have put a temporary shield where the walls come together. If we should fall, the shield will catch us. If we are followed, it may slow our pursuers. I have released the stability field. To keep it up, I would have to cast it all around, and that would leave a heavy trace. We must now depend on each other and our own skills to get out of here."

They continued climbing, boosting each other and using the walls as support. At one point, the walls came so close that they feared Manfred would not make it, but he managed to wriggle his way through with little more than a couple of scrapes. Soon after that, Shawlen called down that they had reached the turn, a near jack-knife in the oppressive stone. Proceeding on hands and knees, for the way did not allow any more room, they moved along this little tunnel at an easier pace, the incline much less severe. Half an hour passed before Shawlen called for a halt in a space just large enough to sit in.

"It gets pretty tight for the next while. Especially for you, Manfred. The best way to get through is like a snake, on your belly and pulling with your arms above your head. One spot in particular, I know, nearly touches my back. I *think* there should be enough room for you to get by, but I can't guarantee it. After that, it opens up and the going gets less difficult."

Manfred nodded an acknowledgement and motioned them onwards. The musty odour of damp rock and mildew coated the back of their throats, overwhelming any hints of fresh air. Grunts of effort, the only sounds in the near darkness, reflected back a dull affirmation of their confining situation, but they moved on with no complaints. The ball of light led them on, although its glow beyond Shawlen's body did little to show Karen her surroundings, and helped Manfred not at all. Time dragged past in agonising slowness and screamed a lack of progress. But when Shawlen slowed to an inching procession, they knew that they had reached the narrowest part.

After Karen had followed the rebel through the narrow tunnel, the walls opened enough to make sitting almost comfortable. The little light hovered between Karen and Shawlen, as uncaring of the welcome space as to the oppressive confines still holding Manfred captive. Karen stopped and turned to wait for her friend. His arms came through slowly, pulling the rest of his body along. He had somehow unslung his sword from his back, pushing it through ahead of him, to give himself as much clearance as possible. The rock above touched his shoulders, then his back, pressing down on the large warrior.

Then he stopped.

Karen could see his fingers scrambling at the ground before him and could hear the scuffle of his boots as he tried to push from behind, but he didn't budge. He let out a muffled cry as he pushed again. A few tiny rock particles fell from the ceiling, but nothing else happened. Karen reached back and pulled his sword through, freeing his hands. She took hold of one of his callused hands while Shawlen waited. She spoke softly,

"Just a little more, Manfred. Come on, you can do it."

"I'm stuck, Karen," he wheezed, trying to get air into his lungs. "I can't move."

"Yes, you can. I am here. I will help." She gave his hand a reassuring squeeze. "Try it again."

He took a breath as best he could, and as he let it out, pushed again. Karen braced herself and tried to pull him along. Years of fending for herself in an oasis of nature had made her stronger than she appeared, yet even with this added help, Manfred only moved forward an inch.

"Again, Manfred," she said gently, taking his other hand. "Come on, my friend." He pushed once more, but didn't move. Karen looked up to Shawlen, but found only helplessness gazing back. She closed her eyes, trying to think, not knowing how to help. They neared the surface and using her magic had extreme risks, but she knew she would take that risk if all else failed. She could not lose him

"One more try, Manfred."

"I can't do it. I'm wedged in too tight," he wheezed. Still, she could hear the scuffle of his boots.

Karen opened her eyes and gazed into the steely greys looking back at her. With a tight smile, she spoke in a slightly accusatory tone, attempting to give him extra incentive.

"Manfred, how am I to get to Nearbrook without my guide and protector?" He blinked, a curious expression on his face. "If you stay here, I will have to go on alone." His eyes took on a more determined light. She gripped his hands tighter. "Come on, man. You have to try again."

He expunged all the air from his lungs and gave a mighty shove. Karen pulled him along as more little rocks crumbled down. He began to move forward, slowly at first, then suddenly found himself spat free of the grip of the rock. Shards of debris showered down. He threw his hands over his head protectively and Karen used her own body as a shield as best she could in the little space. The rain of rubble slowed to a dusting of dry earth, threatening to choke them. When this also stopped and their coughing eased, Karen pulled herself back and Manfred peered through blackened fingers to the tunnel's ceiling. A thin layer of debris covered him, and grime smeared Karen's back, yet the roof remained intact. With a shaky exhalation of breath, Manfred turned an almost boyish grin to Karen and Shawlen.

"Well, that wasn't so bad, was it?"

Shawlen laughed softly and Karen smiled, reaching over to give Manfred's hand a quick squeeze. She looked to Shawlen after a moment and the rebel turned, continuing their journey through the tunnels.

***

"Nearbrook is a half mile west of here. You should reach the town in about fifteen minutes by the road," Shawlen explained. Five days had passed since the small tunnel had failed to consume them, and they had encountered few setbacks since. They had made better time than Shawlen had expected, limiting breaks and taking food on the go instead of stopping for a more relaxed meal. "I wish you both luck on your quest." He turned to the tunnel wall and pushed a concealed panel, a patch of wall looking virtually the same as the rest of the tunnel in the flickering glow from the torch Shawlen held, the last of their supplies. A section of the rock face gave way, letting in the afternoon light, harsh and bright after so many days in the dark depths of the earth. A welcome breath of fresh air wafted in, swirling the smell of unwashed bodies back into the darkness.

"Perhaps," Shawlen said, but paused. He looked at the ground, then back to Karen. "Perhaps we will meet again, under better circumstances." Karen smiled, the light from both the torch and the entrance drawing strange shadows across her face and lighting up her eyes. He doused the flames of the torch, laying it aside.

"Thank you for all your help, Shawlen." She touched his arm, meeting his eyes for an instant. "It is greatly appreciated." She stepped back as Manfred extended his hand.

"Thanks, Shawlen." Shawlen shook the offered hand. Manfred squinted at the entrance. "A half mile west, you say?" The rebel nodded. "Right. Well, see you after the war."

Shawlen laughed and, following the two through the entrance into a dense patch of lilac and spicebush, closed and covered the tunnel. With a quick nod of his head west, Shawlen turned south and set off in a silent jog without another word. He had explained that, for him to continue through the tunnel system right now was far too dangerous if any followed, and he couldn't risk leading pursuit to other rebel bases. He planned to take a cross-country route to the rebels near the town of Sandroga where he would pass on the information about the tunnels near Ildare. Without Karen and Manfred, he would call less attention to himself, though dangers still lurked everywhere for any traveller, and more so for a rebel. Karen and Manfred both admired his courage and wished him luck.

Alone again, the two turned west, toward Nearbrook. They paused at a stream to wash off the dirt of the tunnel from face and hands. Though the spring air blew brisk and cool, the water felt strangely warm, perhaps fed by a hot spring. After a moment's consideration, Karen decided she required a more thorough cleaning.

"Have you been here before?" Karen asked as she struggled out of her tunic. Manfred's face reddened and he turned away from her before answering.

"I have passed through from time to time on my way elsewhere."

"Is it like Ildare?"

"Like Ildare how?"

"The people," Karen said as she knelt in the stream to wash her clothes. "Are they as unhappy and frightened of the world here as back in Ildare?"

Manfred considered her question, staring intently at the reeds lining the stream's edge.

"Ildare is far enough west that the effects of Guardian rule are newer, fresher. The people more easily remember the time when they lived free. Nearbrook has lived under Guardian domination longer. They will have become more used to it, having had time to adjust. It doesn't mean the people are any less depressed, but they have had more time to forget the meaning of freedom and to learn a new kind of happiness, however dampened."

Karen nodded, sorrow filling her eyes. Her clothes as clean as she could manage without soap, she moved on to the rest of her body.

"It is not a good way to live," she said.

"No, but so long as they remain oppressed, it's the only life they have left to them."

Karen nodded again, thoughtful as she stepped out of the stream to dry herself in the sun.

"And that is why I must do what I can to change it." She slipped on a fresh tunic from her bedraggled pack and lay her wet clothing aside, trusting the sun to dry it in short order.

Manfred turned hesitantly and placed a hand on her shoulder. He gazed steadily into her troubled eyes.

"You are not alone, Karen. Remember that. I am here to help. Chanet and Will and Shawlen, they all do what they can to help too. We're all in this fight together."

She stared back at him, her eyes losing some of their sorrow to a new sense of determination. With a small smile, she thanked him.

Then she glanced meaningfully at the water and back to Manfred. The warrior looked down at himself and grudgingly admitted that he was a mess. But he refused to bathe with Karen watching. Bemused, Karen followed his previous example and turned away from him. He mumbled something about modesty that she didn't understand.

After much splashing—Karen had only turned once when a particularly large splash had convinced her that Manfred had fallen, but an indignant squawk from her companion as he hastily tried to cover himself sent her whirling away again—Manfred emerged from the water. Karen tried not to grin at the memory of the big man floundering in water that didn't even reach his knees. He scowled at her, his face an interesting shade of red. They waited just long enough for the sun to leech most of the heavier moisture from their clothes, then the two continued their journey to the little town ahead.

Chapter 8

Sandroga, to a certain extent, was a trading town. A large trading town. That is, if you wanted to take your life in your hands and barter with it. One could make a tidy profit, if one survived the first days in business.

Merchants learned quickly who ruled the town and at what cost. A certain percentage (plus a little something extra) went to the mayor as taxes, as anywhere. What made Sandroga different was the price of protection.

Amrah and Toron ran a good trade in such affairs. If a merchant wanted his business to survive, he made sure he had the siblings to back him up. Without protection, merchants soon found their wares damaged or missing, followed by a late-night visit from masked assailants, and at times, if these hints remained unheeded, a visit to the healer or a one-way trip to the death house. Merchants seeking the aid of the mayor's enforcers found their pockets far emptier than had they simply bought what Amrah and Toron sold.

And as an added benefit of this protection, a merchant could, if he chose, limit his competition—for a hefty sum.

Of course, getting into business in Sandroga in the first place was no easy undertaking. Nor a cheap one. A merchant first had to get approval from the mayor and the head merchant—an unctuous little fat man with the personality of a brick but the brains of a scholar. Also essential, sponsorship from an established citizen of the town (a fellow merchant, a craftsman, or a farmer). Not so much to speak for the merchant's character, but rather to vouch that said merchant wouldn't rock the boat if accepted into the trading arena of Sandroga. But once accepted, the potential profits from this shady little corner of the world were great.

Craftsmen existed on a different level. Although they also paid taxes to the mayor, protection from Amrah and Toron came at a nominal fee. After all, half the craftsmen were already on the siblings' payroll. And the rest offered generous enough deals for their services, grateful of the watchful eyes keeping them safe.

The farmers, of course, everyone left alone. They received special protection at no charge for the simple fact that, without them, Sandroga would cease to exist.

For the past few weeks, Amrah had thrown herself into her work. She collected on debts, saw to it that everyone stayed happy, that no one was cheated (too badly), and that the one or two merchants who did try to cheat her received a fitting response. Yagoth trailed her almost everywhere, trying to get her alone. Occasionally, he brought up a conversation topic that eventually led to the rebels, but she evaded all his questions in such a way that he couldn't claim she intentionally led him astray. Each day he grew more and more frustrated, and with his frustration came that new-found cruel streak and an increasing sense of irrationality from the man.

Toron noticed the change almost as acutely as Amrah did.

"Sweet Spirits, Amrah, what's cooking his stew?"

Amrah looked up at her brother's heavy frame, meeting his hazel eyes. People often underestimated Toron, judging his wits as thick as his torso. He was pure muscle and just about the craftiest man she had ever seen. And, brother or not, Amrah could not have found a more apt business partner. She gazed back to where Yagoth had stormed off, shaking her head.

"Whatever they did to him, I thinks it's affecting his mind," Amrah's husky voice, so similar to Toron's, held a note of pain. "I know he betrayed us, but this can't go on. I don't know whether to kill him and put him out of our misery, or concoct some tale he'll take back to the Guardians and let them deal with the lie. Either way, I'm running out of excuses to keep him at bay. Sooner or later, he's going to figure out we're on to him."

Toron grunted noncommittally.

"Another death last night," Toron said softly, giving her something else to worry about. Amrah turned to him, eyes narrowed and a snarl forming on her lips.

"One of ours again?"

Toron nodded and spat in disgust. "Merchant Gilnor." He left unsaid that Gilnor was one of those under protection; one she had visited mere days earlier.

Amrah cursed, her attention drawn to the street recently vacated by Yagoth. "You think he knows something about it." She didn't bother making it a question.

"As do you," Toron remonstrated. "Don't deny it, sis. There's a connection there; we just have to find it."

Amrah shook her head viciously.

"If it were anyone else, we'd have already dealt with it," she growled. Toron made no reply. She heaved a sigh.

"Alright. I'll deal with it."

She received a raised eyebrow from Toron in return. Anyone else would have asked, but not Toron. She answered the unspoken question anyway.

"I'll let him get me alone, ask his questions. He's so frustrated now, I should be able to get information in return with little effort."

"Where?" Toron asked.

"If you're there, he may not talk—" she began.

"No way, little sister," Toron used his greater height to advantage, not to intimidate (a useless gesture against Amrah), but to make his point. "If his brain's really scrambled more than my breakfast, there's no way I'll leave you unprotected." He quickly waved away her protest before it even made it to her throat. "I know you can take care of yourself, but you said yourself, you don't know what they did to him. What if it's more than just mess with his mind? What if they put some kind of protection on him? Or some other like spell that'll go off if he's found out?"

"And you're going to protect me from magic, brother?" Amrah was touched by her brother's concern, though the strength of his emotions did not surprise her. "If he has such a spell on him, better just one of us is exposed."

"You know I won't outlive you, little fox," Toron grinned. "If we go by magic, so be it. But damned if I let you face Yagoth without me in the background."

"He's my lover, brother. Don't you think he'll be suspicious if you show up when things turn intimate?"

"He'll never know I'm there."

Amrah chuckled, knowing any further argument was futile.

"In that case, we need a plan."

***

Darkness had fallen, bringing with it a cold drizzle, by the time Amrah caught up with Yagoth. She had expected the sullen mood, but not the muttering. They neared the warehouse district. At this time of night, only the whores and those seeking unsavoury company populated the area. Although few covered lanterns on their tall posts were lit—and those mostly to show the way for late warehouse workers—Amrah knew Yagoth spoke to no one; at least no one she could see.

"Yagoth?" she called uncertainly, hating the quiver in her voice that she knew only she heard.

Yagoth stopped under one of the lights. Amrah suppressed a shudder as he turned to face her. His eyes glinted, glowing red. *Just a trick of the lantern fires,* she told herself as he blinked normal eyes at her.

"Amrah," he began with a tender smile. He took a step toward her before his sudden frown stole the warmth. His eyes searched the night and suspicion crept into those dark orbs. Or again, maybe it was just the shadows created by the flame above him.

"Where is he?" his voice grated, sounding like a different person.

"Where is who?"

"You know. Your brother. You've barely left his side for the last few days." Definitely an accusation there. But how could he not have noticed? "And before that, you were always with *them.*"

"Them?" She felt like a talking bird, repeating words back to her master. What was he talking about?

"The merchants," he spat. "You've been spending so much time with them that I may as well not exist."

"I have a business to maintain, Yagoth," she shot back, angry now. Yes, she had kept him at a distance, but it was not

76

unusual when she collected protection pay. Even knowing the cause of his upset—because her distance had prevented him from gaining the information he thought he needed—did not give him the right to question how she did her trade.

"No matter the cost—"

"What are you talking about?" she demanded. The calm flatness of her voice at the moment had been known to send hardened murderers run screaming, but if it affected Yagoth in any way, he hid it well. "You know how I work. Hells, Yagoth, some of the stuff you know well enough to do on your own. It's never bothered you before; why should it now?"

Somehow during the argument, they had come so close to each other that they practically shared the same breath. Amrah made sure to keep that fine line between them though. If they actually touched, she knew they'd come to blows. At least she would.

"They don't deserve your attentions," he whispered. Their nearness should have made that sound intimate. It didn't. It sounded crazy. Yagoth stood a little taller than Amrah, which put the lantern at an angle to create shadows on his face. Amrah was almost glad she couldn't see his expression. She didn't want to know what it would tell her.

"It's just business, Yagoth. They pay, we protect. What is it about that that disturbs you?"

He growled and she steeled herself not to react, though she longed to step away—to put as much distance between them as possible. What had the Guardians done to him? It sounded as though an animal tried to claw its way through his throat, and it sent shivers down her spine that had nothing to do with the cold of the drizzle soaking her body.

"Why do you sell yourself like a common whore?"

Amrah's hands curled into fists and she vibrated with the desire to rearrange his face with a well-placed smack, and the effort it took not to do so. He was trying to pick a fight; but why?

"Are you trying to get yourself killed?" she asked, her voice pitched low. "Because insulting me is a good way of getting your blood spilt."

He let out a twisted laugh, a cat screeching in the night over an old crone's cackles. Amrah stepped back. *He's insane,* she decided, and keeping a greater distance seemed the smartest course after all.

"Don't flatter yourself, Amrah. We both know you don't have it in you."

Sweet Spirits, he is *trying to get himself killed!* No one in their right mind taunted Amrah, and anyone who tried ended with a knife in the belly. *Yagoth knows that, so why* ... A thought struck Amrah. Perhaps he knew she was on to him, and sought death rather than revelation. She would have to proceed carefully.

"No, Yagoth, what we both know is that you're still alive for a reason." She stood far enough back now that she could read his eyes better, though shadows still swirled about his features. What she saw beneath the crazed exterior hinted at confusion, pain and fear. Her heart lurched at the sight. *No. I cannot let his pain affect me.* Thanks to the Guardians, he had betrayed her, and she had to find out how deep that betrayal went.

"A reason?" Yagoth's voice came out as little more than a breath on the wind.

"Tell me about Merchant Gilnor."

He didn't flinch, no sign of recognition. *What does he know?* As a spy, he must have heard something.

"What do you know about his death?" she pressed.

He stood silent for such a long time that Amrah had to stare hard to make sure he hadn't turned into a statue. Finally he nodded, more to himself than in acknowledgement of her though.

"I'll tell you what I know if you answer a question first," he said.

"I don't answer to threats, Yagoth."

"Not a threat. A simple exchange of information."

She tensed, then forced herself to relax. *Here it comes. This is what I need to know.*

"An answer for an answer," she agreed through gritted teeth.

"I think you already know my question," his voice was a caress. "You've been avoiding it for weeks now."

Amrah blinked up at him and he barked a laugh that sounded so close to the real Yagoth that she almost smiled.

"Don't try that coy, innocent face on me, Amrah. I'm not buying," His eyes darkened, flickering red. *No trick of the lanterns, that.* An unexpected stab of fear tightened her chest.
78

"Truth, Amrah. Where are the rebels?"

She swallowed the cold lump in her throat, hating that he could unnerve her so. *I will not let him control me.*

With a deep, cleansing breath, she looked him straight in the eye and lied.

"Their nearest base is a hard day out, due south. There's a natural cave behind Shilton Falls. The entrance is ten paces from the cluster of carnda plants. And you need a password to get in, if you can avoid the traps around the place."

"What kind of traps?"

She shook her head, a smile that didn't reach her eyes curling her lips.

"An answer for an answer, remember?"

He snarled.

"What do you know about Merchant Gilnor's death?"

"Messy," he said.

"And?"

"And what?" he glared down at her. "I've given you an answer."

She cursed.

"Damn you, Yagoth—"

"Far too late for that," he whispered. Again, his face held that confused pain but he shook it off. He frowned in concentration, his words measured. "Let's try this again. You tell me what I need to know about the rebels, and I'll show you what I know about Gilnor."

"Show?"

"You'll understand," he grinned. Except for the spine-chilling glint of his eyes, that smile could spread in a joyous wave to all who encountered it. Amrah shivered. *I don't want to do this,* she realised with a start. But there was no one else. She would not risk Toron; that left only her.

"What did they do to you?" she asked, voice unusually soft.

His hands trembled and she thought he paled, though the dim light made it difficult to tell. Even his jaw quivered as he tried and failed to speak. A strangled sound escaped his lips, and that seemed to bring him back from whichever of the Hells had claimed him. His face shut down and he went utterly still. Amrah wanted to cry. *Sweet Spirits, he's not only my lover, he's my love.* No one had ever brought her close to tears. What was she going to do?

His eyes filled with terror. "You don't know what they'll do to me if I fail," he whimpered. "The rebels," his voice shook and he cleared his throat with a growl. But then his features took on a more imperious cast and he stared down at her, the fear washed away by resolve.

"The rebels, Amrah. What are these traps? And how much resistance will they put up?"

She shook her head. "Yagoth, I can't—"

He grabbed her shoulders, fingers digging in hard enough to bruise.

"Yes, Amrah, you can." The sheer flatness of his tone stilled her struggles. Never had she heard such intimidation hidden in so simple a statement. She knew assassins who would kill to achieve the absolute coldness Yagoth showed now.

"If you don't release me this instant, Yagoth, you'll learn nothing." Amrah kept her voice as level as she could. "And that will leave you to their mercy."

He released her as though fire marched up her arms, and she stumbled.

"Talk," he barked.

Her mind whirled. What would he believe? She had to make it convincing. Yagoth knew how slick her tongue could be and he'd watch for the lie. How much truth could she afford to impart? Spies knew how to sift through information, and Yagoth was the best in Sandroga in his line of work.

Although the rebels weren't her people, they had an understanding. For the most part, they kept out of each other's way. But on some occasions, mutual aid proved profitable. And the rebels fought the Guardians. Anyone who kept those monsters out of her territory deserved whatever protection Amrah could provide. Turning them over to Yagoth, and in turn to the Guardians, would violate her principles. *You don't relinquish access to any asset.*

"Mostly, the traps are simple to avoid, if you know what to look for," she began. "Trip wires, covered pits, that sort of thing. I can't tell you where, because they move them regularly. The places are marked, though. Broken twigs and rock patterns."

She tried to gauge his reaction. Did he believe her? But he had moved back into the shadows and she couldn't read his expression. She could only see the bold lines of his nose and
80

chin where the rain gathered and fell to the dark street below.

"What other traps?"

"I don't know for sure. But whenever I go, they know I'm there before I reach the water's edge. Even with avoiding the other traps, they have advanced warning of someone's approach. They've never explained it to me."

"A look-out, then," he mused. Amrah kept her face blank. She was an expert at body language, how to use it and how to hide it. But he was an expert at reading hidden intentions. She played a dangerous game with an unstable adversary.

"What about this password? Do they change that as frequently as they move their traps?"

"No, they give special access to me and Toron. We have our own words that single us out from the rebels. Since we don't go there often, giving us different words every few days would be stupid."

"And your password?" Did drool glisten at the corner of his mouth, or just more rain? He fidgeted, hands clenching and unclenching around nothing but air as he waited for her answer.

"It's a phrase. 'The game are out in force.' Deer and rabbits wander around the Falls, so anyone who might overhear wouldn't think much of it."

"Is that everything?" Yagoth demanded, and for a moment, it sounded like someone else speaking through his mouth. Amrah frowned, studying his face, but she couldn't make out anything useful.

"Yes," she replied.

His look grew distant, seeing things she could not. It sent shivers down her spine. But the flash of red in his eyes disturbed her more, mirrors reflecting triumph. Eyes that did not belong to Yagoth.

She stepped back, but he took her arm in a firm hand.

"Thank you, my dear," he murmured in a voice not his own. His eyes returned to normal. "My turn." She could only call his grin wicked and she pulled against his grip.

"What's wrong, Amrah?" He looked down at her in concern, pure Yagoth again.

I can't handle this, she thought to herself. *My nerves are shot.*

"You wanted to know about Merchant Gilnor," he said. She nodded, forcing the numbness to lift from her mind. She had no time for weakness. "Then I have something to show you," he continued as he marched them into the rain-slick dark.

They headed deeper into the warehouse district. The occasional lantern should have provided some level of comfort, but instead, the inconsistent light screamed *isolation* to Amrah. *I've never been afraid of the dark,* she chided herself, yet the heavy hand of oppression refused to leave her. Even knowing that Toron kept watch out in the night somewhere didn't alleviate her anxiety.

The scabbard of her sword as it slapped rhythmically against her left leg and her right hand resting on the hilt of the dagger at her belt provided the only comfort. But it was cold comfort; if she had to use either, it would spell Yagoth's death—or her own.

Yagoth stopped at last. The nearest lantern stood several feet away, its distant flicker serving to lengthen shadows rather than show Amrah her surroundings. Night vision was all well and good, but she needed a certain amount of light to make out any details, and definitely a lot less rain. Right now, she could only see the dark bulk of one of several near identical buildings looming before them, and feel the presence of Yagoth at her side. The drip of the weather effectively drowned out any sound, and the smell of the warehouses—grain, leather, steel, even the midden heaps and back-alley defecations—was overlaid by the refreshing scent of falling water. All of which told Amrah nothing she could use.

"Why are we here?" she asked.

"You wanted to know about Gilnor," he spoke, his words breathing across her neck. Under other circumstances, his closeness would have aroused her, but Amrah's nerves had wound into such a tight knot that her stomach churned with the queasy knowledge that she stood with a madman whom she loved.

"So why are we here?" she repeated. "Gilnor was found in his shop, his own silks tying him to the rafters. That's a long way from the warehouse district, Yagoth."

"You'll see soon enough," came his ominous reply.

"I can't see my own hand in front of my face," Amrah complained, adding a few choice profanities to make her point.

"Don't worry about it," he murmured. Amrah felt him move an instant before a blinding pain struck the back of her head.

She tried to blink away the stars fluttering before her eyes, but then darkness once again engulfed her vision as her knees slammed to the ground.

She woke moments later. When she felt the chaff beneath her back and felt the vermin crawling under her shirt and through her hair, she realised Yagoth had taken her into the warehouse; one of the grain dealers. She knew from experience how well grain strewn across a floor could soak up blood. As did Yagoth. That thought made her skin itch more than the biting bugs did. She struggled to sit up, only to find her arms tied above her head.

A small spark leapt from the near dark to a lantern in Yagoth's hands. He tucked the flint back into his belt, crouched down and turned to meet Amrah's enraged glare. He trailed a hand tenderly across her belly and she was startled to feel flesh against flesh. Her tunic was ripped into strips, many pieces missing. She suddenly had a terrifying thought. Her gaze followed her arms up to her wrists, tied with those missing bits of cloth. Tied with her own shirt. Like Gilnor.

And she no longer had possession of her sword and knife.

Her eyes snapped back to fasten on Yagoth's amused stare. Keeping her thoughts from betraying her and writing themselves all over her face, Amrah emptied her mind of all emotion, trying her best to seem as unconcerned and solid as a statue. Inside, her stomach roiled and her heart pounded furiously, but her brain screamed vengeance.

Yagoth killed those under her protection, and her name had just made the top of his list. How had she and Toron missed it? And where was Toron anyway?

"Why?" she demanded, proud that her voice held only cold anger and none of the fear crawling up her throat. "Why would you do this?"

He didn't say anything, just leaned over, studying her. Flames reflecting from his flickering lantern danced over his face. *Is Yagoth even in there?*

"Do you know what they did to me?" he asked, but not as though he wanted an answer. It sounded more as if he spoke to himself.

"I've faced capture before, even being put to the question," he continued. "The body mends." His eyes focused on Amrah for a moment as he idly trailed her own knife down her cheek

83

without drawing blood. "You know that. Sometimes there's scars to remind you, sometimes not," and his eyes lost focus again; or rather, they saw things Amrah did not, sending fresh chills the length of her lithe form. She started testing her bonds. Fabric rips easily enough with the right amount of pressure, but not when it's wet, as Yagoth well knew. It would take some work to free her hands of their damp bindings.

"The body mends," he repeated, "but the mind, now that's a different matter. How do you heal what you can't really see?" He shook his head. "I don't even know how they did it, but those bastards got into my mind.

"We went to learn what we could, me, Vilna and Gorath. Things went wrong almost right away. Like they were waiting for us, expecting us. We did the usual. Vilna went in first, looking the whore. Then me, a semi-respectable merchant wanting a drink. Gorath would come in later, doing his beggar routine. Only, soon as I went in, I knew something wasn't right. Vilna was jus' standing there for one thing. She looked at me, fear and warning in her eyes, but it was too late. I couldn' move. One of them silver-cloaked bastards grins at me and I knew he was workin' magic."

Amrah could see how much the memory frightened Yagoth. He had worked hard to rid himself of his low birth country accent, but it sometimes slipped through when he was scared, and it thickened now as he relived the moment.

"Tha's when I felt this pressure in me head, like somefin tryin' t'git in. I fight it, not even knowin' wha' the Hells it is or how ta fights it. Only it gits worse; hot pokers stickin' in me brain, blindin' me wit such pain as I niver felt before. I scream an' they laugh. I don' know how long this goes on fer, but afer a bit, I kin sees again.

"They got Vilna and Gorath stuck in a corner an' I don' even know when Gorath came in. They's shaken some, but not screamin'. The Guardians are talkin' to 'em, tellin' 'em stuff I don' unnerstand none; somefin 'bout buyin' off the powers of the place so they don' innerfere later. And them two starts noddin' an' smilin' like they'd be happy ta help. The Guardians start smilin' too; 'til they look at me agin."

The terror in his eyes made Amrah want to tell him to stop, but she had to know what the Guardians had done to him. And the more he talked, the longer she had to work herself free.

84

"The only smiles they got fer me are hard-edged an' dangerous," he shuddered. "It feels like they're draggin' the inside of me head through hot coals an' I gits so scared I piss meself. I try ta put me hands to me head, keep the brains from leakin' out all over the ground, but I cain't move. There's nothin' I kin see to fight, but I fights anyway, 'til me brain feels raw an' bloody, only I got no marks to prove it. I scream at 'em to stop, an' they starts babblin' 'bout rebels an' locations an' those who know wha's what. I tole 'em ta go ta the nine Hells, so they starts all over."

His eyes found Amrah's.

"I jus couldn' take it no more, so I tells 'em I'd do it. Only, soon as I do, there's this odd squeezin' in me mind, an' I cain't take it back. It's like I hafta to do what I said. I tried not to when they let me go; only I'd git that pain agin if I disobeyed. The only relief from that pain was givin' pain to others.

"But I cain't bully my way past you, Amrah, an' you're the one who knew what I needed to know. But you kept putting me off, so I tried to get what I needed from others."

The fear drained from his eyes, taking his accent with it. Madness took its place.

"Your merchants are useless. They pay their due, but they don't have the first idea on how to defend themselves. Their superior attitudes got them nowhere, as they soon learned when they tried to put me off. So now they know what I'm looking for; I can't leave them alive to unmask me. But it didn't matter, because you already knew what I wanted."

The intensity of his gaze burned along Amrah's body and she jerked. Her bonds gave a little and she schooled her features to a careful blankness so he wouldn't see the surge of triumphant hope. She needn't have bothered; he wasn't looking at her face.

"And now I have the information; *they* have the information," His knife sliced away the remnants of her tunic and his hand trailed across her breast as the blade worked lower. "But they're still in my mind, Amrah. I can feel the pain waiting in the corners of my head, ready to spring out at me if they want it to. I've only found one thing that stops that pain."

His knife drew blood, a thin trickle down her side. Amrah pulled against her restraints. They broke. Yagoth drew back, hands held out from his sides. Confusion and stubbornness

85

chased with pain flared around his face.

"Run," he whispered harshly. His muscles trembled as he forced his hands to stay far from her. "Spirits, Amrah, run!" Tears streamed down his cheeks as he fought whatever demons the Guardians had put in his brain.

Amrah scrambled to her feet, eyes searching for the door as she moved. A hulking figure stumbled forward in front of her. She just had time to register Toron emerging from the shadows, a bloody lump on the side of his head, when Yagoth tackled her from behind. He roared, a futile defiance against the madness overwhelming him.

"Amrah!" Toron called as Yagoth's weight was lifted from her back. She rolled, seeing Yagoth's fist take the wind from her brother with a strength unnatural in the spy. Toron dropped to his knees, but he managed to fling a knife toward Amrah. It overshot her hand and she scuttled after it.

Yagoth seized her again and she screamed in frustration, the knife a finger's length from her grasp. She kicked at him and scored her nails along his face. He reared back, not releasing her but allowing just enough freedom for her to reach the waiting blade.

He captured her wrist in a grip of iron. His own knife poised above her heart, but his arm wavered as Yagoth fought the compulsion to kill her. His lips curled into a snarl. He spat out a curse, then raised his knife in both hands for the final strike.

But that left Amrah's arms free. She clutched her blade and, with a cry of despair for what she must do, drove it hilt deep into his chest.

Surprise widened his eyes, followed by relief as blood gushed out, covering Amrah in a hot rush of metallic scent.

"It's gone," he whispered gratefully as he smiled down at Amrah.

Then the light of life fled from her love's face and Amrah choked on her own tears as Yagoth's dead weight threatened to crush her.

But then, Toron appeared. He threw aside the corpse and drew Amrah into a fierce embrace heedless of the gore covering her.

She cried herself out on his shoulder while he held her silently, lending what strength he had in his comforting arms.

When there was nothing but a raw hollowness left in her chest, Amrah sat back, scrubbing at her tear-stained face.

"They're going to pay for this," she vowed.

Toron nodded. "I know."

Chapter 9

A lank youth sat on the doorstep of a small but well-built brick cottage. High cheekbones and pointed ears announced his Elfin descent, contrasting his otherwise human features. Jans wore a white tunic tucked haphazardly into brown trousers. His blond hair continued the unkempt look, but his emerald eyes spoke of a sense of experience beyond his youth, a maturity hidden away from an overbearing father. In the long graceful fingers of his left hand he held a wooden pole, and his right gripped a hunting knife, which until a moment before he had used to sharpen one end of the stick. He looked up into the azure sky, letting the warm sun bathe his angular face. A gentle breeze touched his tanned skin, bringing with it the soft sound of flowing water from the nearby brook. His gaze passed with familiarity over the forest to the east and the gently rolling meadow lands, with their plush green vegetation so early in spring, to the west. The air smelled fresh, the scent of sweet spring flowers following wherever it blew. Jans closed his eyes and rested his head against the cottage door, enjoying the beauty of the afternoon and once again pretending he shared a better relationship with his father in a friendlier world. The youth could not comprehend why the man held so much anger toward his son.

Jans had returned from working with his father over at the new mill across town a half hour earlier, but the freedom he felt from that short time away almost overwhelmed him. His father was a mason, perhaps the best for miles around, and he wanted Jans to follow in his footsteps despite every objection the youth made. Jans had just spent the last eight hours laying bricks and erecting wooden supports. The only reason his father had let him off so early was because of the complaints about his rumbling stomach. It wasn't Jans' fault that he hadn't had time for breakfast that morning. Waking before dawn to find a trowel waiting in the impatient hand of the mason wasn't Jans' idea of how to start the day. But that's how things often went around the place, though not usually so early. Jans had always found time to cram something into his mouth before running off to get his hands dirty. But not this morning. His father had practically pushed him out the door despite Jans' protests.

"If you hadn't slept so late, you'd have had time for food," the mason had grumbled.

An hour before dawn meant sleeping too late? That was a new one to Jans. Had he slept past dawn, he could understand the mason's anger. But this new mill was a big thing, commissioned by the mayor himself, and his father wanted it done quickly.

And tomorrow promised equal discomfort. That's when the mason vowed to show his son the new method of roofing. Something about tiles. Jans would rather lay back and pretend he was off adventuring in the world; saving damsels in distress from dragons, wandering the world in search of treasure, hunting in the woods with the spear he was making—anything but building new structures for Nearbrook in the company of his father.

A commotion a short distance off brought Jans out of his pleasant daydream. He opened his eyes and lifted his head, looking toward this new sound. He stood, unable to see what had attracted the attention of the villagers. A young man hurried by as the youth walked to the end of his cottage. The man called out:

"Have you seen the strangers? A large man and a goddess."

Jans shook his head. "What are you talking about?"

The man clutched at the boy's shirt in excitement. "Come on, you got to see them. I hear she's more beautiful than Ella." Jans couldn't imagine that. Ella was by far the most beautiful girl anyone in Nearbrook had ever seen. "She's got to be a goddess! He must be her earthly protector." The man's eyes

89

turned distant as he grabbed the boy's shirt again. "Come on, Jans, you've got to come see them!" The young man pulled at Jans' arm then took off at a run to the centre of town.

"Wait, Boran," Jans called. When the man didn't stop, Jans just shook his head. "A goddess," he muttered. He put his hunting knife into its holder at his belt. Going back to the doorway, he put his half-finished spear down and reached for his beige cape. Wrapping this about his shoulders, he decided to head for the heart of town, where he would surely see this goddess and her protector. Probably a joke, he thought to himself. Nearbrook had grown pretty dull lately. Boran had likely blown things all out of proportion just for something to do; although he had seemed so excited. Maybe these strangers were part of an acting group, hired to alleviate the boredom of the little town. Well, he didn't have much else to do at the moment. He certainly didn't want to go back to the mill to work with his father. Why not see what all the excitement was about?

It was not difficult to find them. A small crowd had formed about the Nearbrook Inn, the people all trying to get into the tavern to enjoy the specials on drinks that the innkeeper extended when strangers arrived. The boy tried to see past his fellow villagers into the small inn, but soon realised the futility. Too many people blocked the entrance. Normally only a half dozen or so people tried to get in on drink specials. Everyone else usually found the exercise hopeless. But there had to be three or four dozen here now. It wasn't as if no one ever came to Nearbrook. What differed about these strangers to warrant such an assembly of onlookers? Maybe the man was a Guardian, but then why such a crowd? Guardians didn't come often anymore, but they were not uncommon. *A goddess,* he reminded himself, reconsidering the situation in that light. *No,* he chided himself, *that's ridiculous.* Even if goddesses took human form, they certainly wouldn't stop in Nearbrook.

Oh well, he thought. *No use staying here. Might as well go back home and finish the spear.*

As evening approached, Jans' father returned from the mill.

"Father, did you see the strangers?" he asked.

"What of them?" the man responded gruffly, wiping a callused hand across his forehead. He glared at his son. "Is
90

that what you did all afternoon? Gawked at strangers instead of doing an honest day's work?"

"No sir," Jans protested. "Of course not. I looked after things here." And he had too. He had tidied up the house, repaired the loose stair on the porch, and prepared supper. All stuff he could do without the hard stare of his father looking over his shoulder, waiting to find fault.

Jans waited a second, then spoke again before his father could move past him into the house. "What were they like? The strangers? Who are they?"

"I don't know. Just travellers I guess," said the man in an annoyed tone that seemed almost natural. "They'll probably leave tomorrow. So you can't use them as an excuse to shirk your duties."

"Are they still at the inn? I'd like to see them."

"Why? They're no different than the rest of us."

"Then why such a big crowd? Boran said she was a goddess. I thought maybe they were actors or something. Or maybe even Guardians."

"Boran is more a fool than you are, boy," the man sneered, casually cuffing the side of Jans' head. "And you are not going to any inn. If you have so much time on your hands to go wandering to the inn instead of doing an honest day's work, then I can easily fix that."

"But—"

"No. That's my final word on the matter." He stormed into the cottage, slamming the door behind him. The boy stared after him a moment, then sank to the ground and leaned against the wall, his eyes closing. Sometimes he just did not understand his father, but he had no wish for the beating he would get if he disobeyed the man. Jans wondered for the umpteenth time if the man's bitterness to his son had to do with the death of Jans' mother. Jans knew his Elfish features reminded his father of her. He just wished his father would stop living in the past and recognise his son as an individual and not as a reflection of his mother.

A half-hour later, he stirred from a light sleep to the sound of his name. He opened his eyes, but saw only darkness. He shivered in the chill of early night and wrapped his cape about him, waiting for his vision to adjust to the shadows. Two figures stood silhouetted a few metres away, one a large form, the

91

other a slight shadow.

"Jans?" a female voice repeated.

"Who wants to find him?" the boy replied cautiously.

The figures neared and the large one, quite obviously male, asked evenly, "Are you Jans?"

"Well ... yes. Why? Who are ... Oh! You must be the strangers, the ones at the inn? The goddess and her protector."

The man barked a laugh before the girl spoke again.

"I am Karenrana, daughter of the Druid Draimar, and I have come a great distance to find you, Jans. We have much to talk about."

***

"You're crazy!" Jans exclaimed. He sat across from Karen and Manfred at a table in Nearbrook Inn, his hands mottled from his too-tight grip on the table's edge. "What do you think I could possibly do against," his voice lowered, "against the Ebbrings?"

"You have magic," Karen stated.

"Yes, but I don't see how it would help. I don't think the little things I can do would impress, let alone destroy, an Ebbring."

"You'd be amazed what simple things can do," Manfred said. "It is, after all, the simple things that best add to a surprise."

"That may be, but do you realise what you're asking?" Jans' voice cracked. "You want me to just leave here and set out with you—total strangers no less—to kill Ebbrings? That's insane! If they catch me, the best that I could hope for is a quick death. I'm barely sixteen! I want to live a little before I throw my life away."

"So you'd rather sit in this stinking hovel, tail between your legs, instead of fighting the curs that have you so firmly crushed under their boots," Manfred challenged. Jans jerked like he'd been stung, his whole body quivering. He pushed back from them so violently that Manfred's ale sloshed out of the mug and over the table. Karen stopped him with her quiet words before he could gain his feet.

"The choice is yours of course," her eyes barely flickering

92

in warning to the warrior as Manfred stared at the boy. "I understand your hesitation and I will not force you into this. I will, however, warn you not to use your magic. Should a Guardian find out ... well, you know what will happen. Whether you use your magic or not, they will eventually find you and you won't have any means to stop them. With us, you at least have a chance to face them before they find you. But even that is not certain. As I said, the choice is yours."

She stood and looked at Jans. "We will be here until morning should you change your mind." Then she turned and, followed by Manfred, left through the inner door leading to their rooms.

Jans sat a moment longer, staring at the vacant chairs in front of him; then he too left the table and headed for home on leaden legs.

It took several hours for Jans to doze off. Talk of Guardians and rebels and Ebbrings echoed in his thoughts, sometimes in Manfred's voice, sometimes in Karen's, and sometimes in his father's. Karen's words kept repeating in his head, over and over.

They will eventually find you and you won't have any means to stop them.

She was right, he realised. There was nothing he could do. But he hadn't used his magic in a long time. Too many people feared it, himself included. What would the Guardians want with a boy who didn't use his magic?

He awoke with a start in a cold sweat, breathing hard. He looked around, wide-eyed. Upon finding he had dreamed, that no Ebbrings or red-eyed dogs hovered near his bed, Jans lay back down. He stared at the ceiling, his dream fading as he watched the shadow of a nearby tree branch reflected by the moonlight.

The whine of a dog followed by voices drifted into his room from the open window. A dog. Maybe he hadn't just dreamed after all.

"She was here. It's a faint trail, but I can definitely sense her presence," spoke an unfamiliar voice nearby.

Jans slid out of bed and crept to his window. At the front of the cottage, barely visible from where he stood, he caught a glimpse of a man nearly the size of Manfred. He wore dark clothes and a silver cape that shimmered in the light of the moon. A Guardian? What did he want here?

"And the Stalker?" a second voice inquired.

"Him too. Both were here."

The Stalker, Jans thought studying the floor. *Isn't that Manfred? That means he and Karen are in trouble!* His head snapped up to see the Guardian again.

"They must have been here for a reason," the second voice said. "Search the house. See what's of value here. I'll tell the others of our progress."

Jans sprang from the window, tore off his sleeping garb and yanked on his tunic and trousers. See what's of value? Karen and Manfred had come for *him!*

A resounding crack reached Jans' ears. The front door to the cottage crashed to the floor and Jans could hear the surprised shout of his father in the next room. Jans grabbed his boots and the belt with his hunting knife. Without stopping to put them on, he vaulted through his window and ran toward the centre of town, to Nearbrook Inn.

He burst through the door, gasping for breath. Glancing down, he finally figured out why his feet felt so uncomfortable. Trying to put boots on while he ran in panic, Jans had put them on the wrong feet. Muttering to himself about stupidity, he fixed the problem and looked around. For the most part, the inn held silence, only a couple of men in the far corner. A single torch gave small comfort to the main room. Jans moved into the corridor leading to the sleeping chambers.

"What are you doing here?" Jans jumped at the sound of the innkeeper's voice, his heart slamming against his ribcage as he spun to meet the man.

"I'm looking for Karen and Manfred. Uh ... which room are they in?"

The innkeeper eyed him suspiciously.

"Jans, isn't it? Mason Thomas' boy?" Jans nodded. "What do you want with them?"

"I ... have to tell them something very important. It can't wait until morning." It sounded lame, even to him.

The innkeeper hesitated. He studied Jans appraisingly. Finally, he said, "All right. They're in rooms two and three, down the hall." He pointed them out. "Just make sure you don't disturb the lady. I've problems enough keeping the rest of this riffraff away from her room." He jerked a finger to the two

94

men now laughing drunkenly in the far corner, then retreated behind the bar in the main room. Jans took a breath to steady himself, then moved to the rooms, asking himself all the while just what he thought he could accomplish.

He came to room three first and pushed open the door. A large bulk lay on a bed too small for it, silhouetted by the moonlight streaming through the window. *Manfred,* Jans thought. Too dark to tell for sure, but who else was so massive? Except maybe that Guardian at his house. Jans hurried forward, preferring the towering Stalker to the frightening Guardian.

"Sir? Manfred, sir?" Manfred did not stir. Jans cleared his throat nervously and spoke louder, although his voice wouldn't rise above a choked whisper. Manfred *was* better than a Guardian, but he still scared Jans something awful. "Stalker?" He stood right beside the bed now. He leaned forward to shake Manfred's shoulder when a massive hand encircled his neck from behind. Jans' hands instinctively went to the wrist of the restraining hand as he lifted off the floor, his feet kicking. He squirmed and twisted just enough to turn himself around, but that only made the grip about his neck all the tighter. With his eyes, Jans followed the wrist to an arm, then to the intimidating body, and finally found the face of Manfred. Behind him. Jans rolled his eyes, trying to see what lay in the bed if not Manfred, but then decided it didn't matter. The hand about his windpipe mattered more than a bulk in the bed.

"Manfred! It's me! It's—" He choked, barely able to breathe. "It's Jans!"

The hand released him and he fell to the floor with a thud, gasping for air, his hand at his throat.

"Sorry kid. Didn't expect to see you here. You shoulda knocked." When Jans made no response, Manfred continued, his voice only a little less gruff. "You're out late. Why?"

"To warn you," Jans rasped, his eyes searching for anything to stare at that didn't include the steel gaze in the Stalker's face. In the corner beside the door, barely visible, lay a bedroll and Manfred's gear. "They're here. The Guardians, they're here."

"Where?" Manfred's voice turned deadly.

"They were at my home. It won't take them long to find

95

you."

Manfred turned and gathered his things from the corner. "We must wake Karen, quickly." Jans followed Manfred out, resisting the temptation to bolt for the exit.

They found Karen already awake and standing at her window. She turned when they entered. Upon seeing Jans, she glanced at Manfred. "Guardians?" Manfred nodded once.

"They were at my home," Jans said, feeling he should say something, but not knowing what. He felt incredibly awkward and his hand kept reaching for his throat.

"Did they say anything?" she asked calmly.

"One said he was going to tell the others of the progress they had made. The other ..." Jans paused.

"The other?" Karen urged. "What did the other say?"

"He was told to see what's of value at the cottage. He said he could sense that you had been there and they wanted to know why. I climbed out the window as he smashed in the door. I ran all the way here." Jans' eyes narrowed. "They probably have my father."

Karen lowered her eyes.

"I am afraid we can do nothing for your father if the Guardians have him."

"My father wouldn't care. He'd tell them in a minute where you are."

Karen raised her eyes and looked straight at Jans.

"Then the Guardians know of your magic."

"I don't think so," Jans said slowly. "When father found out I had magic, I was only five years old. He ordered me never to use it again, saying he would beat me if I did. And he meant it, too. As far as he knows, my magic's gone because he's never seen me use it since."

Karen nodded and looked back out the window.

"We must hurry. They will be here soon."

Jans backed toward the door. "Well, it was nice meeting you," his voice squeaked. "Maybe our paths will cross again."

"You can't stay here Jans, not now," Karen said.

"Why not? They're only after you!" A fine trembling started down his arms and turned his legs to jelly.

"Not any more," Manfred said at his back. Jans whirled to find the Stalker blocking his escape. "They will find you and know you're of some importance to us."

96

Sweat poured down Jans' face, despite the chill in the night air. He felt like a trapped rabbit.

"But if you leave without me, they'll think you have no use for me," he shrilled, his hand again reaching protectively to his throat.

"No. They'll think you know something and that we've made plans with you."

"They will kill you if you stay." Karen spoke evenly as she went on. "You are no longer safe here. Your father has made sure of that."

"My father?" Jans stammered, thinking it was these two who had brought such danger, not his father. "How?"

"By telling the Guardians everything they wanted to know," Manfred replied. "Guardians have a way of getting information long forgotten. Maybe he didn't tell of your magic but he will have told of your eagerness to meet us."

"My eagerness ..." Jans began, confused.

"I saw you outside the inn this afternoon," Karen explained. "I could practically read your thoughts when we approached you at your cottage. You are in danger. If you do not come with us, you will die," she said as though announcing that it would rain tomorrow.

"Or worse, if the Guardians think you know something. You'll wish for death long before they kill you," Manfred added.

Jans stared open mouthed at Karen, then at Manfred, and back to Karen. He swallowed hard, trying to clear the lump in his throat. He looked helplessly past Manfred to the door.

"Come on kid," Manfred said gently. "It'll be an adventure."

Chapter 10

Three large men approached the Inn, their torches bobbing up and down. The door opened quickly behind the quaking hand of the little innkeeper as the Guardians reached it.

"Where are they?"

The innkeeper slowly raised his head to see the face of the Guardian who had spoken.

"The Stalker and the girl. Where are they?"

The innkeeper took a quick step back and pointed down the hall toward the rooms with a shaking hand. He gave a little bow, though likely more to hide his face than out of any deference. The Guardians had seen it all before.

"Numbers two and three," the innkeeper said, his voice trembling in fear.

The Guardians pushed past the little man with contempt and headed for the rooms. The one who had spoken motioned one companion to take the Stalker's room and the other, the girl's. Once positioned, he nodded and the doors flew into splinters. The two entered and made a quick survey of each room.

"Well?" the waiting Guardian growled.

"No one here," replied the first, leaving the Stalker's room and joining him.

"Empty," the second called from the girl's room. "But her trace is here, Garcouk. It's different now, though. I think another may have joined her. Couldn't have been more than ten minutes that they left."

"Damn," Garcouk cursed, sending a fist through the nearby

wall. He glared at the two, his gaze settling on the one who had searched the girl's room. "Find her trail. Find it now! Leave the hounds; they'll only slow us and alert her to our presence. Don't lose her, Carnier." His voice boomed, full of rage. If anyone could hunt her down, Carnier could. The man had a unique ability to track magic without its being used. *If only he had been available at that rebel camp,* Garcouk thought bitterly. *We would have wasted less time finding her tracks.*

The other Guardians hurried to the front door to begin their search while Garcouk walked into the room that the girl had occupied, kicking aside loose slivers of wood. He dropped heavily upon the bed and looked around, a scowl etched upon his visage. Every time he got close, this girl would somehow slip through his fingers. Ildare, the rebel's camp, Goran, the passages under the Alberion. He pounded the bed in frustration.

His scowl curled slowly into a small smile of admiration. She was good. She was very good—an opponent worthy of this little cat-and-mouse game. Seemingly without effort, she continually evaded him. Without Carnier's rare talent, they would have lost her long ago, he thought irritably. The hounds were only useful in open stretches, and then only until the traces of their prey became confused with other scents. It took too long for the beasts to find the trail again. Not so for Carnier. But they were close now. Not more than ten minutes ahead, Carnier had announced. So close and yet so far. But he would find her. Garcouk spat, wiping the saliva from his lips with the back of his sleeve as he glared around the room. He wondered, not for the first time, who this girl could be, where she acquired such vast powers and, most importantly, if she could be stopped.

Chapter 11

The branches of the forest met and intertwined like a protective net high above them. They headed east, into the depths of a changing world where, with each passing day, evil grew more prominent. Karen could feel it like a malevolent hand weighing her down. Her vision had implied that the heart of this atrocity lay in the east and that they must find it. This evil had to stop. These three, so different in appearance and mannerisms, were the only hope for the world—the world of goodness.

The undergrowth grew thicker the further they went into the forest, casting odd shadows in the glow of the moon. Soon it became so thick that Manfred had to draw his sword to hack it away.

"Won't they be able to follow this trail? I mean, it isn't exactly hidden," Jans complained. Manfred ceased his cutting motions and allowed his sword to drop slightly.

"You could go back," he growled but paused at a frown from Karen. Moderating his tone slightly, he went on, "If you have a better idea Jans, I'd love to hear it. Besides, they would find us whether we left a trail or not. If we had more time, I'd choose a different route, but we can't double back now."

Karen touched Jans' shoulder lightly.

"Manfred is right. We do not have much of a choice," She looked up as a breath of wind whispered in the trees. "But we could stall them." She smiled at the confusion on their faces.

"How?" Manfred asked, dividing his attention between Karen and the undergrowth he now continued to push against.

"We could split up, give them two trails to follow."

"Two?"

"Yes, two." Karen replied. "You are a tracker and can move well, no matter the conditions, and you have your sword. Jans is ... well, he's not as experienced. I will go with him and we can use his knife to cut a path." She paused. "But one thing bothers me. Jans said they could sense I was at his home. I used no magic there. That can only mean they can somehow track auras."

"So they'll know which trail is yours," Manfred said, his eyes narrowing as his sword stopped again.

Karen nodded, pulling a strand of her long hair behind her ear as a stray breeze tugged at it.

"I did not know it could be done, but I have no other explanation." She shrugged uncomfortably. "To see an aura is rare. To track one ..." She shook her head, her hair falling back across her cheek. "If that is what they do, perhaps I can use it against them. I can give you a trace of magic. Hopefully, they will not be able to tell the difference." She glanced at Jans, then back to Manfred. "Well?"

Manfred pursed his lips, then nodded once. "It's worth a shot." There was an opening in the undergrowth and they hurried ahead. "Where'll we meet?"

"There's a pool of silvery water in the forest," Jans offered. "Silben, they call it."

Karen felt a jolt of recognition at the name, a familiar lake from her runic map, but even more familiar from an important lesson from her father. Perhaps the most important lesson he had to offer, though she did not realise it at the time. Silben was the source of Balance where, long ago, the cast-off emotions of the world were drawn. In the time of enforced goodness, Elves and Druids had tried to eliminate evil by forcing the races to follow the paths of righteousness. The build-up of discarded evil shifted the Balance of Silben until the lake itself became a source of evil. That evil had hunted Draimar's teacher Gorlon, and to try to end that corruption, Sadricha had given her life. The beings of Karen's vision—they had risen from beside a silvery lake, perhaps this same Silben Jans spoke of.

Manfred merely stared at Jans, disbelief plain on his face.

"Well, it seems you could be useful after all," the warrior

101

muttered, then louder, "I know of the lake. It was once said to have been beautiful, but something happened to change it." The undergrowth sprang up again with a vengeance, seeming almost magical in its sudden vigour, and Manfred again resorted to force, trying to untangle a path. "I'd almost forgotten it lay near here."

"Things haven't changed," Jans said. "It's nothing but a dead zone. About ten miles further east."

"Due east?" Manfred glanced over his shoulder.

"It's a little to the south, too."

After a brief moment of silence, Manfred asked, "Do we just guess how far south, or do we start walking and hope to reach it?"

Karen gave the Stalker a warning glance.

"Ah, I'm sorry kid," he said. "How exactly do we find this lake?"

Jans sighed. "The land changes. It sort of dies. The trees have no leaves and their bark is ash white. I've heard that most of the lake's edge is guarded by thick patches of thorns. The pool itself is in a valley so you can see it from far away. You can tell if you have the right water 'cause it's still as ice."

"Have you ever seen it?" Karen asked, thinking this *must* be the same Silben her father had told her about, a land dying of evil.

"We were forbidden to go anywhere near the place, but I saw it once from a distance. It'd be a perfect place to meet."

"Yeah, I guess it would," Manfred murmured. "When do we meet?"

"Two hours after dawn," Karen replied. "But not at the shore. Too exposed."

"Right," Manfred said. "You two head for the southern shore; I'll head east. When you reach it, head west around the lake. I'll find you."

Karen nodded. Manfred hesitated, his fist clenching around the hilt of his sword as he avoided Karen's glance. With a deep breath, he voiced the one question that for some reason he feared.

"What if one party doesn't show?"

Karen looked him in the eye and held his worried glance a moment. Her eyes flickered to Jans, but it seemed as though she looked right through him. She blinked, shaking her head,

102

her hair lashing the air.

"I do not know." She looked back at Manfred. "We must hope it does not come to that."

"And if it does?" his voice trailed off. She said nothing. "Look," Manfred drew a deep breath. "If I don't show by midday, leave. Head east or south. If I'm still alive, I will find your trail and follow. If not ... it won't matter. And if neither of you show ..." He clutched the hilt of his sword tighter in an effort to keep his hands from shaking. "If you don't show by midday, I'll assume the deal is off and go on my own way," he finished in a rush, surprised by the heaviness in his heart at the thought.

Karen stared into his eyes, saying a hundred things with that look, but Manfred didn't understand any of them. He had fallen too deep in his own inner turmoil. His chest felt tight, like he had run for a long time and now couldn't catch his breath. Why did he find this so difficult? He took a long breath to steady himself and gazed deep into Karen's wondrous eyes, willing her to agree with him.

Finally, she did, nodding her assent. With a grim smile, she extended her hand to bestow a trace of magic upon the large warrior. Manfred flinched. He couldn't help it. Magic and he were unfamiliar allies and he wasn't sure he trusted it on him, but he didn't feel any different when Karen announced she had finished. She told him the effects would wear off in a few hours, then turned south with Jans. Manfred continued east, looking back over his shoulder as they parted until he could no longer see them.

***

Manfred moved in silent contemplation, clearing twisted undergrowth and strangled tree branches from his path with swift, sure strokes of his blade. One question repeated itself over and over in his mind; what would he do if they did get separated, if Karen and Jans didn't show up? Despite his words, he didn't think he could just leave. It's the why he couldn't figure out. He couldn't shake the feeling that something would happen, something not good.

Before Manfred had met Karen, he only looked out for himself and wouldn't have stuck his neck out for anyone. Sure he was a tracker, but he chose his clients and did things his own way. From time to time, he would take a risk, but for his own gain, not someone else's. Now though, he found himself daring to take a risk for someone else—for Karen. There would be a gain, and not just for him. Success meant the destruction of the evil in the East, the Ebbrings. Yet that alone did not urge him to help. There was something special, something unique about this girl. He had only known her for a short time yet he felt he could trust her—something Manfred couldn't say of anyone else alive. And he knew he would help her with almost anything, something he could not say of anyone else, alive or dead. She was beautiful, but the Stalker had known beautiful women before. No, something else reached deep into him, something more.

He stopped, his sword dropping to his side. Nearly a mile from where they had separated, Manfred realised at that moment that he would give his life and soul to help her.

***

Jans listened to the cutting of Manfred's blade through the thick vegetation until it faded into silence as he and Karen journeyed further south. The only sound now was his own small knife hacking awkwardly at the undergrowth, mixing with the occasional hum of night creatures. He looked back at Karen, easily making her way over the roughly trampled path he had cut. She had immense powers within her and ancient knowledge, the knowledge of all the Druids and Elves. He wondered how she carried such a heavy burden and couldn't even begin to imagine what it must be like. His own small magic sometimes seemed a great weight even though he seldom used it. His father's dislike of magic had taught him the pain of any power long ago when Jans' magic had first manifested itself. He strongly warned Jans several times against using it, and Jans still had a few scars to remind him of that. He tried to imagine how different his life might have been had his father allowed him to practice this magic. Would the people of his village still have accepted him or were they like his father, fearing what they did not understand? He didn't know, and remembering the Guardians at his home, didn't know if he would ever find out.

***

Karen also remembered the Guardians at Nearbrook. She knew they had tracked her and Manfred from Chanet's camp and wondered whether the blockades had succeeded. Chanet's people had been helpful and kind; she hoped her actions had not caused casualties, but feared they had.

The Guardians were much closer than she liked. That they had caught up so quickly disturbed her. That they could follow her magic frightened her. The two trails would confuse them, but there would likely be several Guardians now, enough to cover both paths.

The cry of some beast sounded in the distance, silencing nature's night songs. Jans jumped and turned quickly to Karen.

"What was that?" he asked, his voice a hushed quiver.

"The Guardians are getting closer," she replied, masking her own anxiety. The call was human, disguised as a forest creature. She had spent her life with nature and wasn't fooled. "We have to hurry."

Jans turned back to the gnarled and twisting branches in front of them and renewed his cutting. The branches gave way before his blade only to reveal more densely packed vegetation. Another cry rang out, closer now.

"They're gaining on us," Jans cried. "We can't lose them and we can't move any faster. What are we going to do, Karen? What can we do?" His voice nearly broke with terror. Karen felt the same sense of dread. She had no idea what to do. Not long ago she had been shielded from this outside world. How trivial her little problems seemed, her biggest worry whether a wounded bird in her care would last the night. Now, in fear for her own life as well as for Jans, she looked within herself for an answer. She found a slim possibility. She grabbed onto that thought and acted.

"Jans," she called softly. "Stand back."

He cringed at her side. She sent out a wave of magic to slice away the vegetation in front of them, cutting out a wide swath. Before Jans took off along the path though, she grabbed his arm.

"Not that way. Follow me."

She turned and retraced her steps a few yards, easily making her way back over the freshly cleared path, Jans tripping along behind her. She found a small thicket and then heard a third cry. She stopped and silently motioned Jans to crawl in, following a moment later.

After a brief pause, several pairs of legs thundered past.

"The trail leads this way," one Guardian called to his companions. "It's still fresh. We have them now!"

Karen quickly crawled back out, Jans at her heels, hoping that the darkness would mask their escape. She stood and ran in the opposite direction to that which the Guardians had taken, tearing through the undergrowth as only one of Elfin blood could.

"Stop!" bellowed a voice not far behind. Her hope shattered. "Fall back men; they're behind us."

Jans stole a glance over his shoulder and nearly fell. Six burly men stormed *en masse* toward them, moonlight outlining the harsh angles of their faces like something out of a nightmare. He faced front again and tripped on a tangle of vine, falling face first into the dirt. Three more men had appeared before them, seeming even larger than the first bunch. Karen did not have time to slow down. A Guardian grabbed her with an iron grip before she could slip past.

"Pick him up and bring him," he said. Then quietly, he said to Karen, "You have proven to be quite an opponent." He looked up at the six figures that had approached from behind. "And the Stalker?" he asked. "Where is the Stalker?"

"He's not with them."

"Ah, then the other path was a true trail. Very clever indeed. It will make no difference though. We will find him soon enough. And you," He glared meaningfully at Karen. "You and I have a lot to discuss. I look forward with keen interest to learn how you managed to dispose of one of my men without a weapon. You've avoided us so far, but now your luck has abandoned you." He raised his voice, tone commanding. "Take them to the dungeon tower."

***

Manfred parted the leaves before him, foliage that became sparser as he neared Silben. About ten feet away stood a large oak tree, completely barren and ash white, as if drained of life and energy. Even the undergrowth had faded to practically nothing. Jans had aptly described the land dying. Manfred wondered briefly how they fared, but the snapping of dried branches underfoot somewhere behind him interrupted his thoughts. Too far from the lake for Karen or Jans and unlikely some poor fool who had taken it into his head to wander into an accursed land in the middle of the night. That left Guardians.

He crouched low and listened. Yes, there it came again, distant yet, but approaching quickly. *Four, maybe six men.* Armed with his broadsword and his stealth, Manfred still stood at a disadvantage, the Guardians being armed with magic. Against one, Manfred had fair odds, but four would be more than he could handle. His only chance lay in his continued motion and a hope to outdistance them.

He angled slightly south, moving at a quick pace. He passed several more dead and dying trees in his flight. What else marked Silben? He tried to remember Jans' description. Thorn patches, dying land, a valley, and still, silver water. Such an obvious marker, he acknowledged belatedly. The Guardians could easily determine their destination by the paths. However, they would still have to reach the lake first in order to capture them. Unless, Manfred thought, he missed the way altogether. The dying trees gave proof to his nearness, but he had no idea just how far this dead zone extended. For all he knew, he had already passed the lake.

Manfred paused, listening for sounds of pursuit. He heard nothing, yet that did not give him much comfort. They were still out there, searching. The trace of magic Karen had given him had faded by now, but they could still find his trail. He wondered if Karen and Jans still lived.

A thought came to him then. He could purposefully go in circles, cross and re-cross his path to throw the Guardians off his trail. It hadn't worked so well for Trayon, but then, these Guardians weren't half the tracker Manfred was. But he would have to move fast. The night would soon make way for day, making his path more visible. If his plan had any chance of success, he would have to keep moving, constantly make new trails to confuse his pursuers, at least enough to provide him with more time to come up with a better plan.

Manfred took a deep breath, then retraced his steps and started to make a maze of tracks.

Chapter 12

His shoulders screamed in agony from the awkward angle of his arms chained behind him to the chair at his back. His face ached and he could feel bruises forming beneath the oozing blood. More blood trickled down his back, even though they hadn't whipped him today. But try though he might, he just couldn't keep still under the barrage of fists pummelling his body, and the movement had reopened the lash marks that had barely begun to scab over. Hells, he hurt everywhere, but he'd be damned to let them see just how much pain they brought. It only angered them more, but Joanha didn't care. He wasn't about to tell these bloody Guardians anything.

They had moved off for the moment, leaving the rebel in a temporary haven of solitude. These were strange Guardians, Joanha reflected. All three wore black uniforms, but no capes. At first, he had assumed they didn't want to get the capes bloody, but now he had other thoughts. None had tried any magic on him, relying on physical torture to get what they wanted. Seeing as they hadn't gotten any information, Joanha kept waiting anxiously for them to take it the next step. But no magic ensued. He was both grateful and troubled.

After the raid on the tunnels, Joanha and a couple of the others were captured and hauled off to Jadathe dungeon. It seemed a long way to bring prisoners, but not everyone taken had ended up here. Splitting up the captives made some sense, but to bring them so far ... Joanha didn't understand. But he didn't have to. He was here now, for whatever reason, and he intended to stay alive long enough to escape.

Joanha jerked his head slightly at a sudden movement at his side and silently cursed himself for letting the Guardians see any weakness. There were two now; the third had disappeared to question some new arrivals. Two Guardians was still two too many.

"This girl," the shorter, though broader man began. "She went to a lot of trouble to get to Nearbrook. Why?"

Joanha spit at him, blood mingled in his saliva to make a messy little splatter of red on the man's face. The man's dark eyes flashed as he slammed his fist across Joanha's jaw. Joanha's head spun and he spit a mouthful of blood onto the cement floor. Not the first of his blood to end up there. Probably not the last either.

"Who is this boy she wants?" the second man demanded.

Unlike most of the Guardians Joanha had seen, this one had pale blue-green eyes. The nearly black eyes on other Guardians usually held anger or hatred, but these lighter eyes were somehow worse. They showed absolutely nothing; no anger, no hate, no anything. They were so devoid of anything resembling emotion, even life, that Joanha knew this man was more dangerous then anyone he'd ever met.

"Why him? What is special about him?" The voice carried no more emotion than his eyes.

Staring up into those icy orbs, Joanha could almost swear he stared into the eyes of a corpse. It was more than uncomfortable; it was damned scary. Joanha bit his lip to keep from screaming and schooled his face to show as little emotion as possible.

Joanha didn't know anything about *her*. Didn't know who she looked for or why the Stalker travelled with her. Whoever she had hunted, obviously she had found him by now, or the Guardians wouldn't have asked. Joanha sat mutely. He refused to even think her name. He had known a magic-user once who could read minds. If a rebel magic-user could see into his thoughts, Joanha had no doubt a Guardian could do the same. They didn't know her identity and he wasn't about to tell them.

"You still refuse to talk?" The shorter man sounded more eager than disappointed. Then Joanha saw the glint of metal as the Guardian pulled a knife from his belt. So, it came to this. The whip and knuckles hadn't worked. Now they'd try steel.

109

Joanha wondered what they'd cut first, but didn't think it mattered. He could only concentrate now on keeping his mouth shut. He licked the coppery tang of blood from his lips and hoped he had the strength.

***

Jans slowly opened his eyes. He lay crumpled on a hard cement floor. Though dark, he could discern a small, damp, cold room. The air felt stale and heavy. Vague shadows jumped out at him, a couple of rough planks for beds and a high barred window. Stars winked at him through this window from a sky softened by moonlight. He tried to sit up and immediately felt dizzy. Holding a hand to his head, he discovered a nasty bump and dried blood. He squinted at his hand, trying to remember what had happened. Images of running with Karen and being captured a few hours before dawn flashed through his mind. The leader of the Guardians had said something about taking them to some tower—a dungeon. That must be where he was. But he didn't remember anything resembling a tower near Nearbrook. It was dark though. His leg muscles ached, suggesting he had walked a long way.

Spirits, how long had he slept? He glanced back at the stars. They twinkled in a sky that promised to darken, not lighten. That would mean they had left Nearbrook the night before. Or maybe even longer. Everything after their capture remained either a blur or a complete blank. Had he been unconscious for the whole day? He wondered if maybe he had lost more time than that. Putting a hand to his head again, he encountered the bump anew. When did he get that? A hazy memory showed Karen fighting against their captors and him trying to help, of Karen glowing red and frying one of the Guardians before the big one hit her, his fist blurring across his vision to strike her. Perhaps that same fist had hit him too.

Again gazing around the little cell, he wondered what had become of Karen. He seemed to remember that they had both arrived here, but he had no idea where she was now. Probably in some other dark and gloomy cell.

He curled one leg under him to push himself up and then slowly stood. A very dim shaft of torchlight shone through a tiny crack near the bottom of the door, about a foot up. A small

110

platter of food stood before this crack. His vision swam for a moment as he swallowed back nausea and concentrated on keeping his balance. From the hall beyond his door, he heard someone approach, banging each door with a fist. As he listened, the footsteps receded down the passageway.

"Hey!" Jans shouted, his hand clutching his head to stop the echoes of his own voice. "Wait! Where am I? What's going on? Where's Karen?"

The footsteps slowed and then stopped. Jans listened to the silence wondering if the guard would come back.

"Hello?" Jans called again, his voice breaking in uncertainty. "Are you still there?"

"Jans?" Karen's voice called faintly, from the next cell he thought.

"Are you all right?" he asked, relieved that she was there. At least now he wasn't alone.

After a brief pause, Karen replied, "For now."

"Quiet," the guard called from the corridor. "You'll wake the rats." He banged on another door further down the hall and laughed harshly.

A few moments of silence followed, then Jans heard more footsteps as the guard left their cellblock.

"Karen?" Jans called hesitantly.

"I am still here."

"Where are we?"

"The Guardians' dungeon tower."

"What are we going to do?" he asked.

No reply. Jans looked down at the platter of food on the floor before him. A plate held some mouldy bread and dried meat, and a small cup of dirty water stood beside it. He wondered again just how long they had been there. Looking at the food, he tried to remember when he had last eaten. Judging by the gnawing hunger of his stomach, it had been quite some time.

He brought the food to the bed, sat on the lower bunk. The water tasted flat and the food less than palatable. From the odour, he was just as glad he couldn't really see what he forced past his lips, but he knew he had to put something in his stomach. Despite the blandness and obvious age of the food, he felt somewhat better having eaten. Setting the plate on the cold floor, Jans lay down, crossed his arms behind his head, and began thinking of ways to escape. He stretched and winced as the hard board beneath him pressed on his wound.

After a time, an idea occurred to him. He sat up and moved to the wall.

"Karen?" he called.

"Yes?"

"How thick are these walls?"

"I don't know. Why?"

He paused before responding, wondering if he had stumbled across such a good thought after all.

"I could try to move something, see if it works."

"See if what works, Jans?"

"Well," he hesitated. He had never tried what he thought of doing before, at least not on people. "I might be able to teleport us out of here." He looked around for something to use as a practice test, not wanting to send Karen flying in six directions at once by accident. He had seen it happen to a water bucket once, and the memory of that container splintering into several pieces cautioned him against trying to transport Karen without a trial run. He looked to his food tray and decided that would prove a good test object.

"I'm going to try moving my tray first. It should appear somewhere in your room, if it works." He turned and concentrated on the tray, willing himself to teleport it.

It took more energy than he thought, but after a time the tray disappeared. He closed his eyes and willed it to reappear in Karen's cell. A minute later, he lost the image in his mind. A wave of dizziness washed over him and he thrust out his arms for support, scraping his knuckles on the wall. When he caught his breath, he called out, "Is it there? Did it work?"

"Yes, it's here."

Just then, they heard footsteps coming down the corridor again, two pair this time, though one very uneven, as though someone dragged his feet. The steps stopped outside Jans' door. For a moment, he thought the guard had come back to keep them quiet. Then he heard a key slide into the keyhole and the door swung open. The guard shoved a dishevelled man into the cell, pulled the door closed, and locked it again. His footfalls retreated up the hall.

Jans looked to the gaunt man sprawled face-first upon the floor. He crouched down, his Elfish eyes examining his new cell-mate despite the dark. What he could see showed a man's face, cut, bruised and swollen beneath a fall of dark shoulder-length hair. A wound in his arm oozed, dribbling onto the floor. His torn shirt had moulded itself to his back, slick with blood. Jans reached forward to check for a life-pulse when the man suddenly jumped up, ready to fight. Jans toppled back with a startled cry and scrambled to the nearby wall, pursued by the man.

"Wait," Jans cried as his back slammed against the cold cement wall. "I'm on your side."

The man hesitated, his swollen eyes narrowing in suspicion. After a moment, he spoke in a harsh whisper, voice rough as though recently more used to screaming than talking.

"They won't get anything from me. Throw me back in a cell will they? And with a roommate too. What did you do to end up here?" He glared at Jans, sizing him up.

"I ... I ran." Jans stammered. The stranger's eyes narrowed further, making Jans wonder if he could see at all now.

"You ran," he repeated.

Jans shrugged and nodded, his eyes wide and helpless.

"I don't understand," The man glanced sidelong at Jans. "You got thrown into the depths of the nine Hells, for running?"

Jans opened his mouth, ready to reply, but thought better of it. He had no idea who this person was. He could be working with the Guardians. And Karen! She'd be waiting to hear from him. Jans looked to the stranger again. He couldn't just disappear right in front of the man's eyes. He'd have to tell him something, but what?

"How, ah," Jans swallowed hard. "How did you come here?"

The man laughed roughly. "Oh, no. They're not going to get me that easily. You think I'd tell you? You're not getting word one out of me." He turned and, limping stiffly a few paces, sat on one of the beds, leaving Jans against the far wall.

After a time, the man looked across the cell to Jans.

"Don't trust nobody kid. You stay alive longer that way. Even in the tunnels, trust is limited." He stopped speaking. Jans waited, but his companion said nothing more.

Screwing up his courage, Jans asked in a small voice, "The tunnels?"

The man glanced at him sharply and winced, his hand probing the swelling at his jaw.

"Running, huh?" he said, returning to a previous thought. "I knew someone else who was running. What did you run from, kid? Why did they bring you here?"

"We ran from Guardians."

"We?" The man looked around, then fixed his gaze upon Jans once more. "Why were you running? What did you do?"

"I didn't do anything! They came searching for us in Nearbrook and we've been running ever since."

The man sat straight up.

"What did you say?" he growled.

"I said I didn't do anything!"

"No, no. After that. They came searching for you where?"

"To Nearbrook," The man jumped up at Jans' words, cursing. "Why?" Jans asked, his courage fleeing in terror, leaving him trembling.

"Of all the ..." the man muttered to himself. "Who was with you?"

Jans shrank back, but said nothing. The man stepped forward, his eyes aglow with emotion. The darkness did nothing to hide his dangerous glare.

"Who?" he hissed.

Jans shook his head, eyes wide. The man loomed over him, staring down, a wild expression on his battered face. Suddenly, he nodded and his features grew less menacing.

"It was her, wasn't it," he whispered. "It was Karen."

Chapter 13

Manfred paused, his back pressed firmly against the rough bark of a dead tree. He peered around the trunk. About fifty feet away, three Guardians passed, searching a new path. So far, Manfred's plan had worked. His various pathways and backtracking trails confused his pursuers. These three, however, came a little close. He'd have to exercise more caution. He glanced toward the setting sun; nearly dusk and still no sign of Karen or Jans.

To his left lay Silben. Jans had not exaggerated the water's stillness. Manfred had never seen anything quite like it before. Nothing moved in the cold water. A few dead and broken trees and clumps of old, dry bushes skirted the shore, giving the impression of life suspended in an endless deep winter. The whole area, laid deep in a valley, supported ashen white and deathly tints. Around the upper lip of the valley, as Jans had described, grew thorn bushes, the only thriving form of life Manfred had seen. Other than the Guardians. The whole place left an eerie sensation under Manfred's skin. He couldn't shake the feeling that the lake was unnatural, evil even, and that something as dead and barren as that place should not exist. He shivered now just remembering it.

"This way," he heard one of the Guardians call. Thinking perhaps his inadvertent shiver had alerted them to his presence, Manfred watched with relief as the Guardians turned away from him.

Slowly, though, apprehension replaced amusement as his eyes darkened. Where were Karen and Jans? It was far past their scheduled meeting and Manfred feared for their safety. He may have said he would go his own way if they didn't show, but he was just fooling himself. No way could he leave them. They knew nothing of the world. Karen had told him bits of her life before Ildare, and none of it had included anything beyond the Farrange Mountains. And Jans ... well, Nearbrook had suffered under Guardian control half his life. The kid didn't know much beyond his own town. Certainly nothing that would help if Guardians got hold of him.

Manfred pictured two mangled bodies, Guardians laughing over them, a sweep of golden hair fluttering to reveal her face a ruined mess. He gasped and forced the image from his mind. They had to be alive; they just had to be. But where?

Determined not to lose hope, the large tracker turned toward Silben, preparing to re-search its perimeter and look for any sign of his missing companions.

Then he thought of another possibility. They had made two paths. These Guardians would have known that, so they might know what had become of Karen and Jans; if they had eluded capture or not. He would just have to find a Guardian who would talk, and survive in the process.

The Stalker set off in pursuit of his foe.

**

Jans stared at the man looming above him.

"How ..." Jans' voice failed him.

"It was her, wasn't it? Where is she?" The man's gaze swept the cell as if he expected Karen to step out of the shadows. He looked back at Jans, waiting for a response.

Jans gathered his resolve and asked instead, "Who are you?"

After a moment's hesitation, the man drew himself up to full height. If he noticed the wounds in his back, Jans didn't see it.

"I am Joanha."

"Joanha? Part of the ..." Jans stammered, biting his tongue to keep from blurting anything out. It wouldn't be very smart to give anything away, especially knowledge of the rebels. After all, Jans had no reason to believe this man was the same Joanha that Karen and Manfred had encountered,
116

except his knowledge of Karen and his mention of the tunnels.

Joanha's eyes darkened a shade at Jans' outburst, but he nodded, more in approval, it seemed, than in agreement, when Jans paused.

"You're not bad, kid. You got backbone. A little slow maybe, but you know enough to listen when someone says not to trust anyone. Yes, I'm that Joanha." He paused and regarded Jans with a sort of curiosity. "You have magic." He presented it as a statement, not a question. "Karen went to Nearbrook to find you. What sort of magic would she need to help her?"

Jans remained silent. He remembered what Manfred had said about Joanha's suspicion and mistrust of magic. However, he had asked himself that question many times since he first met Karen in Nearbrook, all of what? Two days ago? If that. What could his small feats of power do that a Druid could not?

Joanha edged closer to Jans, whether to appear more menacing or to try to appear less of an enemy, Jans couldn't tell, although the latter seemed more likely at this point. In Jans' mind, Joanha could not seem more frightening right now if he were the leader of the Guardians.

"Come on kid. What can I do to you in here?" His eyes flickered to the door. "Especially if *she* found out," he mumbled under his breath.

'*Jans,*' the boy heard, but not from Joanha, nor through the wall from Karen. He heard this voice in his mind, yet it was not his own. He jumped. Joanha stepped back, uncertain of this new tactic. Jans shook his head and put a hand to his forehead. The voice sharpened and he heard it say,

'*Trust him, Jans. Tell him your plan.*' The voice, he realised, belonged to Karen. There was an echo to the sound, as though she spoke from across a large, empty room.

"What ... how ..." he stammered.

Joanha's eyes narrowed as he stared at the boy.

'*I will explain later. We do not have much time.*' He felt her sense of urgency. Not fully understanding, Jans told his cellmate the plan of escape.

"I can teleport things. I was going to try and get us out that way."

"Teleport, eh? How far's your range?"

"My ... what?"

"Your range. How far away can you get us?"

"Who said we were taking you?" Jans blurted out. Had he thought it through though, he would have seen Joanha's usefulness. The man was a fighter; a rebel and a valuable ally against the Guardians, and Joanha knew it.

"I can lead you to wherever you're going. The question is, how far can you get us?"

Jans thought for a moment. He had never tried to teleport people before. The only living creature he had teleported had been a cat trapped between two fences, and that took place more than eight years ago. Luckily that had ended more successfully than the splintered water bucket. However, thinking back, the cat had never been the same since, having acquired a strange fascination for wandering into walls. Jans had felt dizzy when he teleported his tray to Karen's cell. How would he feel after teleporting three people?

"I don't know," he said slowly in response to Joanha's query. "I may only get us out of the cells and no further. I've never actually teleported people before."

Joanha considered Jans' confession. "We'll need a key then, if we only make the hall. There's still the main entrance to get through."

Jans regarded him with wonder. Here stood a man who held little trust for anyone and had no liking for magic, yet willingly took take Jans, a stranger, at his word. A smile broke across Joanha's face, as though he could hear Jans' thoughts. He shrugged.

"What have I got to lose?" he said.

***

Jans closed his eyes and concentrated on the form of the man standing in front of him. He took a deep breath. Joanha's battered face came to mind, but after a minute, it shimmered and slowly faded. He heard a faint gasp of surprise. Jans felt the room go empty. He had Joanha somewhere between the cell and the hall outside. Jans concentrated on the door and the hall beyond, only now realising he had no idea how wide a space stood on the other side of the door. He did not want Joanha to appear in a cell opposite his, nor in the middle of the door. But he couldn't panic or worry about what might go

118

wrong.   Instead, Jans renewed his concentration, his will strengthening; he imagined Joanha on the other side of the door.

Suddenly Joanha's face hovered before him, then shot through the door. It wavered, and became solid on the other side of the frame, then faded. Jans opened his eyes, only now discovering he had seen all this in his mind's eye. He glanced quickly about the room. Joanha had disappeared.

He looked at the door and moved toward it. His vision swam. A soft tap came from the door and a muffled voice. "Kid? Hey, you all right?" A pause. "You did it. I'm in the hall, but you gotta hurry."

Jans leaned against the wall and took several deep breaths, gulping in stale air. He staggered to the bed. Sitting gingerly on the edge of the hard mattress, he pictured Karen, her golden hair and her sparkling mauve eyes, and he again closed his eyes, maintaining the image. He projected his thought and perception into Karen's cell. It didn't take long before he felt her presence. It felt as though they shared the same room, her image seemed so clear. He concentrated on this presence and enveloped it in his thought. Slowly, the presence faded and Jans hoped he had Karen safe in the midst of his teleport. He thrust his thoughts to the hall between cells and allowed her image to reappear there.

"Karen?" he called when the image faded, his voice a raspy whisper, but sounding loud to his ears. No response reached him, either from the hall or the cell. "Karen?" he called louder in panic as something wet and sticky fell down the side of his face. He put his hand to his head and found blood trickling from his wound. Remembering Karen's voice in his mind, he projected a thought out to her. At first, nothing happened and he wondered if he even could mind read to her, or if he had imagined things before. Then her voice came in a short message.

'*Hold on.*'

Jans didn't know what to make of it until he heard footsteps growing steadily louder as the guard approached. Now Jans understood why silence had met his calls.

The guard banged on the door with his fist. "That's enough noise from you, hear? Not another peep. You're disturbing the rats." Jans heard a grunt and another bang on the door. Next, he heard the jingling of keys as one slid into the lock. The door slowly opened and the guard fell in, unconscious. Joanha slipped in behind the guard, a grin on his face.

"Way to go kid. Come on, let's go before they miss him."

Jans blinked and stood. A wave of nausea and dizziness washed over him as he stumbled forward and almost fell. Joanha, at his side in a flash, supported him.

"There's no time for this. We have to go, now." Joanha's voice was calm, yet stern. Jans found it somehow encouraging. Gulping for air, his nausea retreated and the dizziness subsided. Outside in the hall, Karen gave him a brief hug. She had a cut lip and a greenish-yellow bruise puffed out her jaw. Jans smiled shyly, relieved she had made it. He had been unsure of teleporting people, and with Karen, she hadn't even been in the same room. He had feared it wouldn't work. He had discovered a new aspect to his magic, and for that, he was also grateful, grateful that he could use it without others always fearing him. Why then did *he* still fear it?

"Now for the gate," Joanha said. A hint of mischief lit his battered face as he led them off, the guard's keys in one hand and the other encompassing the hilt of the guard's sword.

***

A glow in the clearing ahead caught the Stalker's eye. Manfred peered cautiously around one of the large rocks sheltering the clearing's perimeter. The evening had darkened and the horizon swallowed the last traces of remaining sunlight. The glow Manfred saw did not come from the sun, though, nor from anything he would consider natural. It came from a fire that burned with neither wood nor leaves. This was a Guardian-fire, one that burned with magic. As Manfred watched, the flames turned from red to pale blue, then shimmered into a sort of green. A pretty enough display, he supposed, though one that would give away their position. But these were Guardians. Who did they have to fear? They had no reason to hide; except that they were supposed to be searching, either for him or for Karen and Jans.

He glanced over his shoulder, wondering if he should put more distance between himself and the Guardians. What he saw surprised him. The light barely illuminated beyond where he crouched. So that was the secret. No one would know about such Guardian encampments until they stumbled upon them. For someone without Manfred's skills, that would be too close to escape. He looked back to the clearing. Two Guardians sat by the fire's edge and another three lay nearby, silhouettes in slumber. The two on watch had a difference of opinion.

"I don't like it, not one bit," one said.

"Listen, those are our orders and you will follow them, like it or not."

"But it's not right. We don't even know what we're up against. If we—"

"They're probably being questioned as we speak. We'll find out what we're up against. They got caught, didn't they? Did magic help them escape? No, that's why they're in the tower now. How much of a threat can they be?"

"Yeah, but what about Ildare? You saw Anda's remains. It takes something powerful to do that. No, that girl is more than she seems."

That girl!? Manfred had gotten a lucky break. What had the one said? *They're in the tower.* But what tower?

"It doesn't matter right now what she is. What we have to do is find the Stalker, find out why he's here, what his part in this whole thing is." He paused. "I can't figure it. From what I've heard, he's always been a loner."

"Maybe she forced him."

"No one forces the Stalker," the Guardian snorted. "No, he's helping her on his own. But why?"

The two fell into silence. Manfred sat, his back to the boulder, facing away from the clearing, and thought about the same thing. Why? He had no obligation to her. The most she'd done was bring a little adventure his way, but his life revolved around adventure. Why then? Certainly not just to frustrate Guardians. He had done that well enough before she came along. And that Guardian had spoken true; he had always been a loner. No one forced him to do anything. Especially after that business with Trayon. Hadn't he determined to step back after that?

Then Karen had appeared and he found himself traipsing across the land with her. He'd had plenty of opportunities to get away, but constantly stayed by her side. So what did he feel toward Karen? Why stick with her? Sure, she'd become a friend, a travelling companion, even someone he would risk his life for, but did it go further than that? He glanced over his shoulder at the clearing. Yes, he realised. He did have feelings for her. He knew so little about her, yet he knew as he gazed into the Guardian-fire that he would do anything for her. Manfred, the Stalker, loner tracker, the giant of a man who seemed to have feelings for no one, found himself vulnerable. He found that he loved Karen.

Manfred sat back. He felt the air sucked out of his lungs. Love. He barely knew her, but even in their short time together, he had come to love her more than life. He had to get to her, help her escape from whichever of the Hells they had thrown her into. But where? Manfred searched the deadened trees, as though they held the answer.

"Maybe she's helping him," the one Guardian ventured. After a moment, the other said,

"He's a tracker, a natural. He wouldn't need any help." He hesitated, considering. "For all we know, he's at the dungeon tower now and not here at all. We're probably wasting our time."

The dungeon tower. Now Manfred had a place to start. Only two actual dungeon towers stood nearby. The one, Sheol, required more than two days hard travel. Since they had separated only the previous day, that left Jadathe. A shiver crawled down his spine. He had heard tales of that hellish place, unpleasant recountings of nightmares. About five years ago, he had ventured near the edge of the forest guarding Jadathe in pursuit of a particularly nasty cutthroat, and the screams which echoed from the place chilled the heart to its core, if not deeper. If the Guardians had taken Karen and Jans there, they faced more danger than Manfred cared to think about. Especially Jans. He was, after all, only a boy, an inexperienced one at that. The most danger he had faced came from the lash of his father's belt. Now, subject to the wills of Guardians, beings without mercy or feeling, he stood in great peril. Manfred didn't want to think what they might do to a magic user like Karen. Just the thought of her in danger tightened his chest, and he had to concentrate on his breathing to keep it steady.

Manfred gazed up through the thin web of tree boughs to

the stars glimmering faintly above and wondered if his companions would ever see those stars again. His hand reached unconsciously for the hilt of his sword as he retreated quickly into the forest, plans forming as he hurried toward his love, fervently hoping he did not arrive too late.

***

Three figures crouched in the shadows of the dungeon, waiting. A well-armed guard, not a Guardian, passed them. He remained unaware of the hidden trio, since the torch on the far wall did not have the power to reveal them. Joanha crept forward, peering around the next corner, searching for any other sign of guards. He motioned for Karen and Jans to follow, and led them down the corridor to where another hall crossed their path. He paused, looking for signs of life. A shriek disturbed the stillness, causing them to jump back and blend with the cold grey of the walls. Not the first such wail of despair to send them cringing into shadows, their hearts beating a furious rhythm as they swallowed their own dread. Jadathe seemed full of such sounds, the screams and cries of terror, all the tormented souls the Guardians enjoyed bending to their wills. Karen grew cold just thinking of what the Guardians practiced in their own sick way. She looked around. Jans cowered behind her, lost and frightened. The wound on his head had stopped seeping again, but blood crusted the side of his face. She worried about him. He was an innocent, but she needed him to help her cause. She did not know whether she had the right to bring him into this though. Still, he had featured so prominently in her vision. He retained more importance than either of them guessed. Karen knew that somehow Jans held the key to the defeat of the Ebbrings. If only she could keep him alive long enough to find the lock.

She looked then to Joanha. So much skill and so little trust, yet still a courageous rebel. His caution kept him at a distance from everyone, even Chanet and Will. He turned toward her. His face held old scars and new wounds—did she cause those too? He met her gaze, his dark eyes unable to conceal the breadth of his experience. He looked then to Jans. *So untrusting,* Karen thought again, *and yet so worthy of trust.*

"Come on," Joanha whispered and set off through

123

Jadathe's maze of corridors. Already, they had searched for an hour, seeking escape. The tower spanned more area than she had thought.

They headed down the hallway, turned a corner and ran into a door. Karen watched as Joanha glanced around. He tried one key and then another until it opened, revealing a staircase descending into darkness. They remained motionless for a time, unsure of whether to follow this new path or retrace their steps.

"We *are* in a tower. The gate should reside below," Karen reasoned. Joanha hesitated, then nodded. He stepped forward and slowly advanced into the gloom, Karen and Jans a breath away.

All around, the walls seemed to whisper, calling to Guardians. Karen grew more nervous. The stairs narrowed and spiralled down with only the wall on the left for support and emptiness to the right. The air warmed and the darkness grew stifling. Karen glanced over her shoulder, past Jans. She could feel the tension building. It seeped through the whispering walls and wrapped about her like a shroud of impending danger. She put a warning hand on Joanha's arm. He turned. A shout from below shattered the silent darkness. Looking down, Karen saw the faint glimmer of a torch held by a Guardian. Jans gasped and edged closer. She followed his gaze to the stairs above. Several men in black advanced, trapping the three.

Above and below, the enemy gathered, corralling them. Karen stepped in front of Jans, shielding him. He tried to retrieve his place as protector despite his fierce tremors, but Karen refused to give way. The Guardians had magic too powerful for Jans to defend against, and he still recovered his strength from his teleportations. Karen gathered her power and allowed it to grow, prepared to do her bidding.

She looked down the stairwell. The torches steadily closed in on them, revealing the faces of those who carried them. Joanha's sword rose, his face set and grim, ready for battle. Karen returned her attention to the men above. Six, maybe seven up there. She could not tell for certain in the dim light. They all wore uniforms, although not all had the silver accents she had seen on other Guardians. She raised her arms, ready to prepare a shield.

124

Everything went still. Karen grew cold.

A dark shape snaked up the stairs through the tableau of soldiers. It wore a human form, but there the resemblance stopped. Crimson slits marked its eyes in a face of shadows. A black cowl wrapped its body, mostly hiding the muddy folds of its clay-like flesh.

"Ebbring," Joanha hissed.

An Ebbring? Karen thought. But this was not the same creature she had seen in her vision. This was something different. She could sense the power of the Ebbring, the evil seething from the foul being and filling the narrow staircase with its stench, yet this unnatural horror did not rival her enemy in its depredations. What, then, did she truly fight?

Time ceased. Only this sinister creature moved.

Then Joanha lunged forward with his sword, plunging it into the heart of the nearest Guardian.

The Ebbring stopped, but Karen could feel the force of its magic and knew it prepared itself for battle.

The Guardians came to life, swords drawn, ready for bloodshed. The Ebbring brought up a hand formed of mud, aimed at Joanha. A jet of red flame from Karen's magic blocked its attack.

The warriors from above were almost upon them now. If Karen turned to fight, the Ebbring would have them. If she continued to fight off the Ebbring ... either way, they were lost.

Suddenly, Jans pushed past her, arms raised. She did not have time to stop him, having to counter the Ebbring's next attack on Joanha. Three more of the enemy had fallen under the rebel's whirling blade, but Joanha had not escaped unscathed. Blood welled from yet another gash on his left arm and he favoured his right leg. Considering his injuries before all the sword-play began, it amazed her that he could still fight as well as he did.

Joanha knew what he faced; he understood the power of the enemy. Jans, on the other hand, was not a seasoned fighter and lacked a means of defence.

Yet, to her surprise, and no doubt to the surprise of the Guardians, Jans did not need a sword, at least not yet. His magic became its own weapon. As Manfred had said back at the inn in Nearbrook, the simple things best add to a surprise. Jans now used a variation of levitation on his foes, or more

125

precisely, on their blades. He had disarmed three of them and held them at bay with their own weapons. One, more daring than his companions, took a step forward, and met with a sword to his gut. Another gathered his power, about to throw a wall of fire at the boy, but his blade, too, prevented that.

Unfortunately, Jans lacked the strength of the Guardians. His stamina began to falter. *I will lose the boy,* thought Karen, *unless ...*

She projected her voice into his mind.

'Jans, lean against me, back to back. Draw strength from me.'

She heard his protest, but could not let him die. She did not bring him this far to have it all end here before they had really begun.

'Do not argue Jans. You need the strength. Just do it.'

He did so and the battle continued, Joanha thrusting with his sword, Karen and Jans wielding their magic.

The Ebbring had turned its attention from Joanha and now fully concentrated on Karen. She had not anticipated an attack in such a confined area, nor so soon. Still, she made due as best she could, attack and defend, three against many. She did not like their odds.

Chapter 14

In the shadows of Jadathe's blackened outer walls, a figure hid, sword bared from its scabbard, grey eyes watchful. Manfred knew he had to find a way into this tower of death looming before him. It had taken nearly five hours getting here and had no desire to waste more time. He could see the gate, lit by two torches, one to either side of towering silver-black bars. Two guards stood below the torches and a third patrolled the outer confines, Guardians to the dark dungeon. Silent strokes from Manfred's blade had dispatched two other sentries earlier. Guardians were powerful in face to face confrontations, but taken by surprise, they were as vulnerable as anyone else. For the moment, Manfred gave no thought as to how he would rescue Karen and Jans, nor what he could do once he passed the entrance. For now, he merely concentrated on finding a way in.

He lay in wait, searching for other signs of defence, but no other guards appeared.

Strange how light the protections are. In the past, he had heard of whole legions securing this tower, this mighty fortress of evil. He himself had seen many more soldiers than this from a distance years ago. Did evil now think itself strong enough to withstand minor attacks? Or simply that no one would risk an assault on such a fortress? No one save Manfred. Of course, they would easily spot an army's approach, and a one-man invasion screamed insanity. All the better for a surprise attack, thought Manfred, but surprises only lasted so long. The longer he waited, the more chance of discovery. Time to make his move.

He watched the patrolling Guardian make his rounds of the tower, waiting only long enough for the man to wander out of sight of the other two guards. Then, with movements giving credit to the name Stalker, Manfred crept up behind the lone man and slit his throat without a sound from either hunter or prey.

Keeping his back to the cold stone wall, Manfred stole his way to the gate. The remaining Guardians, oblivious to his presence, stood at attention, staring off into the distance.

Manfred's chance had come, but some sound or movement must have given him away. The nearest Guardian turned his head. Manfred crouched and leapt, grabbing him about the waist. As they fell, the second man whirled, bringing his sword up with one hand and extending the other in front of him, preparing to send some sort of magic into the unexpected intruder. Manfred and the one Guardian struggled upon the rocky ground, rolling this way and that, each seeking an advantage over the other. The solitary guard, finding no clear shot at Manfred, merely stood at the ready, unsure of what to do—help his companion, call for aid, or maintain his post at the gate. Even now, his eyes searched the near vicinity, fully expecting others to appear out of the darkness in Manfred's defence. Only the grunts from the two grappling men and the ring of sword against stone broke the silence of the night. Not even a crackle from the torches above the gate gave evidence of anything beyond the existence of these two adversaries.

Manfred brought his fist up and landed a powerful blow across the jaw of the Guardian. The blow barely fazed the guard, though it brought blood to his lips. The man retaliated with a knee to Manfred's gut. Manfred hunched in on himself, feigning the extent of his pain, while searching for the Guardian's fallen weapon. In the same motion, he brought his head smartly against the bridge of the other's nose, feeling a distinct crack as the nose broke. He raised the sword, ready to strike, when its metal erupted into flames. Manfred dropped the burning blade with a curse and glanced up to see the other Guardian advancing, readying another burst of magic. Manfred returned his focus to the Guardian below him. The man's face, covered in blood, revealed eyes that glowed a fierce red, forcing Manfred to feel the hatred that had long ago consumed

128

this shell of a man with whom he fought. The other Guardian had a similar hatred. In truth, all of Jadathe vibrated with such ill feeling, and the thought of Karen and Jans locked somewhere within its miserable confines gave Manfred the strength to fight his way past the evil in his path.

The free Guardian released a mass of magic, sending jagged fire daggers at Manfred, just as Manfred pulled his other foe to a sitting position, in effect creating a shield for himself. The magic reached the Guardian and tore into his flesh, sending reeking smoke flying from him with a screech of tormented agony as life fled from his body. Manfred lifted the fiery corpse with surprising ease and threw the charred mass into the other Guardian, pushing his enemy off balance. The Guardian fell with one arm pinned behind his back.

Manfred wasted no time. He dropped his knee to the man's chest, using just enough pressure for the Guardian to know that one little movement would snap his ribs. Then Manfred grabbed the man by the nape of the neck and pressed a dagger to his prisoner's throat.

"Where are you keeping the girl and her companion?" Manfred demanded, his glare as potent as the Guardian's.

The Guardian's eyes narrowed, but he said nothing. Manfred shifted his weight. The man winced as a rib popped, then growled as a trapped beast might. Manfred pressed his dagger closer to the man's throat, drawing a thin trickle of blood.

"Where are they?" Manfred hissed again.

The Guardian spit at him and grinned wickedly, trying to kick out with his legs. Manfred dug his knee deeper into the Guardian's ribs, breaking more of them and puncturing the man's lung. The Guardian gasped and coughed, bringing up blood. When he still refused to answer, Manfred slit the man's throat, ending his pain and hopefully sending him to a better life.

The Stalker glanced around. Jadathe's guards lay dead and no others had come to help. Did no one watch from the tower's heights? Were these the only defences for the gateway to the east? It did not seem possible, or likely, yet it certainly appeared so. Still, Manfred knew he had to proceed with extreme caution. He grabbed the dead man's sword and put it in his belt. Then, he entered the blackness of Jadathe's halls.

For a moment, the stench stopped him. The reek of mould permeated the stone, but over that, Manfred smelled worse things: the tang of blood, the odour of unwashed bodies, even fear and misery had left a scent in this place. And underlying all those, he smelled the rot of death. It clung to his nostrils and slid down his throat when he swallowed. Taking shallow breaths, ignoring the taste clawing on the back of his tongue, he pushed on.

It would take time to find the right room. He had to locate the access to the cells first and avoid any guards, and he expected close-quarter combat at any moment. The dungeons would be higher up, easier for defending and more difficult from which to escape. Arrows and hot oil from above could slow a direct assault. In this type of tower, Manfred knew the barracks lay closest to the ground, so any attack would have to get past soldiers before reaching the cells.

He crept forward warily, but quickly. A movement out of the corner of his eye caught his attention. A rat scurried past. Manfred heaved a silent sigh and immediately regretted it. Bile rose in his gorge as Jadathe's fetidness tightened his throat again.

A shriek echoed off the stone. Manfred leaned back against the wall, eyes bright and watchful, muscles tense. The scream had emanated from above and to the right. Manfred edged in that direction. He moved forward, crouching or running as necessary, always in the shadows of the walls. Ahead, he spotted a great wooden door. Stooping to the keyhole, constantly checking around him, he worked at the lock. After a minute, the lock sprung open. He eased open the door, keeping out of the way of the entrance, not revealing himself to whatever lay in wait beyond. When nothing moved, he peered around the corner. Stone stairs. Empty. Manfred's uneasiness increased. He felt as though he had walked into some sort of trap. And still, he saw no guards.

The stairs ended in a landing opening both right and left. Which way now?

A long hallway to the left led to an open door where a faint light shone. A sudden clash of swords. Shouts of battle and cries of pain pierced the air. Manfred saw Karen's red flames of magic. He now understood the lightness of defences. A prison-break was underway.

Manfred set his jaw and tightened his grip on his sword. He charged to the door and ascended the stairs. He killed three Guardians and maimed two more, throwing them into confusion. He saw Karen far above. Behind her, crouching low on the stairs, stood Jans. A third figure also fought the Guardians. Manfred struck out as a Guardian turned, the evil being crying out a warning. When Manfred glanced up again, he saw with a start that he recognised the third figure—the rebel Joanha.

Chapter 15

They would not survive much longer. Every time one foe went down, two more took his place. Or so it seemed. Exhaustion was setting in.

A commotion from below added to the confusion. Startled shouts and cries of warning drifted up into the fighting mass. Karen glanced down, but could see only black uniforms.

The Ebbring also paused to look, as though feeling a shift in the battle. Karen took the opportunity to attack. She pitched her red flames into the dark form. It recoiled at the force, unable to bring up a shield in time. She followed with another burst of magic before it could recover. Behind her, Jans found a renewed strength as two more Guardians fell and Joanha, too, redoubled his attack as the Ebbring sank to its knees, smoke rising from its body.

Looking down past Joanha again, Karen saw that they might win this fight after all. Below her on the stairs stood Manfred, his great sword slicing with morbid grace into the thicket of enemies as he fought like a man possessed. Hope warmed her heart. She hurled one final burst of power into the clay-formed body of the Ebbring. It flew apart with a horrifying wail that clawed deep into her soul, its final attack failing before it began. The Guardians staggered, set back by the death of the Ebbring and its last soul-wrenching cry. Karen seized the opportunity to rush down the stairs, Jans and Joanha close behind. She pushed her way through the Guardians, shoving some into the emptiness on the right and smashing others into the wall on the left. Manfred cleared a path below and the foursome emerged from the crowd at a run.

"This way," Manfred called as he retraced his steps to the gate. Each cast the occasional glance over their shoulder, but none slowed.

The Guardians began a pursuit, but were slow to organise. For now, their biggest disadvantage lay in their numbers.

Dawn hovered in the east as they burst out into the open. The soft beginnings of morning light chased the stars and silhouetted the nearby forest. The four ran toward the trees in the hopes of losing pursuit. As Karen neared, she felt a presence oppressing her, a thousand voices just beyond hearing calling out to her, trying to force their thoughts into her mind. But her companions had nowhere else to flee, and she pressed on.

Moments later, when they broke through the outer line of trees, she identified this presence as the forest itself. The undergrowth sprang up thick and twisted in the manner of a net, ready to trip the unwary. Branches extended from trunks at low and awkward angles, grabbing at shirt and pants, clutching at cloaks, searching for some way to slow the intruders. Here and there, thorns sprang up where emptiness had appeared before, and sturdy thistles pricked their leaves into tiny crevices, eager to jab at weary feet. The leaves moved without a breeze, echoing the voice of the woods deep in Karen's consciousness, a voice haunting, searching, hoping ... and crying out as Manfred swung his bloodied sword as an axe, trying to clear a path through the dangerous plants.

Karen felt each thrust as a wound unto herself, heard the cries of the forest repeated by her own voice. Manfred turned, startled by her outburst. She clutched at her arm as a slash of red trickled between her fingers, mirroring the trickle of sap running from the broken underbrush at the end of the Stalker's blade. He stared at her arm in horror, his heart in his throat, seeing pain in her eyes.

"Don't stop now," Joanha rasped, brandishing his own weapon. "It won't take them long to follow." He slashed ahead into the forest. But as soon as his sword sliced into the undergrowth, Karen screamed in pain, another cut digging into her flesh. Joanha looked back, nearly dropped his sword at the sight of her unexpected blood.

"What the Hells is going on?"

Karen stared at the two men then looked beyond, her eyes focusing on something neither could see. Behind her, she sensed Jans looking with her, seeing beyond the physical forest to its magic, power calling power to itself. The strength of the forest surrounded her, infusing every tree, every bush and crawling plant, each insect and animal, with a magic potential that filled everything it touched to near bursting. The sheer intensity forced Karen to her knees.

She thrust her awareness outward, past the immediacy of the injured plants and her own pain, toward the heart of this magic. A second presence flitted at the edge of her awareness—a smaller, individual mind. A mind watching, waiting ... and completely unprepared for Karen's address. Karen stretched out her thoughts to this watching mind, as she had stretched out her thoughts to her father in the past and to Jans in the dungeon.

'*Please, we need your help.*'

A startled silence answered her before a reedy voice whispered above them in the language of trees, a language Karen knew well.

'*We help not tree cutters.*'

'*We meant you no harm,*' Karen sent. '*We did not realise our actions would cause pain.*'

'*Why do you intrude here?*' the voice hissed.

'*We run from the dungeon and its keepers,*' replied Karen. '*Please, we need somewhere to hide.*'

The leaves rustled in muffled argument, becoming a blurred babble to Karen as other smaller voices joined the first. Manfred, beside her, studied her with deep concern. He could hear nothing of this conversation, save the eerie rustling of the trees in the still air, and he did not understand the distant look in her eyes. He knew it dealt with magic, and he dared not interrupt. Joanha, however, felt a growing unease as his thoughts shifted from the still form of Karen to the pursuers he knew would soon find them. With a glance over his shoulder to Jadathe, he turned back to the trees, sword raised.

"We don't have time to stand around here. Your sword Stalker. Let's go."

"No, wait!" called Jans. Joanha frowned at the boy, his blade hovering over the choking undergrowth. Jans spoke on. "I think she's speaking to someone."

134

"Who?" Joanha asked, glancing around.

"The forest," Jans sounded perplexed.

"What're you talking about?" the rebel demanded.

"There's a lot of magic here. It's gathering around Karen. Even I can feel it. When you cut the forest, it cuts her."

Joanha looked to Karen dubiously and shook his head.

"That's foolish. It's just a forest."

"Look at her," Manfred snarled, tearing a strip of cloth from his tunic to bind her wounds. "She didn't just scratch herself. These wounds are deep."

"A forest can't hurt people like that."

"Then how do you explain this?" Manfred wiped at the blood dripping down Karen's elbow. Her eyes remained glazed, unaware of his attention.

"There are Guardians coming for us, men with magic, creatures who would do this without a thought. The longer we stand here waiting, the shorter your life-span, Stalker." Joanha gripped his blade tighter and turned to the trees. Manfred's broadsword crossed his path.

"If you touch even one plant ..." Manfred's voice hovered in the air, low and menacing.

Karen, only peripherally aware of the conflict around her, concentrated on trying to diffuse the tension the forest emitted. The presence spoke again.

'From the blackness you run? The dark that spreads hate in our depths?'

'If you mean the Ebbrings, then yes.'

'Why run you?'

'We fight them. They want to stop us.'

The leaves stirred in consultation. At least two factions argued about what to do. One group seemed grudgingly willing to hear what Karen might say, but the other felt so violently opposed to the presence of the companions that Karen feared the outcome of the argument. She listened with a sinking feeling as the opposing sector gained dominance. It was this second voice which then addressed her contemptuously.

'And who are you that challenge what we must fear?'

Karen stood, pulling herself up to her full stature, letting her wounded arms grace her sides in a stance of proud determination and defiance to this inhospitable creature. She spoke aloud, her voice clear and powerful.

135

"I am Karenrana, daughter of the Elfin High Priestess Sadricha and the Druid Draimar." The sharp intake of collected breath as the forest recognised the names caused Manfred and Joanha to stop their struggle and glance uneasily at the woods around them. Karen ignored their questioning stares and continued speaking to the forest. "I challenge what you fear because no one else will. I live to bring light to the shadows. But I cannot do that alone. So I say again: we need your help."

For a long moment, nothing happened. The forest was silent, and frighteningly still. Karen's companions glanced nervously back toward Jadathe and the Guardians tumbling from its dark maw, but Karen kept her gaze straight ahead. Finally, she saw movement, a slight stirring of foliage as plants parted to provide a path. Several charcoal-coloured stick-thin creatures no taller than Jans strode forward, their large leaf-green eyes shining brightly. Manfred and Joanha levelled their swords at the advancing beings until Karen waved the two warriors aside. The central figure studied the four companions, then addressed itself to Karen in a quiet, almost gentle reed-like voice so that all could understand its speech.

"If challenge the dark any have a right to, then you are she. We will help as we can. I am Whooshea of the Forest Fey. The outer limits of the forest we guard and from immediate pursuit, you we can conceal. But hurry we must. Please follow."

Whooshea turned and dissolved into the trees with a breath of wind, but the path the Fey had created remained to lead the four. The forest closed behind them, guiding their steps and masking their flight. Karen followed without hesitation, forcing the men to either join her or remain to face the pursuing Guardians. They crowded behind her.

Manfred watched Karen for any further signs of wounds. He did not understand what had happened, but he could keep his curiosity in check for now. His anxiety, however, he could not hide.

Joanha's glance shifted between the girl and the Fey leading them, his eyes dark with distrust and a scowl on his face. Only the slight pursing of his lips when he looked at Karen betrayed his concern for her.

Jans was full of wonder and curiosity, but he didn't want to show his ignorance. Ebbrings and Guardians were one thing—everyone knew of them—but a Forest Fey? He had

136

never seen the likes of what walked before them now. Whatever else these creatures were, however much they helped, Karen's bloodied arms proved them dangerous.

Karen alone seemed unconcerned about their escort. She swept along the path Whooshea left as though it were the most natural thing in the world.

The Fey all but ignored the group they led, never turning to see that they followed or kept pace. Yet they were all well aware of the companions. The forest itself whispered of their passing, just as it howled at the intrusion of the Guardians. Karen understood the call of the trees. Her friends only heard the shivering of the leaves in a wind they could not feel.

The group never saw the Guardian patrols, but they could hear the soldiers crashing through the tangle of trees. When the third such search party passed out of hearing, Joanha spoke up.

"What in all the Hells is going on?" he growled. Karen glanced at him, but did not slow her pace. The rebel gestured at her wounds. "I mean, what happened here? How did these Fey cut you, and how do they keep those bastards from finding us when we can point out their patrols with our eyes closed by sound alone?"

"Magic calls to magic," she replied. "The forest is very powerful, and it reached out to my magic as the strongest here. When we maimed the trees, they thrust the wounds onto me. As we harmed their power, so they harmed ours."

"And now we follow them? After they've proven their willingness to hurt us?"

"When Manfred and I came too close to your tunnels, you threatened us. Then, when you learned we intended no harm, you helped us. The Fey are no different. Once they learned that we fight the same battle, they turned their threats to help."

Joanha shook his head, peering cautiously at the trees surrounding them.

"What kind of strange forest is this?" he whispered.

Manfred answered softly.

"We walk through the cursed forest Crownawn."

Joanha gave the warrior a sharp look.

"You've been here before?"

"I have skirted its edge," Manfred replied. "Strange that you, Joanha, a member of the rebellion, know nothing of it."

"What do you imply Stalker?"

"Why were you in Jadathe?" countered the large man.

"You think I'm in with the Guardians?" Hatred flashed in Joanha's eyes and he struggled to keep his voice low and his stride even.

"Just answer my question; why were you there?"

"For saving your hide."

Complete silence followed Joanha's outburst. They had stopped moving, lending weight to the silence. It seemed even the wind would not shatter the stillness. Another enemy patrol finally dared move nearby.

Joanha held his breath as he and Manfred stared at each other. The dark soldiers tramped out of range, unaware of the proximity of their quarry. Finally Manfred spoke.

"What happened?"

Joanha relaxed, his tension easing away. He drew in a deep breath and glanced to Karen, then returned his attention to the Stalker. They started after the Fey once more.

"Like you said back in the tunnels, Guardians did follow your trail, well hidden though it was. They had Death Hounds with them."

"Death Hounds?" Karen asked.

"A special type of blood hound, bred by the Ebbrings themselves. Or perhaps created by them," Joanha explained. "They are merciless and vicious. Can tear a man to shreds, bones and all, in a matter of seconds. But they're well trained. They know when to kill and when to capture.

"They found the entrance. The tracks to the second entrance worked, but not for long. Most of us had left by then, but Will and I and some others had remained well hidden in case we had to stall them. The bastards broke through the blockade and those damned Death Hounds picked up your scent again. They went into a frenzy, started howling like mad. That is a sound I would not wish upon anyone, the piercing cries of a Death Hound." He shuddered.

"The Guardians were so intent on following you that they didn't notice us. They must have expected a lot of resistance because I saw at least twenty of them.

"We waited for most of them to pass, taking out the rear ones first. Their magic is practically useless when they're caught unprepared. Unfortunately, it didn't take them long to

138

figure out what we did. Some tried to double back. We knew all the ins and outs, all the best places to attack and to retreat. Still, we were too few.

"Maggie fell first, then Honres. Will went down, but still alive when last I saw him. We scattered. They set the Death Hounds on us, but not to kill. The lead Guardian bellowed to the others that he wanted us alive.

"I don't know what Death Hounds are made of, but it can't be flesh and blood. The first one to reach me had teeth of iron. My blade made no dent. I didn't even faze it. Still, it took three of the bloody beasts to bring me down and two Guardians to convince me to behave myself." He grinned at that.

"Convince you?" Manfred asked, raising an eyebrow.

Joanha pushed his hair from his face to reveal a large bruise faded to a sickly yellow-green above a scabbed-over gash in his cheek. "Had a lump the size of a Mangrat egg here, too." He gingerly touched a swell of purple-speckled skin beneath his left ear. "And that's what's left after a week and more."

"What about the Death Hounds?" Jans asked, his voice full of curiosity and his eyes wide as he stumbled. "Did they hurt you?"

"Not really, kid. They may have a grip of iron, but they didn't even break the surface. Left some nice marks though." He rolled up his sleeve to show his upper arm, covered with ugly bruises fading to a memory. The teeth marks were unmistakable, despite the intact skin. "The legs were worse. Can't tell now, though, with what ice-eyes and his buddies did.

"Anyhow, when I came to, I found myself in Jadathe, clamped in irons. They thought the whip would make me talk, then moved on to knuckles and finally the edge of a knife. But they learned nothing from me."

"What did they want to know?" Manfred inquired.

"Mostly about you two. They began by demanding to know who I was and about the rebels and all. But then they asked about you. 'Who's the girl?' they wanted to know. 'What are her powers? Why's the Stalker in her company and where are they going?' That sort of thing. They're real keen on knowing about you, Karen. And why the Stalker would risk his already endangered life to help. You ..." he said, nodding at Jans, "they don't understand at all."

"They asked about Jans?" Karen asked, startled.

"They asked why you'd be in Nearbrook, why you'd go looking for a child. I had no idea myself." He looked to Jans again, then Karen.

"Why is he here? Was it just so that you could escape Jadathe, or is there something more?"

Karen glanced at Jans, and at Manfred. Such a difference—the inexperienced, naive young man and the warrior, wise in ways even he did not realise. Then she gave the only answer she could.

"I do not know. There is something more, much more. But I do not know what it is."

She met Jans' eyes. He held her gaze and for the first time, Karen saw great power in the depths of those green eyes. Within this child, dormant for the moment, lay a power of which he knew nothing, a power that would somehow help bring about the downfall of the Ebbrings. At that moment, Karen knew her quest could not possibly come to a successful conclusion without the boy.

"Jans is very important. His role in this fight is not yet over." She squinted at the sun, almost directly overhead now. "We must go east. There is little time."

"East?" Joanha repeated. "We don't even know where we are. How are we going to be able to find our way out of this forest, let alone make our way east? These Fey may lead us in circles for all we know."

The flash in Karen's eyes silenced any doubts the three men may have had. Questions faded and somehow they all understood, as Karen did, that the seed of evil lay in the east, the domain of the Ebbrings.

Before she could call out to the Fey, Whooshea appeared before her.

"East we will take you, daughter of Draimar, though power there we have no longer. Your safety we can guarantee no further than the distance you walk before the sun sets. There, must our protection end."

"I understand, Whooshea, and I thank you."

"Once, to our very heart we could take you, but no longer." Whooshea's thin voice grew quiet. "Accursed your friend called this place, and truth we hear in his words. For millennia, evil has the Forest Fey kept from entering or leaving our home.

140

Now our powers weaken. In the inner depths of our land, evil has lived long, and creatures of good enter at great risk. Spreads now that evil. Our home it leaves and yours it enters. You send your light into that dark and we can but watch, and hope. Care follow you and guide you, Karenrana, daughter of hope, but we cannot."

Karen gazed long into Whooshea's eyes, eyes tinged with worry, and fear. Finally, she nodded.

"It is a blessing beyond compare that your people have guarded our world for so long. I thank you for your help, and your warning. We will do what we can to restore your lands and answer your hopes. Life and growth in all summers, Child of the Forest."

Whooshea blinked in surprise at hearing that treasured phrase of his people from an outsider. Then his thin lips spread into a gentle smile and he bowed his head.

"Honour us you do, friend to the Fey. Our ways few know, and fewer bother to remember them." *'Life and growth in all summers,'* he said in the language of trees before turning to lead the way once more.

***

When the sun touched the earth behind them, Whooshea slowed, then stopped. He peered uneasily at the forest ahead. Gesturing to the Fey accompanying him, he spoke softly. The others then faded back the way they had come, leaving Whooshea alone with the four companions.

"No further can we go," he said, eyeing the deepening darkness of the end of day. "Our limits we have reached. For this night, safe will you rest. Until the sun rises, over you will we watch."

"Thank you, my friend. We have nothing which with to repay your kindness, but—"

"Payment enough is your will to fight the dark, friend to the Fey," Whooshea interrupted, not unkindly. "May the trees shelter you. In the morning, a path you will find that leads where you go. In sight keep it, but no foot set upon it. Avoid prying eyes you might, but this I know not. Have our hopes, dearest daughter." With that, he faded into the trees, leaving the companions alone once more.

Chapter 16

Jans woke, feeling better than he had in a long time. Stretching with a yawn, he sat up and took in his surroundings. Considering the injuries of the past few days, everyone looked in good health. Joanha's bruised and battered face seemed much improved though far from fully healed. Karen's arms looked unscathed, and the lump on Jans' head had disappeared. When he asked Karen about it, she smiled, gazing into the forest.

"The Fey have given us a gift. They can heal their woods in times of sickness. Whooshea has extended that healing to us."

They had started out after that, walking on through Crownawn, trusting the new risen sun to guide them in the right direction. The path Whooshea had mentioned stretched wide enough for six men to walk abreast. Keeping this path in sight but moving through the tangle of undergrowth, Manfred led the way, Karen a step behind. Jans ambled along behind her and Joanha brought up the rear. Although they did not see Whooshea or his people again, the Fey had left a supply of food from the forest for them. About midmorning, they stopped for a meal, then continued on their way.

By late afternoon, Jans caught up to Karen and broke the silence.

"Um," he began. Karen looked at the boy. He bowed his head and his eyes searched the ground.

"What is it Jans?" she asked.

"About that mind reading ..." he muttered, uncertain how to

proceed. Karen smiled.

"You want to know more about it."

"Well, yes. I mean, it's something I've never done before. I'm not even sure it really works."

"You must be fairly certain, or you would not have asked."

"I know it exists, if that's what you mean. You can use it. I just don't know if I can. Does that make any sense?" He glanced up at her.

"Yes, I think so. You have heard me use it and you tried it yourself, but you do not know how it works. You want to understand it."

"Yeah. Maybe if I knew what I was doing ... I don't know." He looked directly at her this time. "Can you teach me?"

Karen smiled again. She remembered her father teaching her of mind speech, of their conversations without sound. One occasion in particular leapt to mind, walking through the woods of Farrange with her father as the dazzling fire of the sun crested the mountains and sent its light to burn away the shadows and early morning mist. She had learned mind speech three months earlier and still delighted at its beauty—providing she did not try to probe her father's mind. Such things were dangerous, he had told her, though it had not stopped her from trying anyway. Just once. The backlash of the mind trap Draimar had set for her, knowing she would try to probe, was enough to teach her not to force a person's thoughts.

On that day so long ago, she had studied the serenity around her with open joy and caught herself daydreaming once or twice, mostly about the outside world that she had never seen. At one point, she heard her father's voice in her mind, helping her practise this relatively new skill.

'What are you thinking?' *He asked through this inner speech.*

'About how beautiful the world is,' *she replied. He gave her a strange glance, then looked ahead into the forest as she continued.* 'How peaceful everything is here. Is it so wonderful in the outside world?' *The outside world, the world of man that she had only ever heard about. She was always curious about that world, yet fearful too.*

'Some places are, though far too many now have changed.' *Draimar replied, his eyes lost in shadows and his*

143

posture stiff.

Karen understood that now, looking around at the trees of Crownawn. Whooshea had spoken of such change. The emergence of the Guardians and Ebbrings, the existence of a rebellion, the possibility of her vision coming to pass, all spoke of how things changed.

She looked back to Jans and answered his question.

"Of course I will teach you. Jans, you need not be nervous about your magic, or about asking my help. It is not the sign of a coward to admit he does not know a thing; it is the sign of a wise person. We all need help now and again."

"You don't," he protested.

She laughed. "Don't I? What about Jadathe? Do you think we could have escaped without you? Or without Whooshea to lead us this far? And the reason I sought you in the first place ... Jans, I may have powerful magic, but I need help too. So do Joanha and Manfred, though it may not seem so at the moment. None of us are perfect."

Jans stared at her for a few seconds, then smiled.

"Thanks," he whispered. Then louder: "Will you teach me?"

"It is mind communication, a form of telepathy my father taught me," she began. "I was not sure if you possessed the ability, but when you mind-read to me in the tower, I knew. To project your voice into the mind of another, just form your thoughts. You can almost see the words in front of you. Imagine the person you want to talk to and do so, only in your mind. Do you understand that much?"

"I think so. That's what I did before."

"It works on those without magic, but only one way. Some may have the ability to respond with their unformed thoughts, while others simply become aware of your presence. Some will not even consciously sense you, but none can initiate mind speech."

"Then how will I know if they hear me?"

"Consciously or subconsciously, they will let you know. You can sense some of their emotions, especially strong ones. I felt your surprise, so I knew you had heard me. It is not what one expects to happen, to suddenly hear someone who is not with you. It can be disconcerting to one who is not used to it."

Jans thought about this for a moment. "Can I read

144

someone's mind without them knowing? You know, read their thoughts?"

Karen regarded the boy. She remembered her father's warning about reading a person's mind without their permission. The cost could be high if that person found out.

"It is possible, but you must exercise caution. Should that person discover that you invaded their mind ..." she shook her head before continuing.

"The other danger to reading thoughts unbidden is what you may find out. Some thoughts can be overwhelming, even deadly."

"How do you mean? A thought could kill me?"

"That is exactly what I mean. My father taught me about such thoughts. They are so full of malevolence that their very presence is devastating. Those would be the thoughts of such minds as the Guardians or the Ebbrings."

"Have you ever tried to read the thoughts of others?" Jans asked.

Karen shook her head. "I tried it on father once," she said. "He knew as soon as I did, as though he could feel my mind in his. He gave me such a pointed warning, I never tried it again."

"What did he do?"

Karen smiled. "He had a trap set in his mind. It felt like a sharp slap to my face, but in my mind, one that left an impression. Then he told me it was just a warning, that others would not be so kind. My pride was hurt more than my thoughts, but I learned my lesson." She looked Jans in the eye. "If you ever try reading another's thoughts, Jans, promise me you will be careful. Do not try it on the enemy. They are much too powerful. A wound of the mind is not easily mended. Will you promise me that?"

Jans nodded. They walked on in silence. Jans fell back a step, lost in thought, and Karen moved ahead to Manfred. He glanced at her, but kept his pace, not saying anything. Karen easily matched his stride. He looked ahead once more. Finally, Karen spoke in a quiet voice.

"Do you know how far this forest stretches?"

"I've heard too many answers to that question," he replied, savagely swatting at the insects of the evening. "Some say it covers fifty miles, others say five hundred. I am inclined to believe it lies somewhere between the two, provided we do not

145

walk in circles. The sun is an excellent guide, but night approaches and we may lose our way." Manfred took in his surroundings. The trees grew tall and twisted, nearly blocking out the sky, and insects infested every inch of the increasing shadows. Manfred again slapped at some crawling on his arm and Karen brushed others from her face. Behind them, Joanha and Jans did likewise with muffled curses.

Manfred continued: "We have to find a place to spend the night." He looked at Karen. She sighed, agreeing with him.

Shrubbery stood slightly apart from the path ahead of them, still far enough from the main path to keep an eye on what might pass by. Karen pointed it out and they stopped for a rest, discussing when and where to sleep.

"We will have to post guard," Joanha said, looking to Manfred as though expecting an argument. Manfred merely nodded and glanced around. Joanha went on. "This clearing is too near the path. We should move further into the trees, yet stay near enough to the path so as not to lose it." The rebel glanced at his comrades, his gaze finally returning to Manfred.

"What do you suggest Stalker?" Joanha asked the large man.

Manfred eyed him a moment then slowly smiled.

"You're right Joanha. We should move further away. I suggest that direction." He pointed south to an outcrop of rocks. "It appears to have some protection."

Joanha followed Manfred's finger to the rocks and signalled his acquiescence.

The four made their way to the chosen site and fashioned a meagre camp, each taking turns on watch.

**

Jans jumped, fear slamming his heart hard against his chest as he gasped for breath. Shadows loomed before him, tall and hideous. He spun, stumbled, and fell to the ground. Nameless faces leered at him. Advancing black clad Guardians and their Death Hounds encircled him, cutting off his escape. Hands grasped for him and voices called out, laughing all round. He squeezed his eyes shut. Something clawed into his shoulder and he swallowed a yelp.

"Come on kid," Joanha's voice intruded in the midst of the

146

nightmare. "Wake up, will you?"

Joanha shook him again. Jans' eyes popped open. What he could see of the night sky revealed only stars and he sucked in air with giddy relief. He could see the sleeping forms of Karen and Manfred across from him. Jans looked up to the figure holding his arm—Joanha. A shaky sigh escaped his lips before he could stop it.

"It's your watch kid," said the rebel with an encouraging grin. "Don't worry Jans. It was only a nightmare. We all have those now and again."

Jans sat up, scrubbing at his eyes as though he could erase the dream with his hands.

"It was so real," he said breathlessly.

Joanha nodded. "They usually are." He sounded troubled. He shook himself, staring into Jans' eyes. "You okay, kid? You think you can handle a watch?"

"Of course," said Jans, his own voice shaky.

Joanha smiled crookedly. "Sure, kid. If you say so." He pulled Jans to his feet. "If you see anything or need anything, I'll be just a few feet away, okay?"

Jans nodded and Joanha moved off to find a place to rest.

Jans circled the camp, trying to order his thoughts. What a nightmare. This whole experience with Karen, the adventure, the excitement, the danger—mostly the danger—really had changed him. And it had only begun a few days ago. So much had happened in so little time. As he thought about it, he knew he would not want to change what had happened or what could happen in the near future. *Except maybe to erase the memory of all the blood and a cracked head.* Here, on the run and in constant peril, he had friends, the only people who really accepted him for who he was and what he could do. His little magic tricks didn't frighten him so much, and he felt he could almost take on the world with these people—almost.

A breeze rustled the leaves of the trees surrounding him. Jans paused, and finally sat, his back to one of the large rocks where he could still see the camp. He pulled his knees to his chest and rested his hands on his forearms, rubbing at them a bit for warmth. A small bush quivered nearby as a tiny rodent rushed out, only to be swooped up seconds later in the great claws of an owl. Jans flinched at the sudden appearance of the bird, slamming his head on the rock behind him. He winced,

147

rubbing against the pain. Watching over a camp was something completely foreign to him. Sure, he had often played hiding games with the children of his village, but there, if you were caught, you weren't killed. He knew he had to keep a sharp lookout. Guardians would likely slip in as silent as that owl, and as deadly.

Crickets hummed in the woods and other insects buzzed all around. In the depths of the trees, the calls of night creatures rang out. He had not heard those sounds last night, when the Fey guarded their sleep. Or if he had, they had not alarmed him so. The darkened sky held a waning moon. Stars floated behind and between wisps of clouds. As he looked up, Jans noted the dark forms of birds flying overhead, but soon realised they were not birds, but bats. Dozens of them swooped below the treetops and soared into the air once more, their wings silvered by moonlight. Jans shivered and hugged his knees tighter to himself. Perhaps adventure did not suit him after all.

He longed for the comfort of his bed back in Nearbrook and wondered briefly what had become of it—indeed, what had become of his house or his father, the whole village even. He thought about what he could have done to save them from whatever horrors the Guardians had devised. Jans finally reasoned that his choice to go with Karen and help her was the only way he would accomplish anything for them. Had he stayed in Nearbrook, he would have been on his own, afraid—if he had been alive at all. At least here he had friends, people he felt he could trust. And he had his magic, even though he knew so little about it.

He stretched, yawned, and shuddered at the screech of an avis. It sounded more like a mournful wail than the cry of a bird. Jans glanced to his sleeping companions, then up at the moon. He rose, walking around the camp again, eyes searching for any disturbance. This was going to be a long watch.

***

After an hour or so, Manfred stirred from his sleep. The moon had set, but the stars provided enough light for Jans. He watched as the warrior sat up and took in his surroundings.

148

The large man stood and soundlessly approached Jans. He sat down beside him. Jans peered up at him in curious wonder.

"You're becoming quite a young warrior." He offered it as a compliment, not a condescending statement, and Jans took it as such. Manfred glanced at him, then to the trees beyond the camp.

"Listen, Jans. I know I haven't exactly been friendly with you. I'm just used to working on my own." He faltered. "Anyway, I just wanted to thank you."

Jans frowned. "For what?"

Manfred flinched. *Whatever he wants to say,* thought Jans, *is obviously not easy for him.* The boy leaned forward.

"For helping Karen, for being there for her, at Jadathe. For ... I don't know ... being able to protect her I guess." Manfred met his eyes a second time, his gaze penetrating.

"Promise me something," Manfred said at length. He waited for Jans to nod, then said, "Promise that, no matter what happens, you will look after her, keep her safe."

"But what about you? Won't you—"

"If something goes wrong," Manfred interrupted. "If I'm not there. Just," He sighed. "Make sure she's okay. Can you promise me that? Or at least that you'll do your best?"

Manfred's eyes shone, reflecting something that looked to Jans like a plea. The boy nodded uncertainly. So much emotion emanated from the man.

"I'll look after her," Jans promised. Manfred relaxed somewhat. He smiled and patted Jans on the shoulder.

The two sat in silence for a time, staring up at the sky as the stars wheeled slowly across the blackness of the night. Finally, Manfred spoke again.

"If you want to get some sleep, I can take over watch."

Jans glanced at him.

"Are you sure, sir? I mean, I don't want to impose or anything."

"It's no problem. My watch would have been next anyway. And don't call me sir, Jans. My name is Manfred." He fell silent, but a moment later added, "I just thought maybe you'd like to get some rest. You have, after all, been through quite a lot in a short time."

Jans nodded. It sounded as though Manfred needed solitude for his thoughts.

"Thanks sir. I mean, Manfred, sir." Jans stood and looked down at him. Manfred smiled, then stared out into the darkness of the forest. Jans followed his gaze, but saw nothing, so he turned and found a somewhat comfortable place to rest. He burrowed his face into the fabric of his cape to ward off the chill of the night, hoping to protect himself from his nightmares as well as from the cold.

Chapter 17

Vilna sat unconcerned at the corner table with two men and a woman, thieves all, when Amrah strode in to the Ivory Chip Tavern. Although Amrah appreciated a good toss of the gaming chips as much as the next cheat—and the Ivory Chip provided the least rigged games in Sandroga—today, she went after a larger prize. The means to that end sat laughing at her leisure in the corner, far too comfortable with herself.

"Amrah," the pretty spy greeted in that false sweet tone Vilna usually reserved for unsuspecting targets as Amrah wove her way through the half-full tavern. "What an unexpected surprise." The hostility heating her brown eyes didn't touch her voice.

Not as unexpected as this, Amrah thought as she brought her fist slamming across the other woman's face without a word. The gratifying smack of her knuckles scoring on Vilna's temple sent a thrill of satisfaction through Amrah's otherwise cold fury.

The three thieves jumped to their feet, bench scraping and ale sloshing from the mugs on the table at the sudden motion. The taller of the men reached for his dagger while Amrah's attention focused on the fallen spy, but he thought better of drawing steel when Toron stepped up beside his sister.

"Ah, meat for a Guardian stew," Toron said into the silence, rubbing his hands together like a child eager for a Birthing day gift. Low murmurs of disdain spread through the small crowd. The thieves looked nervously down at Vilna, then to Amrah's agate stare.

"This is how we deal with Guardian spies," she said. At this confirmation, the thieves turned hard eyes to the stunned woman at their feet. No one liked a Guardian informer. The two men began reciting every colourful curse they had ever heard and the woman spat on the prone body. Amrah fixed the three with a piercing glower.

"Bring her," she said as she spun on her heel and strode from the tavern without a backwards glance.

The thieves looked askance at each other, then at the feebly groaning Vilna. Under Toron's heavy gaze, the taller of the men scooped up the spy and tossed her over his shoulder, none too gently. He followed Amrah out the door, his companions at his heels, Toron bringing up the rear.

A large number of merchants crowded the street in front of the Ivory Chip. Even dressed down to avoid notice, most failed to blend in to the shabby surroundings across town from their places of business. Many clutched hands to belt pouches, though their eyes followed Amrah and her entourage. The tension of malice, fear and smug relief thickened the air like yesterday's porridge.

Amrah marched her mob over a few blocks until they met a second mob in one of the lesser market squares. A willow-thin young woman detached herself from this group, her chestnut hair tied back in a braid. She stood face to face with Amrah, her expression grim until a smile softened the angles of her mouth.

"Laurana," Amrah greeted. "Did you get him?"

Laurana nodded, absently brushing back some stubborn strands of hair that had escaped their confinement. She turned to address someone behind her.

"Bring him," her voice sounded like a child's, but no one would mistake the authority it conveyed. A remarkable trait Amrah respected in the rebel woman.

Two men stepped forward, carrying a third. They dumped their bloodied and dazed load unceremoniously between the two women, then moved back, dusting their hands now that they were free of their unwelcome burden. Amrah gazed at the dishevelled figure of Gorath, her features impassive. She signalled to the thief with Vilna and he dropped the spy beside Gorath.

Murmurs arose from each mob as they examined the two

152

prisoners. Some voices shouted hostility, some sounded indignant, but most were simply puzzled.

"Tie them up," Amrah ordered.

Laurana moved to obey, Toron at her side, securing leather straps tightly around the captives' wrists and ankles. When Amrah was satisfied Vilna and Gorath had nowhere to go, she crouched and brought them fully conscious with some well-timed slaps and buckets of cold water prepared for the occasion. Gorath sputtered, trying to get his bearings and attempting to look as innocuous as possible, failing at both. Vilna glared at Amrah with murderous intent. Amrah studied each with a chill smile that left her eyes frosty. Those close enough to see her expression pulled back while those behind pressed forward for a better view.

"Now, let's talk about Guardians, shall we?" Amrah said, her voice pitched to carry. "How their magic twisted Yagoth into a murderer, but seems to have left you unscathed, yet corrupted nonetheless. And how you two sold us out."

Dark murmurs from the crowd. Gorath whimpered before a venomous glare from Vilna silenced him. *No matter,* Amrah thought, drawing her knife with care, her eyes fastened to Vilna's. Amrah had a talent bordering on magical for extracting information, sometimes through sheer determination. If she concentrated hard enough, people usually broke. *They will tell me what I want to know.*

***

Amrah felt cold inside, empty, a hollowness centred around her chest. All through Yagoth's torture, these two had merely watched, letting the Guardians do as they pleased. Gorath at least had the decency to feel shame. Vilna ... Amrah wondered if Vilna felt anything beyond pleasure at seeing another's pain. Laurana had had to pry Amrah's fingers from Vilna's throat when the spy finally broke and admitted to willingly aiding the Guardians and enjoying what they did to Yagoth.

"If you want to kill her, I have no problems with it," Laurana kept a strong grip on Amrah's shoulders, holding her away from the spy. "But she said herself that a Guardian would return to pay them. Better to use her as live bait than rat food."

"She'll never play along," Amrah spat full in Vilna's face,

but made no move to attack the woman again.

"Who says she has to?" Laurana relaxed her grip. Amrah studied the rebel, one raised eyebrow saying she would listen. "All the Guardian has to see is that she's waiting for him. If she happens to be discreetly bound, how will he know?"

"How do you hide a gag around her mouth?" Toron moved up beside the two women. "I assume you have an idea to keep her quiet?" he went on at Amrah's wicked grin.

"She doesn't need a tongue to act as bait."

Toron nodded as though he expected such a statement from his sister. Laurana seemed briefly surprised before a pitiless smile crossed her lips. Vilna looked close to tears, a defeated yet panicked sheen watering her eyes. Gorath, however, looked almost happy. Amrah walked over to him, crouching to meet his gaze.

"You'd better wipe that smile from you face, traitor," she growled. "What makes you think you'll escape her fate?"

His eyes widened in terror and he began to whimper. Amrah had had enough. She drew her knife again, and set to work preparing the two spies for bait.

***

The Guardian strolled into town like he owned it; which, in a way, he felt he did. By now, those three idiots would have done what was required, putting Sandroga into Ebbring hands, though all they had seen were Guardians. They thought they were so smart, these so called spies. *What were their names again? Goranth? Gory? Ah yes,* he thought with a sneer; *Gorath.* And Vilna. He hadn't forgotten her name. She had been so simple to turn. Her hatred and arrogance so easily fed into corruption, and betrayal was second-nature to her. And Gorath's spinelessness and need of purpose left him open to tampering.

That other one, though. *Yagoth, wasn't it?* He had proved to be one of those creatures who required more than a little push to put him on the desired path. Who would have thought a spy and a thief had morals? But they were sometimes the most challenging, the Guardian thought. To push someone over the edge, take away his will, yet leave his ethics, twisting him to be a Guardian tool ... The Guardian's lips twitched into a

154

wolfish grin. To force someone to do things against his nature was the sweetest torture. A shame so many forced went mad. But even a madman had his uses.

He wondered if Yagoth was dead yet. Very likely, considering the false information he had passed along. Garcouk himself, leader of the Guardians, had lain in wait in Yagoth's mind while the spy learned of the rebels' whereabouts. Then Garcouk abandoned him, leaving the spy room to take his pleasure with that woman. The others Yagoth had killed were nothing, but killing a town's leader, even one as brutal as that whore, would leave too many questions for a clean get-away. Yes, Yagoth must have died for that. With his task complete, he was no loss to the Guardians.

But the information proved faulty. No rebels nested near Shilton Falls, no cave big enough for more than four people existed there. The Guardian scowled as he remembered leading the preliminary force to assess the strength of the base, only to find no evidence of the enemy. He had wanted to storm Sandroga and lay waste to the town for their impertinence. But Garcouk's instructions were explicit. *Stick to the plan.*

So now the Guardian had come to ensure Gorath and Vilna had followed through on their promises and there were no more betrayals. The rest of his force he had sent back through Asturban Forest to rejoin the army and await further instructions. He wouldn't need their help for a couple of turncoats.

No one paid him the least bit of attention as he made his way to that same stinking inn where he and his comrades had first encountered those simple spies. Of course, without his uniform, no one had any reason to think him anything other than a mere traveller. Assuming any traveller would actually want to stop in Sandroga.

It was dim inside, like he remembered. Flames in the blackened fireplace provided more smoky haze than light, and the lamps with their rancid, cheap oil made his eyes water for a moment. There were more people than before, but it was later in the day, closer to supper time. *Easier to lose yourself in the mob,* the Guardian thought, his gaze taking in his surroundings.

He saw them cowering in the deepest shadows of the far corner. Only two. So, Yagoth *was* dead. The Guardian hid his contempt behind a false smile as he wound his way through the

155

crowd. He paused briefly as a warning hummed in the back of his mind. Something didn't seem right. But what?

He studied those around him as he continued toward the pair. A few merchants—not unusual for businessmen who wished to avoid the notice of their neighbours to use this less-than-savoury inn—a handful of craftsmen and the normal percentage of cutthroats. Nothing out of the ordinary. Certainly nothing a Guardian need fear. So why the warning?

He pushed the thought from his mind. The sooner he got this business out of the way, the sooner he could rejoin his comrades.

"So, what's the word?" he asked, swinging a wobbly chair around from a nearby table and straddling it. Neither spy spoke. He frowned. Fear danced in their eyes, apparent even in the poor light. It was only right that they should fear him, but he had thought Vilna at least knew how to keep her fear under control. So why did it show now? Unless they, too, had failed.

"Speak," he demanded. Gorath made a noise in his throat and Vilna shook her head, her mouth working without sound. The bitter-sweet odour of blood scented her breath. His eyes narrowed and his scowl deepened as he noted their rigidity. Their arms trembled as they tried in vain to move. His eyes widened as he finally comprehended his situation. Someone had bound the spies, and their refusal to speak combined with the smell of blood could only mean one thing; after all, one could not speak without a tongue.

He jumped to his feet and spun, sword already in his hand and magic singing at his fingertips. But not fast enough to stop the feathered shaft that lodged in his throat. He just had time to acknowledge the presence of two females—the one's bowstring still quivering, while the other's grass green eyes filled his vision with their pain and fury—before the filthy ground rushed up to meet him and darken his world forever.

***

Amrah stared down at the Guardian. The death of one could never replace the loss of Yagoth and others like him, twisted without remorse. Her glare rose to Vilna and Gorath. Even at the end they had struggled to warn the Guardian. Such betrayal could not go unpunished. A glance to the cutthroat at her side sealed their fate.

Amrah turned to Laurana.

"We may not always agree on everything," she began. The rebel met her cold gaze evenly. Amrah smiled without humour. "But if you ever need us against this scum, Sandroga will stand with you."

Chapter 18

For the next two days, Karen and her companions made their way through the depths of Crownawn forest, encountering little opposition. Now and again, a group of Guardians passed by, but the companions easily hid themselves in the undergrowth. On the night of the third day in Crownawn, they shared a dismal meal of what little remained of Whooshea's provisions and discussed their options while setting up camp.

"We've been wandering through these accursed trees for three days now, and we haven't seen an end to them yet," Joanha said.

"What choice do we have?" Karen countered. "We cannot go back to Jadathe. The only thing left is to continue east, to where Whooshea said the darkness lies. It is there that the battle awaits us. Besides, the forest cannot go on forever."

Joanha scowled at the ground, knowing she was right. He just hated the idea of not knowing their destination or what awaited them once they got there.

For the first time that day, Jans spoke.

"I don't understand."

The other three glanced at the boy, waiting for something more. When Jans didn't speak again, Manfred asked, "What? What don't you understand?"

Jans started, as though he hadn't realised he had spoken aloud, then replied, "Why haven't the Guardians found us?"

"Would you prefer they had?" Joanha's sarcasm was hard to miss.

"No," Jans paused, gazing at Karen. "If they can sense

magic, then why are we still free?"

For a moment, no one uttered a sound. Without taking his eyes off Karen, Jans continued:

"You said that the Guardian could sense your magic in Ildare. They followed our two paths near Silben because they could somehow feel the magic. So why can't they find us when we stay so close to the path? They should sense us, both of us. I may not have much power, but I do have some," He caught his breath, as though he meant to go on, but merely sighed, "I just don't understand." He lowered his eyes.

Karen regarded the boy thoughtfully and nodded.

"I have wondered the same thing," she said. "How we have eluded them this far is a mystery. Perhaps they are too wrapped up in the search that they simply haven't thought of using their magic to find us. Or perhaps the magic of the forest hides our own. I do not know. There is nothing we can do about them for the moment. What we must concentrate on is finding the heart of this evil, even if it takes us out of Crownawn."

"What about Death Hounds?" Jans asked, determined not to let the subject drop. "Joanha said they were well trained, that they knew when to kill and when to capture."

"They may be leading us into a trap," Joanha mused quietly.

Manfred raised an eyebrow and cocked his head, considering the possibility.

"Still," Joanha went on, "they really don't know which direction we headed from Jadathe, and there have been many forks in the path. To trap us, they would have to know where we're going. Since we don't know ourselves..." The rebel's voice faded and he shrugged, letting each of the others finish the sentence in their thoughts.

Silence surrounded them as the twilight sky darkened into night. Finally, Joanha broke the stillness.

"Well, they haven't found us for whatever reason and we can but hope it remains that way. We should get some sleep. Who knows how much farther we have to travel."

"I'll take first watch," Jans stated and moved off before anyone could argue. Joanha stared after him a moment, then shrugged again. He found a fairly level patch of earth and readied himself for sleep. Manfred and Karen soon followed.

159

Jans watched over the makeshift camp, aided by a half moon draped with gossamer clouds. Uneasy thoughts plagued him. Something didn't feel right, but he couldn't put his finger on what. The creatures of the forest still sang their eerie songs and the whole woods seemed alive. Only when enemy soldiers passed through did the noise stop. The fact that the Guardians hadn't found them disturbed him, but that wasn't all. Something in the air frightened him. Jans looked to the east, to where they headed. Whatever went on there felt terribly wrong, and he and his friends were walking straight into the heart of it. Jans trembled.

**

Nearly two hours later, Jans looked up to see a graceful shadow walk toward him. Karen sat quietly. At first, she said nothing, merely watching the trees. Then she turned to study Jans.

"What do you see?" she asked.

Jans shook his head. "Nothing," His voice quivered slightly.

"Jans?" Karen said softly. "What is it?"

He took a breath, then looked into Karen's eyes, dark in the moonlight, and whispered, "There's something not right. I don't know what it is or how to describe it, but the further east we go, the more sure I am that we're approaching something sinister. Whooshea may have called it evil, but it's more than that. Or less. I don't know. I don't understand what I feel."

Karen held his gaze. A cloud flickered over his eyes briefly and Jans shivered, an act barely noticeable. Karen, too, seemed to sense something then and asked again, "What do you see?"

Jans' lips trembled and his eyes moistened. He fought to regain control over himself before he answered.

"Death." The word caught in his throat. He coughed quietly and Karen could see pain in his eyes. "I see death, Karen, and it scares me. It scares me more than anything ever has." He bit his lip, holding back the tears.

Karen lowered her head, her hair falling in front of her eyes. When she spoke next, Jans had to strain to hear, her voice had gone so quiet.

160

"I know, Jans. I have seen it too." She looked up. "But I have not seen who," She shook her head, her gaze drawn toward the sleeping forms of the men, toward Manfred, and she trembled. "I don't know who or how to stop it or ..." She hesitated, taking a breath to steady herself. "It scares me, too."

"Something else frightens me," Karen said after a moment. Jans looked to her, waiting. "I came to find you because of a vision," she went on. "A glance at the future we would suffer if the Ebbrings win. Only, it is not just the Ebbrings." She paused.

"The Guardians too," Jans mumbled. "They fight beside the Ebbrings."

"But there's something else. Some other creatures we have not seen yet."

Jans stared at her, eyes wide.

"Who?" he asked. "What?"

"That's just it," she whispered. "I do not know. When I saw them in my vision, I thought they were Ebbrings, but they were not what I saw in Jadathe. The Ebbring there seemed more a creature fashioned out of clay, something far removed from human. The things in my vision were something different. I thought I knew who and what I fought, but now ..." She shook her head and met his stare. "I do not know what I face, and that scares me."

They lapsed into silence. The moon escaped the thin clouds to cast a strange glow on the camp. Jans peered around. He turned back to Karen and saw her start, eyes wide. He examined the camp again, wondering what had startled her, then heard it too. A shrill cry, distant but audible to Elfin ears. It came from the north-west, followed by the sound of raised voices drawing closer. The two sprang up. Karen woke Manfred while Jans went to Joanha. Soon, all four had gained their feet, listening to the wild calls.

"We have to move," Karen said. Although she spoke in a whisper, anxiety tainted her voice.

"What is it?" Manfred asked.

Karen looked at Jans, but the boy just shook his head.

"I don't know, but it might be after us."

"Are you sure?" Manfred responded.

"You want to wait and find out?" Joanha asked. Manfred turned to Joanha, about to retort, but did not see sarcasm on the rebel's face. He saw fear. The shrill outburst sounded again, trailing into a frightening wail.

The four gathered their things and headed east at a run. Fear pushed aside fatigue and they moved with great speed. As they fled, the voices diminished and faded. Even the blood-chilling wail came to them from a greater distance, yet it still followed.

The companions ran on, their breath coming in ragged gasps, their lungs afire. After several long minutes at this gruelling pace, they slowed, but did not stop, refusing to give in to their weariness and agony.

Up ahead, the trees ended in a tiny clearing. They halted, panting heavily. The clearing actually marked the edge of the tree line. Five feet of bare ground ended in a sheer cliff overlooking a wide valley. They were trapped.

Almost instantly, all thoughts of fleeing the creatures behind them faded from the mind of each companion as they regarded the vista before them in horror. From the cover of the trees, they could see the valley floor. Trees jutted out from the ragged cliff face at varying angles, and scattered boulders ringed the valley's edges. Hundreds upon thousands of campfires littered the valley, lighting up the area as though it were day. A haze of smoke clung to the area. An army of evil gathered in this vale, perhaps larger than the Druid's forces of ten years ago in the war that had claimed so many lives. An army from the east.

Dark tents stood in innumerable rows, parting only to allow access to the fires, all surrounding one large, central tent. Thousands of soldiers lay rolled up in blankets outside the tents, or sat talking quietly among themselves, their fires casting eerie shadows on their forms, making them look hideous. Hundreds of other soldiers guarded the perimeter of the encampment. The stink of the fires mingled with burned food, the sharp scent of oil used for cleaning and honing weapons, and the cloying stench of sweat-soaked armour. And over that, the reek of evil; an almost sulphurous odour that burned the nose and stung the eyes. Even Manfred and Joanha, untutored in magic, could feel the hatred all around them. *Evil guards itself,* Whooshea had said. But more than that, it guarded an entire army, hidden in the deepest depths of this haunted realm.

Standing in horrified silence, the four friends stared at each other. Jans' face held a mask of pure terror, having never seen anything so frightening. He wished he stood anywhere but here. Even a fate back in Nearbrook seemed preferable to this.

Karen, having never seen an army, of good or evil, felt her doubts rise sharply. How could she stop this abomination? Hope fought against despair within her as she struggled to maintain her self-control. Her soul cried out silently: 'Father, I cannot do this; I don't know how to go on. I am scared, Father.' She wondered how the Druid had kept his faith in such a world of evil, and she wondered if she would ever find equal faith.

Joanha glared into the army of the enemy with disgust and hatred, an intense loathing burning in his dark eyes. So this was what the rebels faced; legions of Guardians and other corrupt beings obeying every foul order the Ebbrings thrust upon them. His hand brushed the hilt of his sword as though he would strike down every last creature in that cursed valley on his own.

Manfred's steel grey eyes narrowed in anger. While the rest of the world sat huddled in bars and taverns like Ildare, muttering in hushed whispers about ridding the land of Guardians and Ebbrings, the enemy gathered in vast numbers, patiently readying themselves for the complete and total destruction of every last bit of resistance. The few who spoke openly of rebellion would be killed outright for all to see, a warning to others. Once fear stilled enough hands, the armies of evil would face little opposition in the conquest and plunder of the land. The large warrior now realised just how important this quest was. If Karen failed, none would remain to quell this darkness.

He glanced at the Elfish-Druid and saw sadness and despair fill her eyes. Manfred could almost feel her doubts, her questions. He moved over to stand beside the girl. She seemed so lost and frightened. Her head bowed as she stifled a sob. At that moment, Manfred felt the pain of love pierce his heart more surely than any arrow, and he longed to hold her in his arms, to comfort her. But he dared not touch her. She could never love him. They were as different as sun and moon; she, the child of such power and he, the warrior-tracker. No, he thought, he could only help her and keep his emotions buried deep within himself. Those feelings could only lead to despair.

163

Right now, they had more important things to worry about than his tortured heart.

Behind the small group and still slightly to the north, the eerie wail echoed anew through the trees. This time, an answering cry rose up from the large encampment. Karen crouched low in the undergrowth and crept to the edge of the drop-off, her comrades following suit. A dark figure emerged from the large tent near the centre of the military compound, so tiny in the distance as to seem an insignificant insect. Two other forms accompanied it, firelight glinting off silver capes coloured by the moon—Guardians. The dark figure moved closer to the outskirts of the stronghold. All parted quickly before this being, giving it a wide berth as though it carried a disease. It let out another shrill shriek.

Manfred looked to Karen and she nodded, mouthing one word. Ebbring. Another dark shape detached from the shadows of the trees lining a path down to the valley, attended by seven Guardians. This second Ebbring, the source of the eerie signal, walked the long distance to the first and said something. Then the two hurried back to the large tent and disappeared.

***

"We don't know what they plan," Manfred said. "Until we know their next move, we can do nothing." The four crouched in the woods near the clearing above the valley.

"Exactly," Joanha replied. "That's why we have to go down there."

"We can't just walk up to one of them and ask what's going on. We need a better course of action."

"Can't we take one of their guards?" Jans asked hesitantly. "There's so many down there," he shuddered. "Surely they won't miss just one."

"We can't take that chance," Karen said. "But I agree with Joanha. We have to get closer."

Manfred made an exasperated sound deep in his throat.

"Fine," he said. "Than I say Joanha and I go down. You two stay here." Before Karen could object, he continued. "If something happens to us, you will at least be free."

"But ..." Jans paused when the Stalker's steely eyes met

his. He swallowed. "How will we know if something happens?"

"You can go with them," Karen suggested. "Not physically," she amended when both Manfred and Joanha started to protest. Jans merely stared at her with terror in his eyes. She smiled reassuringly at the boy. "I mean with your mind, Jans." His fear turned into puzzlement.

"My mind?"

"Yes. You can use mind-speech to ride either Manfred's or Joanha's thoughts." She turned to the other two. "Jans will, in a way, become just another thought. He can project his consciousness into one of your minds, see through your eyes. He will be in two places at once, here with me, telling me what he sees, and with you, seeing what you see and hearing what you hear."

She herself could not risk her magic being sensed. Jans' magic lacked the strength of hers, so she hoped that the Guardians would not easily detect him. Mind-speech held more mental will than it did magic, hopefully enough of a difference to keep him safe.

"I can do that?" Jans asked, his face growing more animated as excitement stretched into a smile across his mouth. Karen nodded.

"Then I volunteer," Joanha said, bringing their attention to him. "Jans can ride with me."

It seemed to Karen that the rebel had grown protective of the boy, an interesting deviance from the distrust he held for everything else. Perhaps Joanha saw something in Jans that reminded the rebel of himself, an innocence cruelly shattered by the harsh reality of this world.

"Good," Manfred said. Now that they had decided, he seemed resigned to their plan. "Then let's get going."

As the warriors left, using the trees as cover, Karen reflected on how Joanha and Manfred had changed in their feelings toward each other. At one time hostile, each had learned respect for the other and now tolerated each other's presence. Joanha still held doubts and little trust for anything, yet he had opted to remain with the group and to help Karen in her quest. Manfred had by now given up any pretence of wishing to work alone in this adventure. He knew the worth of Joanha's skill and regarded the rebel as a valuable ally against the enemy. Once they overcame their personal differences,

Karen believed that Joanha and Manfred would make a formidable pair.

Now, using mind-speech, Jans watched through Joanha's eyes as the rebel descended into the valley with the Stalker. Near the edge of the encampment, two guards stood sentry. They wore dark armour, but not the uniforms of Guardians. Normal foot soldiers, then. One stood transfixed by the distant bulk of the Ebbrings' tent, while the other, taller than his companion, gazed with half-lidded eyes around the camp. He yawned. Neither noticed Manfred or Joanha.

"I wonder what they're up to," the shorter guard mumbled in a country accent, still staring at the large tent.

"Whatever it is they're always up to, I 'spect," replied his friend dully.

"But they been in there a long time, Cuffer."

The taller guard sighed irritably.

"They're always in there a long time, Frax."

"I don' know, Cuffer; it's been an especially long time," Frax said, trying to sound mysterious.

"Will you shut up," Cuffer said harshly. "They're prob'ly tryin' to figure a way to get all them rebels in one place."

"Why would they do that?" Frax asked.

Cuffer's eyes narrowed.

"Ha' you been asleep all this time, idiot? I figured you'd at least ha' heard our orders!"

Frax's face took on a sullen look and he muttered something only Cuffer heard.

"I'm gonna tell you once, and that's it, so ya'd better listen." Cuffer took a deep breath, then proceeded as though speaking to a child. "The army is marching west in five days. You an' me and the rest of our section stand guard here for them days."

"I know that part," Frax interrupted. "It's the bit about the rebels I don' remember."

Cuffer scowled, then continued.

"Them rebels is becoming a pest to the Masters. We're to wipe them out now before they gets any stronger. The trick is to get them all together so we don' have to do the job twice. Once the rebels are gone, no one'll be left to try an' stop us. Got it? I know that's a lot for your small brain to comprehend, but I think I made it clear enough."

166

"That ain't fair Cuffer," Frax whined, chewing at his lip. "Besides, what about the girl and her friends?"

For a moment, Cuffer didn't speak. He just stood staring at Frax.

"How do you know about her?"

Frax blinked in confusion. "I thought everyone knew."

"Well they don'." Cuffer retorted. "If I was you, I wouldn't say anything too loud about her."

"Why?"

"'Cause she's gonna be a problem, that's why!" Cuffer lowered his voice to a whisper and leaned forward. "The Masters don' know who she is or what she kin do, but they're real scared of her. She's got some kind of magic they don' like. What's worse, they can't seem to find her."

"Why don' the Guardians find her? They got their own magic."

Cuffer shook his head. "Few Guardians can be spared right now, or so I hear. They sent out foot patrols, but there's been no sign of the girl since she escaped Jadathe. Besides..." Cuffer paused and jerked back. "Wait a minute, why am I tellin' you all this?"

Frax looked around, perplexed. "Why shouldn't you?"

"It's an NTN subject, that's why."

"What's NTN?" Frax asked, scratching his head.

"Need to know. And you don't need to know. You don't even ..."

Manfred and Joanha glanced at each other from the cover of the trees. Manfred shook his head. At least now they knew something of the army's plans. The two withdrew into the shelter of the brush, leaving Cuffer to lecture Frax on army procedures. Manfred spoke quietly.

"We have five days. Somehow, we've got to do something to stop them, but I don't know what."

"If only the whole army were as thick as that Frax fellow," Joanha grinned. "It would be so much simpler." His smile faded and he bit down on his lower lip. "We have to get closer to the tent of the Ebbrings. Whatever plans are being made, they're being made in there."

Manfred nodded slowly, a thoughtful look creeping over his features. He glanced at Joanha.

"They have to get the rebels together," he said. "How will

they do that?" Joanha's brow furrowed as he gazed into the military setup of the valley. Manfred went on. "How would you do it, Joanha? If you had to get all the rebels together, how would you do it?"

Joanha's eyes widened.

"A spy," he said softly. "They've planted a spy in our midst." He paused. "But it would have to be someone with power, someone who could call Council."

"Council?" Manfred asked.

"To discuss unified action. Almost every member of the rebellion would attend Council once it had been called. Certainly all the leaders. Of course, how stupid." Joanha berated himself, shaking his fist impotently in the air. "We'd be so busy planning some sort of resistance that the thought of being captured together might not even cross our minds. A nice little trap. All the rebels conferring while the entire enemy army waits on our doorstep," he said bitterly.

"Who can call this Council?" Manfred inquired. "You said something about power."

"Yes. Only the leaders can call Council. But our leaders are all trustworthy. None would betray us."

"What if he were forced to, if there were some kind of ransom?"

Joanha shook his head. "No. We know when we join that the rebellion comes first. Whatever happens, keeping the rebellion alive is the only thing that matters. Not even a hostage can come before the survival of our cause, unless that hostage can help further our plans. Brutal, but necessary."

The two men stayed in the cover of the trees a while longer, studying the army installation, taking count of numbers and supplies.

Meanwhile, Jans relayed the information to Karen in the clearing above them. Karen considered their situation. Four against an entire army was obviously suicidal, but there had to be something they could do to slow the enemy down long enough to warn the rebels. She agreed with Joanha; they must find out what went on inside the Ebbrings' tent. It was too dangerous for any of them to enter the compound. Even disguised, the odds would not favour them.

Jans regarded Karen as she thought the matter through. He could see the doubts on her face and watched as despair crept into her eyes by the light of the half-moon. *If only there were something I could do.* Jans thought back to what Karen had said, that he was meant to do something important. He just wished he knew what that was.

Then, an idea came to him.

"Karen, what about the mind speech?"

The girl gazed at him without comprehension.

"If I can see through Joanha's eyes," Jans continued, "why not look through someone else's? One of the guards?"

Karen began to shake her head, but Jans pressed on.

"The foot soldiers don't seem to have magic, so they won't know I'm there. When one approaches that tent, I could get into his mind and see what's going on."

Karen stood irresolute. Jans could practically hear her questions, her thoughts on sending him into such danger.

"It's a risk, I know," Jans' voice held a maturity beyond his years. "But I think it's one we have to take."

Karen opened her mouth, about to object, then hesitated. Looking into Jans' eyes, she saw the hidden power, not so hidden anymore. She saw his strength, his willingness to confront this danger. The memory of her vision suddenly burned in her mind and she realised that this was what Jans had to do. The means to destroy this oppression before her waited inside that tent and Jans was the only one who could learn the secret.

She bowed her head. *I cannot do this to him, but what choice do we have? It is why I searched him out. So why is this so difficult?* Finally, she nodded. "Yes Jans. You must do this thing, though it grieves me to say so." Karen looked up into the boy's Elfish eyes. "But you have to get closer, down to where Manfred and Joanha wait. It will be easier if you see your target. Tell them you are coming, what you will do. They can guard over you in case someone should discover your presence."

"What about you?" asked Jans. "How will you know what's going on?"

She smiled sadly. "Do not worry about me. I'll know." She gave him a playful shove. "Go, now. And good luck." She watched him climb over the brim.

"Be careful," Karen whispered. Jans flashed her a smile of encouragement, telling her he'd be fine. As the boy disappeared, Karen's eyes filled with tears. If only she could be so confident of his success.

***

'*Joanha,*' the rebel heard in his mind. He started at the sound. Manfred turned to look at him.

"It's Jans," Joanha replied to Manfred's unspoken question. Joanha had almost forgotten the boy's presence. Karen had been right; Jans was just like another thought in his mind.

'*I'm coming down, Joanha,*' Jans continued. '*We have an idea, a way of finding out what's going on in that tent.*'

Joanha tried to ask what this idea was, but Jans went on before his friend could form the thought.

'*I can enter the mind of one of the guards and get in that way. Karen says you and Manfred should watch over me and make sure nothing happens.*'

Joanha's eyes narrowed in doubt as he told this to Manfred.

"But Karen said that would be too dangerous," the warrior said.

"You tell him that. He's on his way down," Joanha replied.

"He's leaving Karen by herself?"

"Apparently so."

Manfred's eyes darkened.

Jans crept silently down the hill behind the two, following Joanha's directions. When he reached them, Manfred turned and demanded in a harsh whisper, "Where's Karen?"

"She said not to worry about her, that this was something I had to do." Jans' voice was calm and level. He explained his plan, ignoring Manfred's anxious expression. Then the three sat and waited for a promising opportunity.

After a time, a young guard exited the tent carrying a pitcher. He walked to a nearby barrel and filled the jug, then turned to go back to the Ebbring tent. Manfred and Joanha looked to Jans, but the boy had already lost himself in concentration.

Chapter 19

Jans opened his eyes. He did not see Manfred or Joanha. Instead, he watched the Ebbring tent loom larger and larger as he approached. It worked! He could see what the guard saw. A sudden rush of thoughts assaulted him and he quickly stilled his own mind, erecting a barrier to keep his thoughts separate—and unnoticed.

The host's name was Alhor, page to the Ebbring Da'Harnak. Alhor performed his duty efficiently, knowing the Ebbring could replace him at any time should Alhor lack diligence. He had seen it happen and it left an unpleasant memory.

Jans was surprised at how much information came to him from Alhor. Jans had not felt such emotion or heard such thoughts from Joanha. But Joanha had known the boy was there; Alhor did not, and so Jans experienced everything the guard did.

Alhor opened the tent flap and entered the makeshift headquarters. A huge drape divided the tent into two sections. The area he could see, about the size of a typical room in a modest house, boasted a makeshift table littered with maps and papers. Two lanterns lit the walls and a third illuminated the central section, yet shadows still crawled across the dark canvas. Despite the lack of smoke from the lights, a heavy pall still permeated the confines. Alhor found this comforting, mostly because, to him, the dark mantle reminded him of Guardians.

Several Guardians surrounded the table, including their

leader, Garcouk. He was formidable, strongest in magic, brawn, and cunning. It was he who had followed that mysterious girl from Ildare to Nearbrook; he who had led the attack on the rebel base and captured many of those dissidents, including their second-in-command.

Alhor looked now to the unconscious rebel tied in the questioning chair beneath the far lantern. Abrasions covered his body and his clothes hung in tatters. Dried blood made the creases of age lining his face seem all the deeper. Grizzled grey hair with only a little of its original sand colour left stood up in all directions, also streaked with crusting runnels of blood. Alhor knew the only reason he still lived had to do with the plans to crush the rebellion. Whether the other rebels that were seized still lived, Alhor didn't know. Jadathe was a powerful fortress. The young guard caught himself. But it could not be that strong if the girl and her accomplices had escaped.

The Ebbring Ing'Lahar stood amidst the Guardians. He had arrived only an hour before, straight from Jadathe, Alhor thought. He had brought no servant, merely more Guardians. As a result, Alhor filled in, running errands for Ing'Lahar as well as Da'Harnak. Alhor glanced at the draped off section. Da'Harnak would be back there, conferring with the Master. The guard involuntarily shivered at the thought of that Ebbring. None could go back there. Only Ebbrings ever saw the Master, but everyone heard him. Alhor could only assume it was male. The voice chilled the blood and filled the soul with fear. Although Alhor had heard the Master speak many times, the effect never quite wore off. He honestly could not remember exactly what the voice sounded like, only the command of its words and the fear they conveyed.

Alhor walked to the table and began filling glasses with the water from the pitcher he carried. The Guardians paid him no heed. Alhor had learned long ago to remain inconspicuous.

"It must be done tonight," a Guardian reiterated. The dark blue accents of his uniform denoted him as one of the Changeling Guardians. They were the smallest unit of the army, as few creatures had the ability to take on the shape of another.

"Rainier is right," Garcouk voiced. "We march in five days and if the rebels are not gathered by then, we will lose our chance. If they catch wind of what we're planning, this Council

172

idea will be useless."

"But five days may not be enough time," a third Guardian protested. "They have a lot of groups, small though many may be. It will take time for them to gather."

"Perhaps it is too much time," another Guardian said, this one in the red cape of a Beast Keeper. "They may be more organised than we give them credit for. Remember their base, Garcouk. I was there too. They did not have much notice of our approach, yet they managed to put up two blockades, make false tracks, cover any signs of recent occupation, and organise for both evacuation and defence. They'll have some sort of procedure for Council, some way of getting together in a short span of time."

"I will need time to find their most recent base," Rainier said. "Taking on the form of this rebel is easy enough," he said, indicating the man bound in the chair, "but he is strong-willed. We do not want another set-back, like those in Sandroga gave us. The directions the rebel gave are vague and there are many gaps in his memory. But five days is time enough, if I leave tonight. It will take time to move the army, more time than to gather the rebels, no matter how far strung out they are."

The Guardians continued their deliberations, each trying to convince the others his way was right. Alhor filled the last glass, then retreated to the corner of the tent where he could watch the proceedings. He felt his attention wander. These arguments were old news to him. Instead, Alhor glanced at the rebel tied to the questioning chair. *What a pathetic looking soul,* he thought. Surely it would have been easier on the man if he simply told the Guardians what they wanted to know.

As Alhor watched, the prisoner moaned and stirred, beginning to regain consciousness. Alhor moved to him and grabbed a handful of bloodied greying hair. He pulled hard, forcing the man's head back. The rebel suppressed a cry of pain and glared at the young guard with intense hatred. Alhor pushed the head forward, releasing his grip. He walked over to Garcouk and whispered to the Guardian:

"The rebel is awake. What shall I do with him?"

Garcouk, recognising the evil pleasure Alhor took in seeing the rebel's pain, smiled.

"Leave him be for the moment. Once we have reached our decision, I'll let you know."

Alhor nodded and returned to his corner of the tent, cuffing the rebel on the back of the head as he walked past.

Jans could feel the baseness in Alhor's mind and longed to escape, but dared not. He had to know the Guardians' plans. His friends counted on him. So he stayed and concentrated on the proceedings.

Alhor shook his head, still glaring at the rebel. Movement caught his attention near the back of the tent. Da'Harnak stepped out from behind the curtain and approached the table. His orange-red gaze searched for Alhor with a puzzled expression, then signalled for the guard to advance.

"It is decided," Da'Harnak hissed. "Rainier will become this rebel and call Council within three hours. You must ensure all rebels are gathered in five days. None are to leave the Council. Stall if you have to, but we believe you will have few difficulties." Rainier nodded. Any who had doubts kept them to himself, knowing that to argue against the orders of the Master meant death. Da'Harnak spoke again, watching Alhor out of the corner of his eye.

"We do have a problem. The Master senses opposition, someone from within this tent." All eyes looked around suspiciously, searching for the traitor. The Ebbring proceeded in an even tone. "All will be scanned, starting with you, Alhor."

The guard's eyes grew wide.

Inside Alhor's mind, Jans' own fear mingled with the guard's. He had to escape before they discovered him, get back to his own body where Manfred and Joanha waited for him. Jans fought for release from Alhor, but something prevented him from fleeing. He was trapped.

Alhor swallowed hard and gathered his courage. He forced himself to appear confident. After all, he was no traitor. For the first time, he would see this Master; he'd be the first non-Ebbring to do so. The thought both frightened and excited him. He strode forward, following Da'Harnak. When they reached the drape, the Ebbring pulled the fabric back. Alhor took a deep breath to steady himself, then entered.

***

Manfred sat concealed in the shadows of the trees, his eyes glued to the large tent in the centre of the army camp.

174

Joanha crouched beside him, guarding the body of Jans. Several long minutes had passed since the boy had entered the mind of the soldier, but Joanha could not say for certain how much time had elapsed.

Suddenly, the boy jumped and trembled.

"Jans?" Joanha said softly, but received no answer. Joanha shook his head. "I don't like this, Stalker," he said. "I don't know what Jans has gotten himself into, but I have a bad feeling. Something's going to happen."

Manfred grunted and looked back to the compound without saying anything. He knew Joanha was right. Something was going to happen, very soon.

**

Alhor could only stare at the figure before him. It was not an Ebbring, as he had previously thought, but he couldn't say what it was. Except that it was beautiful in a most horrifying way. For the most part, it seemed human, but its skin was too pale, its hair too dark, its eyes too bright. An intense and powerful menace swam in those eyes, a depthless sea of evil. A magical aura surrounded the being, so strong that even Alhor's untrained senses could perceive it. Alhor could see it as male now, but that distinction made no difference to the young guard. Male or female, demon or human, the creature in front of him could not have produced more terror in Alhor had it been dredged up from the nine Hells. Maybe it was a demon. Alhor fell to his knees, trembling. Then a panic not his own overcame Alhor. A slow smile spread across the Master's face, the most wicked grin imaginable.

Jans cringed within Alhor's mind. Any minute now, Alhor would become aware of the boy's presence, but Jans no longer cared. His only thought now was escape, no matter what it took.

Suddenly, Jans felt his mind relax. For a moment, he thought he had freed himself, but then realised in horror that the Master was pulling his senses from Alhor's mind. He fought for control and freedom, but it was a losing battle. The Master had too much power.

Jans knew he was lost. Once this being caught him fully, he was done for. So he did the only thing he could think of. He

175

turned all his attention to the Master and concentrated, forcing his presence into its mind. The move surprised the creature, but not for long. However, Jans had just enough time to discover the truth, a truth that shocked the boy to his very soul.

"She is nearby," the Master stated. Jans shook violently. The voice was not natural and Jans, like Alhor, could not begin to describe it except to say it seethed with malice and extreme loathing. Jans felt his mind go numb and his perception turned ice cold.

Da'Harnak's eyes burned.

"Is that her? Do you have her?" the Ebbring asked greedily.

"No. This is but a child, though a child with some power. Yet she is here, with him. Find the body which encompasses this soul and we will have her."

'NO!' Jans screamed silently. He fought with renewed vigour, again surprising his captor. Then, Jans lost consciousness altogether.

***

Joanha grabbed Manfred's arm in an iron grip, his eyes focused on Jans' stiffening body. The warrior turned, startled at the sudden motion. Joanha just pointed. Manfred looked to the boy and gasped. A mask of fear and dread distorted Jans' visage. The half-elf's eyes flew open and his mouth formed one word—NO. Manfred again glanced at Joanha, but the rebel didn't notice. Instead, Joanha reached out for the boy. Jans' body shook fiercely, sweat beading on his face and soaking his hair.

Then his eyes rolled back in his head and closed.

A cry rose from the large tent, hideous and terrifying. Both Manfred and Joanha glanced sharply to the enemy encampment. Jans' eyes fluttered open and his spoke one word before losing consciousness.

"Escape."

Joanha didn't hesitate. He picked up the comatose boy, slung him over his shoulder, and ran up the hill to where Karen waited. Manfred followed close on his heels.

***

The two men broke through the last bit of brush, emerging at the top of the drop-off point of the valley. At the sight of the fleeing warriors and Jans' limp body, Karen rushed over to them. Gasping for breath, Joanha laid Jans down and crouched beside him. Karen paled.

Suddenly, Jans opened his eyes and whispered,

"Trap! Rebels ... calling Council ..." He spoke in broken sentences, shaking so violently that his teeth chattered. "Changeling Guardian ... must stop, three hours," Jans choked, swallowing. His eyes squeezed shut, but he forced himself to continue, knowing he had to pass on the Guardians' plan. Karen tried to calm him. She put her hand to his forehead, but snatched it back quickly. Jans burned to the touch. He went on.

"Captured ... second-in ... second ... tortured ... the evil!" He drew in a ragged breath. His eyes opened, suddenly clear. "Changeling will be second-in-command ... leaves tonight to gather rebels." Jans' eyes focused on Joanha for an instant, but they clouded with each word. Jans coughed, falling back. He lay still.

Karen agonised as she searched for a life-pulse. She found it, a frantic fluttering against his throat.

Manfred looked to Joanha.

"Did you get all that?"

Joanha nodded.

"I think so. They're using a Shape-shifter to impersonate one of the rebels."

"The second-in-command," Manfred stated. "Who is the second-in-command? Who do they have, Joanha?"

Joanha leaned his head back and closed his eyes with a sigh, resting on his heels.

"They've got Will. He survived, and for what? To be tortured and used." Hatred replaced the sorrow in Joanha's voice as he pushed himself to his feet. "Those bastards won't get away with this." He glanced down at Jans' still form. "I'll make them pay. Somehow, I'll make them pay."

"We have to leave," Karen said. "They'll be coming soon."

"What happened to him?" Joanha asked, eyes riveted on the boy.

"He entered a mind of great evil, I think against his will,"

177

Karen replied. "We must get him out of here. They may be able to follow his mind now that they have discovered his presence. We have to move."

Joanha glared down at the enemy camp, now swarming with movement. He took a step forward, but Manfred restrained him.

"That's not the way, Joanha," he said. The rebel scowled, but Manfred didn't let go. "What would you accomplish by going back down there? You'd only throw your life away and right now, we need you." Joanha paused, staring grimly at the large warrior blocking his path.

"You're right Stalker. This is not the time to die." He nodded to Karen and picked up Jans. "Karen's also right. We must hurry."

Without another word, Joanha slipped into the forest. Karen and Manfred raced to keep up.

***

"When can you reach the rebels?" Karen asked Joanha.

"Jans said something about three hours. It will take me a little longer if I have to pick up the Shape-shifter's trail, but I think I can be there before daybreak."

The companions huddled together in a small cave a few miles from the army. The sky had grown overcast and drizzle dampened their already burdened spirits. Jans regained consciousness a few times, but only long enough to cry out or mutter something unintelligible. Presently, he lay against a large rock, sheltered for the moment from the rain.

"What if they don't believe you?" Manfred asked. "Will is the second-in-command, while you—"

"I know," Joanha said with a wry smile. "I'm the troublemaker, the dissident. But I am a rebel. I will convince them, whatever it takes." He stood, his eyes moving to Jans.

"Will he ..." Joanha faltered. "Take care of him. I'll meet you with the rebels in a fortnight."

"Remember, north end of the lake," Manfred said as he stood to face the rebel. Joanha nodded, then offered his hand to Manfred, who returned the handshake.

"A fortnight, then," Karen said. Joanha met her gaze with a tight smile. After a final glance to Jans, he slipped into the night.

For a time, silence reigned. Manfred sat glumly, staring off into the distance. Karen studied the warrior-tracker for long minutes before she spoke.

"What is it, Manfred?"

Manfred did not meet her gaze.

"It had to be Silben, didn't it?"

"What do you mean?"

"For all the running we've done, we end up returning to the beginning. Silben is where it all started and that's where it's going to end." Manfred's voice seemed to come from a distance.

"It started before the lake, Manfred." She sighed. "We have run a long time. But Silben is the best place to meet with the rebels. I do not know why, but we have to return there. There is something about the place, something I do not understand. My father told me once that Silben balanced the forces of good and evil in the world, but the balance had been destroyed. You said it used to be a place of cold beauty; somehow the loss of balance changed that. We have to return."

"The place is evil." Manfred stated. "I have never felt the presence of death so clearly as I did at that lake. I know we have to go back ..." He blew out a hearty breath. "I just wish we knew what we faced here. An entire army to kill all the rebels ... there has to be more to this whole thing than that. I hate not knowing. And Silben is, well ..."

"The heart of all evil," a voice said from behind the two. Karen and Manfred turned to see Jans leaning on shaky elbows. He spoke again. "Silben is where they came from."

"Who?" Karen asked.

"The Two," said Jans. Karen glanced at Manfred, then back to Jans. The boy fought for consciousness. His fevered eyes held a wild sheen.

"What two? What are you talking about?" Manfred demanded. But Jans slipped back to the ground, his arms no longer supporting him. He coughed painfully, bringing up a splatter of blood. Karen moved to Jans' side, wiping the blood from his lips.

"Can you hear me?" she asked quietly. Jans tried to focus on her. He nodded. "Who are the two, Jans? What are they?"

179

Jans swallowed hard and coughed again. Fear darkened her eyes as she whispered, "Did they do this to you? Was it their minds you entered?"

Jans cried out, then nodded again. When his coughing eased, Karen continued, her voice soft. "Can you tell me who they are? Jans? Can you hear me?"

But the boy had lapsed into unconsciousness once more.

Karen stood, sighing. She walked over to where Manfred sat and joined him.

"Things are going to get worse, aren't they?" the warrior asked, subdued.

"Yes. Much worse, I fear." She bowed her head, her next words so quiet that Manfred had to strain to hear them.

"I don't know what to do, Manfred." She glanced at Jans. "I have brought him to this. If it were not for me, he would be safe back in Nearbrook. The Guardians would not have found him if they had not followed us. Followed me."

"You don't know that," Manfred said. "Guardians have swept the countryside for years. They would have found him sooner or later."

"But it's my fault. I should never have dragged him into this. My father would have known better. He would have protected him. I should not have let him go into that valley," she sobbed.

"Stop it Karen," Manfred said. "You can't blame yourself. It was Jans' decision to come this far. You just made it possible for him to make that choice. And you can't know if your father would have done any different. I hate to say this, but had he known better, he would still be here and this might be his battle. Your father's not here, Karen, and this is *your* quest. Don't slip into his shadow. You must do what you think best. If Jans didn't agree with your decision, he wouldn't have done it."

Karen looked up into Manfred's steely grey eyes and smiled.

"Thank you," she whispered, leaning against his side. "I am tired."

Manfred put his arm around the girl and pulled her close.

"We can rest here for maybe an hour," Manfred said. "Then we'll have to move on. The rain will cover our tracks and slow any pursuit. But don't worry, Karen. Sleep now. I'll watch over you."

Karen nodded, her head resting on his shoulder. She soon fell asleep in Manfred's arms.

Darkness sucked her into its cold embrace. Her lungs squeezed tight under future's oppression, terror clutching at her heart as despair threatened to overwhelm her. Evil surrounded her. Dimly, she saw the slumped form of Jans, the heavy shadows of death obscuring his light. She screamed in silence, a wail contained within her mind, clawing for release. She strained to reach the boy, to protect him, even as the forces of evil fought to steal his soul.

If he dies, all hope is lost. She didn't know where the thought came from, but she recognised its truth. She also knew that, for all her power, she stood helpless against the forces surrounding Jans. He fought his own battle now, a struggle for life, and she was nothing more than a bystander. His part in this struggle had not ended, but the decision to stay and fight to the finish no longer lay in Karen's hands; perhaps never had.

Nevertheless, the violence of her vision continued, a forewarning of a disastrous future if Jans died, if she failed, if the forces of goodness faded without a fight.

Once-fertile lands burned, charred husks left to mark the past. Cities fell into ruin; villages turned to dust and ashes blown across a barren landscape. Ildare was but a smear against the mountains; Nearbrook a smudge of wilted land. Towns she had never seen, cities she had only noted on maps, all suffered and died.

Fear powered mankind, greed and ignorance ruling weak hearts. Hatred dominated, and two creatures stood tall over the wretched survivors, staring out from impossibly beautiful faces etched with cold contempt over the chaos they had wrought. Karen watched as these creatures commanded Ebbrings, Guardians, and thousands upon thousands of ignorant humans, bending them to their ugly will. Joanha, Shawlen, Chanet—all the rebels—writhed in unimaginable agony under the weight of oppression. Manfred screamed and bled, and Karen cried out at the utter despair that suffused her body and stole her breath.

"Karen," Manfred called, trying to wake her. He pulled her into his lap, folded her shivering body in his arms, desperate to warm her cold flesh. "Karen, wake up. Come back to me."

"Cold," she mumbled, her teeth chattering.

Heart pounding in dread, Manfred reached for his pack,

drew out a blanket. He held her close, wrapping them both in what warmth he could.

"Dark," she whispered, clinging to Manfred, as though seeking to anchor herself. "It's so dark. I can't see the light."

The terror in her voice nearly shattered Manfred. He yanked a small lantern from his pack, lit it with a quick strike of flint—all the light he dared in the cave; wishing he could build her a roaring fire to light her path and warm her flesh, knowing he dare not.

Karen stared at the tiny flame, taking comfort from this little spark against the coming night. She snuggled deep into Manfred's embrace, borrowing the warmth he held against the cold possibility of so bleak a future. She sighed, allowing tense muscles to relax, dark and desperate thoughts to fade. The horror of her vision revisiting her eased. The terrifying prospect of watching the world spiral into such dark and evil times transformed to a promise of hope brought by Manfred's warmth and light. She quieted, her trembling stopped, her hope restored.

"Thank you, dear friend," she murmured.

Manfred kissed her hair with a quiet tenderness.

Karen let herself drift, grateful for Manfred's support, needing it in a way she didn't truly understand. She stayed curled in his lap, his arms encircling her with the promise of protection, and finally she fell into a dreamless slumber.

The large warrior gazed at her in wonder for a time and finally smiled. Here at last, so close to what could be the end, Manfred had found contentment and peace, unified by this girl, the Druid's daughter.

Chapter 20

Garcouk watched the Ebbring servant Alhor take a deep breath before moving behind the curtain leading to the Master. The leader of the Guardians wondered again at the quizzical expression Da'Harnak had given the young guard when the Ebbring had re-emerged from the divided section of the tent. No one was ever called before the Master, but Da'Harnak had spoken of some sort of opposition. Yet Garcouk found it difficult to believe Alhor could be a traitor. The youth took too much pleasure in causing pain.

Garcouk forced the issue from his mind and focused on Rainier's role in the war effort. The Changeling Guardian regarded the rebel's second-in-command. Even as he studied Rainier, Garcouk found himself seeing two rebel leaders. Rainier looked to Garcouk, waiting for approval. Garcouk scrutinised the two men, comparing them. The only difference was the predatory anticipation in Rainier's eyes. He nodded and without another word, Rainier, in the rebel's guise, withdrew into the night.

Garcouk had no doubts about Rainier's abilities. The Changeling would reach the rebel camp in less than three hours, provided the information was correct. This time, it better be. That vixen in Sandroga had already duped him; there would be no mistakes with this rebel.

Which brought the Guardian leader's attention to the scum secured in the questioning chair. The man had served his purpose and had no further use. Garcouk signalled to another Guardian who drew his blade. A sudden movement from the curtain brought the bloody act to a halt as Da'Harnak swept out, eyes ablaze with anticipation. All eyes turned to the Ebbring.

"She is near. She travels with a boy who also has magic. Find his trace; find them both. We need them alive." Da'Harnak's voice flowed with excitement and deadly intent. Rushing out of the tent, the Guardians hurried to obey. In a matter of seconds the whole valley clattered to life. Garcouk remained behind with Da'Harnak.

"Which direction?" the Guardian asked.

"West."

"Who else is with her?"

Da'Harnak grimaced.

"The Stalker still travels with her and this boy from Nearbrook. There is a fourth, most likely the rebel from Jadathe."

Ing'Lahar emerged from behind the drape with the crumpled form of Alhor and dropped him unceremoniously in a corner. Garcouk waited impatiently for the Ebbring, then asked in a low voice,

"What did the intruder learn?"

Da'Harnak frowned, an unnerving expression in his dark clay-like face. "He caught the Master by surprise. There is no telling how much he learned in those seconds. But to enter a mind such as this is dangerous, as you know Garcouk. He is a child meddling in things too deep for him. Any information he gained will sound muddled and confused."

"But she may know our plans," Garcouk insisted.

"She can't know anything," Ing'Lahar stated. "The boy is in no condition to be of any help to her."

"We can't assume that," Garcouk said. "We don't know what he can do. He surprised the Master; let's not aid them further by underestimating them."

Ing'Lahar snarled, his teeth bared. The growl crawling up his throat sounded petulant rather than threatening.

"The girl may know our plans," Da'Harnak overrode the other Ebbring's objections, his brow pulled down in warning. "We must find her and stop her."

"Who is she?" Garcouk demanded, also ignoring Ing'Lahar.

Da'Harnak's eyes narrowed at the Guardian's tone, but the Ebbring responded, "We do not know. The boy carefully kept that hidden, as does this rebel leader. All we know is that she will be a problem."

"She has already been a problem," Garcouk reined in his temper at Da'Harnak's warning glare. The Ebbring would only tolerate so much insolence. "How am I to fight someone whose power even the Master does not know?" Da'Harnak said nothing. Garcouk sighed, then continued, his voice more controlled. "You said they are west of us, is that right Da'Harnak?"

The Ebbring nodded. Garcouk took a breath and closed his eyes. After a moment, he exhaled and spoke again.

"If the boy learned of Rainier's role, he will warn his companions. They travel with a rebel. He will try to stop Rainier. The girl will no doubt devise a plan for this rebel's success. She cannot risk being detected by us and will not leave the boy in his condition, provided he still lives, so she is not likely to accompany the rebel. Which means they will have to split up. The Stalker has barely moved from her side and is unlikely to now. That leaves the rebel to Rainier's mercy." Garcouk paused, enjoying this moment of power he had over the Ebbrings as they listened mutely to his reasoning.

"They will plan to meet later," Garcouk concluded. "What we have to do is figure out where. Then we will have her."

"So where is this meeting place?" Ing'Lahar sneered. "It is fine to know what they will do, but if we do not know where they head, these conjectures are useless."

Garcouk had to fight hard to control his frustration. It all fit so clear in his mind; why could these Ebbrings not see the simplicity of it?

"We caught the girl heading east, toward Silben. They're drawn to it. What better place to meet? The rebel could have his companions there in time to meet our armies should Rainier fail. That is the obvious choice."

"Then it is the least likely one," Ing'Lahar snapped. "She is not so stupid as to fall for such a trap."

"And if the boy learned Silben's secret? What of that, Ing'Lahar? Go to the heart of power to destroy us. Even if she doesn't know the lake's history, to go to the obvious is perfect because we will think it impossible."

An uneasy silence filled the tent. Da'Harnak sat down, a hand to his mouth, thinking. Ing'Lahar muttered under his breath until Da'Harnak's withering glare silenced him.

And then, the Master stepped from behind the curtain.

For the first time in his life, Garcouk knew the true meaning of fear, and he stood in awe of that feeling. The Ebbrings were visibly unnerved by the appearance of their leader before a non-Ebbring, but if the Master noticed, he said nothing. He walked gracefully to the table and sprawled into a chair. He was tall and beautiful as a bird of prey is beautiful; stunning until he sinks his talons into flesh, captivating unto the point of destruction. He studied each Ebbring in turn, then looked to Garcouk with eyes blacker than deepest night and colder than the icy heart of winter. Finally, he spoke in a low, even tone.

"So, you are the Guardian leader who has served these wretches, and through them, me, for so long." Garcouk forced himself not to betray his fear to this almost human creature. The Master smiled and nodded before continuing.

"I can see why you were chosen to lead, Garcouk. Few can master their feelings as you have. Even the Ebbrings sometimes have trouble with it." The Master slowly gazed from Garcouk to Da'Harnak, then on to Ing'Lahar. "You should learn to trust this man's intuition, Ing'Lahar. Garcouk has served loyally for long enough and brought back sufficient compensation to be listened to. His conjecture is adequate and should be followed. The girl will go to a familiar landmark. Silben is a logical choice."

"And what of our army?" Da'Harnak inquired. "Do we march now or send a scout team to see if she truly goes there?"

The Master appraised Da'Harnak, but the Ebbring didn't flinch. Obviously Da'Harnak had also learned to control his emotions, assuming such a creature had any.

"The army will move as planned. We can no longer rely on Rainier's success, so we will have to act quickly." The Master turned back to Garcouk. "However, send out a small scout force. You will lead them, Garcouk. As for who this girl is, Da'Harnak was not quite correct in saying we do not know her identity. The truth is, he does not know."

Da'Harnak glanced sharply at the Master.

"You know her, Sharnac?" Ing'Lahar blurted out, then clutched at his throat as though being choked. His breath rattled and his knees slammed to the ground. One arm flailed while the other clawed at his neck, trying to remove the unnatural obstruction. The Master slowly rose to his feet, watching the struggling Ebbring through eyes narrowed to dark slits.

"Never use my name," the Master rasped, his tone acid. "That was agreed upon. None shall have that power over me. You draw close to the line, Ing'Lahar. I have tolerated too much," He regarded the thrashing Ebbring, his countenance smoothing to a dispassionate mask. "One more mistake and I will obliterate you. I created you and I can destroy you. Remember that."

After a moment, Ing'Lahar gasped, drawing in a desperate pull of air as the Master released his magical stranglehold. The Ebbring ceased his frantic motions, regaining his feet despite his trembling.

Sharnac turned to Garcouk and continued calmly, "I know the identity of the girl, but that changes little. She is still a great threat. She is the daughter of the last of the Druids."

A shocked silence followed Sharnac's revelation. Garcouk broke the stillness.

"And her powers?" he asked in a small voice. He cleared his throat and added, "What of her powers? Are they the same as Draimar's?"

"They are not," Sharnac said simply, leaning forward as though taking Garcouk into his confidence. "The blood of the High Elves also flows in her veins, along with their magic."

"Can she be stopped?" Da'Harnak whispered softly.

Sharnac looked to the Ebbring, then back to the Guardian. He said nothing. Instead, Garcouk spoke.

"She is young and inexperienced. She must have some weakness, something that will work in our favour."

"And that, you will learn," Sharnac hissed, a strange fury in his words. "She cannot be allowed to fight us." He pushed back from the table, head held high, and stared down his aristocratic nose at them.

"But she is just one person," Ing'Lahar murmured, his gaze downcast and his tone obsequious. "Surely even with her powers, she is not enough to stop us."

"We said the same of her father," Sharnac snapped. "And he very nearly destroyed us. He may have had an army, but to all intents, he stood alone. She does not. She fights with these people, not just for them. Never underestimate the power of loyalty. The Stalker may have no magic, but he has skill. The rebels will join them. With the help of this girl, they make a formidable match for our army. If the boy tells what he learned through his mind talk, she may learn the secret of your own powers, Ing'Lahar. We cannot allow that.

"You will leave by dawn, Garcouk. She must not reach Silben."

Garcouk nodded and prepared to leave the tent, but he paused a moment.

"One last question," the Guardian said. "How do you know who she is? Da'Harnak said the boy kept it secret and we learned nothing from the rebel."

"Not quite true," Sharnac smiled, the malice of which twisted his exquisite features into a gruesome mask. "The boy did not betray her, but the rebel did."

"What?" Garcouk looked to where Will sat. The rebel shook violently and beads of perspiration etched crooked paths through dry blood as sweat dripped down his deathly-pale face. "How?" Garcouk asked staring into the rebel's panicked eyes.

"He was not prepared for an interrogation, at least not by me. I entered his mind, blasting away his pitiful defences. His thoughts tore open before me like a spider's web shredded in a storm. But he is of no more use."

Garcouk watched as the rebel fought in the chair against an unseen force. Blood splattered from Will's mouth onto his tunic as he choked. His eyes turned back in his head. A wet gurgling erupted from his throat. His muscles convulsed fiercely under a tormented strain. Finally, his body slumped forward in the chair as the rebel raggedly breathed his last horrified gasp. Blood ran in little streams from his nose and ears.

Garcouk shuddered slightly at Sharnac's dispassionate show of power. A mere glance had sealed the rebel's fate. Sharnac's face held no emotion as he turned to watch Garcouk leave the tent.

Once outside, Garcouk heaved an uneasy sigh, then quickly gathered a team of his men together. When dawn's first light kissed the sky, he was already moving west in search of this daughter of the Druid.

Chapter 21

Joanha ran most of the way. He had retraced enough of their trail to find the Shape-Shifter's path, barely visible in the mud. The tracks had turned south and west, and the Shape-Shifter's trail had escaped the forest about forty-five minutes earlier. Two rain-drenched hours had passed since he left Karen and the others. If the outbursts of Jans' tortured fever were right, he had another hour of travel before he reached the nearest rebel base.

As Joanha ran, his thoughts turned to Jans. What the boy had done to learn what he had, Joanha could only guess. The discovery of the plot against the rebels was merely the beginning. Now, thanks to that cursed evil, Jans lay fighting for his life, and Joanha prayed the boy won that struggle. Something about Jans had deeply touched the rebel. He could not say exactly what, but Joanha felt a kind of protectiveness toward the boy. If anything happened ....

Joanha forced his thoughts to concentrate on the trail he followed. The land looked more familiar now. Gentle hills and pastureland had taken over beyond the forest, and farms now began to grace the land. Crownawn had a different name around here. Joanha recalled the tales of the haunted forest of Asturban, the tales of death and fear. Yet even the worst rumour-mongers had no idea what really waited in the depths of those woods.

He approached Sandroga, a place noted for its thieves and cutthroats, scandals and general ill-repute—and the source of the stories of Asturban. It was also a valued source of information for the rebellion. One could learn anything here—for a price. A rebel base hid three miles west of Sandroga. The Shape-shifter would have arrived by now.

Not wanting to attract attention to himself, Joanha slowed his pace and skirted the edges of Sandroga, keeping to the shadows. He was exhausted and sick with worry over Jans. Mud had splattered most of the way up his legs more than once, and the layers of grime threatened to stiffen and tell on his pace. Though his wounds were healing, his back itched where the whip had scarred him, and the fading bruises and cuts on his face ached in the damp. The last thing he needed was for some cutthroat to think him easy prey.

Even at this late hour and with the drizzling rain, Sandroga did not sleep. Her residents were always on guard and wary of everything. As it happened, Joanha was only stopped once. A large, bedraggled man ambled out of the darkness in front of him. He had a lantern fastened to his belt. Probably an enforcer. A sword hung loosely at his side and a knife flashed in his hand. As he neared Joanha, the man's resolve seemed to slacken.

Joanha's eyes gleamed with intensity and he held himself loose, ready for battle. The man before him took this in, recognising the fact that Joanha was a man to be reckoned with despite his slim figure. He nodded. Joanha narrowed his eyes but returned the greeting and continued on his way with no further interruptions.

If the rebels needed help against the Ebbring's army, they could count on the citizens of Sandroga. As vicious and dishonest as they were, they had no love for Guardians or Ebbrings. It might cost the rebels more wealth than they had to convince Sandroga to fight so soon, yet their allegiance would be worth such a price. But Joanha had other things to worry about at the moment. He had to prove to the rebels that the man they thought was Will was in truth a Shape-shifter.

***

The door opened at the top of the stairs. Laurana peered up in apprehension. No one was expected in this section of the rebel tunnels, but she had trained for this sort of thing. One of her tasks was patrolling the two entrances to the Sandroga tunnels, doubly important now that the Guardians had expressed such an interest in them. She cast her torch aside and nocked an arrow to her bowstring, fading into the gloom. A dishevelled figure toppled in, covered in abrasions. Laurana aimed her weapon. The person in the doorway looked up, the flickering of the torch marching shadows across his features. Laurana gasped. She recognised that face.

"Will?" she called.

The figure peered into the darkness through one eye, the other swollen shut.

"Who's there?" he rasped.

"It's me, Will. It's Laurana." She rushed up the stairs and caught the man as he fell.

"Laurana?"

"We were told you fell at the raid!" Laurana exclaimed.

"I was captured. They took me to a camp and questioned me." He spit the last with venom. "I have to see the others. We must call Council."

Laurana sucked air through her teeth.

"Are things that bad?" she asked.

Will nodded and pointed down the stairs. "We have to hurry. There's not much time."

Laurana sealed the entrance and retrieved her torch before it guttered completely. She escorted Will to a large chamber where some of the other rebels worked. Silence fell when Laurana brought Will in.

Will took in his surroundings. A young man emerged from the background.

"Will," he called enthusiastically.

Will looked him up and down, squinting through his good eye. The man wore a white tunic, dark pants and a green cape.

"Shawlen? Is that you?"

With a teary grin, Shawlen grasped Will in a hug. Laurana silently slipped away back to her post.

"I thought you were dead, brother. How did you survive?"

"They took me captive," Will said simply.

"To Jadathe? We had reports that some of us languished in that bloody dungeon. But we hadn't known you were among them."

"Not to Jadathe. They took me to an encampment north of here."

Shawlen stepped back, regarding the older man.

"You escaped?" he asked.

Will nodded. "They thought me unconscious. There was only one guard and I guess they figured I was in too rough a shape to try an escape. They were wrong."

Shawlen grinned.

"What of the reports of Jadathe?" Will asked suddenly. "How did you get reports?"

"Same as always," Shawlen said, a quizzical look crossing his face.

"I mean, who brought the reports?"

"They came through the chain, of course. Will, are you okay?"

"I'm fine," Will snapped. Then, quieter, "Sorry Shawlen. I've had a few harrowing days, that's all. I don't mean to take it out on you."

"That's all right, Will," Shawlen said uncertainly. "Listen, you need some rest and those wounds have to be treated."

"There's no time," Will said, his voice barely above a whisper. "I have to call Council."

Shawlen stared at him in amazement.

"Council? Now? Will, are you sure this is the time?"

"It must be done. The enemy has an army, not yet very strong, but enough of a threat to warrant Council. We have to call a meeting now."

"Why so soon?"

"They plan to march within the week. We will strike when they least expect it." Then Will announced to all in the room, "The enemy has gathered an army. We must call Council. All rebels must meet within these walls in five days time."

Murmurs rose throughout the chamber, suddenly silenced by another voice.

"Don't listen to him; he's an impostor."

All eyes searched for this new speaker. Joanha stepped from the shadows, Laurana at his side.

"That's not Will," Joanha said.

Startled gasps followed his statement and confused eyes shifted from Joanha to Will and back again.

"Joanha?" Shawlen called uncertainly.

"Step away from him Shawlen; he's a Shape-shifter," Joanha advised.

"What is this nonsense?" Will demanded. "We don't have time for this. Send word. Council must meet."

The rebels hesitated, wanting to trust one of their leaders, but no longer sure of his identity.

"What are you waiting for?" Will cried. "Are you taking this troublemaker's word over mine?"

"I may be disagreeable at times," Joanha acceded, "but I am a rebel. I have sworn the oath. My word is honour-bound."

"As is mine," Will spat. "Were you not captured also, Joanha?"

"I was."

"You weren't at the army camp. Where did they take you?" Will challenged.

"Jadathe."

More startled whispers spread through the room.

"Jadathe," repeated Will, his voice hard. "The impregnable fortress of the Guardians. Tell us how you escaped such a place."

Joanha glared into Will's good eye.

"With help."

"He's in league with the Guardians," Will snarled.

"Not the help of Guardians, Shape-Shifter," Joanha countered, moving forward. "But with the help of Karen."

Shawlen gasped and Will's eye narrowed.

"You remember her, don't you Will?" Joanha asked.

"Of course. She travels with the Stalker."

"But do you remember who she is?" A brief pause. "Come now, Will. Surely you haven't forgotten her identity?"

Will scowled, his eye flashing red.

"No," Joanha continued. "I didn't think you'd have gotten that from him. Will's too strong for that. You've failed, Shape-shifter. Your army may march in five days, but we'll stand ready."

Will growled deep in his throat and lunged for Joanha, catching the rebel by surprise. The two fell to the dusty ground. Laurana raised her bow and Shawlen drew his sword, yet neither struck. The two men rose and disentangled, but Will was nowhere in sight. Instead, two Joanha's faced each other, identical in every way—except their thoughts.

One Joanha dropped to a crouch, ready to spring, while the other merely stared at his opponent, waiting for the attack.

The first leapt forward and the two grappled, their limbs flailing, their frantic struggle blurring their movements. Shawlen looked to Laurana, but she shook her head.

"I cannot tell them apart, Shawlen."

The second Joanha shoved the first away.

"Joanha," Shawlen called. Neither man looked at him. "How can we tell them apart?"

The first Joanha spoke, his finger pointing at his mirror.

"He's the Shape-Shifter. Kill him."

Shawlen glanced at the second Joanha, still hesitant. Then this second man, devoid of emotion, said, "Kill us both. It's the only way to be sure."

In the next instant, the first Joanha fell, a feathered arrow lodged in his throat.

The man writhed in a brief spasm of pain, then lay silent. Joanha's features faded from his face, leaving the Changeling Guardian Rainier dead on the floor.

Shawlen turned to Laurana, his eyes wide.

"Joanha is a rebel," she shrugged, brushing her braid back over her shoulder as she lowered her bow. "He knows the rebellion comes first. The only way to be sure, as he said, was death to both. The Shape-shifter failed to see that and paid with his life."

Joanha smiled briefly. "We must gather all the rebels we can. The enemy has an army of incredible numbers. In two weeks time, we must meet with Karen at the lake called Silben." All eyes focused on Joanha as he spoke. "Have the magic users summon our people. We'll send others to find help in what towns they can. In two days, I will tell what I know. Hopefully all the leaders will arrive by then. Those who can't make it must meet us at Silben's north shore within a fortnight. We don't have much time."

The rebels, believing now in Joanha's words, came alive with action, quickly devising the best way to follow these new orders.

Shawlen and Laurana, however, waited to talk with Joanha in private.

"Is it true what you said about Karen?" Shawlen asked. "Did she help you escape Jadathe?"

"Yes; she, the Stalker, and the boy from Nearbrook, Jans."

"Is this the daughter of the Druid?" Laurana inquired. "The

one who brought the Guardians to the tunnels?"

"That wasn't Karen's fault," Joanha said quietly. "We brought her and the Stalker there. The arrival of the Guardians had been long expected. She merely provided a convenient excuse for an attack on us."

"One that landed you in Jadathe," Laurana said, her arms crossed beneath her breasts. Though Joanha outweighed the willow-thin woman, her disapproval made her a dangerous person to cross.

"I'm surprised it took them so long to find me. No, you can't blame Karen, Laurana. Besides, had I not been there, the discovery of the enemy army may have come too late. At least now we have a chance."

"Can you tell us what happened at the dungeons?" Shawlen wanted to know.

Joanha recounted the events at the tower, the discovery of the army plans and the role of the Shape-Shifter.

"Now Karen and the Stalker journey to Silben, looking for help and doing what they can for Jans," Joanha's voice choked off at the mention of Jans' illness.

After a brief moment of silence, Shawlen said, "You should rest now, Joanha. The others won't arrive for a while. Get some sleep, my friend. You look like you need it. We'll wake you if anything happens."

Joanha gazed at the young man before him and allowed a smile to play across his lips. He sighed.

"You're right. Sleep will do me some good. Thank you, Shawlen."

Shawlen and Laurana exchanged a quizzical glance, noting the change in Joanha. A sense of gratitude had replaced his usual standoffishness. It seemed to Shawlen that whatever had happened between Joanha and Jans had altered his old companion, for it was not until his meeting the boy that Joanha's reluctant kindness had reappeared. Shawlen had seen this kindness only once before, five years ago when Shawlen himself had joined the rebellion. Joanha had once remarked how Shawlen reminded him of himself, and at the time, he had taken on a similar affection for the young rebel. But Shawlen had had Will to watch over him. Perhaps this Jans had rekindled Joanha's emotions and protectiveness, a child with no one to look after him. Whatever the cause of the change, Shawlen was glad to see it.

He took Joanha to the resting chambers and showed him to a spare bedroll. Joanha was asleep as soon as his head touched the pillow.

Chapter 22

Joanha dreamed. Or perhaps he merely remembered.

He was sixteen again and the war had ended, but life still went on as always at the farm. Even in the worst of times, people needed to eat. The war had taken most of the young men, but not Joanha. With his father's death and his brother's absence, Joanha was left to care for the farm, and with so little help, that included working the land. Though in truth, he didn't mind the exertion.

Joanha had toiled in the field since before dawn. He had worked up a good sweat in the summer morning breeze when he heard a shout. He looked up to see Tourn, one of the servants, running toward him.

"Lord Aldan has returned," Tourn barked, slowing his onward rush an instant before colliding with Joanha. "Young Lord, your brother is home."

With a whoop of excitement, Joanha dropped his scythe and took off at a run for the farmhouse.

"Aldan!" he called as he burst through the door.

A broad-shouldered man with dark hair turned from the hearth. Aldan, home at last.

"Brother, we were so worried," Joanha said, grabbing Aldan in a fierce embrace.

So many questions and emotions tumbled through Joanha's mind, struggling to escape, but not a sound passed his lips.

And then their mother walked in.

Tishan's usual calm shell broke but a moment at the sight

of both sons together again after a year. Then her features returned to their statue-perfect stillness; her outer beauty born from a gentle soul.

She took Aldan briefly in her arms, then stepped back to study him.

She frowned, a crease forming between her delicate brows.

"The war has changed you."

Aldan smiled, but not the open and friendly smile Joanha remembered. There was more menace now, a hard glint to the eyes.

"Wars change many things, mother," Aldan said, his voice deeper, more grating. "The whole world is changing. Why does it surprise you that I change with it?"

Tishan stepped back, hugging herself as though cold. It was late summer; Joanha knew she wasn't cold. Like Aldan, their mother was a magic user, and the only time Joanha had ever seen her close in on herself like this was last summer when a Guardian had come to the farm. That was before Joanha knew that Guardians were capable of the atrocities proven by the war. The Guardian had come to recruit Aldan, by force if necessary. He hadn't counted on Tishan's power. She had explained to Joanha later that she could feel the Guardian's magic building and that it had a dark aura. She had wrapped her arms about herself then, as though trying to keep the darkness away. She huddled in on herself now in the same manner.

Joanha glanced toward the entrance. Had the enemy followed Aldan home? Did a host of Guardians approach the farm even now? Were they in danger?

When he turned back to Aldan and his mother, his apprehension grew. Aldan had their mother by the arm, his grip tight enough that Joanha could see the mottled indentations on her skin.

"Aldan, what ..." Joanha began.

"Everything changes, mother," Aldan said, his eyes intent on Tishan. "If we do not follow where those changes lead, we die."

Tishan's eyes were so wide that white showed all around the dark irises, but her voice betrayed no fear.

"Release me."

198

"Add your strength to mine, mother, and we can rule the world."

"I said, release me." A sharp flash bit the air and Aldan gave a shout, wrenching his hand from Tishan's arm. For a moment, his eyes flared red. Joanha quickly pulled his mother behind him, for what good it would do. He couldn't protect her from magic.

"Aldan, what's going on?" Joanha asked.

Aldan stared hard at his younger brother, his chiselled features grim. Then his face softened, looking more like the fun-loving prankster Joanha remembered from earlier days.

"I haven't gone mad, Joanha," he assured. "But I have seen the folly of my ways. Of our ways. I have come to recognise the truth."

"And what truth is that?" Tishan demanded.

Aldan shifted his attention beyond Joanha.

"That we were wrong to hate the Guardians. They are the future. The ways of the Druid are gone. Draimar failed because he did not see the power of the Guardians, the power that will rule the world. But I see that power, mother. And you can too."

"Follow the path of butchering tyrants?" Tishan spat. "This is the future you wish to live?"

"It is the only future that exists."

Tishan firmly pushed Joanha aside and faced Aldan.

"I will not live the life of a traitor, and I will not have a traitor living under my roof. The war has killed my son."

She turned her back on her eldest. Joanha stared in disbelief. And then in alarm as Aldan's face distorted in fury. Before Joanha could do anything, Aldan backhanded him hard enough to send him flying across the room to crash into the wall beside the hearth.

When he regained his senses, Joanha stared into a nightmare. Flames crawled at the carpets and licked across the wooden furnishings. A sickly greenish fire ate greedily at stone walls and swirled in little eddies, hanging impossibly in midair. But worst of all was the sight of the two humans locked in mortal combat. Aldan's rage had so transformed him that Joanha only recognised his brother by his size and clothing. Tishan, covered in blood, her face ashen, continued to fight. Bolts of magic flew around the room; winds howled out of nowhere, flaying everything; invisible forces impacted the air or rent bits of stone from the walls and floor. Joanha had never seen a battle of pure magic, and certainly had never expected to see one waged within his own family. He tried to rise, but a sharp pain in his leg sent him crashing to the ground again. A shard of stone had lodged in his calf. He cursed, digging at the fragment, trying to see through tears made worse by smoke.

Just as he worked the stone free, Joanha heard his mother scream. His head jerked up as Tishan crumpled to the floor. Aldan towered above her, triumph in his eyes.

"This is what we do to all enemies of the Guardians," he growled. He had taken a sword from somewhere.

"No! Aldan!" Joanha cried.

Aldan glanced at his brother, grinned, and swung his sword. It met their mother's throat with a horrible wet sound. Joanha shrieked.

The door slammed open as four men burst in. Joanha stared in numb confusion, but Aldan seemed to know the strangers. He snarled and ripped his sword from Tishan, trailing a splatter of blood.

The sword flew from his hand at a gesture from a man with pale curly hair. Another magic user then? The other three men closed in on Aldan with their own blades. A streak of flame erupted from Aldan's fist toward the nearest man. The fire seared his face and the man screamed. The other two kept moving. A sword skewered Aldan in the gut, another severed his right arm, but he merely grinned, his glittering eyes wide.

And then Aldan erupted in flames. For a moment, Joanha thought the magic user had attacked. Then he heard Aldan cackling over the screams of the two men nearest as they burned with him. Aldan had set the fire upon himself.

Aldan's laughter hung in the air even after the screams had faded, a sound that would haunt Joanha for years.

The magic user and the other man, his face red and blistered from Aldan's strike, came to Joanha's side.

"Who are you?" was all Joanha could think to say.

"Later," replied the burned man. "This building is about to fall down around us." He reached for Joanha's hand, then he and the magic user helped Joanha from the blazing house.

Joanha watched in shock as his home burned. The servants who had worked in the fields gathered with him and the two strangers.

"What about Lady Tishan and Lord Aldan?" cried Tourn. "We must help them."

"They're dead," Joanha said, his voice strangely flat to his own ears. A cold hollowness ate at his chest. His own brother. How could this have happened? If you couldn't trust your own blood, who could you trust?

He turned to find the strangers regarding him sympathetically. At least, the burned man watched him. The magic user tried to heal the other's face.

"I'm sorry we weren't fast enough to stop him."

"Who are you?" Joanha asked again.

"My name is Chanet. This is Derek." The magic user didn't pause at the introduction.

"What in the nine Hells is going on?" Joanha croaked. "Where did you come from?"

"We've been tracking Aldan for some time now," Chanet said.

"Why?"

"You were his brother?" Chanet asked.

Joanha nodded, swallowing past the lump in his throat. Chanet sighed heavily, his shoulders slumping.

"I'm sorry you have to learn this about your own blood, but Aldan turned. The Guardians corrupted him."

"He went to spy out enemy numbers," Derek spoke, finished now with Chanet's wound, though impending scars would forever mar his face. "He didn't return for several days and we feared the worst. Then one day, he came back to camp, a little cut and bruised, but nothing out of the ordinary for someone who had seen and survived a skirmish. We didn't think anything of it when he told us just that—that he had a bit of trouble with some soldiers.

"But things started to happen; small at first. People would become sick for no apparent reason; food would go bad—all things that might happen in an army. But it started happening in the farms and towns that supported us." Derek paused and Chanet took up the tale.

"Then the killings began. By the time we discovered that Aldan was behind them, the final battle was upon us. Now the Druid is dead and our army is decimated. We have done what we can to keep the Guardians from taking over everything, and that includes chasing after Aldan."

"We had but to follow the trail of bodies," Derek snarled. Chanet glanced at him sharply then turned back to Joanha, a sympathetic hand to the youth's shoulder.

"What will you do now?" Chanet asked.

Joanha looked back to the inferno that was his home. Smoke clung to his nostrils.

"The only thing I can do," he whispered bleakly, walling up his emotions even then. "Fight back."

***

And he woke, still smelling smoke. A lantern sat on the floor a few bedrolls over, its flame flickering as rebels moved about the Sandrogan tunnels. Joanha shuddered. He turned, clutching the blanket to his chin, and tried very hard to forget the past.

Chapter 23

The chamber grew more crowded with each passing moment and Joanha began to wonder if the small space would accommodate all the rebel leaders and any fighters they brought. That was not to say that there was a plethora of his people; it merely proved the small size of the room. Two days had passed with surprising speed for Joanha. Since exposing the Shape-shifter, the other rebels had turned to Joanha for guidance and orders, and it still unnerved him.

"Joanha," a familiar voice greeted him enthusiastically from one of the three entrances to the chamber. Joanha rose from a large rock he had claimed as his own and moved to embrace the newcomer.

"Chanet, it's good to see you again," Joanha said sincerely. "Have you seen Shawlen yet? He's been on pins and needles to see you."

Chanet let out a bark of laughter and replied, "Shawlen is always on pins and needles. But I saw him at the entrance. Laurana just relieved him so he'll be down soon." The smile faded from Chanet's scarred face as he continued in a quiet voice. "Do we know what happened to Will?"

Joanha shook his head. "I'm afraid his chances of surviving that place are slim. I wanted to go after him but ..."

"You know that wouldn't have done any good. At least with you here to tell us of the army, we have a chance to avenge him. Had you gone after him, you know what would have happened."

"I know," Joanha sighed.

"How's Shawlen taking the loss of his brother?" Chanet asked, quite subdued now.

"He hasn't given up," Joanha shook his head. "Until he sees a body, Shawlen won't lose hope. You know how stubborn he can be."

A moment or two passed, filled with the hubbub of the gathering rebels. Shawlen came to stand with Joanha and Chanet. From the far entrance, a heavily built man walked in, followed by a lithe middle-aged woman, both well armed. Chanet touched Joanha's arm and nodded toward the two.

"May as well get started, Joanha. Now that Amrah and Toron are here, all the leaders are accounted for."

Joanha nodded. He moved to the platform provided for the Council and began speaking.

"You know why we're here. The enemy has raised a vast army and will march within three days. We must be ready for it. By that time, all rebels and all who fight in our cause must be prepared to move, if they have not set out already. We will gather at the north end of the lake known as Silben. There we will join with one who will add greatly to our forces, able to fight the magic of the Ebbrings with her own magic. She is the daughter of the last of the Druids." A scattering of murmurs washed over the assembled peoples, quickly fading to hear the rest of Joanha's speech. He relayed an approximate account of enemy numbers and weapons. After a few pointed questions, the leaders broke into smaller groups to discuss the matter and offer suggestions. Joanha took this time to speak with Amrah and Toron.

"Well Joanha, you've got enough toppings here for a reasonable salad," greeted Toron, his gesture sweeping around the gathered rebels.

"I just hope it's enough," replied Joanha. "Tell me, Toron, can we count on the help of your people?"

"You get right to the point, don't you?" Amrah laughed, her husky voice similar to her brother's.

"I don't have time to dance around it," the rebel said simply.

Amrah grinned, but the expression didn't reach her grass-coloured eyes.

"Five hundred await your word now, and we can have another five hundred by nightfall tomorrow," she explained. "We will be at Silben and ready for battle."

204

Joanha nodded, impressed at these numbers. A thousand Sandrogans comprised most of the cutthroats in town. "And the price?" he asked.

"Not this time," Amrah said, her features as hard as he'd ever seen them. "These people know the consequences of failure, of what will happen if the enemy wins. We've lost enough to them."

At Joanha's puzzled expression, Toron spoke up.

"They tried to use Sandroga, take her from the inside." Joanha's brow shot up.

"Yagoth died for it, as did two of his network for betraying us to Guardians," Amrah spat out the last. Joanha knew better than to delve deeper. Laurana had said Sandroga would fight, but hadn't elaborated. No wonder, with the ache in Amrah's voice. Something painful had happened to secure Sandroga's allegiance, painful enough to override the fear and hatred of magic, of Guardians. For some reason, Joanha remembered his brother's betrayal in that moment.

"Our people will fight for the kill, and they will kill until the last enemy lies dead," Amrah continued. "When you need us, we will fight for the price of freedom."

"And don't worry about loyalty," added Toron. "Every one of our folk would rather die than fight for them, especially with the traitors' blood still fresh in their minds. We will not betray you, Joanha. You can count on us."

Each rebel leader expressed the same sentiment. For the first and hopefully last time, every rebel would join together in battle, and the people of allied towns would fight by their side. They would present a formidable force, but would it be enough?

Chapter 24

Jans floated in torment. He didn't know whether he lived or had drifted into an endless breach between worlds. He remembered hearing voices and seeing shapes he couldn't understand. *Shades of the dead,* he thought, his mind following the sentiment back to the first encounter.

"He does not belong here," a shadow had whispered, the voice a heavy rasp from the grave.

"It is not his time," another man's dead voice confirmed, though other shades objected.

"He stands at the cusp of our world—"

"He is but a step away—"

"But he cannot pass to us," the first voice interrupted. "He must not."

The second voice added to the first: "She still needs him. The world still needs him."

Jans tried to follow the conversation, hearing the voices, seeing the dim shades that spoke, but he could not move, had no body *to* move.

Am I dead?

A lithe shade detached itself from a darker clump and drifted near. She reached out a shadowy hand, but did not touch him. For a moment, Jans could see her as she must have looked in life; silver-streaked golden hair, green-flecked eyes shining in a glimmering face with the high-swept angles and grace of the elves. Love so bright it held the shadows of death at bay—until she seemed but a spirit again, a form cloaked in shade and standing across the abyss in another world. Tears blurred Jans' vision, though he had no eyes to shed them. He had never seen her, for she had died giving him life, but Jans recognised his mother nonetheless.

"You yet cling to life, my son," she whispered, her voice a strange mix of music and the grave. "A single step will take you from that world to this. Do you wish to cross?" Her palm up, she spread her fingers in welcome, but she did not take his hand. Jans hesitated, torn between embracing the mother he never knew and clinging to the memory of life. His felt himself shift a fraction, a thought of movement without action, and the shades who had spoken for his life hissed in mockery of drawing breath. His mother pulled back, just out of reach, though Jans did not see her move.

"Know that to cross over is easy," she said. "Your pain, your suffering, will end. We can start anew, you and I, share what we never had in life.

"To go back, to return to the world of the living, will bring you agony and fear. You will see anguish and bloodshed; those you have come to know will suffer in their struggle for survival. But you will have the opportunity to make a difference, if you remain strong. You must choose, my son. To return to a life with an uncertain future, where you will experience terrible pain and torment, or to cross over to peace and end your suffering."

Jans thought about it, his bodiless mind trapped by indecision. To end it all, to escape the fevered torture Sharnac had inflicted upon him, to flee a world falling into eternal night. It would take but a single step, one clear and concise thought. What would he leave behind? A father who cared little for him, a land turning to madness, a world, as his mother warned, full of anguish and bloodshed. Would it be so bad?

Karen, he thought. Joanha and Manfred. Creatures like Whooshea. All those who fought to keep the light, to keep the forces of evil at bay. That one step into death would betray them all. He had known the risks when he stepped into the Master's tent, though he hadn't understood just how deep those risks ran. He wasn't prepared for Sharnac, for something so base and evil. But he knew now. He couldn't leave his friends to deal with that unprepared, unaware of the true nature of the enemy. If he had a chance to change the future, to influence the outcome of the approaching war in Karen's favour, then he had to take it.

He gazed at his mother's face, at the shade she had become, and saw the knowledge of his decision written in her peaceful expression.

I wish to live, he said without a voice, without lips to utter the words, but with such conviction that a mere body became superfluous. The clump of shades, almost pressed against him now, wailed in what sounded like pain as a wall of shimmering white light flung them away from the presence of Jans and blocked their reaching hands. They wavered and dispersed, their cries fading as they vanished. His mother smiled at him before she too disappeared. Jans stared in wonder, then in fear as the two shades that had not left stepped through the protective light. Then the light also faded, leaving Jans with two ghosts, and no knowledge of whether or not they would cause him harm.

"You have much to learn, and little time," the first spoke. "We will show what we can; the rest is up to you."

The rest of what?

"My daughter must know what she faces," the second shade said. "Thank you for having the courage to do what is right."

Karen's father and his mentor strove to finish in death what they could not accomplish in life, and Jans would serve as their conduit.

That had been ... Jans didn't know how long ago. Sometimes it seemed like mere minutes, sometimes days or even years. He remained vaguely aware of his physical body moving, most often carried on someone's back or slung in a litter between his friends. Joanha had disappeared, leaving only Karen and Manfred. With him as a burden, Jans felt the desperate vulnerability of the situation. Yet though his body lay helpless, his mind filled with knowledge, information imparted by the dead to save the world of the living.

"We thought we knew everything," the spirit of the Druid Gorlon told Jans. "Druids were supposed to be the guardians of life, of magic, of the world. Instead, we destroyed the Balance."

"We forced goodness on the world and disregarded the consequences," Draimar continued his mentor's tale. "While outwardly, the world appeared to gain from the Druids' efforts, in fact—"

208

"In fact good and evil must check each other," Gorlon interrupted, as though trying to impress upon Jans an issue others had ignored. "Without one, the other cannot exist. By trying to abolish evil, we only helped it grow. By acting without full knowledge, we gave birth to an era of darkness. Through the arrogance of some and the clever plans of others, the Druids allowed the rise of the Masters."

Jans shuddered as the claws of malice from Sharnac's touch tightened in his gut. He had known somehow, through that brief contact with Sharnac, that the Master called Silben home, but he did not understand how a lake could birth such evil.

How? he wondered, and Gorlon heard him and answered.

"Every system in nature has a series of checks and balances. In this case, that system resides in the lake known as Silben. It is a magnet for the forces of good and evil, and the source of Balance."

"When the Druids tried to eradicate evil," Karen's father went on when Gorlon paused, "they in truth perpetuated it by saturating Silben with that which they sought to destroy. All discarded emotions find a home in Silben, and those who once guarded and protected its spelled shores would ensure against any flux that might damage the Balance."

"But when anger, hatred, greed—any emotions the Druids deemed as a form of evil—were forcibly quelled, they had to go somewhere," Gorlon said. "Through nature's system, that somewhere was Silben. Those who guarded the shores grew disillusioned as their charge was inundated with more ill-will than they could handle. They became corrupt or were destroyed. Evil grew where Balance should exist."

"When Silben could no longer hold the evil forced within its waters, it spewed forth a new race," Draimar spoke, his voice gravel dragged across glass. "Silben's Children, the Masters."

Jans suddenly saw it all, the cool silver of Silben erupting in jagged shards of glassy ice. Seven beings formed of shadow and hate, coalescing into creatures of impossible and deceptive exquisiteness. Hair of midnight, skin of snow, eyes of molten coal, their grace hypnotic and their nature wholly immoral. The irony of beauty hiding evil weighed heavy in the air. It all swam through Jans' mind in a flash, leaving him dizzy and nauseous.

The scene swirled, showing Silben just before the eruption.

A hazy figure stood on the shore enveloped by the glow of magic. Without being told, Jans understood that this was the one who had orchestrated the birth of the Masters. *The Druid who betrayed us all,* whispered Gorlon and in an instant, Jans knew Gorlon's story; his struggle to prevent Silben's fate, and his death, a sacrifice to buy time for the future.

The betrayer used those who guarded Silben—Guardians, Jans realised with shock, creatures of good twisted by the whims of those who abused their charge—to augment his power and bring about the birth of Sharnac and his kin. But the Masters would suffer no rule save their own, and they destroyed those who gave them life, tore them apart in wailing strips of agony. The Masters saw a world ripe for the taking, knowing through stolen knowledge that Gorlon lay dead.

What they did not see was the threat of Draimar. The last of the Druids waged war upon the Masters and their legions of twisted Guardians, the dark creatures of the world, those who fought to suppress and dominate the forces of good. With his army, Draimar destroyed more than half the ranks of Guardians and vanquished many of Silben's Children. But the strongest survived. Sharnac and his sister took advantage of a momentary weakness and killed Karen's father. The Druid's forces scattered, yet so too did Sharnac's, their numbers decimated by the bloody struggle.

Sharnac did not despair, for he knew he could rebuild his army. Together with his sister, he set out to replenish his ranks, returning to Silben's shore to give birth to something new. With clay and blood, the Masters created something to strike terror into the hearts of men; six beings imbued with the powers of the Guardians, those yet living, and those torn asunder. The Ebbrings would lead the army and the Masters would rule the Ebbrings.

But again, Sharnac failed to see the greatest threat. Though he continued to send his minions to corrupt or destroy those who might stand against him—those with magic enough to thwart his vile plans—he did not see a thirteen-year-old girl learn of her father's death. Nor would he recognise the resolve of that child now grown and on the path to fulfilling the tasks begun by her father and his mentor.

"She needs you," Draimar's eerie voice whispered, tearing Jans away from the cold visions of the past and back to the strange place between worlds. "Despair chases her and doubt seeks to choke the life from her. Do not let that happen."

Jans nodded, though without his body, the sensation left him disoriented. He blinked without eyes and the shades from Karen's past faded. He had a moment to ponder what they had imparted before he recognised the feel of his body around him again, the cool kiss of the air and the concerned touch of Karen's hand—before the torment of Sharnac's taint slammed fists of agony through his body and mind. He screamed, and then the pain stole his breath and left him in darkness.

Chapter 25

Nearly five days they had travelled and Jans continued to deteriorate. Karen glanced to the tops of the concealing trees twisting together above them and watched the afternoon sun drift further west. How many more days would Jans have to suffer so? The fact that he had survived this long proved there was more to this boy than one might think. Jans referred to the evil mind as the Master and it was a mind so overwrought with abhorrence that it would take incredible strength to endure. Jans, it seemed, had that strength. As to the identity of the Master, Karen could only understand part of Jans' confused outbursts. What she did comprehend was the importance of the Master in the coming war. It appeared he ultimately led the army and even the Ebbrings turned to him. To stop the Ebbrings, they had first to stop the Master.

Masters, Karen amended, for Jans had spoken of two from Silben. But Karen still did not know just who or what these two were. The only thing she knew for certain about these Masters was that they were the creatures from her vision. Only, her vision had shown seven figures rising from the lake, not just two. So where were the other five? She fought a power she did not understand, and until she knew what she faced, Karen could do nothing for Jans. She felt so frustrated.

She glanced at Manfred as the warrior eased Jans to a sitting position, leaning the boy's back against a tree. He managed to pour a little water into Jans' mouth, but most of it dribbled down the boy's unresponsive chin. The Stalker met her gaze but said nothing. Karen sighed and looked back into the forest's depths.   Suddenly, she dropped to a crouch, sensing magic in the air. Manfred reached her side in seconds.

"What is it?" he whispered, then saw the trouble. Several men in the black garb of the enemy appeared in the distance, led by a silver-caped Guardian. Karen and Manfred retreated to where Jans sat. The boy's eyes remained closed and his breath came in laboured gasps. Both knew they could not run, but Karen did not want to have to fight yet. Other Guardians could be nearby and the use of her magic would draw them closer. Yet, it seemed they had little choice. A confrontation appeared imminent.

Karen stood and leaned against one side of the tree, Manfred on the other, Jans partially concealed by the trunk. The Guardian paused, turning to his men. He said something quietly, then moved forward alone. Karen recognised him as the Guardian who had captured her and Jans. He stopped a few feet in front of Karen and folded muscle-bound arms across his chest.

"We meet again," the Guardian said. "I'm afraid we did not get to have our little chat in Jadathe. I should have questioned you right away, but the Masters had different ideas on the subject."

"Yes, I suppose your Master is not to be questioned." Karen emphasised the capital.

The Guardian smiled, peering past Karen to what he could see of Jans' prone form. "So the child still lives? No matter. There's nothing you can do now. You are too late."

"Are you going to kill us?" Manfred asked coldly, eyeing the Guardian's companions.   "Not very sporting, eight Guardians against two."

The Guardian laughed.   "Would it make you happier, Stalker, to know that I am the only Guardian here? The only one with magic? These are but some of my foot soldiers. The odds are a little fairer that way. Besides, it would have to be eight against three; that is, if your young friend doesn't fall down first."

Manfred turned to see Jans on his feet, resting heavily on the tree trunk. The boy glared at the Guardian before him.

Then Jans spoke, his voice thick. "The uniforms. The army wears black. The Seekers, the ones with the most magic, wear silver capes, like Garcouk here." Jans drew a haggard breath, ignoring the baneful stare of the leader of the Guardians. "Blue means Changelings and red, the keepers of Death Hounds and Summoners of the beasts." He paused, coughing up blood.

"Go on, child," Garcouk spat. "Tell her the other colours." When Jans did not respond, Garcouk grinned maliciously. "The greens of Knowledge, Guardians who know the weaknesses of man; the violets of Mind Control who can twist a mind past usefulness; the ambers of Weather who kill with a storm; the orange of Soul-Splitting who make you wish you were never born. Go on boy, surely you learned of them too," Jans coughed uncontrollably, blood dribbling down his chin as he sank to his knees, but Karen heard him continue in her mind.

'They're dead, Karen. Those other colours are gone. Your father ... he killed them. Only the Ebbrings who use those powers remain; the Ebbrings that the Masters created to lead the Guardians.'

Karen nodded and looked at Garcouk as he laughed.

"Enough," Karen said in a powerful voice. Garcouk sneered at her. "He is not the one you were sent to find."

"True enough," Garcouk said, regaining his composure.

"You said before you enjoyed this little cat-and-mouse game," Karen said. "It is time now to end it. No more games." She felt her power gather within her, but then Garcouk spoke again.

"I also said you were a worthy opponent. At the time, I had no idea how wrong I was." Karen frowned. Garcouk smirked before continuing. "The Druid was a formidable enemy, but not strong enough, for he failed. We still live. He may have crippled us for a time, but he was too weak to destroy us." The Guardian's voice grew more acerbic. "Now he sends his daughter to complete what he could not. What could you possibly do that your father did not do already?"

"She could win," Manfred said. Karen's gaze flickered to the warrior, then back to the Guardian, her stomach fluttering. She had known that her father's quest and hers were the same, that she fought the same evils he did. Garcouk had even now confirmed that in his taunts, as had Jans. But her father *had* failed. How could she presume to accomplish what the most powerful of Druids could not?

Garcouk saw her uncertainty and allowed himself a faint

smile. *So she does have a weakness,* he thought to himself. *Her father.* He glanced at the Stalker. "She could win, you say. Against our entire army? Even with the rebels, should your friend reach them in time, you are hopelessly outnumbered. You saw the size of our camp, Stalker. How do you propose to deal with that? This girl does not have the strength. She is as weak as her father."

"No," Manfred shot back. "You are the one who is weak."

"Me? Now how can you believe that? This is the second time I have captured her and I have yet to see any reason for me to believe she has any strength."

"Then why are you here?" Manfred challenged. "Unless she is a threat to you and your Masters, you have no business with her."

"She is a threat only because she has some use of magic. You, on the other hand, do not." With that, Garcouk turned on Manfred, releasing a volley of flames. They never reached him.

Karen extended her hand and closed her fist, as though catching a ball. The flames vanished.

"Ah, so the kitty-cat can fight," Garcouk sniggered at Karen. "What else can you do, child?" he continued with a leer.

Karen did not move. She did not want to take the offensive position, not yet. She had to find out more about what she faced. This Guardian might know.

"Who is the Master?" she asked. "Why do you follow him?"

"He defeated your father, brought him down with a thought." Garcouk watched in triumph as Karen's eyes widened. "He has more power than you could even dream of, born from the very heart of power." Karen slowly shook her head, much to Garcouk's amusement. "And you thought you had a chance against us. Foolish girl, your cause was lost before it even started. As much a fool as your father."

"No," Karen retorted. "You are the fools. Your Master cannot be so powerful, else he'd have no need of you."

"Of course he has no need of us. He tolerates us because we have the same purpose. We are his subjects—"

"You are his slaves," Karen stated. Garcouk's eyes flared red.

"Ignorant girl. Your father didn't understand either. That was his weakness; a weakness that killed him."

"He was not weak," Karen said, sorrow filling her voice.

215

Garcouk smiled. He had her now.

"Oh, yes he was. Your father failed because of his weakness. His powers were feeble and his mind inferior. They dared call him the most powerful of Druids. They were sorely mistaken. If he was so powerful, he'd have no need to send a mere girl-child to do what he could not. You cannot win. The strength is not in you, nor was it in your father. He was a poor excuse for a Druid and a poor excuse for a man. You will fail as surely as he did."

"No," Manfred said quietly, but loud enough to stop Garcouk. "He destroyed enough of you to thwart your plans for over a decade. He didn't lack power; he lacked friends. Karen doesn't. She'll finish what her father started." With that, Manfred drew his sword and stepped in front of Karen. Garcouk smiled.

"You are as foolish as she," the Guardian said with a dismissive shake of his head. "You think your blade will ever come near me? I can stop you with a mere flick of my hand, yet you stand there, thinking to protect those weak children." Garcouk pointed a finger at Manfred and the warrior doubled over with a grunt as if struck.

Garcouk gestured again, but Karen's voice stopped him as she stepped in front of Manfred, assuming his protective position. "Why fight strength with magic Garcouk? Do you fear your inferior might, or enjoy wasting your power? You are not the one Manfred must fight," She indicated the foot soldiers behind Garcouk as Manfred regained his stature. "They are. Your fight is with me."

A bright red flash accompanied her last statement, temporarily blinding Garcouk and his men. Neither Manfred nor Karen lost this chance. With a slight stumble as he shook off the fading influence of Garcouk's blow, Manfred roared past the Guardian and slammed into the enemy soldiers beyond. Karen dodged to another tree so as to draw Garcouk's retaliation away from Jans' crumpled form. Then she sent her image to an opposite shelter on Garcouk's right, concealing her true self in a magical camouflage. The invisibility took effect seconds before the Guardian's sight returned. She did not attack yet, determined now to find the strengths and, more importantly, the weaknesses of this and other Guardians as he had sought to learn her own.

216

Garcouk regained his sight and oriented himself on the image of Karen.

"Not bad, but you accomplish little. That sort of magic is mere child's play. But I expected no more from the child of a weak man."

Garcouk watched the girl raise her arms, preparing an attack. He didn't give her the chance. Summoning his own power, the Guardian leader let fly such a fury of flames that the girl fell to her knees and the tree behind her ignited in a violent burst of fire. Garcouk relaxed his stance, thinking her neutralised. In an instant, he found himself enveloped in flames seemingly from nowhere. The Guardian howled in pain and rage, unprepared for such an attack. Yet even as he turned toward the source of the assault, the flames withdrew into a small pinpoint in his fist, then fell, dripping like water to the ground, and vanished. Garcouk peered intently in the direction of Karen's attack, his cape singed by her flames, but he found no trace of her.

"That's more like it," he said. "But still not enough to stop me. You want to play with fire?" He spoke a word and gestured with his hand, summoning a mist to form around Karen, revealing her position. Anticipating this, Karen hurried to another tree, but not before the edges of the mist betrayed her. With a satisfied cry, Garcouk hurled his power at the girl, throwing ice darts with such ferocity that everything they touched froze. "Then feel the pain of ice."

Karen dropped to the forest floor, but not before one of the darts caught her cloak as it followed her down. The material froze instantly, the clasp at her throat threatening to cut and strangle her. She tore it off. As soon as the cloak left her fingers, it became visible, a sudden splash of taupe against the green and brown of the forest. Garcouk let fly a second volley of ice darts toward the cloak. Just as this barrage reached their destination, they stopped, hovering motionless a moment. Suddenly, they turned and shot back at Garcouk like arrows. The Guardian glared at the points of doom, melting them with his hatred.

"So you turn my magic against me. We'll see about that." He vanished.

Behind the Guardian, another battle raged. Three enemy soldiers lay dead, but the other four had Manfred backed against a large tree. The warrior fought well, yet he had not escaped untouched. Blood stained his left arm and covered a section of his right leg, but he continued to do battle heedless of these wounds.

Despite their advantage of four to one, however, the soldiers of the dark army could not seem to concentrate their attack, each man mindful of the powerful, stinging blade of the Stalker. Manfred, his broadsword held mightily in both hands, cut arcs in the space before him, keeping his enemy at a distance. Sword clashed against sword, and the sound of metal on metal rang out in the fading afternoon air, joined by the laborious grunts of the struggling parties.

One soldier watched as Manfred's blade moved away from him, then stepped closer to take advantage of this opportunity. Manfred didn't give him the chance. Before the man knew what hit him, Manfred's weapon swung around, crashing heavily on the soldier's helmet. The helmet cracked and Manfred kicked at the man even as his sword moved to block an attack from a second soldier. The one fell, sorely wounded, leaving the Stalker with three able opponents.

Suddenly, another soldier fell, eyes wide with surprise as the life drained from him. Behind the dead man stood Jans, bloodied sword grasped tightly in whitened hands. The boy dropped to his knees, unable to maintain his stance. Manfred slashed with his own weapon at the two remaining men, then charged to a new location, drawing the enemy after him and leaving Jans free from harassment.

The Stalker stopped and turned of a sudden, taking on the nearest man with a powerful stroke. Manfred ducked under the cutting edge of the man's sword, then, barely avoiding the other fighter's weapon, rammed his adversary against the trunk of a stout tree. Spinning about, the Stalker watched to his dismay as the remaining enemy dashed at him, sword raised and ready to deliver a killing blow. Manfred didn't have a chance to move.

Yet even as he awaited his death, a bolt of red lightning seared through the woods to discharge into a tree limb above him. The bough snapped and fell crashing onto the enemy soldier, crushing him beneath its weight, inches from where Manfred stood.

Garcouk watched this show of power also, fully aware of its origin. He had now found a second weakness in the girl; her

218

concern for her companions. This weakness he would exploit, first on the Stalker, then on the boy. The girl was sure to give up then and he, Garcouk, would ensure security for his forces. Once the daughter of the Druid and these two companions of hers were out of the way, nothing could stand against his army. He would crush the rebels and subject everything to the strength of the Masters, the most powerful beings of this world.

Garcouk stretched out his invisible hand and closed his fist, as though picking something up.

Manfred had returned his attention to the final soldier and felled the man. As his foe slumped to the earth, Manfred felt a strange sensation, as though his whole body had become wrapped in the clutches of a mighty hand. He rose from the ground and in the next moment, found himself flung backwards through the air, overcome by Garcouk's magic. The large warrior fell near to where Jans leaned against a tree, landing upon a bough on the forest floor, a thorny branch protruding through his left side.

"No!" came Karen's anguished cry from the air on Garcouk's right. The Guardian smiled maliciously and prepared a fresh assault on his wounded opponent. Sending forth a tunnel of flames toward Manfred, Garcouk even allowed himself a laugh, but the sound caught in his throat. Before they reached the injured man, the flames dissipated into a fierce red glow surrounding a human form. From the midst of this glow, Karen appeared.

"Well, girl," sneered Garcouk, holding to his concealment. "It seems your friends are as weak as your father was." Karen said nothing. Behind her, Jans pushed himself from the tree and crawled to where Manfred lay, helping the man, but also acting as a shield. He sent his thoughts out to Karen again.

'The Masters, Karen. Draimar killed them, all but two. But they're strong, stronger than any of the others. Your father wasn't weak, just outnumbered.'

Garcouk continued, unaware of this exchange. "I tire of this game. You're right; it is time to finish this."

Karen stood, still silent, but the luminescence surrounding her increased. Her gaze remained riveted on Garcouk, despite his invisibility. Garcouk frowned, then sent a stream of magic toward her. Her light took in this power, yet Karen remained untouched.

Garcouk hesitated before resuming, unsure of this turn. Did the girl deflect or absorb his magic? Apparently, he would have to reassess the situation, find a more appropriate means of destroying her. So long as she stood before her companions, he had little chance of attacking them physically. Mentally, he dare not touch the boy, for the child's mind still held the venom of the Master Sharnac. As for the Stalker ...

A thought struck Garcouk. Why not use the Stalker's pain against her? Not physically, but mentally. She cared for her companions; should one die, she would be vulnerable.

"Come girl, surrender. It's just you and me now. Make it easy on yourself and give up. Follow in your father's footsteps and abandon this hopeless quest. Surely you know by now that you cannot win. You are as weak as your friends. You only waste time while the Stalker dies."

Tears welled up in Karen's eyes, and then she spoke, her voice carrying a power Garcouk did not understand; a power that frightened him.

"You are wrong Garcouk. My quest will succeed and goodness will prevail. My father did not abandon this quest; he made it possible. By defeating all the Masters, save two, and by destroying your other races of Guardians; the greens, violets, ambers and oranges you seem so proud of." Garcouk glared at her, as though demanding an explanation, but when Jans stood behind her, he knew the answer. The boy had learned the secret, known how the Druid wiped out four of the seven ranks of Guardians and destroyed most of Sharnac's race. Now he had told the girl somehow, and she knew her task was not hopeless. Difficult and improbable, yes, but not impossible.

Karen spoke again. "You say we are weak, mere children. Perhaps you should fear the children." Garcouk involuntarily stepped back, struck by some magical force in her statement.

Karen's glow increased to a blinding intensity as she summoned the full strength of her powers into a concentrated stream of lightning. The charge of her magic shot out with a terrible crash and ripped into Garcouk, penetrating his disguise and melting past his shield of protection. The Guardian shrieked in intense pain, every bone in his body feeling the power of the Elves and the Druids, of Karen's compassion and resolve, blended into a force one so corrupted by evil could not understand. Garcouk's flesh tore apart and disintegrated into a pile of dust, free now to blow in the wind, and the cruelty of his mind fled, retreating to its origin.

***

Manfred swallowed past his pain and looked up. With a mix of horror and fascination, he watched as Karen gathered her magic and destroyed the leader of the Guardians. Staring at her in that moment, with tears staining her face and the red glow of her magic encompassing her, Manfred knew he had never seen anything so beautiful. Or so terrifying.

***

In the large tent of the army encampment, Sharnac sat in his curtained off section. He looked up from his work as if listening to something, then summoned Da'Harnak to him. Sharnac did not look up when the Ebbring entered.

"Garcouk and his men are dead and the girl heads toward Silben," he said. "Mobilise the army; we move tonight."

Da'Harnak nodded and left. Sharnac paused, considering the best plan of action against the Druid's daughter and her powers. Then, through a mind-link, he advised his sister, the last of his race, of the situation, instructing her to meet him at Silben when the army arrived.

Chapter 26

Joanha hurried forward, a fleeting shadow in the dead land surrounding Silben. A half-hour before sunrise he judged, on a day of reckoning between the forces of good and evil. Although he could not see them, he knew the other rebels made their way to the meeting place at the lake.

Most will have arrived by now, he thought. They would station themselves around the northern perimeter until Joanha made contact with Karen, then they would finalise the plans for attack and defence. Already, warning mechanisms and primary defence contraptions guarded their paths, devices set up by an advance party of rebels who had set out immediately after the conclusion of the Council.

Joanha had passed the outer line of defence five minutes earlier and had not seen any of his people since. He deemed it unlikely that he would see them until Karen came and he gave the signal.

He stopped now, standing just within the last ring of trees before the lake. Even in the darkness, Silben's silver waters glowed like an unnatural sheet of ice. He didn't know when he would see Karen and the others, but he knew it wouldn't be long.

Dawn of the fourteenth day since the discovery of the enemy army loomed ahead. Joanha didn't kid himself; this day would see the end of thousands of lives, his friends as well as his foes. At last report, the enemy army lay half a day's march east and had constantly moved for more than a week with little rest, making incredible time for so many men. Something had happened to provoke this haste and it would cost the rebels valuable time.

While he contemplated the situation, Joanha watched as a figure detached from the shadows about twenty feet away. He recognised it at once as Karen's slender form. With a quick glance around, Joanha stepped forward to meet her. She stood alone.

"Well met, old friend," she said guardedly.

Joanha, noting her apprehension, replied, "You've no need to fear, Karen. The Shape-Shifter is dead and the rebels are here, ready for battle, as we planned." Karen relaxed a bit, but remained on her guard. Joanha looked past her briefly, then asked, "Are they ... Are you alone?"

Karen smiled sadly. "They are here, Joanha. Both still live, despite injuries."

"What happened?"

"We encountered the leader of the Guardians and some of his men. And we have learned something of utmost importance, a possible means to destroy the enemy. They are ruled, not by the Ebbrings, but by two creatures with incredible powers called the Masters. If we can defeat them, we stand a better chance against the army."

"What kind of powers do they have?"

"I do not know the full extent of their magic, but it is from the mind of one that Jans suffers," Joanha's eyes darkened. "And that is merely a small show of its power."

Joanha glared at the ground then asked in a subdued voice, "Can you defeat them? Is there a way?" He looked at her then, met her eyes and held her gaze. She opened her mouth to speak, her lower lip trembling.

"We will soon find out." Her eyes, clouded and unsure until that moment, suddenly cleared, and a confident determination shone in their mauve depths. "I believe there is a way, and I will find it." She smiled and the beauty of that smile warmed Joanha's heart and heightened his own confidence.

The sky lightened with the coming of dawn, yet clouds masked the rising of the sun. The beginnings of day brought the promise of rain, and the knowledge of death.

Karen turned and nodded. Manfred emerged from the concealment of the dead trees, Jans supported at his side, but walking on his own. A strip of taupe cloth torn from Karen's missing cape dressed Manfred's wound. Joanha smiled briefly, his grim features softening. Relief at the sight of Jans able to stand on his own touched the rebel, but time would not allow for a fitting reunion. The enemy would soon arrive. Joanha raised his hand in the air and closed his fist, chirping out a signal to the others. Soon all the rebel leaders stood at the edge of the ring of trees, Chanet and Shawlen among them. Joanha led Karen and her companions to them.

"How many fighters do we have?" Manfred asked.

"There's a thousand Sandrogans and six hundred horsemen from Rischa village with our rebels. Thirty of our people are magic users," Joanha said. "Four hundred archers have concealed themselves in the thorn bushes along the southern rim of Silben's valley. We plan to have five hundred or so fighters here in the valley, barely hidden, to draw the enemy in. Horsemen will trap those who enter the valley by blocking the northern entrance. Foot soldiers will guard the south and east entrances to the valley; these are the passages accessible to larger numbers, while the north passage could accommodate most of a small army. The archers will then fire upon those who enter the valley."

"We know not all the enemy will enter the valley," Chanet continued. "In fact, we can only pray enough enter it to make a difference. The rest of us will disperse around the lake. We'll use a strike and fade method, do the best we can to throw their army into disarray. We must find vulnerable points in their ranks, strike at these and fade back into what cover we can find. This will hopefully leave gaps in their defence and cause enough confusion to give us an advantage."

"We have little chance in concentrated assaults using all our warriors," Joanha said. "If we keep to smaller numbers, attack in many places at the same time, we can at least buy more time for you, Karen. Smaller numbers make it more difficult for the enemy to learn the size of our forces. Besides, we're more accustomed to fighting in smaller groups."

"What of us?" Manfred asked. "What's the best position for us?"

Joanha glanced anxiously at Jans, noting how pale the boy looked. Then the rebel looked down to Manfred's wound. "Are you able to fight?"

Manfred grimaced and replied, "The wound's not bad. I

can still fight." Karen glanced sharply at the warrior, then quickly away, but Joanha understood the meaning of her expression. The Stalker had serious injuries, yet the desire to fight against this accursed enemy far outweighed Manfred's pain. Joanha looked again to Jans.

"What about the boy?" he asked.

Jans raised his head, his eyes clouded but determined. "I will fight," he said, clearing his throat with some difficulty.

"But ..." Joanha began, "can you?"

"I will fight." Jans repeated.

After a brief pause, Chanet spoke. "What of you, Karen? Where will you be?"

Karen perused the landscape before speaking. "I will look for the Masters, the real leaders of the army. When I have found them ..."

She left the sentence unfinished, gazing toward the east where the enemy would soon appear. With little debate, the leaders moved off to prepare for the coming battle.

Karen moved away alone, searching the eastern sky for any sign of disturbance. Manfred watched her, the wind growing stronger, caressing her golden hair. Jans leaned against a tree a few feet away, lost in his own thoughts. Joanha came up behind the warrior-tracker and followed Manfred's gaze. After a moment, the rebel spoke softly.

"She's something special, isn't she?"

Manfred nodded, a faint sigh escaping his lips.

"How is she handling everything?"

Manfred looked at Joanha, a frown creasing his forehead.

"I ask," said Joanha, "because I'm worried. This is a big venture she undertakes, a matter much larger than anything I would want to carry."

Again, Manfred nodded, his eyes refocusing on Karen. "I know." His voice held a slight catch. "I worry for her too. I'm afraid ..." He hesitated, then turned away from Karen.

"What, Stalker?" Joanha asked quietly, his voice gentle. "What do you fear?"

Manfred shook his head and gazed into the distance. With a deep breath, he replied, "I'm afraid I won't be able to protect her, to help her in her quest. I fear leaving her, but even more, I fear her leaving me." A minute passed in silence, then Manfred, his voice barely audible, whispered, "I love her."

Manfred felt Joanha's eyes searching his face, but he didn't turn.

"Does she know?" Joanha asked finally.

Manfred's eyes closed and he leaned back against a tree. "She deserves so much better. No, I can't ..." He shook his head. "It's best that she doesn't know."

"Why?"

"I'd just be a burden to her. I don't want to make her choose."

"Choose between what?" Joanha asked, confused.

"Between looking out for me and fighting the enemy. She already has Jans to protect. I'm afraid that if I tell her my feelings, she'll feel obliged to protect me also. I can still fight, but this wound," he touched his side, "will slow me down. I don't think she knows, but she suspects how bad it is. She needs all her strength to fight these Masters."

"And if she knew you loved her ..."

Manfred nodded. "This isn't the time to tell her."

"What if you never get the chance?" Manfred appreciated the implication of Joanha's soft-spoken question, but he had thought about that answer too long to change his mind.

"Then I will have saved her undue grief. I cannot bear to part with her, but if I must, at least she'll be spared the pain of knowing how much she means to me."

A moment passed before Manfred felt a hand on his arm. He turned and found himself confronted by Karen. His gaze flickered briefly to Joanha, then back to the Elfish-Druid. She said nothing for a time, her eyes softer than usual. Then, faintly, she began,

"Manfred, I—"

A sudden fit of coughing from behind interrupted her. Karen turned as Jans jumped up, his face contorted in a mask of fear. Karen looked quickly to the east again, searching. In the distance, thunder rumbled. A flock of birds winged overhead, crying out as they flew; the first warning of what approached. Yet beyond that, Karen's keen Elfish ears detected the dim sound of the advancing army.

"No!" Jans cried out beside her as he became more aware of the Master's presence. Karen sensed that Jans still had a connection to Sharnac, and as the Master neared, Jans grew more and more agitated. The army must have started their

226

march early, before sunrise, to arrive so soon. Or perhaps an advance party had been sent out to scout the area. Whatever the case, Karen knew that the battle had begun. Very soon, she would see her enemy face to face and finally understand the nature of the last of the evil beings calling themselves the Masters.

Jans coughed again, an uncontrolled outburst. Karen moved quickly to him and grasped his shoulders firmly.

"Jans, look at me," The boy tried to focus on the Elfish-Druid. "Fight this Jans. I know it is difficult, but you must force him out of your mind. Do not let this Master control you. Block him out, Jans. Put a wall between yourself and him. You can beat him. I know you can." His eyes cleared and his cough slackened. Karen smiled faintly.

"That's it, Jans; keep him away." The cough subsided entirely and Jans nodded, once. "Don't let your barrier fall. It is your protection. Draw strength from it." Without another word, Karen released Jans.

"The enemy is almost upon us," she whispered. Looking to Manfred and Joanha, she continued, "I must go." She stepped toward the two hesitantly, but made no further move.

"You can do this, Karen," Manfred said gently. "I *know* you can."

Karen smiled, her eyes lowering briefly before she turned and started out to find the heart of the enemy. A single tear slid down her cheek. Karen made no move to wipe it away; the only sign of emotion she allowed herself.

Manfred watched her go with a heavy heart. Then, with only a glance to Joanha, the three companions faded into what little cover Silben's valley provided.

The sodden sky wept.

Chapter 27

The troops advanced along the north-east boarder of Silben's forests, led by the Ebbrings Da'Harnak and Ing'Lahar. A cloaked and hooded figure walked with them, tall and proud in his concealing garment. Sharnac did not show his face to any save these Ebbrings, and to the other three Ebbrings who commanded the second detachment of the army marching to Silben's southern entrance. The detachment led by the other Master, his sister. Sharnac knew the rebels had all gathered by now, but he had little concern for them at the moment. Finding the Druid's daughter occupied the Master's mind. Finding her and destroying her.

A shrouded figure hovered in the trees ahead, waiting for the army. Sharnac moved away from the Ebbrings, commanding them to continue the march while he greeted the newcomer. Da'Harnak and Ing'Lahar carefully avoided looking at this form, knowing her identity. Having only dealt with Sharnac's sister a few times, the Ebbrings knew her as a formidable creature.

"Well met, Aerieanna," Sharnac said, greeting his sister.

Aerieanna nodded. "Sharnac. What do you plan?"

"Our army will rout the rebels, strengthened by the Ebbrings. The Guardians, though they now lack a leader, will supervise the army and do what damage they can. You and I, sister, must find this daughter of the Druid and destroy her before she can destroy us."

"Is she that strong?" Aerieanna asked in her wintry voice.

"She is," Sharnac replied, equally cold. "But she does not

yet realise her full potential. We might flush her out through her closer companions, the boy and the Stalker. Attack them to get to her."

"And if that doesn't work?"

"It doesn't matter. She will show herself sometime. That just may hasten her movements, put her off guard. We must find her first. Wait until our army engages their resistance before acting."

"Of course. I will search near the water's edge." With that, Aerieanna disappeared.

Sharnac stood a moment longer surveying his surroundings, searching for the girl with his mind. The boy who had entered Alhor's thoughts languished nearby; Sharnac could sense his presence. The fact that the boy had survived this long bothered Sharnac, but the Master put the matter from his mind, concentrating on the Druid's daughter instead. She would not likely go far from her companions, but he could not guarantee that. But if the boy was here, so was she. He grinned.

***

Joanha crouched beside Jans, waiting in the sparse cover of the valley floor. The Stalker, he knew, waited somewhere to his right, but Manfred well understood the tactics of war and stayed out of sight. Joanha knew he would not see the warrior until the fight began. Jans was the only person he would see until the enemy emerged, but Joanha hated these waits.

The uncertainty of the location of their foe merely added to his tension. The army had to fall for their trap. Otherwise, the rebels with Joanha in the valley would be at the mercy of the dark forces. The rain fell in torrents now and would hide their position if it continued unabated.

The call of a bird disrupted Joanha's thoughts and he quickly responded to the rebel signal with his own, thus passing on the message to his companions nearby. Jans glanced at him, an unspoken query on his face.

"Their army has reached the outer defences," the rebel whispered. "The call came from the north; that's where the first attacks will come."

Jans nodded and turned his face to the north, searching

229

the rim of the dying forest above as though his eyes could penetrate to where the enemy now marched. They would not have long to wait.

***

Da'Harnak glanced furtively at the figure waiting for Sharnac, remembering his last dealing with Aerieanna's callousness. She was a true incarnation of evil despite her incredible beauty, and Da'Harnak knew that all the Ebbrings feared her. Sharnac, although equally vile, at least tolerated those under him. Not Aerieanna. She had no mercy. As Sharnac moved to greet his sister, Da'Harnak looked away, not wanting to come under the scrutiny of Aerieanna. He and Ing'Lahar continued the army's march. They would soon come within sight of Silben's valley where the rebels were sure to have some sort of force assembled. Nothing the army couldn't handle, especially with himself and the other Ebbrings strengthening the army's actions. That is, if Sharnac destroyed the Druid's daughter. With her abilities, the rebels had a chance; faint, but a chance nevertheless.

Da'Harnak paused, moving to one side and allowing the army to proceed without him. He intended to fade back to the middle ranks and confer with the Guardians in that section in order to inform them of his desired strategy. Before the troops had moved far, Ing'Lahar called for a sudden halt, but his call came too late.

The front line triggered a trip wire set up by the rebels. Rough spears thrust up from the ground impaling a dozen front line men. From the trees came a barrage of arrows before the army had a chance to put up their shields, striking down more soldiers. Da'Harnak crouched low and examined the trees, but found no rebels. The arrows, already notched and waiting, had discharged with the trip wire, same as the spears. Da'Harnak silently cursed the carelessness of the men, and of Ing'Lahar. The Ebbring should have kept a closer lookout. These were the very setbacks that could, and should, be easily avoided, yet the dark army had foolishly blundered into this trap.

Da'Harnak glared at his fellow Ebbring. The soldiers all stood at arms, looking for any other signs of attack, yet none appeared. The rebels would most certainly be alerted to their
230

presence, if indeed they had not known already. Surprise on the army's part did not figure into the overall plan, but such petty traps did not help.

"A trip wire?" Da'Harnak's icy voice grated fiercely as he pulled Ing'Lahar off to the side, away from prying ears. "You were fooled by a trip wire?"

"A simple mistake—" Ing'Lahar began.

"Silence, fool," Da'Harnak kept his voice low, though he longed to strangle the idiot. "If this army didn't need your strength, I'd turn you over to the Masters. I might anyway, have done with your fool blundering."

Ing'Lahar seethed, his outrage at Da'Harnak's upbraiding palpable.

"You don't command me," he grumbled.

Da'Harnak backhanded him hard enough that dark fluid oozed from a split lip.

"Do you have any idea how lucky you are the Master didn't see this? 'One more mistake,' remember? He'll kill you."

Ing'Lahar wiped a hand across his mouth. Da'Harnak watched him without pity. Ing'Lahar's weakness disgusted Da'Harnak, but Ing'Lahar had always proved the weakest of the Ebbrings. Despite the army's need of the Ebbrings to increase their strength, Da'Harnak knew the Masters would not hesitate to kill any one of them. The fact that they could obliterate their creations at any time without warning kept the Ebbrings in line, but Ing'Lahar came close to the edge. He represented a danger to the whole operation, and Da'Harnak did not want to be anywhere near him if he overstepped the boundary of Sharnac's tolerance.

Finally, Ing'Lahar nodded.

"You're right, Da'Harnak. No more mistakes."

Da'Harnak curled his lip in disgust. He turned back to the troops, Ing'Lahar following like a whipped cur. Da'Harnak wondered if saving Ing'Lahar was worth the trouble.

The march of the black army resumed, Sharnac rejoining them. Thunder rumbled in the wake of their march, accompanied by the splattering of rain. A dismal day for a dark deed, and, Da'Harnak hoped, a dark victory.

***

Sharnac stopped in his tracks. He could sense her, Draimar's daughter! She had avoided his scans until now. Why would she suddenly become apparent? Unless to lure him somewhere. She had obviously lowered her defences enough for Sharnac to find her. And he intended to do just that.

"Da'Harnak, Ing'Lahar," the Master called. With barely a glance at the Ebbrings, he said, "Take your squads and take over." Then he walked to the trees and vanished.

Moments later, a rebel emerged from the trees and moved purposefully to the Ebbrings. As he walked, his image wavered, revealing a Changeling Guardian who saluted his masters. The man had taken the form of a rebel to scout ahead.

"There are rebels on the valley floor," he reported. "They have taken what cover they can, but the valley provides little shelter. That is the only sign of resistance visible, though they will no doubt have more scattered throughout the woods."

Da'Harnak nodded and dismissed the Guardian, then turned to an enlivened Ing'Lahar.

"Our first catch," Ing'Lahar piped up. "We will flush them out."

"You fool," Da'Harnak hissed back. "It's too obvious. Most likely a trap."

"Then I will catch them in their own net. The valley is easily blocked. We can defend the entrance. They will prove easy prey once they see our greater forces."

"What nonsense is this?" Da'Harnak snapped. "Our greater forces have done little to deter them thus far, and I doubt the rebels will balk at them now."

Ing'Lahar ground his teeth, then asked in a spiteful tone, "Do you fear them, Da'Harnak?"

"I fear the Masters. The rebels are a mere inconvenience; the Masters are lethal. I'd remember that if I were you, Ing'Lahar. He won't tolerate any more failures from you."

To Da'Harnak's astonishment, Ing'Lahar started to laugh.

"You are afraid I can do this, destroy those rebels in one shot. Then *I* will have the approval of Sharnac and *you* will feel his wrath. I will take the valley floor Da'Harnak, and you will be left with nothing on your side."

"You go to your death," Da'Harnak stated.

"I go to my ultimate glory," the Ebbring retorted wildly.

Ing'Lahar turned and called loudly over the pounding rain, "Men of the second company, take up arms and follow your leader. We go to crush the rebels." With one final crazed look at Da'Harnak, Ing'Lahar led his men forward.

Da'Harnak shook his head and went to speak with his Guardians. With Garcouk dead, the Guardians lacked a leader, but Da'Harnak felt them capable enough to reorganise, at least to some degree. Garcouk's death had weakened the position of the Guardians. He had symbolised the uniting force behind them. Now Da'Harnak had to rely on their common sense and loyalty to the cause. He spoke first to the Changelings.

"There could be rebels anywhere. Find them, find their weaknesses and exploit them. You know what to do to get close. The rain will act as an ally and keep you hidden longer. Spread out and go, now." The blue-caped Guardians moved off in different directions. Next, the Ebbring addressed the Seekers, the silver-caped Guardians.

"Each of you will take a legion and work your way south. I want the whole forest secured. Leave the valley floor; Ing'Lahar and his men are there. When you meet with the rest of our forces from the south, team up and make sure all resistance ends. I will take a detachment of soldiers as my personal guard to hold the north end. From there, I will strengthen our troops. Use mind speech for emergencies only. Go."

As these Guardians gathered their men and left, Da'Harnak turned to the Keepers of the Death Hounds, his eyes blazing red as their capes.

"You will wait until I give a signal to release the Hounds. Until then, fight hand-to-hand."

"Sir," one of the Keepers spoke. "If I may make a suggestion?" Da'Harnak nodded for the Guardian to continue. "We could form a rough circle so that when we call forth the Hounds, they will surround the forest and keep the rebels within the trees."

Again, Da'Harnak nodded and replied,

"You and three others will hold the north and east borders. The rest will stagger themselves in a semicircle on this side. Do not go past the valley; that is for our other forces. When I give the signal, the Hounds will move in toward Silben itself. Instruct them to kill any rebels on sight; and be sure they know which are rebels and which are not. Understood?" The Ebbring looked around, and finding no opposition, sent these Guardians out also.

Da'Harnak then took his personal guard and moved to a secure location. His own instructions demanded that he use his powers to strengthen the foot soldiers, give them might beyond ordinary human strength so that it would take at least twice the effort to kill them. This division of his magic to so many men would put the Ebbring at a severe disadvantage if any rebels should find him, yet the guardsmen would deter any attack, so Da'Harnak felt relatively safe from such threats.

However, should any find him, he could call upon a reserve of magic for personal protection, at least for a short time. The Ebbring grounded himself, legs firmly and squarely planted beneath his shoulders. As his men formed a circle about him, Da'Harnak closed his eyes in concentration, readied his strengthening magic, and spread his powers to his regiment of the army.

Chapter 28

Karen stood in the middle of the clearing. She had re-strengthened her inner defences, carefully fortifying a barrier around herself so that Sharnac could not poison her mind as he had Jans'. After allowing Sharnac to detect her presence, she had made her way to this spot, shielding it from all save one, the Master for whom she waited.

Into the clearing walked a creature of impossible beauty, his hair so black that it sucked in any light, and his dark eyes emphasised the snowy paleness of his face. Karen pushed away the sense of fear that threatened to overwhelm her and confronted Sharnac with determination. She recognised the powerful aura surrounding this being, intense even in the rain, as a show of malevolence meant to intimidate her. It did not. Instead, Sharnac's audacity strengthened her resolve to complete this quest and rid the world of the cruelty of the Masters. Sharnac stopped in front of Karen and eyed her up and down. With an unearthly grin looking almost bestial against his unnatural beauty, he spoke.

"We finally meet, Druid's daughter." Karen merely nodded, saying nothing. She did not flinch at the power in Sharnac's voice. "Do you really think you will win? Do you believe you have the power your father did not?"

"Yes," Karen replied, a cold smile flickering across her lips.

The strength of her confidence dismayed the Master. He recognised in this mere child such vast power. Even if she did not yet realise her potential, Sharnac well understood that this girl could bring the downfall of his plans. She must die, and he

235

would do everything possible to ensure her death.

"Really?" Sharnac tried to sound amused. "Well, we will see." A bolt of lightning seared toward Karen. She side-stepped this blast of strength and sent her own magic soaring toward the evil being. Just as easily, Sharnac avoided her explosion and the two stood facing each other again. Karen felt a slight presence at the edge of her mind, barely noticeable amid her thoughts. She knew Sharnac attempted to find a way past her guard, and Garcouk's insinuation echoed in her head: 'He defeated your father, brought him down with a thought.' Whether true or not, Karen did not intend to give Sharnac the chance to destroy her power of reason.

With lightning speed, she hurled a wide sweep of magic at the Master, then crouched to present a smaller target for retaliation. Sharnac reacted instantly, putting up a shield of protection around himself, yet some of Karen's fire circled around to lick at Sharnac's less protected back. His eyes red now with rage, Sharnac doused his opponent's flames, but he did not counterattack. Instead, Karen felt the strength of his mind as it tried to penetrate into her thoughts. *'You cannot win, child. Give yourself over to me. It is the only way you will survive.'*

Karen stood, abandoning her protective crouch. The implication of Sharnac's mind speech told her he did not intend to physically attack her yet. This fight would involve a struggle of wits, a battle of minds. Karen understood the enormity of such a fight. One can kill with a thought, or leave a mind so crazed and tortured that the body becomes an undefended and easy target for obliteration.

Maintaining her barrier, Karen replied with one word only, but so imbued with conviction that it had a power all its own: *Never.*

'You lack strength, as did your father. The Druid failed as surely as you will fail.'

Sharnac searched for a weakness in her inner wall, but Karen would not allow this creature to undermine her in the same way Garcouk had tried. As Sharnac attempted to locate a weak point, Karen laid various traps within her thoughts, illusions and deceptions that would hinder Sharnac should he find a way in.

When Karen did not respond to Sharnac's innuendo of the

Druid's failure, he took a slightly different approach.

'Do you want to know how your father died?'

'Brought him down with a thought;' Karen again heard Garcouk's words and felt herself waver ever so slightly. Sharnac felt her hesitation and pressed on.

'I can show you how he died, his last breath, his final wasted effort to survive.'

She could feel his mind searching, pressing in on her thoughts. Karen reflected on how precious little she knew about Sharnac's origin, in comparison to how much he seemed to know about her. Scattered images from Jans' confused communication with Karen filtered into her consciousness, as did images from her vision, and she grasped at them hopefully. What she saw consisted of Sharnac and six more of his kind rising from the depths of Silben's silvery waters, drawing energy from the cool surface of the lake and also from Silben's protective forest, draining the trees of life and leaving them ashen, woods barely clinging to life. In a subtle shift of scenes, Karen watched as refuse from the muddy shores of Silben gathered into six dark forms, each receiving a different magical force from those who created them. Karen recognised these creatures as the Ebbrings, their powers those of the Guardians, past and present: a Changeling, a Summoner of beasts, a seeker of Knowledge, the power of Mind Control, controller of Weather, and the ability of Soul-Splitting. The Seekers, Garcouk had led. Yet Karen did not see how that information could help her in a battle of wits with the Master. She had to keep searching.

'Open your mind to me and I will show you what you want to know.' Sharnac's mind communication sounded dangerously smug and sure of itself, but Karen detected the faintest reservation in his stance. Something in the way he held himself, a trapped animal ready to bolt at the first chance of freedom, made Karen reassess his tactics. Like Garcouk, this being did not attack her outright—merely a few comments on her youth and inexperience. Instead, they relied on her feelings for her father, on the fact that she did not truly know how he had perished. Now Karen realised Sharnac's own weakness, so similar to hers. She altered her own tactics, placing herself on the offensive and pressing in on Sharnac's mind. A dangerous move, yes, but one she felt necessary.

'*And I will show you what you most fear.*' Her mind-thought made him pause. Karen watched as his eyebrows rose, whether in curiosity, surprise, or fear, she could not tell. With a slight crook at the corner of his mouth, Sharnac made his response.

'*I fear nothing, child. Not even death has that power over me.*'

A disturbance in the earth behind Karen caught Sharnac's attention. Karen watched the Master as Sharnac's gaze faltered and his eyes widened in disbelief. She knew what he saw and understood his reaction, for she herself had summoned this image, forming the features from the memory of her past.

The muddied ground shuddered without a sound and took on the appearance of waves parting in a pool of dark water. From the centre of this upheaval a dark form slowly rose. First, a head appeared, its features concealed beneath a heavy hood. Its shoulders and upper body followed, mud and dead leaves falling from the tightly wrapped cowl around the figure. The earth stilled as the mysterious being wholly emerged, and the wound in the ground closed over as though it had never existed. The cloaked figure advanced silently, head bowed and face hidden. Only its hands showed, strong and tanned, belying the close relation to Death's spectre.

"Greetings, father," Karen spoke aloud. The covered head lifted with deliberate care and a sudden flash of lightning illuminated the face of Draimar.

Sharnac's lips curled in loathing fury. He glared at Karen, but before he could say a word, the Druid spoke.

"We meet again, Sharnac."

"It's not often I talk to the dead," Sharnac replied with a smirk. He looked back to Karen. "This is what you think I fear, child? The prospect of seeing a dead man?"

"No," the Druid spoke. "You fear that you have failed."

"Have I?" Sharnac scoffed. "Yet I stand here with victory in my grasp. A mere child and her father's shade have no dominion over me."

"You fool," Draimar's voice stung like a whip and reverberated with the thunder. "Do you really believe you have destroyed me? Do you think I, the most powerful of Druids, could be so easily defeated?"

238

"I know it," Sharnac countered. "I watched you die. I brought you down. I bent your mind and scattered your soul to the four winds. And I will do the same to your daughter."

Draimar laughed, a strong yet haunted sound. "You cannot touch her; she has too much power to allow that. As for myself, yes you delayed me, but you did not defeat me." Sharnac's eyes narrowed in challenge to this. The Druid continued. "Remember, Sharnac, why you are the *last* of Silben's Children. I will destroy you as surely as I destroyed those who once stood by your side. Without you, your creations, the Ebbrings, are nothing. Without the strength of the Ebbrings, your Guardians and their army will fail. So I say again, you fear that you have failed. And now, that fear will become reality."

In the blink of an eye, Sharnac found himself enveloped in flames; not the red of Karen's magic, as he had first believed, but the blue fire of the Druid. At that moment, Sharnac felt fear. Even in his discourse with the figure of Draimar, Sharnac maintained his disbelief in the reality of his opponent's presence, thinking this just a trick of the girl—an impressive trick, but unreal nonetheless. However, the heat of this power surrounding him, the blue Druid flames, changed his impression of the situation. He knew these flames, recognised their power as one he had thought long gone. The magic gripping him was the power of the Druid. Sharnac knew from his first glance at Draimar's daughter that she had power enough to at least disable him, but combined with her father's strength, Sharnac did not stand a chance. Somehow, Draimar was right; Sharnac had failed.

With a shriek of pained rage, Sharnac fought off this blue death that threatened him and sent his own power surging toward the Druid. Yet somehow, Draimar had vanished. Only the girl stood before Silben's Child, waiting as Sharnac's magic sailed uselessly past her.

Sharnac stood in hesitant confusion. What had happened? Where had the Druid gone? Sharnac knew from past experience that Draimar could disappear and reappear at will. The Master whirled to look behind him, but nothing presented itself. He turned angrily to face the girl again, then felt her presence in his mind.

'You have failed Sharnac. Now I will complete the quest

my father began.'

A red-hot spear of power exploded in a resounding mass of sparks inches from Sharnac. His defence barely met it in time to save his life. Now, the real show of force between good and evil began.

Chapter 29

Ing'Lahar signalled the attack. His men flowed smoothly and swiftly into the valley, ready to engage the rebels. A battle cry arose from the dark army, a terrifying sound echoing off the valley walls. Ing'Lahar moved with his men, a grin of appalling delight spreading over his visage as his army began flushing out rebels. A quarter of his soldiers defended the northern entrance, but Ing'Lahar felt that he would not require their presence. With his soldiers able to so easily flush out the enemy rebels, the only escape route lay south. Ing'Lahar planned never to let them get that far. The Ebbring suppressed his urge to laugh aloud at the rebels' meagre display of defence, the pauses in flight to turn and attack his men. It seemed so pitiful an attempt, so few rebels against his greater army. Even as some of his own men fell, Ing'Lahar couldn't help his wild glee, for in the end, he would surely hold the victory.

A flash of lightning streaked across the sky, glinting off the torrents of raindrops ... and the tips of two hundred arrowheads. Ing'Lahar gaped as several of his men fell dead around him. A second barrage, points of doom, flew from rebel bows far above at the top of the valley, felling more dark soldiers. With a shriek of outrage, Ing'Lahar turned to the northern entrance in an attempt to evade the rebel arrows, but stopped at the sight that met him. The soldiers he had left to defend the entrance had broken formation in haphazard confusion as the six hundred rebel horsemen bore down upon them. All around Ing'Lahar, chaos engulfed his men. What should have been a simple,

241

clean-sweep operation had turned into an all out melee, and Ing'Lahar knew his men, though greater in number, stood a fair risk of defeat. The rebels fought with great vigour and determination—and organisation. Too late, Ing'Lahar understood the nature of the trap the rebels had set. Not a mere attempt at an ambush, as the Ebbring had previously surmised, but the very net Ing'Lahar had planned to close. He had not considered a rebel cavalry, nor archers from above, whose deadly weapons continued their assault even now. Worst of all, Ing'Lahar had underestimated the abilities and organisation of the rebels. This realisation only served to further enrage him. Da'Harnak had warned him; Ing'Lahar would find no help from him this time. He had failed the Masters again, and this time Ing'Lahar knew there could be no escape.

Behind him, Ing'Lahar felt the presence of Sharnac and the Ebbring slowly turned, awaiting his inevitable fate. Yet Sharnac did not appear. What Ing'Lahar saw instead were two rebels fighting back to back, one younger than the other, a mere boy. The boy had magic, and for a moment, Ing'Lahar stood relieved, thinking he had foolishly mistaken the child's magic for the Master's. Then Ing'Lahar watched as the figure of a large warrior appeared from the haze of the rain to strike down a soldier who had assaulted the boy. Ing'Lahar recognised the warrior as the Stalker, and then the Ebbring started in disbelief. The boy! This was the same child whose mind Sharnac had drawn from the servant Alhor. The presence Ing'Lahar felt was indeed Sharnac's, but only a reflection from the boy's encounter. If Ing'Lahar could capture and defeat these three, escapees from Jadathe and close companions of the Druid's daughter, perhaps his mistake would be overlooked and his life spared. With this thought in mind, the Ebbring focused his power and threw a blinding mass of magic surging toward the three.

***

A battle cry arose from the valley floor, signalling the presence of the enemy army. The rebels above smiled grimly to themselves, knowing that at least some of the enemy had fallen for the bait. But there was no time to celebrate.

Guardians and their soldiers approached from the north and reports of a second invasion force from the south indicated that the rebels would find themselves surrounded within the hour.

Shawlen waited in a clump of dried brush with five other rebels until a small troop of dark soldiers passed. They slipped up behind the rear men and quickly and quietly slit their throats. By the time anyone missed these men, the rebels had long since disappeared from view. Similar strike and fade attacks took place all through Silben's dying forest.

The few magic users among the rebel numbers laid traces of magic where none would normally appear. They also conjured various images to confuse the Guardians, reflecting these forms in the rain, thereby adding a further sense of chaos to the forces of evil, and gaining time both for Karen and for the rebels in the valley.

Everything seemed to flow smoothly for the rebels—for a time. But then the tide began to turn and the chaos infiltrated the rebel ranks, allowing the dark army to regain the advantage. The effects of Da'Harnak's strengthening powers took hold. The strike and fade tactics turned disastrous as rear guards sounded warning cries and rebels found themselves confronted by a whole troop instead of a few bewildered men. After a confrontation with maybe a dozen soldiers whom the rebels had barely bested, Shawlen called his remaining allies aside to discuss another strategy.

"They're getting stronger," he began. "We've already lost three of our original six, and we were lucky to kill those soldiers. I suggest the arrows; shoot them first then attack physically and hope that slows them down before they can raise the alarm again."

His two companions nodded in agreement, but one spoke a moment later.

"We're going to need more people, Shawlen. If we have to face another attack like the last one, the three of us don't stand much of a chance."

"I know," Shawlen agreed, glancing toward the three dead rebels among the enemy bodies. He wondered at that moment if his brother still lived or if he lay as dead as those three companions. "The problem is finding more of our people before finding more soldiers." Shawlen sighed, then with a tone of confidence said, "Let's go. Have your weapons ready, just in case."

The three had set out when out of the corner of his eye, Shawlen spotted something moving. He stared hard to make out the form through the pounding rain, then stared in astonishment as it approached.

"Sweet Spirits, Will! Is that you?" The memory of the Shape-Shifter Guardian at the Sandrogan tunnels flashed through his mind as Will neared.

"Shawlen, my brother, you still live! I can't tell you how glad I am to see you!" Will moved to embrace his brother, but Shawlen stepped back, sword raised. "Shawlen, what is it? What's wrong with you?" Will asked, confused.

"How can I believe it's really you?" Shawlen answered. "How can I tell you're not a Shape-Shifter?"

"Of course I'm not a Shape-Shifter," Will said distastefully. When Shawlen didn't move, Will continued, "How can I prove it to you?"

Shawlen thought of how Joanha had uncovered the Shape-Shifter in the tunnels and asked the same question Joanha had then.

"Who is the girl from Jadathe?"

"From Jadathe? How would I know?"

Shawlen nodded, remembering Will had not known about Karen's capture, but still, he was not convinced. "The girl we took to the tunnels in the Barren Plains, after she and Manfred escaped Ildare." He purposely used the Stalker's real name. "Who is she?"

"The Druid's daughter? Is that who you mean?"

Shawlen lowered his sword, a grateful smile lighting up his face. The Shape-Shifter in the tunnels had not known Karen's identity. Yet a hint of uncertainty pervaded Shawlen's mind. He asked one more question. "What is her name?"

With a hurt expression, Will responded, "Her name is Karen."

With that response, Shawlen quickly slipped his sword into its sheath.

"I'm sorry Will, but I had to be sure."

"I understand," said Will. As Shawlen took Will in his arms, a sharp pain shot through his left side. A glance down revealed a knife just below his ribs, Will's hand at the hilt. Shawlen looked up sharply into Will's cold, hate-filled face as he sank to his knees, weakness washing over him.

"Will?" he whispered.

"You simple fool," Will hissed, his voice slightly deeper. "You give up too easily. Your own thoughts gave me her name." He jerked the knife up and ripped it from Shawlen's side. The rebel suppressed his anguished cry. Shawlen slipped lower to the ground, the pain almost unbearable. Will watched with undisguised hostility. Shawlen drew in a haggard breath as Will grabbed him by the back of the neck and brought his face close. "Before you die," he spat cruelly at the rebel, "you must know that your hopes are futile. Your brother is dead." Shawlen's eyes widened in disbelief at the man before him. "And now, you can join him." Shawlen felt himself thrown down and everything began to grow dark. The last thing he heard was an evil laugh, at first sounding like Will, then deepening. Shawlen struggled to open his eyes, but they wouldn't heed his wishes. Cold seeped into his bones and the mud bubbled as he strove to breath. Then he lay still and allowed the black to take him.

The man who looked like Will stopped laughing. As he turned, Will's guise faded, and a Changeling Guardian walked back into the mist of the rain to seek his next victim. Find their weaknesses and exploit them, those were Da'Harnak's instructions. His process was simple enough; look into a rebel's thoughts until a trusted friend or relative emerged, then mimic that person, get close, and kill the rebel. To make the rebel feel that moment of betrayal before death gratified the Changeling.

He stopped. In front of him crouched a group of a dozen rebels. A middle-aged man with the scar of a burn marking his face spoke to the others, an air of leadership about him. Quickly, the Changeling concealed himself and sought to enter the man's mind to find his weakness.

***

Chanet glanced at the rebels with him.

"I know it's risky, but it's a chance I think we have to take. They've grown in strength with the help of the Ebbrings. That is what you meant, isn't it, Derek?"

The magic user beside the rebel leader nodded, his curly

white hair dripping rain. Chanet went on.

"The Ebbrings will no doubt be well guarded, but the majority of their guards won't have the use of magic. The Guardians won't expect us to circle back for their leaders—or rather for the Ebbrings. The Ebbrings also don't expect us to attack them. Do we agree?"

The rebels nodded solemnly. Then he spoke again. "We will split into two groups. Derek will lead one group to the east of the Ebbring we know of. I will lead to the west. Gather as many of us as you can find and tell them our plan. Shawlen's group moves west of us, I know, and Toron with a group of his Sandrogans waits east. Go to them first." Chanet caught a warning look from Derek and paused.

"Guard your thoughts," the magic user whispered cautiously. Immediately, Chanet put up a wall in his mind as Derek had taught him long ago, trying to make his thoughts a blank. "There is a Shape-Shifter nearby," Derek continued when he was sure of Chanet's barrier. "He searches your mind even now to find a weakness. Use caution with whomever we next encounter." Chanet nodded.

"You know your groups," Chanet said to the men and women with him, keeping his eyes upon them, and avoiding the temptation to glance around. Then he pulled himself and Derek back from them with a signal to his people to stay put and not to interfere with whatever happened next.

The two had barely gone ten feet when Shawlen crept from the underbrush, a hand trying unsuccessfully to cover a knife wound in his left side. Out of the corner of his eye, Chanet noted Derek's minute nod. With a hesitant step, Chanet moved toward the fallen man, but halted just out of reach.

"Shawlen, what happened?"

"The troops ..." he paused to draw in a haggard breath. "They're stronger. My men, they're all dead."

"How did you manage to escape?" Chanet still remained far enough back from Shawlen's now outstretched and pleading hand to avoid the man's touch.

"If you can call this an escape," his hand tightened on his wound, "then I did so with luck."

"Did you see the Shape-Shifter?"

Shawlen's eyes narrowed. "He posed as Will. He's dead, Chanet. The bastard thought he had me when he told me of
246

Will's death. But I'm not that easy to get rid of. Even as he pulled out his blade, I took his life. The Shape-Shifter, like Will, is dead."

Chanet nodded. "Good work, Shawlen." But the rebel leader remained motionless.

"For mercy sake, help me! This wound is deep and I can feel the life draining from me as we speak!"

"Move your hand," Chanet said, indicating the hand covering the wound.

With a pained look, Shawlen did so, using his other hand, previously outstretched, as a support. The wound seemed real enough to Chanet, but then, so did the disguise.

"It does look bad," Chanet said, pulling a dagger from his belt. "I'll have to cut your shirt away." He stepped forward, careful to keep his gaze on Shawlen's hands. The man on the ground shuddered slightly, but made no other move. When Chanet bent down, a knife appeared like magic in Shawlen's grip. But Chanet was faster. His blade cut deep into Shawlen's abdomen and his free hand grabbed the wrist holding the enemy's knife. Chanet quickly pulled his weapon from the startled man and neatly slit his throat, relieving the pain and misery in Shawlen's eyes. For an excruciating moment, Chanet feared Derek had made a mistake, and that he himself had just murdered a valuable friend. However, as the blood drained from the man before him, Shawlen's features faded, and within seconds, the Changeling Guardian lay dead at Chanet's feet.

***

Ing'Lahar's rage quickly turned to fear as his magical bolt dissipated like leaves in the wind before reaching their objective. Surely the boy ahead of him lacked the strength to dissolve the Ebbring's power, especially considering the condition of his mind. Then how ...

An armed and stunning figure materialised out of the air in front of Ing'Lahar and suddenly, with a sinking feeling, the Ebbring understood the source of his opposition. Aerieanna, a glacial look of disapproval and loathing etched upon her impossibly beautiful features, moved purposefully toward the terrified Ebbring. Her voice, the tantalising and deadly call of a siren, echoed in Ing'Lahar's ears, a sound meant for him and him alone.

"You had your warning, Ebbring. No more failures."

"But Mistress," Ing'Lahar began. "The boy, the Stalker—"

"Cannot save you," Aerieanna interrupted. "Neither their capture nor their destruction will erase your blunder. Sharnac was much too lenient with you, Ing'Lahar. Now your mistakes have cost the lives of your soldiers. And for your failure, you will receive your punishment."

Looking into Aerieanna's cold eyes, Ing'Lahar saw evil pleasure and a cruel satisfaction. All the Ebbrings knew the tremendous and awful strength of their creators, and now, Ing'Lahar felt the full force of this power. He well understood the disgust Aerieanna had for the necessity of the Ebbrings. After the Druid had destroyed the Masters of her kind, all save her and Sharnac, the two siblings had to augment their strength. They did so in the guise of the Ebbrings. Both Sharnac and Aerieanna had made it clear that the loss of one more Ebbring—for the Druid's daughter had already disposed of one of them—would not slow down their efforts in this struggle. Ing'Lahar knew Aerieanna would not spare him.

A surge of venom filled Ing'Lahar's veins, heating the substance that served as his blood. A tingling sensation invaded his body, tightening into a fist that promised to crush him from within.

With a desperate attempt to survive, Ing'Lahar called into play his strongest magical attribute, the ability to control the weather. Gathering rain into a torrential downpour and winds of hurricane strength, Ing'Lahar focused this frenzied and unnatural storm around Aerieanna. Forks of lightning speared into the midst of his storm, followed closely by stinging ice pellets and rock sized bits of hail. He summoned every form of damaging weather and sent it into Aerieanna, hoping to somehow destroy her, and for an instant, Ing'Lahar thought perhaps his pains were worthwhile.

Then, the Ebbring saw his error. The crushing of his innards ceased and his blood stilled, but something also happened to the focus of his magic. Ing'Lahar watched with helpless despair as Aerieanna reversed the flow of his power, causing the unnatural and brutal storm to surround and tear at *him*. He tried to stop his magic, but found that he no longer had control over his abilities. Through a brief window in the

248

deafening weather, Ing'Lahar saw Aerieanna, her eyes coal black, outlined by red flames. She held her icy face still and regarded the dying Ebbring spitefully.

The window of his sight closed, and Ing'Lahar heard Aerieanna's final statement, painfully loud in his mind: *'Your punishment.'*

In a violent flash of white light, Aerieanna ended Ing'Lahar's existence. Only a bit of scorched earth testified to the Ebbring's passing.

Aerieanna turned indifferently to study the scene that had caught the late Ebbring's attention. The large warrior known as the Stalker fought valiantly despite a reopened wound in his side, taking on Ing'Lahar's men, yet remaining close to the boy and a battered rebel. Aerieanna sensed the boy's crazed mind and wondered briefly at his strength. Sharnac's inner blow should have debilitated the boy far more than present circumstances suggested, even to the point of the child's death. Yet somehow, he continued to live and fight her army.

Curiosity fringed by anxiety compelled her to investigate the powers of the boy. She started forward, unhurried in her purpose. With a Seeker's magic, Aerieanna probed Jans' mind, but she found a barrier blocking her way. At first, the Master thought this wall inconsequential and attempted to overcome it.

Upon further experimentation, however, Aerieanna discovered a surprising solidity to the boy's defences. Her intrusion on his mind alerted the child to her presence, and she met his uncertain and frightened gaze coolly. Yet something in the depths of those green eyes disturbed the Master; the remnants of an ancient and powerful magic lay dormant in the boy. No wonder the daughter of the Druid had sought out this child. The boy did not realise the full potential of his abilities, much like the girl, and Aerieanna did not intend to allow him to discover his strength. She gathered her energy into a bolt of flame and concentrated on the boy.

Chapter 30

Derek crouched low, peering around the dead and broken limbs of an old oak that hid him from the handful of enemy ahead. A large handful, mind you, he thought, considering that he only had five rebels with him to their fifteen. The Sandrogans were not far beyond this obstacle. He could feel the presence of Amrah's magic. Not that she would admit she had magic, and Derek was not about to force the issue with someone who out-muscled him. He had to get to her and her people.

He pulled back out of sight of the dark troops who approached. Derek couldn't move his people now. They were too close to the enemy. But if he didn't move, they would be discovered. He needed help.

He cupped his hand over his mouth and blew out a sound, transforming the noise into a bird's call. Risky, being so close to the enemy, but at least it attracted less attention than an assault of magic would have. And right now, he was gathering rebels for a larger attack, not trying to announce his presence to every Guardian in the area.

"What was that?" Derek heard from a soldier.

"Jus' a bird," another answered.

"They ain't no birds 'round 'ere. That's a call a some kind."

"It come from over there, sir."

"C'mon men, this way."

Derek winced. Well, he'd taken the risk. Now it came back to bite him. He'd have to use magic, come what may. Signalling for his companions to stay put, he gathered his power. He wasn't a strong magic user and it took time to replenish his strength, but he had enough to deal with this lot. After that ...

He stood, presenting a target for the enemy, and then heard a whistling hoot just beyond them. Another cry, like a field mouse came from the right, answered by a weasel's hiss to the left. Derek smiled. The Sandrogans had heard his call.

The dark soldiers paused at the noise. One took a hesitant step forward, calling back,

"They's jus' one of 'em. 'Es a magic user, thrown 'is voice. The old man can't take us all." He took another step closer to Derek, followed by most of his men. They got no closer.

Wild calls erupted from the rain shrouded forest followed by the emergence of a group of madly grinning cutthroats from Sandroga. A hulk of a man swiped his axe across the abdomen of a surprised soldier and crushed another's skull with his spiked club, painting the trees with spurting blood and grey matter. Beside him ran a lithesome woman, muscles rippling under the weight of a sword. An already bloody dagger clenched between her teeth flashed with gore as she pulled it out and across the throat of a soldier without missing a stride. The rebels with Derek leapt into battle, surrounding the enemy.

In less than a minute, the fifteen men opposing Derek lay dead in their own blood. A second group of soldiers had appeared in response to the cries of their comrades, but the Sandrogans, driven by bloodlust, ran them down too. The mammoth figure of Toron and the graceful build of Amrah, blood dripping down her chin from the dagger again in her mouth, came up to Derek as their people continued to slaughter the enemy.

"We've found an Ebbring, north end, about a mile from the lake," Derek said without waiting for either of the siblings to speak. "Chanet's circling to the west, gathering whomever he finds. We're to take its east side, kill it and weaken them. How many of your people are close?"

"We can get fifty right away," said Toron. "Others can come from the north, take its back." Already, Amrah had turned and chirped out a signal. Without a word, she ran to the north, attracting a group of Sandrogans to her as she went to fetch those she could find to come at the Ebbring from behind. Others flocked to Toron and Derek. They turned east, moving out to surround the Ebbring and its guard.

***

Jans saw the female warrior gather her energy. He knew somehow, and by more than her inhuman beauty, that this being was of the same nature as the Master in that enemy tent a couple weeks ago. Terror clutched at him as he realised this Master probed his mind, but he kept up the defences Karen had taught him, blocking the search. Then he watched, paralyzed, as her power fused into a deadly fire bolt aimed directly at him.

A bolt that never reached him.

Jans prepared himself for his doom when Manfred suddenly stepped in front of him, in the path of the flames, before Jans could react. The Stalker took the full force of Aerieanna's magic. For an instant, the large man stood bathed in the fierce heat, and then he lifted off the ground and sailed into the base of a nearby tree with a terrifying crash. His landing caused his reopened wound to turn from a trickle to a full-out gush, the blood mingling with fresh wounds from magic and tree matter alike. Jans watched horrified as Manfred sputtered blood and lost his strength. The man's large hand quivered, then weakly released the hilt of his broadsword and fell motionless to his side. Manfred's breath slowed, becoming more ragged, and he lay helpless as an infant.

Jans looked again to Aerieanna. Disappointment and a faint rage gleamed on her face as she glared at the dying form of the Stalker. Then she returned her gaze to Jans and her expression changed, becoming thoughtful. She turned her attention to Joanha.

Jans suddenly understood what new plan must have formed in the beast's mind; destroy his friends and make him more vulnerable. Well, Jans did not intend to let her do that.

But he had to act quickly. Even now, she gathered a second magical flame for Joanha. Jans turned to Manfred and concentrated on the sword lying forgotten at the man's side. He grasped the handle with his mind, using his levitation skills, and sent the blade flying at Aerieanna with such speed that Jans wondered at his own strength. The Master must have sensed his magic though, for she turned just in time to see the glinting steel aimed at her heart and some sort of shield prevented the blade from reaching its goal. It was a small diversion, but long enough for Jans to get closer to Joanha.

Jans watched as Joanha felled a man-at-arms, then grew still. Aerieanna's magic halted the rebel's movements, rendering Joanha as helpless as Manfred. She sent forth a blinding fork of her magic lightning, but Jans could not let it reach Joanha as it had reached Manfred. So he did the only thing he could think of, the same Manfred had tried for him. He stepped forward, intending to take the magic into himself, preserving Joanha's life as the rebel had so often saved Jans'.

The fire came closer and closer, seeming to move in slow motion. Time stopped for Jans as he awaited death. Inch by inch, the heat drew nearer, until finally, it reached his body. He squeezed his eyes shut, trying to ready himself to join the shade of his mother after all. Strangely, he felt little of the heat, and no pain as the flames surrounded him. He slowly opened his eyes, then started in surprise. He could see the fire all about, but tinted with white, a symbol he recognised intuitively as possessing protective qualities. What was happening?

He could see through the smoke of the blaze to where Aerieanna watched, as confused as he. The flames died, the white aura with them, and Jans stood unscathed. He noticed that Aerieanna, amazed though she appeared at her failure, had not given up. She snarled. All about her, the air shimmered and her long, dark hair whipped back from her face. There was no wind; only her own aura lashing out in frustration.

Although Joanha still stood frozen by Aerieanna's magic, she concentrated her attack on Jans alone. He felt a tingling in his limbs and a crushing feeling in his chest as the Master sought to tear him apart from the inside. Yet, this eerie sensation quickly dissipated and the white glow again surrounded him. Aerieanna seemed to struggle, attempting to push her way past this barrier, but with no success.

Jans wondered at this aura, at first frightened by it. But it didn't harm him. On the contrary, the glow appeared to help him, like when it had chased away the hands of the dead that had tried to claim him when he lay on the cusp of two worlds. For a minute, Jans thought Karen had somehow protected him, but then he realised what this truly was. White, the colour of protection—this was his own magic. A force that protected him from danger. But if that were the case, why had Sharnac been

253

able to poison his mind?

Perhaps this magic had only recently grown strong enough to manifest itself. Yet Jans knew he was lucky to have survived this long against the torment in his mind, and Sharnac had not tried to kill him directly. The Master had wanted information first. Aerieanna meant to kill him.

Jans suddenly understood a new aspect of his magic as though he had known all along, but only now remembered. He had inherited a very special and rare magic from his Elfin blood, a magic which protects the user and keeps him safe against unnatural threats. It was this ancient magic that Aerieanna vainly fought.

Aerieanna screamed her rage at Jans, both aloud and in his mind. She let loose a vicious volley of power, trying to harm the boy, but nothing could break through his defences. The white light continued to protect Jans, and he came to understand it more as Aerieanna kept trying to work past it. Neither could she attack Joanha, for Jans maintained a continual guard over the inert rebel.

But Jans began to feel his strength wane as his mind grew more clouded from its own inner struggle. He knew his protective abilities would save him even in unconsciousness, but Joanha would suffer if Jans fell. He searched desperately for some way to counterattack the Master, but he could think of nothing that would not require his full concentration. His practised magic simply was not that strong.

He grasped at a fleeting thought and held onto it with great determination. Jans had surprised Sharnac in the tent when he had forced his mind into the thoughts of that Master. The result had led to his crazed and tortured reason, but he had managed to survive. Now, with his present state of mind, what if he turned his thoughts on Aerieanna? At the least, it would surprise her, perhaps enough to forget about harming Joanha.

He had to do something, and no other ideas presented themselves. So Jans gathered his scattered thoughts, focusing on the turmoil and wildness within his head, and with the last of his strength, he flung this tortured jumble into Aerieanna's mind, then sank weakly to his knees.

The result of this endeavour staggered Jans. Aerieanna's attacks stopped and the Master stood bewildered for a moment, then she grew full of fear, an odd emotion etched on her face.

Her hands flew to her head, as though trying to still the chaos within, and her jaw became slack, but no sound erupted from between her parted lips. She staggered back, her body slamming into the trunk of a dead elm, and then she went rigid.

For a long moment, nothing happened. The sounds of battle faded into the background and the drumming rain ceased to have any impact on Jans. Beside him, Joanha twitched and fell, released from Aerieanna's power. The rebel turned over and stared uncomprehending at Jans, then at Aerieanna. But Jans knew Aerieanna saw none of this.

She was created out of pure evil, born of the imbalance of Silben's waters, but not even her vile nature could have prepared her for the cruel torment born from her brother's mind. The pain had grown in Jans. Torture and anguish had taken on a new life and intensity within the boy, and now that foul life invaded Aerieanna, penetrating her very being. Jans' magic and the goodness of his soul provided a Balance within him which had enabled him to survive, a Balance between Sharnac's evil poisoning and Jans' natural goodness.

Aerieanna did not have Jans' Balance, nor his protection, a magic for which Jans found new appreciation as he watched her struggle with this evil. She had no way of stopping the destructive spread of pain. The poison seeped from her mind into her body, spreading like a plague. Now she did make a sound, crying out in agony and fear. Her voice grew shrill, then abruptly ceased. Jans, horrified at the sight before him, found he could not look away. Aerieanna crumpled to the ground, her form convulsing in spasms of uncontrollable suffering. With a final moan, she lay still. A slight disturbance made the air about her waver as the last shreds of her magic left her. Her body shimmered and turned into a mass of black ooze that faded into a fine dust. Jans stared at the sprinkling of matter slowly trickling away in the falling rain, then collapsed in exhaustion.

Chapter 31

Chanet gave the signal. With a loud outcry, the rebels and Sandrogans made their presence known to the foot soldiers guarding the Ebbring. Several voices sounded together, making such a noise that one might think a thousand men and women had the enemy surrounded instead of a little over a hundred. Rebel arrows invaded the ranks of the army mob, each finding a mark. But the additional strength of the Ebbring held for these defenders, and it took more than one arrow to fell an enemy. Chanet had suspected as much however, and the rebels continued their assault, hoping to draw some of the guards away. Derek used his magic to present false images to the enemy, again hoping to lure some into the woods where rebels waited.

This strategy began to work as the front ranks of guards pressed forward to engage the rebels, both real targets and the images of Derek's magic. Yet only a small portion took this bait.

Toron led his people forward, challenging the enemy in hand-to-hand combat while rebel arrows flew overhead closer to those soldiers immediately surrounding the Ebbring. With battle-axe in one hand and spiked club in the other, Toron's great bulk presented a formidable target. Although the teeth of his weapons drank heavily of the lifeblood of his foes, the Sandrogan leader did not escape the blades of swords seeking his own life. The guards, seeing the obvious threat of this one man, swarmed over Toron, taking him down with the strength of their numbers. The Sandrogans responded quickly, ripping apart the men holding Toron down.

Then, a mountain of a man rose, throwing off his attackers, his face badly cut and left arm hanging limply at his side, no longer able to hold onto the spiked club. But the gleam in his eyes where his own blood did not blind them told of Toron's blood lust, roused to the point where only the total destruction of the enemy could douse it.

From the north side of the Ebbring, Amrah made similar charges, the rebels and Sandrogans with her equally willing to kill or be killed in their efforts to reach the evil figure in the centre of the dark masses. The dying trees of the forest looked down on the dying men and women below, watched as the carnage grew, as bright blood mingled with the falling rain to soak the earth with a wet slickness.

Chanet, his bow drawn, aimed his missiles at the Ebbring and the guards closest to it as best he could with the weather warping the wood of his weapon. The shafts fell harmlessly from the creature as it delved into its reserve store of energy. Other arrows hit the men closer to the Ebbring, but they took even more effort to kill than the soldiers who fell by blade, axe, and arrow further from their protector.

The sounds of war, the bravery and the pain, rang from friend and foe. The mud-churned ground sucked at boots and cold rain dripped from faces and weapons, leaving miserable, sodden fighters struggling for their lives. But still, the dark army sorely outnumbered Chanet's people.

The rebel leader was aware of the fighting around him as he concentrated on the Ebbring and its close guard. There must be a way to hinder the foul beast, if only they could find it. They had to keep trying, fighting to the last if necessary, but the loss of even one Ebbring might just swing the battle in their favour, or so Chanet hoped. With fewer Ebbrings to strengthen the army, the rebels had more of a chance of surviving the war.

Chanet aimed at a guard directly in front of the Ebbring, sighting along the arrow's shaft to the man's eye. He released a breath as his fingers left the arrow, hand already reaching for another missile. But what he saw surprised him. The guard moved at the last instant and instead, the arrow hit the Ebbring. Actually hit the beast, embedding itself in the creature's shoulder. Chanet's second shaft whistled through the air, landing inches from the first, closer to the Ebbring's chest. The enemy became disoriented at the wounding of the Ebbring and it became easier to kill the soldiers.

The Ebbring had lost control over its strengthening powers. The rebels and Sandrogans howled at their luck, pressing in on their foes, as the enemy cried out at their sudden misfortune.

Unaware of the death of Aerieanna, part of Da'Harnak's source of power, yet grateful for this opportunity, Chanet ordered a concentrated attack on the Ebbring. Arrows flew and blades slashed as the rebels and Sandrogans flooded over the soldiers. Some of these soldiers, aware of their peril, turned on their own comrades in their confusion. Others continued to fight with determination, though with ordinary strength.

Then the moment passed as Da'Harnak reined in his strength, but the damage was done. The Ebbring reinstated its powers, but it lacked its former potency. A dozen arrows had impaled the body of the Ebbring and its life slowly seeped away. Gradually its power began fading irretrievably and the soldiers again feared for their lives.

An odd chirping noise came from the Ebbring and echoed through the woods; a signal Chanet didn't understand. Then it fell to its knees. Rebels continued to fight intensely. They were still largely outnumbered, but no longer without hope.

The guards, upon discovering the weakening of their charge, scattered and fled, pursued by the rebels. Most did not get far. Chanet's people, along with the Sandrogans, pushed in, killing all resistance. The Ebbring, one hand to the ground to support its sagging weight, looked up through blood-red eyes as rebels fought to reach it.

Amrah was there first, knife raised high to strike the killing blow, but she got no further. A blade ripped through her back, tearing into her chest and splattering her blood into the face of the Ebbring. She opened her mouth to scream, but no sound came out. Her eyes glazed as the sword pulled up, then out of her body, dropping her lifeless form to the rain drenched ground before the Ebbring.

An enraged and grief ridden bellow erupted from Toron as he charged the soldier standing over his sister. Battle-axe clutched tightly in his right hand, he tore into the guard. He swung his weapon, shattering the sword opposing him, and threw his weight onto the man before him. Driven past pain by his grief, Toron ignored the dagger that appeared in the guard's hand and plunged into his side. Toron brought his axe around again, taking off the man's head, even as the enemy's dagger ripped across the Sandrogan's belly, spilling his entrails and draining his life. As the guard's body fell, Toron turned his rage on the Ebbring. He raised his axe, crying out a challenge. Then he brought the weapon down, watched as it drove itself through the Ebbring's shoulder and down into the creature's chest. A horrifying wail sprang from the Ebbring as it helplessly took Toron's dying onslaught. Toron released the handle of his axe and wearily sank to the ground to cradle Amrah's still form in his good arm. With one last roar to the wet, grey sky above, Toron fell over his sister, never to move again.

Chanet watched with a heavy heart. Though he understood the magnitude of the sacrifice he had just witnessed, knew that death was inevitable in war, he could not help but feel pain and anger, and sorrow, for the brave people who would never see another day. Will and Shawlen, Amrah and Toron, people he had known for years, even considered close friends. They had just won a small victory, though at a great price. Still, Chanet knew that their task was far from complete. One Ebbring lay dead. Others approached from the south, and enemy soldiers still continued to fight. The war, then, must go on until Karen defeated the Masters. Or else their cause was lost, but not without damage to the enemy—and to themselves.

***

Manfred's stricken thoughts called out to Karen as the warrior fell to the power of Aerieanna. Sharnac, too, heard the essence of the Stalker's passion and noted the pain it caused his opponent. But Karen quickly buried her reaction and concentrated on the evil presence before her. The rain continued to fall, washing the wounds from this power struggle upon both herself and Sharnac. Neither, however, had found a lasting weapon against the other, and their battle raged on. Yet Manfred's fall, it seemed, would not remain buried for Karen, not if Sharnac had his way. As Karen glared across the open space between her and the Master, Manfred's image came into view, a spectre conjured by Sharnac.

"Your friends all die; one by one they fall, and you, child, cannot stop their deaths," Sharnac spoke through the image of

259

Manfred. "You merely delay the inevitable outcome here. Give up. It is the only way to stop the destruction."

Red lightning answered Sharnac's taunts, fire slamming into a tree and bending the foliage to meet Sharnac's figure. Again, somehow, Silben's Child evaded her attack and his cruel laughter echoed all around her; a laugh suddenly shattered by a chilling wail. The air in the clearing shimmered briefly with a tormented presence, then became unnaturally still as Aerieanna's soul retreated to the sheltering waters of Silben. A moment later, Karen felt Sharnac's brief struggle as he re-established a link with his Ebbrings, a link that soon lost another member as Da'Harnak met his demise.

"It seems that you, too, lose friends, Sharnac. Perhaps it is you who should give up."

"Never." His voice took on a different quality, far removed from anything human. In a growl of tortured hatred, Sharnac screamed his rage and pain and cried out, "With my sister's death, you will feel the wrath of my vengeance."

In the midst of the clearing, a scene of the battlefield appeared, picturing the fallen forms of Manfred and Jans, and of Joanha standing protectively over the two. The rebel writhed in sudden agony, grabbed by some unseen force, and the soldiers of the enemy began moving in on the scene. Karen realised what Sharnac intended. She summoned flames and ice, howling winds and razor-sharp shards of rock, thrusting them toward the Master. She tried any attack that came to mind, hoping to find Sharnac weakened by his effort, but anger had made him more powerful.

Then Karen saw Manfred move. The warrior was not dead. Hope sprang up within Karen. But with a cruel grin, Sharnac reached his arm into the scene and grasped Manfred, the Master's hand as large as the warrior's body. Karen shared Manfred's pain as Sharnac stole the last of his life and she felt her soul drain of energy over the loss. Sharnac's hand released the broken form of the Stalker and moved to the unconscious body of Jans. Karen, despair creeping into her, watched helplessly.

But then she heard a voice, Manfred's voice. Not from the inert body she saw, but from within herself.

You're stronger than him, Karen. I know you can defeat him. I believe in you.

The words echoed in her mind and she clung to them. She gathered her power, but paused. A direct attack would not work; she had already tried that. What could she do? The scene before her blurred and she saw her father's face. His well-loved voice grew in her mind, a memory of his teachings.

Restore the Balance. Remember what I have taught you. Gather energy from nature, the trees, the grass, the earth. Bind with their strength and return your own power to that from which you borrowed.

Next, she saw Jans' face, his boyish smile telling her that he would be all right, that he had chosen this path. And that she must not feel guilty about inviting him to join in this adventure. Karen watched as the faces of those who had helped her in her quest passed before her: Joanha, Will, Shawlen, Chanet, all the rebels, each encouraging her. Whooshea naming her daughter of hope and friend of the Fey. All their voices became a chorus of trust and belief, ending finally with her father's words and with Manfred's smile—and the statement she had heard him reveal to Joanha. *I love her.*

Just as she loved him.

Karen brought her magic into focus. She connected herself physically and mentally to the nature around her, filling herself with its energy until nature's power had seeped into every part. She created a continuous cycle, replenishing the energy even as she borrowed it. Her action caught Sharnac's attention and he paused just as he reached Jans, the soldiers in the scene pausing with him. Karen felt her power growing and became conscious of her own aura steadily brightening, increasing in intensity.

Sharnac, troubled over this sudden accumulation of power in one who should have lost all hope by now, renewed a direct attack on Karen, but his magic had no impact. Even in his rage, Sharnac could not penetrate Karen's shield. He saw in her eyes such tenderness alternating with strength he did not know could exist in this world, and suddenly his fear returned, threatening to tear him apart. It was all he could do to maintain his composure.

***

Da'Harnak's chirped signal soared through the forest,

amplified by the magic of those for whom the sound was intended. Red cloaked Guardians stopped in their tracks in response to the order and gathered their magic into summoning cries. A bellow of thunder followed a fork of lightning, bringing with it the mournful wails of the Death Hounds. Pairs of ruby eyes stepped out from the rain, bringing the feared bloodhounds of the Guardians to their masters, ready for the fight. Their silent orders, kill all resistance. With one voice, the Death Hounds threw back their muzzled heads and howled a blood-chilling challenge. The Keeper Guardians in their rough circle of Silben's sickly forest sent out their beasts of the Hells into the midst of the rebels.

Chanet listened with a sinking heart to the howls of a nightmare. He remembered Joanha's description of the Death Hounds in the tunnels; their grip of iron, how they could easily tear a man to shreds, leaving just enough time before death for the victim to feel the excruciating pain of being torn limb from limb.

Chanet swore softly to himself. He bent to retrieve Toron's battle-axe, still sticky with the substance that had formed the Ebbring. Axe in one hand, sword in the other, Chanet turned and led the rebels deeper into the woods in search of those who stood in the way of freedom.

***

Druid fire tingled in Karen's limbs, eagerly awaiting a release. The magic of the Elves mingled with these flames, strengthening their potency, but Karen still did not loose this power. One thing remained, the Balance.

Until this moment, Karen had not fully understood the importance of Balance, but now, she realised that only a restoration of the disrupted Balance of Silben's powers could destroy Sharnac. She had to confront the evil within her, the dark part of her that longed for Sharnac's violent death, the part that cried for a fierce and bloody revenge for her father's death; for Manfred's. That emotion within her that had coolly enjoyed tearing apart the Guardian leader Garcouk surged forth, gleefully searching for another victim, but Karen embraced this emotion with sorrow, sorrow for the necessity of destruction and for unnecessary death. She united her dark half with her light half; evil and good joined together for a common purpose. With this combined strength, Karen looked to Sharnac's cowering form. She allowed herself to feel pity, sorrow, and joy for the unfortunate creature who even now searched for a means of escape.

And then she released her power. Red flames thundered from her and licked at Sharnac's unprepared flesh. Elf and Druid magic flared around Silben's last Child, invading his body and rending him asunder. No magical shield could prevent the penetration of Karen's power. Silben's forest, deprived of so much life by the Masters, willingly aided Karen's energy exchange with nature, giving her strength to destroy this evil and restore the Balance so necessary to life. Sharnac writhed in pain and tried to fight back, but he could not defeat the Druid's daughter. With a final surge of power, Karen cried out her own sorrow and pain, and in a flash of ruby light and white heat, Silben's Child disintegrated into the ether.

Karen watched Sharnac dissolve into the same dust as his sister as the Elfin-Druid allowed the last strands of nature's energy to leave her body and return to its source. She regarded the Master's remains for a moment. Then, tears streaming down her cheeks, she turned and staggered out of the clearing in search of what remained of her friends.

***

Chanet spun at the sound behind him. A Death Hound sprang up, salivating fangs intent on the rebel's throat. Chanet clutched Toron's axe, using it as a shield, and swung his sword down on the Hound's great head. Desperation and fear lent him the strength to push the beast aside, but as soon as the soft, muddy earth touched its paws, it turned again and leapt at him. Chanet threw himself out of the way. The massive body of the Hound missed his chest, but clipped his arm, bringing Chanet spinning to the ground. His sword flew from his grasp and he gripped the axe with both hands, aiming at the Hound's exposed stomach. The razor sharp edge scored on the tough flesh and the Hound howled in pain.

As it stepped back out of Chanet's range, three blood-covered rebels came to Chanet's aid. The Death Hound glared at them, growling. It leapt at the nearest with incredible speed,

263

sinking its teeth into the man's throat before anyone could react. Chanet pushed himself to his knees, axe at the ready. The two rebels plunged their weapons into the Hound, hacking at it, weakening it. Chanet brought up the axe as the Hound turned to face the others, and thrust the blade down across its neck, severing the head. The body thrashed a moment before finally going still. Chanet looked down to the dead rebel, past the ripped throat, only now seeing the white curls above the blank and staring eyes frozen in a mask of painful fear, the dead eyes of the magic user Derek.

But he did not have time to mourn. Another Hound rushed through the dampness at Chanet and his companions. Bloody eyes glowed and powerful jaws pulled back to reveal red-stained fangs as the beast charged. Beyond it, a group of soldiers ran toward them. Even without the Death Hound, Chanet knew they were horribly outnumbered. If the Hound did not get them, the soldiers would. But Chanet refused to give up. He cried out his own challenge.

The Hound howled in response, but then wavered. It slowed and whimpered, losing substance as the Guardians controlling it felt a loss in their power, the strength of Sharnac leaving them as the Master died.

Chanet did not hesitate. He charged the beast, slicing through its softening hide as he passed, intent on the soldiers behind. Rebels throughout Silben's woods witnessed the confusion of the suddenly leaderless army and took advantage of the situation, just as Chanet did, cutting into the enemy ranks and felling the dark troops, causing as much damage as possible while the opportunity remained. The war cries of the rebels and their allies echoed with the thunder, increasing fear and uncertainty of the army. Enemy soldiers tripped over each other attempting to flee while others stood up to the men and women who fought with a renewed sense of hope. Some of the dark forces even surrendered, looking for any way to avoid the endless motion of rebel blades.

Chanet knew, somehow, that Karen had succeeded, that thanks to her, they would see freedom at last.

With Karen's success came the hope of the future.

Chapter 32

Jans had regained consciousness, free from the torment his mind had suffered these past weeks. But having full use of his senses again brought him a new torment as he recalled the events leading to this freedom. When his eyes finally found the still form he sought, they closed to the onrush of tears, trying to blink back the sorrow of Manfred's sacrifice. Someone had carefully laid a discarded cape over the Stalker's body, protecting it from the moisture dripping from the branches overhead though the rain had stopped.

Jans looked up then and saw her, although he noted that she did not immediately recognise him. A glance in the still waters of the lake had shown that his once blond locks had turned into a shock of white hair. His protective magic had taken its toll, noticeably ageing the youth.

He watched now with tear-filled eyes as Karen emerged from a dense stand of trees and approached the little party. Joanha leaned wearily against the trunk of a slender elm, allowing Chanet to bind his arm. The rain had stopped, leaving only the faint rumble of thunder and a persistent dampness as reminders of the storm.

With the death of the Masters, the Ebbrings had faded into nothingness, for Silben's Children no longer held the fabric of the dark monstrosities together. Many Guardians had lost the majority of their power with the death of the supporting Ebbrings and the foot soldiers had mostly fled in terror. The rebels and their allies hunted down the last of the dark army, aided in part by closely watched converted soldiers.

Chanet had stumbled upon Jans and his companions near

Silben's shore, even as Karen did now. Each man regarded Karen as she advanced, but no one found the proper words to say. Karen greeted each in turn with a weary smile before her eyes fell on the still form covered by a cape. She moved to it, but Joanha stood to block her way. She looked up into his pale face as a tear slid down his cheek.

"Don't," he choked out the word. Karen laid her hand gently on Joanha's arm and stepped past him. She knelt beside the motionless body and slowly drew the cape away. With tears blurring her vision and a hollowness burning at her heart, she traced the rugged features of Manfred's face and silently wished him to a better place.

A crack of thunder echoed through Silben's forest then, followed closely by an eerie silence. The rustling of the dead leaves ceased their wind-driven whispers, and all became still. The three men looked about anxiously, each sensing an unnatural shift in the air. Karen remained motionless, her gaze riveted on Manfred, but no longer blinded by tears. Joanha and Chanet unsheathed their swords and moved to stand one at each side of Karen, ready to protect her despite their exhaustion. Jans took a position behind her, but held no sword, still lacking the strength to wield one. The three waited in silent expectation, not knowing what approached.

Jans saw it first, a faint shimmering in the air by Silben's shore as of a thousand stars clustered together in a midnight blue sky. The disturbance grew in intensity, becoming brighter until a white flash momentarily blinded him. When his sight returned, he saw a dark figure slowly moving forward from the lake. The form flickered, alternating between a solid shape and a ghostlike image as it progressed. Jans could see no face, only a tall form tightly wrapped in a cloak that dragged on the ground, yet the presence felt familiar. His initial fear at the figure's appearance grew instead to curiosity, and a strange sense of absolute safety. He wondered if the two rebels felt the same.

Joanha fought an inner struggle over the appearance of the shape before them, forcing himself to look beyond his feelings of safety. He recognised the offered safety as a magical one and, in light of the evil powers so recently destroyed, he did not trust this sense of peace. He noted Jans' placid countenance and saw Chanet's blade lower, but Joanha refused to yield to the will of the figure as it neared. Not when his companions were put so off-guard, and not while Karen remained so vulnerable, for she had not yet moved from the Stalker's body. If Joanha did not keep up his guard, they would be entirely defenceless. Still, it was only with great difficulty that he maintained his composure or his defences.

Karen watched the figure approach as if in a trance. She knew that form, recognised the man behind the concealing cowl as someone she deeply loved; yet she did not understand his appearance. This was a man ten years dead. Although she had not seen his death, she knew it as a fact. She had felt his life leave the world on that cold night so long ago, felt his presence seek her out in an unspoken farewell. And now, she faced that man again. To her, he looked just as her conjured image of him had, even though she could not clearly see his face. But this was no trick of her magic. This figure before her was the true form of that man, here now through no power of her making.

Karen found herself facing Draimar, last of the Druids, her father.

She felt the same sense of calm as the others, knowing a kind of safety she had not truly felt since leaving her home not so long ago, although she had come close that night when she had lain in Manfred's arms after the discovery of the army. A safety offered by a friend who loved her, a dear friend now lying before her in a valley littered by the dead. Such a short time, but Karen felt as though she had lived an entire life in those weeks. Like Joanha, she recognised this offered safety as a magical promise. She knew nothing would disturb them as long as her father's ghost remained.

Karen watched Joanha take a hesitant step forward, sword raised. Even now, his distrust of magic overpowered the air of safety. She knew he intended to protect her and his loyalty genuinely moved her. The figure slowed, but did not cease his approach. From beneath his hood, Karen heard a deep grumble tainted by a noise like rustling leaves. It grew until it took on a rich sound and finally became a voice she remembered raised in laughter. She saw Joanha's sword hand quiver, yet the rebel stubbornly refused to drop his weapon. It was not until Karen rose to her feet and touched his arm that Joanha lowered his sword.

Karen smiled, a gesture tinged with sadness. The rebel had no way of knowing whom he now faced, nor of the futility of protecting her with a worldly weapon. Karen knew, though she did not understand, that they now dealt with something not of this world, but from the world of the dead.

The Druid stopped an arm's length away from Karen. His whole being held a transparent quality, a reminder that she dealt now with a shade, a memory of a man who once had lived. Pale and thin hands reached for his hood and revealed the dark hair and smiling face beyond. His eyes, unnaturally dark against his pale skin, turned to regard Joanha.

"An admirable effort," the deep voice Karen remembered from childhood intoned, "but not necessary. I did not come to harm, but to help."

Joanha glanced quickly to Karen before sheathing his sword. Perhaps he, too, had come to the conclusion that such weapons here were useless as well as superfluous. Draimar looked at Jans next, his nod of greeting somehow a renewal of acquaintance which the young man returned.

"Well done, young one," his grave-tinged voice complimented, causing Jans to flush, much to Draimar's apparent amusement.

Then the Druid's smiling eyes found his daughter's face. A short time passed in silence while he examined what he saw. When next he spoke, his voice strong for one come back from the dead, the three men with Karen at last understood who this being was.

"You have your mother's beauty, but, I think, my eyes." His smile broadened, filled with pride. "You have done well, Karenrana. You have restored what we destroyed. At last, the land has a chance to heal itself." Karen smiled briefly, but a heavy sense of loss, even regret, overshadowed her sense of accomplishment. She looked down to Manfred's body, the smile fleeing from her features. The Druid followed her gaze, yet his smile remained. "And for that, we must thank you."

Karen glanced up at her father, not understanding. The Druid's eyes, however, had fixed upon Manfred. He bent down, placing a hand over Manfred's heart. As he did so, Silben's surface began to churn. Karen looked to the water, struggling with pain and a hint of fear despite the peace ensured by her father's presence. The air grew distorted around the shore of
268

the lake and through innumerable rifts between two worlds, stars in a night sky, came other figures, dark and silent. They encircled the little group, forming a continuous link and making no sound. Joanha and Chanet stood like sentinels to either side of the body. Jans stepped forward to stand beside Karen while the ghost of the Druid knelt at the other side. The circle of silent watchers, a ring of the dead, made no movement, even when the Druid began to intone a low chant.

Karen studied those figures, apprehension threatening to envelop her. Had they come to welcome Manfred into their ranks? Or for some other purpose? She recognised them as shades, so like her father now. So like Manfred would soon be. But that did not still her fears. Or her grief.

A tear slid down her cheek and dropped to Manfred's hand before she thought to brush it away. In that moment, the ring of shades did move, sending up a wail so piercing that the living had to shield their ears from the sound. The concealing garments of the shades fell from their faces, and luminescent eyes stared out. Karen saw one woman step forward and, although she had never met her, knew it was her mother. Silver-blonde hair framed gold eyes, and sharp Elfin features marked Sadricha's proud bearing. The ghost smiled. That was all Karen saw of her, for with Sadricha's movement, the other shades rushed forward. They converged upon Manfred's body in a flurry of motion and high-pitched shrieks. Dark forms suddenly covered Manfred, but as Karen cried out and moved to stop them, an intense flash of blue illuminated the valley, swallowing noise and stealing sight.

A minute passed before the light died and the four mortals could see again. They stood alone now, with only the Druid's ghost as a testimony of contact between their world and the world of the dead. Karen knelt to Manfred's side and hesitantly touched his face to see what the shades had done. She drew her hand back, startled. She had felt warmth where only a moment before the cold grip of death had ruled. She looked quickly at Joanha, then Jans, then finally at her father. She met the Druid's gaze and held it. His eyes still held the vast knowledge she remembered seeing as a child despite being void of life.

"Father," she began, but paused when she heard Jans gasp. Glancing at the boy, Karen noted the awe and disbelief marking his aged visage. His eyes had fastened on Manfred and he shook his head, not understanding what he saw. Karen looked back to Manfred, then bit her lip in an effort to control her sudden turbulent emotions.

Manfred's eyes fluttered open and found Karen. The warrior drew in a ragged breath and raised a shaky hand to her face, as if to see if she were real. Karen moved her own hand over his and held it tightly, seeking a similar reassurance. She lifted tear-filled eyes to her father, the question mirrored in their mauve depths. *How is this possible?* Manfred turned his head to follow her gaze, and with that motion, the Druid nodded, a gesture seemingly of approval. Then the ghost spoke, his voice more distant now, lacking the rich tone it once had carried.

"A final gift, the only thing I had left to offer. By now you know I fought the same enemy you have defeated. I knew I could not overcome their strength, that I could only delay them until you were ready. This quest was yours all along. Silben herself knew that."

"The lake?" Karen asked, not quite understanding.

"The world once had a precious Balance between good and evil forces, but over time, that Balance shifted. Your heritage, the Elves and the Druids, unknowingly destroyed that Balance, eventually causing Silben to become a source of evil that created Sharnac and his race. Silben's cries for help went unanswered for a great long time, but she never gave up hope. You were that hope, the child of a union between those who destroyed the Balance, a child whose very being symbolised Balance. Through your efforts, the Balance has finally been restored. Your efforts, and those of your friends."

The Druid sighed before continuing. "When the Masters destroyed me, I was able to save a small part of myself, an essence that could still remember what life felt like. Silben's woods harboured that essence, waiting for a time when it might be needed, waiting for you. That is how I can be here now, here to give a gift. I give you Manfred's life."

A stunned silence followed his statement. Manfred rose weakly to a sitting position, examining his body as though in remembrance of Aerieanna's devastating blow, of Sharnac's crushing grip, of his life leaving his body. He gazed wonderingly at the Druid, then looked to Karen and met a sight that warmed his heart. Karen's whole being radiated with a
270

mixture of gratitude, joy, and, Manfred dared hope, love. She reached forward hesitantly, then grasped Manfred in an embrace. After a moment, she returned her attention to her father, although her arm still encircled Manfred's shoulder.

"Father, I," she drew in a breath, containing a contented sob. "Thank you."

"There is a price. I cannot restore life without this one condition, for that is beyond my powers." He waited until both Karen and Manfred turned their eyes to his. "Manfred, you must never again draw a weapon to take the life of another. Your life restored for other lives preserved. There can be no exceptions. On the day you kill another person, your life is forfeit. Do you understand?"

After a brief pause, Manfred nodded. The Druid closed his eyes and nodded once in return. He stepped back, his eyes opening as a gentle wind blew across Silben, stirring the water. The Druid continued to retreat toward the lake although his gaze stayed fixed on Karen. Karen realised then that she was about to lose her father again. She stood, but did not move forward. Her father gestured for her to remain still. The water rose into silent waves and soon caressed the Druid's feet. He stopped then, allowing the lake to churn about him and enfold him in a loving embrace. Manfred stood beside Karen, his arm awkwardly around her shoulder, as she watched Silben claim her father. Just before he disappeared completely, Karen heard his final words in her mind: *Farewell, my child. I love you.*

She turned and buried her face in Manfred's chest. He wrapped his arms around her and held her close as Silben's waters calmed, once more becoming still, but now with a hint of her legendary beauty returning after so long.

After a time, they left the valley, Manfred and Karen hand in hand, Joanha and Jans supporting each other, while Chanet brought up the rear. At the rim of the valley, the thorn bushes lay broken and dying, but the land no longer looked devoid of life. A hint of green poked up from under a nearby tree, a seedling given life by the recent storm. They paused, glancing back down at Silben's silver surface. The sunlight broke through the clouds just then, sparkling on the lake. Things would be different now, a chance for new life. Karen raised her eyes to Manfred's face and smiled.

Thank you, father. For everything.

www.ingramcontent.com/pod-product-compliance
Lightning Source LLC
Chambersburg PA
CBHW020420260626
47156CB00007B/2473